The Thorn Keeper

Penned in Time—Book Two

Pepper D. Basham

Vinspire Publishing
www.vinspirepublishing.com

Pepper D. Basham

ISBN: 978-0-9971732-1-5

PUBLISHED BY VINSPIRE PUBLISHING, LLC

To my amazing family, Dwight, Ben, Aaron, Lydia, Samuel and Phoebe

Dreams become much bigger and better when shared with the ones I love.

Pepper D. Basham

Chapter One

Ednesbury, Derbyshire England
September 1915

There is a distinct difference between a heroine with a promised happy ending and a prodigal who must design her own.

As Catherine Dougall stared across Ednesbury's crowded Main Street at Madame Rousell's Boutique, the French tulle lace and promises of romance taunted her with paper-thin hopes.

Used goods and white lace? Her lips quirked downward. Definitely out of fashion.

Besides, Rousell's tempted Catherine's weakness for the beautiful and extravagant. An old dream, limping beneath the past and reality. *Extravagant dreams have extravagant costs.*

And her purse stood empty.

She turned away from the daydream and pushed open the door to Branson's. The mercantile's welcome scents of coffee grounds and hard candies usually encouraged a sampling, but today, the aroma curled her stomach. She stifled a groan. Pregnancy proved as unpredictable as this prolonged war.

Catherine unhooked the buttons of her coat and visited the small ready-made section of the store. The variety couldn't compare to Lakes down the street or Rousell's with their hand-made designs, but the less expensive clothes fit the budgets of so many in Ednesbury. Catherine smiled. The women who were thrust into the workforce could look stylish without the additional cost. She skimmed a hand over the trip cut of a sleek daysuit, envisioning a bit more embroidery on the sleeves for her tastes.

"Ah, Miss Dougall, I see you've ventured out early."

Catherine closed her eyes and exhaled before turning to the sound of Patterson Dandy's nasal voice. The notorious owner of the local newspaper dabbled in gossip like an epidemic. So adept at sniffing out a story, he often left grown men near tears. Catherine offered her most dazzling smile to the obnoxious man.

"Mr. Dandy, what a delightful surprise this morning."

He shoved his thick-rimmed glasses up on his nose and eyed her with his usual suspicion. "Don't say things you don't mean, Miss Dougall."

"I find those are the only socially acceptable responses I have for you."

His sneer twitched his sleek moustache. "Flattery will only increase my interest in you."

"Flattery?" Her hand went to her chest. "How clumsy of me. I meant to insult you."

He moved closer, his sneer as slick as his oily scent. "It's unfortunate the hospital moved to your family's country house. I should have liked to watch your developing relationship with Drew Cavanaugh continue into dark alleys and midnight romps." Air lodged in Catherine's throat. "Such tantalizing news, only overshadowed by the destruction of Dr. Ross' hospital by the Zeppelin attack."

Catherine kept her stare steady. "I'm afraid I've turned over a new leaf. In fact, I'm certain you'll have difficulty finding anything worthwhile to report in your scandalous and desperate little newspaper."

"You're not the sort of personality who goes undetected, my dear." His gaze slithered down her body, and she had the unladylike urge to slap the glasses off his face. "And my pen awaits the discovery."

The delivery boy caught Catherine's eye from across the store, hospital supplies readied for collection – and not a moment too soon. She tipped her head to Mr. Dandy. "Threats are not very becoming of a gentleman." Catherine gave a mock gasp. "Oh, but you've never been accused of that before, have you?" Her smile returned. "Excuse me, I see my parcel is ready."

Every fiber of her being ached to lash out at the dreadful man and leave a mark on his arrogant smirk. Of course, her terrible compromise with Drew Cavanaugh had been her own fault. Mr. Dandy's intimate knowledge was another byproduct of Catherine's multitude of mistakes, twisting the knife of conviction deeper. How could she protect those she loved from being stained by such disgrace?

A crash sounded from the back of the store and drew her attention away from her self-flailing. Mr. Branson emerged, dragging a young woman by the arm.

"No. Please." Her cry pierced the room with a heart wrenching edge. "I have to eat, Mr. Branson. Please."

"There's nothing for it." Mr. Branson pulled the girl toward the front of the store, his round face red from exertion and his mop of dark hair as disgruntled as his frown. "I can't have your kind here."

The girl's unkempt hair hung loose about her shoulders in a rain of dirty gold, blocking her face, but nothing veiled the desperation in her sobs. Her hands dug into Mr. Branson's thick hold. "I have money. I can pay. I earned it honest-like."

He shook his head "It don't matter, Miss Meredith. I can't risk *her* seeing you here. I could lose my shop."

The girl's plea, the abject desperation of it, fueled Catherine's protective streak, forged over the past few months tending the wounded at Roth. The girl looked young. Her flimsy dress did little to hide the swell at her stomach. Air whooshed from Catherine's lungs. A baby.

"Is she an acquaintance of yours, Miss Dougall?"

Mr. Dandy stood close, too close. Catherine stepped away from him. His implication teased knowledge he shouldn't possess. He couldn't know of her predicament, could he? Few people did.

"I got to eat." The woman tried to pull away, even grabbed for the loaf of bread in Catherine's basket as she passed. "Please, sir. You're a good man."

"Mr. Branson." Catherine stepped forward, but the owner ignored her. "Be reasonable. She can pay."

The door jingled with its customary welcome as Mr. Branson swung it open. There was no welcome in his furrowed brow now. "I can't help you, girl."

"*She* don't have to find out. I won't tell nobody."

What infamous woman controlled this situation without even being present?

A jostle knocked the girl's hair free from her face and solidified Mr. Dandy's insinuation with sickening clarity. The red-rimmed gray eyes, the familiar face smudged with tears and dirt, reminded Catherine of a servant in the Cavanaugh home. Hadn't Mr. Branson called her Meredith? Heat fled Catherine's face, and the picture bled painfully clear. Meredith had been the housemaid who always caught Drew's eye when she entered the room. They'd even exchanged harmless banter to garner Catherine's jealousy and Lady Cavanaugh's ridicule, but had Drew stooped to ruin another woman's virtue? Life?

Catherine lowered her palm to her stomach as if to shield her own little secret from the harshness in the memory. What promises had Drew made to Meredith? How long ago had she been dismissed from service to rummage around the streets alone?

"I can't." Branson pushed the girl out the door and slammed it on her final plea. "I can't," he whispered and shoved a chubby hand through his coarse, brown hair.

Catherine blocked Mr. Branson's passage. "What just happened here?"

"A travesty. Unnecessary travesty." The man's voice rasped with emotion, his dark eyes weary. He walked around her and disappeared into the back of the store.

"But she was willing to pay," Catherine called after him, looking around at the other stunned customers for answers.

"Ah, I see you've not heard." Mr. Dandy's voice slinked into the moment. "Obviously, living so far from town keeps you away from the most current news."

Most of which she never wished to hear. But this....

He waited a few seconds, smile devious, clearly reveling in the attention his reluctance provided.

A woman pushed forward from the crowd. "No one of ill-repute may buy or sell in any public place at risk of losing their leases."

"What?" Catherine looked back to Mr. Dandy for clarification. *Lady Cavanaugh.* How long had Catherine's pride blinded her from the injustice of the Cavanaughs and the harsh social lines set about by the rich. "She wasn't causing trouble to anyone, and she was willing to pay."

"It doesn't matter, Miss Dougall. You saw her condition. No husband?" Mr. Dandy's brow tweaked with the prickle of his words. "Clearly someone…undeserving of compassion."

There was *no* way Mr. Dandy knew of Catherine's similar situation, but from the gleam in his eyes, she wondered. She had always disliked bullies.

"I see you've lived well above the weakness for compassion, Mr. Dandy, but as for the rest of humanity, we are all in need of it. Her mistakes should not condemn her to starvation." Catherine's hand fisted at her side. "It's fortunate indeed that Lady Cavanaugh doesn't own the local church, for she might very well refuse the son of God admittance for displaying such liberal grace."

She surveyed the wide-eyed observers in the room, seeking allies. As she met each stare, the person looked away—all, that is, except Dastardly Dandy. "We can't stand by and let someone decide who eats and who doesn't."

"You can say that." Mr. Branson emerged from the back waving his chubby finger at her. "But your livelihood and your family's existence don't depend on your shop. She owns more than half the buildings in this town. She decides who stays and who leaves."

A mumble of agreement merged through the room. Fire spliced Catherine's middle. No one should have this type of power over another.

She cast a fleeting glance to Mr. Dandy, snatched up her food-laden basket, and then slammed her money on the counter. "We shall see about that."

Dr. David Ross arrived to town in plenty of time to make his lunch appointment with his great aunt. Her unexpected request after a month of silence inspired healthy caution. Though she'd never wielded her power against him, he'd heard her behavior with others proved…tedious at times. After all, she remained the final link to Uncle Jeffrey and, perhaps, a thread of hope for his father's reconciliation with the Cavanaughs.

David simply wished to do his job—offer quality medical services to those in need, without additional drama—but something thwarted his dream at every turn. From the Zeppelin's destruction of his hospital to the reduced finances of many of his former benefactors. Surely God believed in this dream as much as he did?

A flash of red and cream caught in his periphery. Across the street, past the Public Park and tram stop, hurried a familiar figure. The vibrant cranberry hues of her gown beneath the light color of her coat danced in contrast to the colorless buildings lining the street. Though the large black hat with a plumage of burgundy shaded half her profile, it failed to obscure her silhouette from identification.

Catherine Dougall.

She stopped at the street corner, loaded basket pulled against her chest, and sent a furtive glance about her. What on earth was his newest nurse doing? In a wink, she darted down a narrow alleyway and into the dingy shadows.

David didn't stop to think. He checked the street for oncoming vehicles and then dashed after her. He'd known her a grand total of three months, and in that time, she'd transformed from a woman dabbling on the edge of a promiscuous life to a community servant, working alongside him in his hospital with tireless diligence like her sister, Ashleigh.

Except she wasn't her sister.

Ashleigh didn't twist David's emotions to the edge of uncertainty. Nor did the younger Dougall sister keep him guessing about her intentions. He shouldn't follow Catherine, but ever since his involvement in her conversion, he'd accepted the responsibility of spiritual mentor…or at least, that's what he told himself.

The alleyway spilled into another, then another, each time slowing David's pace until he snatched a glance at Catherine's movements and he was able to follow again…all the way to Old Rutland Avenue, a narrow lane far enough from Main to hide the less savory side of Ednesbury. Stripped, clapboard houses, gray and broken from misuse and age, stood in direct contrast to the Georgian-style buildings on the previous two streets.

David swallowed a surge of disappointment. Had she resorted to her old ways? No. Surely she couldn't hide her true nature in the confines and emotional demands of an overcrowded hospital. Then what brought her to Old Rutland?

David stopped in the shadows as Catherine caught up with a young woman on the threshold of a dilapidated building. The girl looked unwell, with the frame of an advanced pregnancy and the pallor of hunger. Her tattered dress barely offered any barrier from the early autumn chill. David couldn't understand the exchange, but Catherine's intentions became clear.

She set the basket of food down at the woman's feet and slipped off her fashionable coat. Despite the obvious objections of the girl, Catherine wrapped the coat about the girl's shoulders, brooking no refusal. David's grin started slow and spread across his face.

Catherine wasn't consorting with people from her past.

She was living graciously in her present.

His chest expanded with a warm rush of relief...and something else less definable.

Catherine turned back toward his direction. He waited for her to step into the alleyway before emerging from his hiding place.

"Miss Dougall?"

"Dav—" She snapped her rose lips closed around his name and blinked those large sapphire eyes at him. "What on earth are you doing here?"

"I was wondering the same about you."

She pressed her palm to her chest and drew in a deep breath. "I...I was completing an errand."

"That took you all the way to Old Rutland?"

She opened her mouth to answer but then stopped. The twinkle in her eyes should have provided fair warning before she unleashed her disarming smile, but it unfurled with unsteadying potency, leaving him a bit mesmerized. She unwittingly wielded it like a weapon, but oh, what a dangerous tool if she ever used it with purpose.

"You have the most impeccable timing, Dr. Ross."

Her sudden change in topic took him off-guard. "Do I?"

She tossed a look over her shoulder as she walked back toward Main Street. "Providential, you might even say."

The pixie glint teased his own smile alive. "Oh really?"

Her gaze took a subtle pleading turn. "Would you happen to have an extra pound? Or several shillings at the very least."

He covered his growing smile by looking away. After witnessing her exchange with the poor woman on the street, he knew very well why she needed the additional funds. "Didn't I give you enough for the supplies this morning?"

"Yes…well, I procured a few additional items." She rubbed her palms against her arms in an attempt to warm herself against the morning breeze, deliberately keeping her gaze from his. "Unforeseen, you understand."

David unbuttoned his coat. "And you lost your coat?"

"Yes, about that." She looked down at her gown as if realizing her loss. Her words formed slowly, and he could almost see the frantic search for an excuse evolving in her pretty head. "I must have left it somewhere."

He wrapped his coat around her shoulders, and a few loose strands of her ebony curls tickled his knuckles. He paused, fastened in place by sapphire eyes, the scent of lavender, and a growing tenderness. "How very careless of you." His words worked out through a whisper.

Catherine pinched the coat against her throat and stepped back, breaking whatever spell held him in place. "I'm afraid it is a rather unlovely character trait, my dear doctor. Yet another flaw to add to my needed reforms." Her smile returned with a little too much brightness. "But about those extra funds?"

He'd give her persistence, as well as a few other distracting descriptions. Their friendship was an odd one, but authentic in ways he'd never experienced. He knew her past and had witnessed her transformation. Somehow, the knowledge inspired an inexplicable protectiveness and exquisite freedom. No games. No social dance. Beautiful authenticity.

"Miss Dougall, you are aware that we have a strict budget during these war times?"

She fidgeted with the edge of her gloves and finally released a sigh. "I... I reallocated some of the money."

"You reallocated it?" He punched his lips tight against his burgeoning smile.

"For the best possible reasons."

"Well, if it is for the best reasons." He took off his hat and dusted the brim. "I suppose we can cut rations for the wounded to make up the difference."

She whimpered, eyes rounding like a wounded animal's. "Over an extra pound?"

She must have recognized his teasing because she narrowed those feline eyes and jammed one hand on her hip. "You enjoy that, don't you?"

"What? Cutting rations?"

"Not once do you torment my sister with your teasing, and certainly not my mother, but me?" She wagged her finger at him, unleashing his smile. "You practically torture me with it."

"No one else is quite so entertaining."

"Indeed." She waved a hand in the air. "I assume then, you know exactly why I need the extra money?"

"And how you lost your coat."

"Yes, that." Her gaze lingered in his for a second longer, tightening the inexplicable bond he had with her. She looked away. "All because of your ridiculous aunt."

"My aunt?"

Catherine resumed her walk with a quicker step, a habit he'd noticed when she was particularly annoyed or thinking. He rushed to keep up.

"The way she pushes people around in this town is ridiculous. The weak. The strong. She doesn't care who they are as long as she holds them under her wrinkled old thumb. How can she be so unfeeling?" Catherine paused to send a scorching glare. "She is such a...such a—"

"Buzzard? Snake?"

Her brows rose. "To name a few."

He shoved his hands into his trouser pockets. "What about viper, or perhaps tyrant, or—"

"Wait." She stopped him with a raised hand. "Why are you helping me come up with insults for her? Aren't you supposed to keep me on the straight and narrow?"

"Admittedly." He looked up to the sky, making a poor attempt at keeping his expression thoughtful. He preferred a lighthearted turn in the conversation, untainted by his aunt's reputation. "But I can only imagine the choices I offered were of a kinder nature than the ones rolling around in that head of yours."

Catherine opened her mouth as if to object and then stopped, clearly revisiting a few unnamed insults. She offered a repentant sigh. "You're right."

"And which of those horrible attributes of my aunt's has inflamed your cause for justice today?

"This time?" Catherine stepped onto Main Street and slid him a glare. "She's in danger of becoming a murderer."

Chapter Two

David grabbed Catherine's arm before she entered Main Street and drew her back into the alley, away from curious onlookers.

"What are you talking about?"

Poor man. David Ross knew a great deal about taking care of wounded soldiers, but managing the likes of his notorious aunt? Catherine doubted he had much expertise. Despite his good intentions, his life had been one of shelter and care, with proper parents as guides. What did he know of manipulation and betrayal?

The less for his kind heart, the better. Which certainly meant keeping her emotional distance. He was the type of man who could make a woman believe in glass slippers and magic – and Catherine had never put much stock in fairytales.

"She's made an edict throughout town."

"An edict?" His grin returned with a hint of disbelief to curl the edges but with no show of his infamous dimple, the one piece of his pristine disposition which hinted at mischief. "Like a king?"

"Exactly." She pointed at him. "It's serious, Dr. Ross. She's taken away a person's right to buy and sell."

"How can she possibly do that?"

"Because, as you said, she practically owns this village." Catherine pinched her fists tight. "Oh, if I had the money I'd buy back those buildings. Hateful woman! What else should we expect from the old…the...the…"

"Tyrant."

The tilt in his smile proved he still doubted the gravity of his aunt's decree. Well, this news should sober him. "If any of her shopkeepers sell to those undeserving, then they are in danger of losing their livelihood."

"Undeserving?"

"Yes. The poor, the outcast." She waved a hand toward herself. "The fallen."

David stared at her for a full ten seconds as if processing the information took more effort than usual. "Why?"

"Why?" Catherine gave a humorous laugh. "Because she can." She pulled the coat to her chest to keep the warmth and scent nearby for sweet reassurance. It smelled of peppermint, a plant he grew for medicinal purposes, but the scent clung to him like a personality trait – refreshing, sweet, and inducing a Christmasy anticipation. "Something must be done before worse things than angry edicts occur." She shrugged out of his coat, reluctant to part with its scent. "Much worse."

His jaw stiffened with purpose as he took the proffered coat. "You are right. Something must be done...and I should be the one to do it."

She turned and stepped from the alleyway, only to meet the triumphant glare of Mr. Dandy. He leaned against one of the few trees in the Public Park, pen and pad in hand, with a smile boasting enough wicked confidence to curl Catherine's stomach.

"Dr. Ross, I'm afraid we have an additional problem." He followed the direction of her gesturing nod. "I can almost promise you that tomorrow's news will not please your aunt one bit."

David pushed opened the door to *Bree's Gallery* and savored the scent of fresh chop from the luncheon bar. His great aunt only dined in the finest places, and *Bree's* boasted the best Ednesbury offered. He'd been on his guard since receiving her dining invitation, and Catherine's news only heightened his suspicion. What could she possibly want?

The host recognized David at once and ushered him to follow. Aunt Maureen's silence since the day he'd moved his hospital to Roth Hall, the Dougall family estate, blared her disapproval. He'd never understood his aunt's long-standing hatred against the family. *Unworthy*, she'd called them. She embraced the societal chasm like a tsar, and her black-and-white thinking skewed her vision. Perhaps he could take up his father's mantle and attempt the impossible—logic. David smiled at the thought of his gregarious father – the one person in the family to shatter the stifling rules and marry outside of the Cavanaughs expectations. The decision had incurred disinheritance and broken his father's heart.

With the recent news about his aunt, David was all the more thankful for the distance which lessened the Cavanaughs influence…lessened, but not extinguished.

David slowed his approach to his aunt. Although his mother had only died a month ago, an ache of loss remained a constant presence. Aunt Maureen had never approved of his mother.

She sat at a table overlooking the rest of the lower level of the restaurant, a perch to keep her aware of all the goings on around her. Her throne.

"Aunt Maureen."

Her steel gray eyes kept their hold on him as he sat. "David."

He never allowed his gaze to waver. Aunt Maureen brandished intimidation with the precision of a skilled surgeon, cutting people down to her will. He would not be one of those victims, for both his parents' sakes.

"I was surprised to receive your invitation. I assumed, after I moved my patients to Roth Hall, I'd lost your favor."

She gestured toward the seat across from her. "I have considered the situation and…regret I made such a hasty decision in not supporting your efforts with more clarity."

David folded his hands on the table, keeping his expression as neutral as possible. Her scripted speech curved with a hidden agenda that squeezed out the slightest hope he'd entertained on his walk across town. "I think your lack of support was crystal clear, Aunt."

She raised her brow and, if he wasn't mistaken, upturned one side of her smile. Maybe his stubbornness impressed her a little.

"I realize you could not have controlled the Zeppelin attack on our village or the destruction of your hospital. And I understand you needed immediate housing for your wounded, a service I could not provide at the time."

Could not? Or would not?

"I've come to appreciate the necessary benefits of having a hospital in town and recognize your giftedness in your occupation."

No doubt the prestige a war hospital brought holds no bearing on her sudden change of heart?

"Even though a doctor doesn't increase one's social status?"

She met his challenge with a narrowed gaze, taking time to stir her tea before answering. "I wouldn't expect you to choose a socially advantageous career with your father as an example."

"My parents taught me to value what matters most. Compassion over social status and kindness over pious edicts."

She took a sip of her tea, unflapped by his response. "I will take your own customary insolence as part of the grieving process for your mother and overlook it this time." There was a distinct warning in the downward turn of her mouth. "And I did send your father twenty pounds as evidence of my condolences."

Because money solved everything.

"Is that all you have to say, Aunt Maureen? Your regret for the negative public response to your lack of support for the hospital and an insult about my family's choices? Your change of heart doesn't have anything to do with the Dougalls allowing me to use Roth Hall as a hospital, does it?"

She almost imperceptivity halted her movements as she dusted scone crumbs from her fingertips. "I've already stated my regret over my lack of support for you. As far as the Dougalls?" She spat out the name. "I've never hidden my distaste for Victoria Dougall and any of her family."

"Why all this anger for a family who have done nothing to you?"

Her fist tightened on the table and then relaxed. "Nothing? How little you know of the power of the heart to forget. It never forgets. Should mind and body fail, the heart remembers." She looked away and drew in a deep breath, her attention returning to him. "I have an offer for you, to make amends for my lack of support and to provide a long-term opportunity for your service."

David remained silent, waiting.

"I am certain the financial stress and emotional demands of not only housing wounded soldiers but also war orphans in her home has caused some... discomfort for Moriah Dougall."

He couldn't deny it. Mrs. Dougall's frayed nerves proved as unpredictable as Germany's movements in this war. She neither had the financial resources, long-term space, or emotional fortitude, to secure his needs for the wounded soldiers coming in from the Front.

"I've made a list of possible facilities for your new hospital, all of which are within the town limits. They each require some form of renovation or repair before they are fit for your medical needs, but I plan to cover those costs for the purpose of ensuring your service as administrator."

She slid a slip of paper across the table to him. David scanned over the names of the properties, each carefully chosen for location, space, and garden areas. Perfect places, and convenient to the train depot and supplies.

"These...these properties are superior to anything I could have imagined."

Her smile teased larger, more confident. "Along with this facility, I plan to provide a regular stipend for supplies and equipment. Based on my figures, I propose this initial amount." She slid another paper to him with a number scribbled.

David blinked at the unexpected generosity.

"And, of course, a comfortable salary for you, to ensure you can complete your tasks but also support a family in your future. I have written the salary below the stipend costs."

"This is quite generous of you."

"I see the need to change my expectations as our village continues to grow. And perhaps this agreement will lead to a reconciliation of your father's position to the family, something we both recognize is a desire of his heart."

David measured each of her words, waiting for the dark unveiling of her well-placed scheme. She'd secured all of her marks, but at what cost?

"It's an overwhelming proposition."

"One over which you shouldn't hesitate, but knowing your mind, I will give you two months to answer. We should be able to come to an agreement before Christmas, don't you think?" She nodded, taking another sip of tea. "Two months. And I'll even make the announcement at my Annual Christmas Gala. You only need do one, small thing for me."

The lynch pin emerged like a scalpel. "Your price."

"Everything has a price, my dear boy, it is the game of life." She lowered her cup to the table, her eyes darkening with her smile. "We all must learn to play it, even clever, good-hearted men like yourself. And this menial price comes with the benefits of the financial security for your future, your father's happiness, and the good of this dear village."

The sense of dread deepened with her summary. "What do you want, Aunt Maureen?"

"Once the hospital property is readied for patients and you take command of your new facility, once I announce your allegiance at the Christmas Gala…"

David braced himself.

"I want you to cease all contact and communication with the Dougall family."

Chapter Three

"I'm so glad you've arrived."

Ashleigh met Catherine at the door. Her sister's calm voice belied the concern in her eyes. Ashleigh's white nurse's hat sat crooked on her dark head, another evidence of a long morning with the wounded, and her pale face marked the remnants of her recovery from pneumonia – a sickness which almost took her life.

Catherine rushed forward. "Are you all right?"

"*I'm* fine." Ashleigh placed a reassuring hand on Catherine's arm and looked to the door as David entered, arms laden with more supplies. "But we're out of morphine. I just used the last gauze." She sent Catherine a pleading look. "And we're in desperate need of more diapers."

Catherine waved the bag she held like a flag of victory. "Ask and ye shall receive."

Ashleigh snatched it away. "I'm not sure what's worse—moaning wounded or screaming infants."

Catherine took a few items from one of the boxes in David's arms. "I'll take the wounded. They're less terrifying." She shot David a triumphant grin before turning back to her sister. "I seem to have a particular interest in the needy."

"I assure you, sister-dear, the infants we have upstairs are quite needy."

"Ah, yes." Catherine lifted a bottle of the morphine and tipped it toward her sister. "But I prefer those who smile when they see me coming as opposed to little eyes which widen in fear."

Ashleigh laughed. "That's not true."

"It feels true. Have you seen how Clara Cramer's nearly bulge when I enter the room? One would think I was out to hurt the poor child."

"She responds that way to everyone."

"Except you." Catherine shook her head. "You're the calming angel to every little lost lamb."

"Come now, Catherine," David interrupted, placing one box on the entry table. "You make a world of difference for those soldiers."

"Is that so?"

"Certainly." David's lips barely twitched to warn of his teasing. "You significantly improve the view of any room you enter."

Catherine's mouth swung unhinged. From the sudden flush of red saturating David's face, he hadn't meant to compliment her…especially in such a flattering way. The smile forming on her lips came all the way from her heart.

Someone ought to rescue the poor man from his humiliation.

She tipped her chin up to pose as she'd seen on an old Gibson Girl poster. "I *have* always enjoyed being admired. Clearly, I've found the perfect occupation." She chuckled and walked toward the West Wing. "I shouldn't leave my admirers waiting."

"Catherine." Ashleigh stopped her. "I need to talk to you about an unexpected change of plans."

Catherine exchanged a glance with David. Sudden tension ignited a swell of nausea.

Ashleigh drew a letter from the pocket of her apron. Her eyes, weary from a long day's work, took on a hint of something more…something worse.

Catherine's hand went to her stomach. "Grandmama?"

Ashleigh nodded. "She's not recovered from her previous illness. In fact, as soon as Sam arrived back home from his visit here, he wrote me straight away. She's not well."

"It would be like her to not tell anyone."

"No doubt where you got your stubbornness." Ashleigh's attempt at lightening the mood only deepened Catherine's regret. So many years wasted on misplaced resentment against Ashleigh. So many lost moments while Catherine chased men's attentions and heightened family status. She'd embrace any likeness to her sensible and gracious Grandmama. Even stubbornness.

"How early can you travel?"

"A ship leaves in three days."

David stepped forward. "You'll have to catch the train by tomorrow."

"Yes." Ashleigh looked back to Catherine. "And pray that's enough time."

The gravity of those words ushered death's reality into the room, as palpable as the wounded's presence next door. It twisted her heart into a helpless patter. "There has to be enough time." Catherine took her sister by the shoulders. "She...she'd want you there."

Ashleigh covered one of Catherine's hands with her own. "She'd want both of us there."

"But she *needs* you, and we can't both leave David."

His name slipped off her tongue as easily as if she'd always spoken it. She pinched her heart against the easy familiarity with a firm grip.

"I'll leave Kara in charge of the orphanage. With Fanny and Michael's assistance, she should be able to manage." Ashleigh shrugged one shoulder, her walnut eyes lighting with humor. "She practically runs it now since I've had to give so much time to the hospital."

"We never imagined the influx of soldiers, or the Zep attack."

She waved away the apology in David's words. "I came to help you serve. I have no regrets. And I plan to leave Catherine in charge of the other two nurses. She has the makings of an excellent administrator."

Catherine's gaze swung to her sister. "Me? That can't be a good idea."

"Why not? You've certainly proven yourself," David chimed in.

"I've only been working with patients for six weeks. That does not give me expertise—"

"You've a quick mind and are a born leader, two very important skills you've always possessed, Catherine." Ashleigh's smile grew. "I think it's time you stop hiding in the shadows—a place you were never meant to be."

"The shadows and I are getting on just fine."

"I have every faith in you." The confidence in David's expression proved his utter insanity. His dimple flickered with mischief. "Your sister wouldn't lie."

"You can't be serious." Catherine looked from one to the other. She wasn't the sort of person to place in charge of nurses? Or anyone, really. "I'm more of a rabble rouser than a bringer of calm."

"You've already taken pains to develop daily activities for the soldiers to keep them occupied. You've garnered more volunteers from the village than David or I have ever brought."

Well placed words at just the right times—and maybe the subtlest blackmail—worked wonders. Catherine cringed. No, not blackmail exactly....more of guilt-induced persuasion.

"You're an excellent problem solver and initiator."

She needled David with a look. Being an 'initiator' had got her into her present trouble in the first place.

David ignored her glare. "Both qualities are valuable to us."

"And calm isn't always what's needed." Ashleigh's dark eyes took on a playful glint. "Besides, you have Grandmama's strength. A fresh pair of eyes and a strong determination offer a whole new perspective." She looked to David. "We need new ideas for bringing more funds into the hospital if we're going to be able to save it."

David's smile lost a little of its gleam, and Catherine perked to the alert. Watching him work day after day with these patients, whether soldiers or people in town, proved his passion for his profession, his calling. She might have lost a chance at her dream, but could she help him save his?

She drew in a breath of determination and faced her sister, the lunacy apparently contagious. "All right, I'll try. But if I fail miserably, I'll blame both of you without hesitation, and you can explain this entire insanity to the patients. Agreed?"

David and Ashleigh exchanged a smile then Ashleigh put out her hand. "Agreed." Catherine took her sister's hand. "But I know you. You won't fail."

David had never realized how much of a buffer Ashleigh provided between him and Catherine until she was gone. Though he'd spent many hours in Catherine's presence, enjoying her transformation from flirt to friend, Ashleigh had usually accompanied them, providing a distraction to his feelings he didn't realize he needed. At Ashleigh's sudden absence, he engaged in hourly consults and close proximity. Her presence dug like a two-edged sword, a constant reminder of his aunt's dream-dangling wager pitted against his deepening friendship.

Then there was the added awareness of knowing exactly where she stood in any room he entered. Like an obsessive need, he found himself trying to locate her and make a mental tap at her well-being before moving ahead with his plans. Maybe her pregnancy added an extra glow to her cheeks, because for some reason her beauty captivated with a longer hold than usual.

Truth be told, he liked her. He admired her focus and quick mind. Her humor appealed to his internal wit, and her transparency proved a refreshing change from the typical pretense in the social world around him...but he'd spent his life determined to stay free of a woman like her—strong-willed, sarcastic, hot-tempered, impulsive...and distractingly beautiful. Nothing he'd imagined for himself, and yet, somehow, exactly what he craved. To indulge in the sheer pleasure of her company.

He drew his attention away. His aunt's ultimatum flared warning, causing a chasm between him and Catherine that left residual discomfort in his chest. How could he encourage such a pairing? Social expectations and his aunt's voice bit into his conscience and braided with his convictions from childhood, sending him back a step and cooling the heat of curiosity. He couldn't afford an attraction to her, not with the hospital and his dream in peril.

But his rebel gaze returned to her face. Instead of greeting him with her usual disarming smile, her expression darkened like a storm cloud with an extra lightning sparkle in those sapphire eyes. "We need to talk."

"Clearly." He took her by the arm and pulled her just outside the doorway, free of curious eyes and ears. Being on the receiving end of her fury was a new experience for him. "Have I done something to offend you?"

"You?" Her brow crinkled in confusion paired with a hesitant blink. "Why would I ever be angry with you?"

The question, so honest and direct, completely unfurled his smile. "Close quarters. Long nights. It will only take time."

"I doubt it." She almost grinned, but must have remembered why she'd stormed toward him with such wrath. "It's about Louisa. She left us."

"Left us?"

"I confronted her about her inappropriate use of the Bipp paste, and she threw a bottle of it at me then stormed from the house."

"Inappropriate use?"

"I informed her if she couldn't perform her job appropriately, perhaps she could benefit from *my* training." She gestured toward herself. "And that didn't suit her at all."

Louisa, a newly trained nurse, accepting help from Catherine? "I should think not." He studied her face and her stormy blue eyes. She looked rather fascinating when she was angry.

"This is no smiling matter, Dr. Ross." She pointed her finger to his chest. "It's quite serious."

"Yes, of course." He wiped the smile from his face but not from his mind.

"She refused to place Bipp on half of our current patients."

"What?" All humor fled him with a cold wave of clarity. The Bismuth iodoform paraffin paste kept the wounds from becoming infected. The nurses had been trained to use either Bipp or Carbolic lotion on any unhealed injuries, particularly the large ones, regardless of the wound's severity.

"She was trying to conserve it for the ones she'd deemed more worthy. But how can she decide who will live life well, whatever their circumstances, amputee or not? If the poor men survived the train all the way from the Front, they deserve whatever chance we can give them." Catherine growled. "And I'm certain she took some of the morphine with her when she left as a little salt in the wound."

26

What a disaster! Losing another nurse and important medicine? Catherine's brow crinkled with worry lines. "I'm sorry, Dr. Ross."

"This wasn't your fault." He attempted to smooth away her concern with his words. "Thankfully, I have another shipment of morphine arriving in two days."

She nodded. "I'll collect it when I gather our usual supplies."

"And visit your friend in the process?" He hoped to tease away a few more of her worry lines.

A waif of a smile touched her lips. "I have no idea to what you refer."

The hint of mischief in her eyes, the shared secret, tempted him a step closer. "Well, should you recall, I implore you to take care. Certain places in the village are less polite to your class, let alone your sex, than others."

She stared up at him. An enchanting tenderness softened her features to display the sensitive, beautiful soul hidden beneath her usual strength and fire. The invisible bond born from the night he'd prayed with her a few months ago knotted tight against his best efforts to fight against it.

She lowered her head and shrugged her shoulder, as if passing off the awkward moment. "Next time I visit Branson's, I'll be certain to heed your advice."

"I doubt you'll be welcome in Branson's ever again." Moriah Dougall's voice hammered into the conversation with its usual anxious edge, eyes narrowed with accusation. "Not after everyone sees Mr. Dandy's latest article in the paper. We are ruined."

She rattled papers at them and shook her golden head, her brow a furrowed wave of frustration.

Catherine's shoulders dropped. "What do you mean, Mother?"

"I believe you have just secured your reputation as a woman of ill-repute."

Even as her mother marched forward, pages in the air, Catherine braced herself, closing her eyes for a moment against her mother's needling implications. She understood the consequences of her previous lifestyle. Being a notorious flirt and compromising herself for the affection of a rich gentleman carried with it certain unhappy residual effects, but when her previous reputation reared its ugliness to impact the people she loved, it brought an added sting.

It was impossible to forget the stains, let alone forgive herself for them.

Her mother shoved the paper into her hands. "I don't know how much more my nerves can take. Wounded soldiers, crying babies, and now, our names are slandered in the paper."

The article wasn't what Catherine expected. Mr. Dandy failed to report about David, a well-respected gentleman, walking out of a dark alleyway with the village flirt. Nor did he mention their close proximity, the mere memory of which warmed her cheeks.

At least David's reputation remained beautifully intact.

He stood near her shoulder, so she turned to give him access to the paper. Mr. Dandy focused the full potency of his verbal venom on Catherine's association with those of ill-repute, bringing into question Catherine's character as well as that of the entire Dougall household.

With a final flair of melodrama, Mr. Dandy reiterated the need to keep Ednesbury's reputation as pristine as its benefactress, which clearly marked the influence for his bias. Catherine almost let loose her own verbal tirade but remembered David's proximity, and out of sheer will, kept her thoughts about his aunt to herself. She never imagined learning to control her tongue could be so exhausting.

Mr. Dandy ended the article with a clear proclamation that "anyone who associates with persons of less moral fortitude should be shunned until they can reform themselves."

Catherine rolled her eyes at the utter arrogance. She could imagine a few very powerful means of reformation she'd like to carry out on Mr. Dandy and his nefarious intentions, starting particularly with some tweezers and his spindly moustache. Moral fortitude, indeed!

"You are too impulsive, leaving the rest of us to suffer from your rash decisions." Her mother snatched back the paper, turned on her heel, and walked down the hallway.

"I would rather do something than nothing at all," Catherine called after her. She sighed and lowered her voice. "How can she ever understand?"

She looked up at David, afraid he might share her mother's disappointment, but she should have known better. Somehow he saw her…truly, in a way no other man did. Beyond the frills and the façade, the past and the mistakes, his intense stare looked into her wretched heart – and still wanted to keep looking. If she had been pure and good, like her sister, she would offer him every part of her for the rest of their days.

But she was nothing like her sister. Neither pure nor good.

"But you understand—and you can make a difference, no matter how small." He lowered his gaze. "You're brave enough, I'm certain."

His smile flickered before he returned to the hospital room. If bravery meant fear mixed with a healthy dose of righteous anger and a reluctant dash of humility, then she had enough courage pumping through her veins to change the entire village.

Or, at the very least, cause some trouble.

And she had much more practice with the latter than the former.

Chapter Four

Branson's delivery boy was an easy sale, especially when Catherine mentioned David Ross' name. Giving Caleb an extra shilling to secure his solidarity around the secrecy of exactly 'who' was picking up the supplies didn't hurt either. She knew his family from long ago. Hard-working, honest country folk.

Before her many failures, she would have sneered at such a simple life. Now? It sounded as welcome as the memory of David's warm coat around her shoulders.

Whether Mr. Dandy's article impacted Branson's choice to allow her into his shop or not, Catherine had no desire to find out. She wouldn't risk losing her chance to get another package of food to Meredith, especially since the poor girl's child was due soon.

Hiding out at Madame Rousell's while she waited came with its own benefits. It tempted a sweet longing. A tug from a past consumed by the search for status, profitable marriages and elegant fashions. She ran her fingers over a white French tulle veil, its intricate scalloped edging and delicate rose designs towed at the ache in her chest. Fragile, pure, beautiful – things she could no longer offer any man. She indulged the broken dream, even tortured herself with it. Daydreaming over a wedding veil?

She sighed and caught sight of a rouge gown which looked like a design from one of the many women couturiers she admired, Jeanne Paquin. The sleeves draped to the elbows in a dramatic fashion with bounds of satin dropping from an empire waistline to the floor in a cascade of reds and golds. The diagonal drape of the midsection of the gown reminded Catherine of similar styles from ten years before, only updated with glamour and an uncorseted look. It was spectacular.

Oh, to bring fashion to life!

30

"I see you have finally found your way back into my shop, *ma chère*. Even if it is only to hide."

"Madame Roussell?" Catherine let the lace slip through her fingers and turned to the sound of the extravagant proprietor's lilting voice.

A middle-aged lady in ravishing purple, she wore makeup like a cloak and a smile like a promise. *You will find something beautiful in my shop.* Her smile appeared more dazzling framed by a deep blush of red lip stain.

"Your heart loves beautiful things, oui?"

Catherine's fingertips still hummed from the touch of silk and fairytales, but her head grounded firm in reality. "It is a weakness of mine."

"*Mais non.*" Madame left her perch behind the counter and moved with the grace of royalty toward Catherine. "It is an appreciation, not a weakness. It is a gift to not only appreciate beauty, but to see it in the most menial of places, perhaps in the most undeserving?"

Her piercing fawn gaze spoke of how news of Catherine's actions the previous week had spread through the village like a plague, but Madame seemed to keep abreast of the most intricate news, even Catherine's.

She challenged Madame's declaration. "Many beautiful things may be more sting than silk."

"Ah." Her pointed finger, almost statuesque, reminded Catherine of a quirky, mustached actor she'd seen in a recent moving picture show. "Those who are wise have learned to sort out the two." She took the veil from the display and folded it over her arm. "Zis lovely veil is beautiful, of course, and to the untrained eye, it appears fragile, *oui*?"

Catherine waited for Madame's point.

"But it is made strong by threads woven together. Even a weak thread, when bound with strong ones, strengthens the entire veil." The woman's painted lips tilted, evidently proud of her subtle—or not so subtle—lesson. "You have made mistakes? I saw you with Monsieur Cavanaugh and I see you now." She blew air through her lips in response. "We all make mistakes. But you are strong. And you can take the strength you've learned from the *qu'est-ce que c'est*...stings, and make something beautiful."

She offered Madame a polite smile, and Madame caught her.

"You doubt me, do you? You do not think a veil is in your future?"

"You are kind, Madame." Catherine glanced around the shop and sighed, taking a step toward the door to escape all the empty promises housed in lace. "But I don't believe in fairytales, especially now."

She took another step forward, unflapped by Catherine's response. "Whether you believe or not does not change the truth."

Catherine conceded her grin in the face of such flagrant optimism.

"The passionate soul has the rockiest road to romance." She released a trill of a laugh and placed her hand over her heart, a conspiratory light of kinship flickering in her eyes. "Rocky, but oh, so magnifique."

The brown eye paste, popular in most social settings, enhanced the tea-color of Madame's eyes in a dramatic sort of way. Passionate soul? Madame exuded it, but her prediction of Catherine's future missed the mark. In fact, it missed the entire target. "Your French optimism, Madame?"

"*Non, non.* The French are realists. Have you not seen our art?" She waved her hand as if to dismiss Catherine's statement. "But Madame knows. God would not give you such passion for nothing. Romance waits in your future. Perhaps with fairytales and French tulle veils?"

She chuckled, clearly happy with her little rhyme and prediction, then returned to her perch at the counter, but her stare rested back on Catherine. "You are not friendless, *ma petite* rebel."

Catherine's face warmed from the compassion in Madame's pet name.

"Your _Grandmama's reputation is not easily forgotten. I see her in you, in your fury to do what is right. To make good from mistakes. Grace breeds generosity…and courage." She nodded her dark head. "I will help you in any way I can. In life and in l'amour. Remember that."

Catherine poised at the door for a moment longer, clinging to one last second hint of promise in Madame's optimism, but as the exuberant woman hummed a melody, Catherine sighed away the daydream. A firm grip on reality propelled her out of the shop door and back to her life. Pondering useless thoughts wasted time and heart, and even if the pull of the veil brought her back to Madame's shop next week, or next month, the mid-morning breeze would chill away the daydream as always.

And Grandmama? How could she be anything like her saintly grandmother? And for what menial mistakes should Grandmama ever atone?

Caleb had just finished placing the packages in the car and greeted Catherine with his gapped smile. "It's all there, Miss."

"Thank you. Here's another pence for your trouble."

"No trouble. You and Dr. Ross are helpin' take care of them soldiers on the hill. I don't need no extra reason to make sure you get your orders."

And David's reputation covers over a multitude of sins.

"I'm pleased to hear chivalry still resides in our village."

He stood a bit taller, tipped his cap, and returned to the mercantile. It was good to know that some hearts remained true, regardless of the bullies flaunting their power from gilded halls.

Catherine turned to Mason, who immediately moved to open the car door for her. She sent a quick glance behind her, as if someone cared about her conversation with the chauffer, but in a village with people like Mr. Dandy or spies like Madame Rousell, possibilities thrived in unexpected places.

"I need to make one more stop, Mason. Do you mind waiting a little longer?"

He dipped his head, acquiescing to her request.

"Thank you." She took the basket she'd brought from the back of the car and filled it with a careful choice of provisions. Then she placed the winter quilt she'd carried from home in North Carolina. Spun by a few Appalachian women, the brilliant rainbow of autumn-hues livened up everything else in her arms.

"I don't plan to be long."

She started up the street and, with another glance around her, took the first alleyway in the direction of her goal.

■■■

David placed his palms against the desk in front of him and released a sigh, bending forward almost in prayer. *What am I going to do, Lord?* One less nurse left the rest of them in dire straits until support arrived. His sister hinted at her return soon, but her last letter gave no specifics.

He massaged his fingers into his forehead, weary from the internal war of making bricks with no straw. His aunt's offer burned a hole in his jacket pocket as well as his conscience. He needed to help these soldiers, along with the people of Ednesbury who had supported this plan for the past year, but how?

He placed the envelope from his aunt in front of him on the table. The morphine was in short supply, the bedclothes in need of repair or replacement, and changing cloths ran low.

And Roth Hall? The old manor house wasn't equipped to be a long-term war hospital, especially due to the stress it inflicted on Moriah Dougall's fragile nerves. Aunt Maureen's wager stung with a renewed sense of urgency. Was this the only answer?

A knock at the door pulled him out of his mental doldrums. He stuffed the envelope back into his shirt pocket. "Come in."

Fanny, the copper-headed housekeeper who basically kept the fragile Mrs. Dougall and Roth Hall in working order, entered. "Dr. Ross, I'm sorry to interrupt what little rest you take for yourself."

"Not at all."

She stepped forward, paper in hand. "This telegram just arrived for you, but it is marked for last week. I believe the postman is falling under the ill-effects of Lady Cavanaugh's particular dislike for Roth Hall."

"I'm sorry, Fanny." His association with his aunt along with the secret wager encouraged his guilty conscience. "I will try to speak to her."

"I don't think she's one to listen to reason, sir, but I'm certain the Dougall's would be obliged for any way you might soften her dislike. It's a bit inconvenient, especially for you today, I should think."

He raised a brow, took the proffered paper, and slipped the card from the envelope.

Coming early. Arrive Thursday. 11am train. Jess

David looked up and met Fanny's knowing gaze. If his sister had made such an impulsive decision, he knew her grief over their mother's death drove her mad. Jessica didn't handle idle time well. She craved distraction. Employment.

His emotions dropped like led in his stomach. "What day is it?"

A hint of a smile softened Fanny's features. "Thursday, sir."

He couldn't keep his own smile from responding. "We were in need of another nurse, Fanny."

"I shall prepare a room."

Catherine knocked on the worn wooden door, its marker made barely visible by weather, erosion, and time. The narrow lane, crooked and dingy, stretched and curved like a bent finger around other similar apartments, each leaving its own blight on the scenery. A stench of sickness and poverty swelled from further down the lane, giving Catherine the slightest gratitude she didn't have to search further down the streets for Meredith's home.

She knocked again, a hollow sound against the thin boards, and moved her gloved hand under her nose to abate the stench, a skill honed at the hospital. The distant clop of footsteps rose from within, halting and slow. An older woman, face creased with age, opened the door wide enough to peer out, her dark gaze riddled with suspicion.

"What'dya want?"

Catherine forced a smile and readjusted the basket over her arm, hoping the gift would curb the harshness in the woman's voice. Showing charity remained an out-of-practice skill, but she kept trying. "I've come to visit Meredith."

The woman gave Catherine another shrewd inspection before opening the door to its full width. She propped her spindly fingers on her thin waist and stood with a strength her waif-like frame defied. "You the one who gave her the fancy coat?"

"I am." Catherine gestured with her chin toward the basket, brimming with bread, cheese, and other staples. "I want to help her, and the child."

With a slight hesitation and enough warning in her grimace to leave a prickle on Catherine's face, the woman stepped aside to allow Catherine into the darkened hallway. Lit by a single lantern in the center of the narrow corridor, the hall rounded more like a tunnel than an entrance.

"She told me you'd be comin'. Blimey, she was right. I owe her a pence." The woman rubbed a palm against her weathered chin. "Told her not to set her cap at you keepin' to your word. Your kind never do."

"'Never' might be too bold a declaration at this point, perhaps?"

The woman stared long at Catherine and then chuckled, a raspy sound. "I 'ave to say, you're the first of your kind that's ever stepped foot in my apartments."

The rift between the social classes glared from the dingy hallway. Months ago, Catherine had embraced the distance, portraying herself as a wealthy heiress when all the while she'd stooped to whatever level she could to obtain a rich husband – only to end up as a castoff. Or she would be, once the news of her pregnancy became common knowledge.

"I hope to provide some help." Catherine followed the woman into the shadows. "It's getting colder out. I thought she might need something for her and the baby."

The woman paused and gestured toward the quilt in Catherine's hand. "I ain't never seen nothing like it before."

Catherine slid her hand over the soft, cool material – the bumps and curves evidence of knotted string and carefully woven seams by aged and experienced Appalachian hands. Patches taken from feed sacks and old garments pieced together in autumn hues to make something beautiful. "It was stitched by some women back home in North Carolina. My grandmother's housekeeper's family are quilters."

The woman reached out to touch the quilt but stopped just before her wrinkled fingers met the material. She curled her fingers back into her fist and continued her walk down the hall. "Something so pretty coming from scraps? Takes a gift to make useless pieces into something so useful and lovely."

Catherine studied the patchwork quilt with fresh eyes. Pieces? Remnants of dreams and hopes pieced together? She almost smiled. Could God make anything beautiful out of the remnants of her life?

The woman continued her conversation. "Meredith's been in good spirits the past two days. Had the wee babe three days ago, and it must've lightened her mood."

"Is the baby well?"

"These walls ain't much for privacy." She patted the thin board as she walked. "Heard him once or twice."

Him. Meredith had a baby boy. Catherine resisted the urge to rest her palm against her stomach, a growing awareness of the little life. When would she feel the little one inside of her? When would it become more than a mental assent?

Shadows, lamplight, and dust led the way to the last door on the right, half-hidden in the remaining shadows. The woman's knock sounded too loudly in the gray swell of silence.

"She must be taking a kip with the wee babe."

"I'm certain she's exhausted." Catherine pulled the quilt close to her chest to stay a sudden chill.

The woman knocked again, louder. A newborn cry rose in response.

"Well, she's inside, make no mistake." The woman shook the doorknob. "Meredith, open the door. You got company."

Nothing. Not even the sound of creaking floorboards. The baby's cry grew louder.

The apprehension building in Catherine's chest must have transferred to the proprietor. She fumbled through her pocket for a set of keys. "I don't understand that girl."

A sudden sense of dread chased a chill up Catherine's arms, her breath skimming shallow.

The key clicked and turned. The older woman pushed the door open, her grumbles dissolving into a gasp. "No!"

Catherine tightened her nerves and peered over the woman's shoulder into the room. Her hand flew to her mouth to ease a sudden swell of nausea, the basket crashing to the floor. Meredith's body swung from a rope in the middle the room, and at the poor girl's dangling feet, wrapped in Catherine's coat, lay the crying baby. A poorly written note, scrawled in large letters, read *Save my son.*

Chapter Five

David drew his pocket watch from his jacket and stepped from the car. Jessica's train arrived in a half hour, enough time for him to ensure Catherine's presence in Branson's didn't bring trouble. For anyone.

One look in the direction of the mercantile sent his hopes crashing. A large crowd had gathered near the front of the shop, and a scattered dissonance of raised voices carried over the cobblestone street.

What had Mr. Dandy's article produced? Where was Catherine?

As if in answer, her voice rose above the throng, a furious storm of American dialect and devil-may-care, sticking out from the rest of the crowd…as she usually did. David hurried forward and pressed into the circle, looking for his trouble-making American.

She stood in the center, facing Dr. Richard Carrier like a tigress ready to strike—eyes narrowed, one fist curled at her side and a cloak cradled in her other arm. Her cloak, in fact. The one she'd given to the woman in the alley.

Dr. Carrier faced Catherine with as much resolution, hands gripped on his hips, leaning from his tall height in a threatening manner. Catherine continued ranting, clearly nonplussed.

David wasn't the doctor's biggest supporter. The older man touted arrogance more than wisdom at times and cared little for new research in the profession, but he had been the town physician since David wore stockings and baby curls.

"How dare you accuse me of injustice?" Dr. Carrier's bass voice boomed each consonant with resounding accusation. "I am not bound to help those who have refused to help themselves." His brow bent in a fury of intimidation.

David released a sigh of resignation. Dr. Carrier clearly had no idea with whom he argued.

"Refuse to help themselves?" Her finger shot up like a dagger, pointing at Dr. Carrier's chest. "You're a physician, for heaven's sakes. You're obligated to help. Falling prey to the influences of higher class morality does not and should never refuse any woman the care she needs...even more a woman with a child."

David pushed forward to break into the circle, but when Catherine turned a little, he saw the bundle in her arms more clearly. A baby, newborn, face pinched as if he liked the argument about as well as David did. What was going on?

Dr. Carrier caught sight of David and his chin tilted in victory. "Ah, Dr. Ross will clarify the purpose of our profession. Not some wench who finds herself in the middle of Old Rutland with a dead whore and her newborn."

David caught Catherine's hand before her claws made a lasting mark on Dr. Carrier's face.

"Catherine." His harsh whisper was meant to calm her, but she ignored him.

"The young woman was not a whore, but even if she was, you had no right to refuse services. She came to you looking for help, for food, and you turned her away because of her reputation?"

The confidence in Dr. Carrier's stance deflated a little, casting truth on Catherine's accusation. David's stomach knotted in response.

"And now? When she's dead in a filthy room with nothing but a cot and a newborn baby, you won't even help me take her body down?" A few gasps from the crowd filled the dramatic silence. Catherine jerked free of David's hold and glared at the older doctor. "You're not even a gentleman, let alone a healer of the sick."

David looked from Catherine to Dr. Carrier then down to the newborn in Catherine's arms. A dead woman hanging? A newborn? The worst scenario emerged in his mind.

Dr. Carrier's snarl hardened the older man's expression. "Gentleman?" He sneered. "I know enough of your reputation, Ms. Dougall, to recognize your definition of gentleman or lady is in question."

David stepped forward, a barrier against Dr. Carrier's insult to Catherine. "That was uncalled for, sir."

He turned the fire of his red-faced fury onto David. "And you would do well, Dr. Ross, to take care of the company you keep."

"Then I shall steer clear of your office from this point on, sir."

The words, a line drawn, sliced into the silence.

Dr. Carrier's smirk deepened. "So, the notorious Miss Dougall has enchanted even you?" He shifted his chin in Catherine's direction. "Mark my words, she's exactly the sort who will ruin you. Like this woman's child. Whether from lapse of judgment, poor morality, or bad blood, they forfeited their right to demand service from anyone of good standing."

Dr. Carrier's words, even his tone, captured the influence of his aunt's cold demeanor.

Catherine pushed passed David. "How dare you. How dare you be judge and jury to them? Who do you think you are?"

"Life is their judge. Their consequences are dim, at any rate. I can do nothing for them."

David found his voice, his shock replaced with a boiling fury. "Dr. Carrier, I won't deny I find your reaction disappointing, especially in the shadow of the devastation we see here, not only from the wounded coming into our town, but even in the wake of the Zeppelin attack." David gestured toward the end of the street where his previous hospital building lay in rubble. "How could this suffering encourage anything but our compassion? Are we not all victims of some sort?"

His own admission pierced his conscience. He'd withdrawn from the likes of Meredith Cooper and her tainted background because of his aunt's previous support. But for Catherine's relationship with her sister, Ashleigh, he would never have sought a friendship with her or realized the beautiful transformation of mercy. Pride in his dreams had erected a ruthless wall in his heart. One cultivated by culture and expectation.

"The wounded of war are quite different than the harlots of the street, Dr. Ross."

"But no less human, nor, dare I say, in need of mercy."

Catherine's look of unfettered admiration urged his confidence and his determination. "You said we shouldn't provide medical care for those who are suffering the consequences of their own choices? But I recall a time when I was twelve and, foolishly, had gone horse racing with my cousin. We'd been told not to go. It was raining that day. I fell from the horse and broke my leg. You shouldn't have helped me, based on your assessment alone. I was suffering the consequences of my own actions. My own rebellion."

"You were a child."

"And how many of these broken people make choices as rash as any child? Or are forced into situations by circumstance or tragedy which have led them to desperate actions?"

"You would condone their choices?"

"No, I wouldn't. And neither would most of them in hindsight. But that should not nullify our ability to serve those in need and provide mercy to perhaps soften the sting of their transgressions. How can we provide an opportunity for hope in future generations if we are not tending to those in this one? How will our children see mercy, if we do not show it to those in the direst need?"

The newborn in Catherine's arms began to protest, as if as insulted by Dr. Carrier's narrow perceptions as David.

"Your optimism is misplaced. Stick with your soldiers and orphans, and leave the people of this town to my judgment."

David didn't waver. "I beg your pardon, sir, but I don't know that your judgment is best."

The man tossed away David's words with a wave of his wrinkled hand. "What do you know? You're still young, green, and arrogant. Someday you'll learn…you can't save everyone."

"I can't save everyone." David looked down at the baby in Catherine's arms and then met her eyes, drinking in the faith he saw in them. His voice caught. "But I can try."

The bundle of life grew more distressed, the tiny face reddening, ready to burst in desperation, which was followed in a second with a pitiful cry. Catherine shushed the child, bouncing with a gentle motion, but his pitch and panic intensified.

"He has to be hungry." Catherine said over the cry. "There's no knowing how long ago he ate."

"Branson's will have something to assist with…with such needs, I should think." A rush of embarrassment replaced the warmth of anger in David's face. "And fresh milk?"

Catherine nailed him with a look to remind him of her unwelcome presence in the mercantile.

"That child has no life ahead of him. With such beginnings and..." The doctor shook his head, turning to push his way back through the crowd. "Bad blood."

"Allez." The French exclamation warned of Madame Rousell's entry into the conversation well before her deep purple gown and exotic hat emerged. "You would be so unfeeling for the child?" She waved her finger at Dr. Carrier's figure disappearing into the crowd unfazed by Madame's question. "Bah. You Englishmen. Your compassion is as dreary as your weather."

Most in the town ignored Madame's antics as nonchalantly as Dr. Carrier. Her shop, with its wide-spread reputation, provided excellent notoriety for the little village – and her generous husband's memory usually calmed any storm Madame's eccentricities brought. But most people couldn't forgive her for being French.

Madame shot a string of French insults after the doctor, who was well out of earshot, then she turned to Catherine and David. "You will need a…what do they call…" She waved an arm in the air as if the word for which she searched could be caught. "An upright feeder."

David had no idea to what she referred, but the word 'feeder' for a hungry baby sounded excellent.

"*Vous comprenez*? For the baby?" she urged, finally giving an exasperated roll of her eyes. "I will go and fetch something."

And off she trotted, spluttering something in half-French related to men's helplessness with babies.

"Thank you, Madame," Catherine called after her.

Catherine's voice had lost its edge from a few moments ago, and her eyes revealed an uncustomary vulnerability. He drew close, grasping for some way to protect her, to comfort her. What had she seen? Witnessed? And most likely alone.

"What happened?"

She blinked from her stare and the momentary fragility vanished with the narrowing of those cat-eyes. Kat? Hmmm, it suited her.

"Do you realize how utterly heartless and...and insufferable this town's doctor is?"

He opened his mouth to answer, to correct the 'heartless' reference to Dr. Carrier, but Catherine wasn't quite finished.

"He left her there." Catherine pointed her gloved hand back toward the alleyway. "He left her in the apartment, swinging from the ceiling. After he looked at the baby, I assume to ascertain that the infant was alive, he turned and left me standing in the middle of the room with a newborn in my arms and his dead mother hanging nearby."

David looked back to the way Dr. Carrier had left, his thoughts searching for excuses as to the doctor's coldness. "Surely he called for a constable to assist in removing the body."

"Surely he did *not*." Catherine marched toward Branson's mercantile, the baby's cries becoming more and more desperate. "*I* called one and he helped...after he interrogated me."

A slice of pain pierced his chest at the sudden quiver in Catherine's voice.

"Interrogated you?"

"Of course. Who was I to be there, in my station, assisting a woman in her condition... and that sort of nonsense?" She turned to face him, her voice growing louder over the baby's cries. "But who else would have been there? No one. She died alone. If I hadn't come..."

Catherine swallowed, emotions fighting a clear battle for her voice. She placed the finger of her glove into her teeth and pulled it from her hand, turning her knuckle to tease the baby's lips. He immediately started suckling. How did she know to do that?

"Why? Why would Meredith do this? Why would she leave her child behind…alone?"

David gentled a hand to Catherine's shoulder. "She must have thought he had a better chance without her."

Catherine's steadied gaze told him she knew his unspoken meaning. Children of fallen women carried the stain of their parents' choices for the rest of their lives. 'The illegitimate son of so-and-so.' 'The tainted child of such-and-such.' David had heard such phrases all his life, regarded them without a second thought…until now. Until he stared down into the face of a crying orphan and this woman, his unexpected friend, who carried her own contaminated reputation with the same dark consequences.

His words rose, raw. "She entrusted him to you."

She searched his face with that unnerving directness and pulled the baby closer, setting her jaw with purpose. Without hesitation, she accepted her assignment…her calling.

A piece of him softened toward her even more. He'd never met anyone like her. In the circles in which he'd traveled, the ones introduced to him by his extended Cavanaugh family, the ladies played their demure and proper part, following the steps of society's dance to perfection.

But her?

An appealing energy pulsed from her, a radiant determination. She lived life on purpose and with an inspiring amount of passion.

"I have it." Madame Rousell emerged from the shop, two green-glass bottles cradled in one arm and a container of milk in the other. She shoved the two glass bottles into David's hands and proceeded to open the milk. "Be useful, Docteur." She gestured toward the bottle. "Vite, vite, remove the rubber teat."

With skilled hands, she poured some of the milk into the nursing bottle. "Something is better than nothing, non? And the milk is not cold, so the babe may take it." She murmured something else in French and handed the remains of the milk to David while retrieving the teat. "Please say you are more useful than Dr. Carrier." She grimaced her opinion of the elder physician.

45

She didn't seem to want a reply but turned to Catherine and gave her the bottle. "Tease the enfant for a moment to let him learn the teat. He will not like it at first, non, but his appetite will soon take control."

So frustrated was the child from crying, the teat sat in his open mouth for long seconds before he seemed to realize it was there. Catherine moved the rubber teat against his lips, teasing him, and after a few inexperienced trials, he began to suck with success. Catherine lifted a smile to him, one of her rare, unhindered smiles that left him unable to do much but stare, befuddled.

"I see, *mon cher docteur.*" Madame Rousell surveyed him with a cautious eye. "I think you have the makings of a good man. Standing up to the Carrier le buffoon in front of the town is no small thing." She tsked. "I'm afraid you may have made an enemy."

David ignored the twinge of concern at his aunt's reaction to his confrontation with her physician. "I'm glad I happened to be by."

"Docteur Carrier has been in this town a long time and is of the old way of thinking. The old English way with all of its…" She gave her hand a toss. "Bad blood and society. Pshh, you have proven today you will not be under the Lady's thumb."

David knew exactly to which 'lady' Madame referred, and his heart sank a little more. The 'lady' waved a dream before him – a dream with a noose at the end, David feared.

Catherine looked up from her musings over the baby. "Why are you in town? I didn't think you meant to leave the hospital today, especially while I was gone?"

"I'd only meant to have a short visit." He looked back toward the station, remembering his reason for traveling from Roth Hall. He nudged the bottles back into Madame's arms. "Jessica. I have to go."

"Jessica?"

"She arrived." He took his watch from his pocket and grimaced. "A half hour ago. Unexpectedly." He returned the watch and sought Catherine's gaze. "Promise me you are going directly home. You and the baby. Mason will help you with whatever you need for the drive."

Could she sense his concern? After discovering Meredith dead and navigating a thoughtless constable, only to face the unfeeling response of Dr. Carrier in front of a curious crowd, there was no telling the impact on her health.

She seemed to read his thoughts and offered a tired smile. "I will."

David bid a 'good day' to Madame, whose expression paused his turn. Her eyes twinkled with a hidden delight, her smile conspiratory. "No worries, dear docteur. I shall see your amour makes it to the auto, tout suite."

His amour? David didn't have time to correct Madame's misguided assumptions. He took off toward the station. His family's expectations, his upbringing, even Catherine's past, shouted to him at full volume. He could not nurture an interest in the lovely Catherine Dougall.

Chapter Six

"Heaven have mercy." Fanny released a gust of air with her exclamation.

The long-standing Dougall housekeeper pushed back some loose strands of her auburn hair, highlighted with hints of silver, and stared down at the sleeping baby in Catherine's arms.

Catherine rested her head against the high back chair, her mind a cloud of doubts and questions. The weariness and weight of the past few hours crashed in on her as she watched the gentle breathing of the baby in her arms. A flood of tenderness, of protection, shocked her with its force, and an unchecked tingle of tears warmed her eyes.

So small. So helpless. How could anyone lay the sins of the mother on his little head? If God healed brokenness and started something new out of a wretched choice, surely he could begin again with the new breaths, the fresh life, of a baby.

"His poor mother," Fanny whispered and stepped closer, placing her palm over the baby's head as if in benediction. "To feel helpless enough to give up your wee bairn. To forfeit her life?"

"The choices for women in her situation are fairly dim." Catherine ran a finger across the baby's cheek, using the silence to reign in the warmth invading her vision. "She's already branded as a fallen woman, which leads to 'proper' individuals shunning her and, in this case, refusing her the most basic services. If she decides to keep her child, she knows the hardships in her child's future. The ridicule, the struggle. The constant barrage of insults. And unless a good, decent man comes along to marry her and somehow curb the tainted reputation, there's little that can be done. Such a man is more fairytale than flesh-and-blood." Catherine smoothed her thumb over the baby's tiny fingers, the sting of renewed tears burning her throat. "But if she gives up the child? What happens to that part of her heart for the rest of her life?"

A daunting silence followed with nothing filling it but the sweet wisp of the baby's contended breathing.

"You've made some hard choices, make no mistake." Fanny knelt in front of Catherine, the compassion in her voice soothing over the open wounds in Catherine's heart. "But your past choices only define what you've done. They don't determine who you'll become."

Catherine gave a humorless laugh. "You're trying to find a ray of sunshine where there are only storm clouds, Fanny dear."

"No." She tipped her chin, the thin coif holding her rebel locks released another strand or two to the motion. "I'm holding out the rainbow in the middle of the storm. Hope. Do you feel the same despair as the young girl?"

Catherine paused, the vision of Meredith's lifeless body still wreaking havoc with her emotions. She shuddered and rubbed her eyes as if to clear the horrid image. "No." She shook her head, the conviction finding residence. "No, I always accepted this as my responsibility and my burden." She pinched her smile tight. "I only forfeited my future, of course, but what is that?"

Fanny's green stare challenged Catherine's declaration. "I wouldn't claim the power of foresight if I was you, Catie."

Fanny hadn't used the nickname in years, and somehow, it seemed to break through the dust and drudgery of her pain like nothing else, reminding her of a time when her future didn't hang limp from misuse.

"And....perhaps your blessing, as well?"

"My blessing?"

Fanny looked down at the infant in Catherine's arms. "When we seek His will, God has a habit of taking our wrongs and transforming them into something beautiful."

A fleeting swell of hope accompanied Fanny's words.

Could it be true, or was it merely a platitude people used to soften the harsh bite of reality? Oh, she wanted it to be true, but she knew all too well the social stigma and ongoing shame associated with someone in her position. Shame enough to...take one's own life. She flinched at the unwelcome memory and looked back to the baby in her arms. Could the Spring not only bring her a little child but also hope for a new beginning? It seemed too much to ask for all of her mistakes.

"I hope you're right, Fanny. For his sake." She placed her palm on her stomach. "And for this one."

"And don't forget you are God's child, and He has great plans for you. He always has. You may have forgotten Him in the midst of your selfish ambition and now, in the middle of your shame, but He has never forgotten you."

"You made a wager with Aunt Maureen?" His sister's wide eyes reminded him of the utter ridiculousness of the entire situation.

He hated feeling trapped…or worse, dependent. He'd worked hard in every situation – school, home, hospitals—to complete his goals on his own, with his wits and hard work as companions, and though he had a floundering hospital, he had the satisfaction of knowing he'd done the right thing. All along. In his own way.

Until now.

"I've not agreed to her demands."

"But you're considering them?" Jessica rolled her eyes behind the motoring goggles as they moved along in the Rover. "Why would you hesitate for a moment?"

"Wait until you assess our current situation before you pass judgment, Jess." His palm tightened around the steering wheel. "Our facilities, though free, are abysmal in space and access to town supplies. And though our hostess is gracious in sharing Roth Hall, it is not without a keen awareness of her sacrifice."

David exchanged a look with her. Moriah Dougall's nerves rivaled any fictional Mrs. Bennet and carried a reputation all the way across The Pond.

"Then we find another way to secure a location."

"And what if this is the only way?" he shot back, his voice competing with the wind. "Aunt Maureen owns most of the village. Apart from a few shops Victoria Dougall sold years ago, we have limited opportunities without her compliance, if nothing else."

"But what about your future dreams? Your happiness?" Jessica leaned back against the seat and groaned. "If Father knew—"

"I'd rather Father not know. It's my decision to make. You alone are my confidante, in the hopes that you might either help me find another solution or…support this one."

"David, it can't be as dire as this."

"I would have opportunity to pursue my profession unhindered by expense and restore Father's standing in the Ross-Cavanaugh families."

"Father would never ask you to give up your freedom for his reputation."

David hesitated. He'd seen his father's grief when he spoke of the severed family connection. There was no doubt his parents had loved each other. He could hardly bear the memory of his father mourning his mother, the pain etched in his father's face. But to know his father was alone, without the comfort of brother or sister in his time of grief, gave David more cause to sacrifice whatever he needed to give his father some happiness in the midst of his pain.

"I assure you, taking her offer will be my last resort."

"After all you've told me about Maureen's iron control over Ednesbury, I think you might be gambling with the devil."

"Too many lives are at stake. Having a hospital in town would not only make medical care available for more soldiers, but perhaps…"

"Oh no, what other scheme do you have in that head of yours?"

"It's clear Dr. Carrier is not providing appropriate care." The argument with the senior doctor burned a fresh wave of guilt through David, and fresh purpose. "I think there is good we could offer for the less fortunate of Ednesbury."

Jessica's eyes squeezed closed behind the goggles. "So you'll use Aunt Maureen's money to treat the very people she detests?" The car puttered to a stop in front of Roth Hall in time with his sister's sigh. "I appreciate your passion for your dreams, brother dear, and the desire you have to set things right for Father, but take care not to dance too close to the fire. Aunt Maureen is not someone to be trifled with. I wouldn't be surprised if her fury scorched the very dreams you are trying to save and singed you in the process."

"How are your grandparents, Jessica?"

The question seemed to surprise David's sister, probably more from the author of it than the question itself. Of course, Jessica had left the hospital months ago to take care of her mother back in the States, so all she remembered of Catherine was the social-climbing, manipulative vengeful woman with designs to snag a wealthy husband at any cost, even at Ashleigh's expense.

Jessica had left well before God had softened Catherine's heart with grace.

It served Catherine justice. She'd created her weary reputation with her own hands, but the constant bombardment proved wearying.

"They are well as can be expected." Jessica replied, meeting Catherine's eyes with an unwelcome stare. "The flood back home couldn't have hit at a worse time, but they're managing."

Catherine ought to look down, hold fast to the label of 'fallen woman' that bit at her heels, but she refused the urge. "I'm truly sorry. Ashleigh always spoke highly of your mother. Ashleigh wrote about some of the destruction around Hot Springs and Asheville from the flood. I can't imagine how difficult it must be to recover from so much such loss."

The stonewall set of Jessica's jaw slackened slightly, as did a bit of the coldness in her emerald eyes. "Thank you."

"I'm happy to see some help has come." Mother's voice drew attention to her place at the head of the expansive dining table. The remains of their aristocratic life paraded in the form of the Dougall family china across the ivory tablecloth. "We lost Ashleigh a few weeks ago and another nurse last week. The wounded are coming in droves, and then there's the orphanage. What was Ashleigh thinking, leaving all this to us?"

Catherine stifled a groan. Ascribing mental energy to work out her mother's rationale proved rather pointless, but one statement among her usual nonsense boiled clear: The wounded came to Roth Hal in a trickle instead of 'droves', but any addition added stress to their confined situation.

Michael Craven didn't help at all. Their childhood friend from the states, now a resident handyman, shoveled a piece of bread into his mouth to keep from making a sarcastic comment which would most likely end in a verbal tirade from Catherine's mother. They always had.

"Jessica is as well-trained as any doctor I've known." David offered an appreciative look at his sister. "Her particular skills will relieve some of the waiting process for surgeries, and she's a capable administrator."

"You can't be serious?" Mother's cutlery dropped to the table. Catherine braced herself. "A woman overseeing those horrific surgeries? That's unheard of!"

Jessica's jaw set, readied to come to the defense of all capable females in the world, no doubt. David covered her hand with his to ease the fight and then exchanged an exasperated look with Catherine before returning his attention to Mother.

"I'm afraid, Mrs. Dougall"—his tone, calm and comforting, soothed her mother's mood like a reed pipe with the mythical Cerberus—"war forces changes peace never would. And desperation of both news and resources provides ample impetus for innovation. By the way, Mrs. Dougall, I do appreciate your choice of the roasted chicken tonight."

Mother retrieved her cutlery and offered a pleased smile, irritation temporarily forgotten. Catherine cut David a look across the table. His raised brows in response taunted innocence in his perfectly placed distraction to curb her mother's erratic reactions. He held her gaze, and a faint glimmer lit the green in his eyes and entrapped her. A flutter, small and momentary, ushered to life a whisper of longing, spreading its quiver to her breath. Daydreams hovered for release.

She nearly cringed and wrapped a fist around her fascination with the good doctor before it became too irrepressible. Being in control of her fate and her emotions had always been her forte...until him. If she didn't govern hope with a steadier hand, his gentleness would be her undoing.

"Perhaps my reentry into the hospital will free Catherine to assist Kara in the orphanage?" Jessica directed the question at Catherine, an edge of warning in her voice. "I wouldn't expect a woman with your..." Jessica raised a brow, making a careful choice of her next words, "...pedigree to continue with the gruesome or menial tasks of a war nurse."

Catherine held Jessica's gaze. "I think working with broken people suits me quite well. It has a remarkable ability to give one perspective on what's important in life."

"And I wouldn't relinquish Catherine's assistance too quickly." David added. "She has a quick mind, and seeks to serve in the most difficult of circumstances. I've been grateful for her service."

Catherine didn't allow the compliment to move into a blush. Common sense and a healthy dose of shame kept her humility intact. Besides, what else could she do when God's grace compelled her to serve and her past closed the door to any former dreams?

"Anyone who has seen the state of our soldiers should be willing to work." Jessica's gaze rose with another challenge. "But it's not for the faint of heart or weak of will."

David's voice emerged between the steely silences. "I don't think you'll find either of those in the nurses we have now."

Catherine tipped her head in gratitude but kept a cautious guard on her feelings. Her friendship with David teetered emotions to a precipice of something much more, but it was an impossibility...wrong. The flagrant warning in Jessica's eyes blasted confirmation.

"I know we've been limping along since the Zeppelin attack." David looked to each person at the small dining table situated at the far end of the massive room. "And I appreciate the work all of you have done. I'm sorry we are still barely living from week to week with expenses."

"There must be another way to seek funds," Catherine added. The weariness in her body had to mirror only a fraction of David's exhaustion. He rarely slept for more than a few hours at a time.

"But no one's going to work for free." Michael chimed in at her side. "Except me, and I'll work for food, of course."

He patted his firm stomach to add some levity to the discussion.

Catherine gave him a congenial nudge. "You've worked miracles on repairs, Michael, but the hospital, an orphanage, and this aging house, might be a challenge even for your incredible skill set."

He looked up to the ceiling as if considering this option anew. "Too bad this wounded leg gives me limits. Just imagine what miracles I could work if I was in the physical condition I was before the *Lusitania*."

Just the mention of the tragedy quelled the tension in the room with the mindlessness of loss. Ashleigh, her fiancé, Sam, and Michael, had barely escaped the sinking with their lives. Oh, what a selfish creature Catherine had been only a few months before. So determined to work society and everyone around to her own advantage. She cringed at the thought, the chill of the *Lusitania's* sinking an added sobriety.

"I prefer you better now than before." Catherine met his smile, an understanding of loss changing both of them in needed ways. "We're the benefactors of your servant heart more than we would have benefited from your arrogance."

He placed a palm over his chest. "You've never been one to mince words, have you?" He shrugged. "I think we've both made some good changes, don't you?"

A tickle of emotion rose into her throat, and she cleared it, turning her attention back to the others. "Well, despite everyone's overwhelming and somewhat saccharine magnanimity, we can't keep adding soldiers to our hospital or children to the orphanage if we barely have enough funds to feed them. Let alone take care of them…and we're all working so tirelessly."

Her mind spun through possibilities, anything.

"I'd be happy to relieve you of the responsibility of Catherine's further training, David." Jessica's stare focused on Catherine, her intention clear. Separation. Then she offered her brother a smile. "It would free you to administer the more advanced care your expertise provides, and it will help me keep an eye on our newest nurse."

Catherine tried to offer a prayer of thanksgiving for Jessica's intervention, but the gratitude fell flat. With Jessica's clear dislike, she'd make every arrangement to keep Catherine from David as much as possible, with prodding resolution from the glint in her eyes. And that's what Catherine wanted, wasn't it? Distance from her gentle friend?

"Well, she's needed in the orphanage too. With all the recent commotion about unwed mothers and abandoned babies, there's no knowing how many orphaned children will end on our doorstep." Mother waved a hand to her neck as if overheated. "What is this house becoming? I don't know how much more I can bear."

"And how is the child, Nurse Dougall?"

Catherine cleared her throat and adjusted the napkin in her lap to avoid making eye contact with David. Jessica's threat made sense, and Catherine preferred logic. Yes. Logic kept her in control. Feelings sent her down paths of…. She shook her head to clear away the vivid memories of her night with Drew Cavanaugh. A night fermenting with regret.

"He's taking to the bottle well."

"Did you name him yet?" Michael asked. "I couldn't wait to learn about Stephen's name."

"Why should she name him?" Mrs. Dougall reacted before anyone else. "It's ridiculous to name a newborn. Give him at least three months to ensure he lives that long."

"Mother."

"Don't look at me as if I'm harsh. It is a fact of life. When you name them, it's much more difficult to part with them."

"I should think it would be difficult to part with them regardless of the name."

"You were so sickly, we didn't name you for six months."

"Well, she's certainly recovered," Michael added with a laugh. "I've been in the wake of her anger or in the thick of one of her schemes more times than I care to admit.

Especially when we were neighbors in North Carolina. She's terrifying."

"Do you use such flattery on all the women, Michael?" Catherine shot back, ignoring the tiny sting in the truth of his words.

"Only the ones who can appreciate it."

His sideways grin smoothed her irritation a bit and drew out a long-suffering sigh. There was such kinship in reformed rebels.

"Oh, heavens." Mother waved her fingers in front of her face. "Catherine has easily taken years off my life with her strong-will and impulsive actions. And the men? It's a miracle her situation isn't worse than it already is."

Catherine stood and dropped her serviette on the table. "I believe that's my cue to leave. After all, one can only handle so many compliments at once."

She kept her attention focused on her mother, ignoring the magnetic pull curiosity for David's opinion played with her will. Did he see her the same way? Terrifying…or worse, a loose, stubborn, uncontrolled woman?

She stopped at the door's threshold and faced her mother. "Nathanael."

Her mother blinked. "What?"

"The baby's name is Nathanael. It means gift from God, so no matter where he goes or what life brings him, he'll always have a name to remind him to whom he belongs."

Chapter Seven

His sister moved about the hospital like a woman with an auto-engine in her boots. From one end of the room to the other, inspecting each patient and cot, she took her time, as if in search of any minor defect. At first, David thought she questioned his abilities, but after further observation, he noted the true issue.

Catherine.

Of course, Jessica's absence over the past few months had deepened her suspicions toward Catherine, but the intensity of her dislike came as a surprise. She launched into a critical examination of everything Catherine did, almost as if she wanted to catch Catherine in the act of...something. Anything.

A heavy sigh breathed from David's chest. Maybe he'd remained clear of a romantic relationship for so long to keep free of conflict, but the twenty wounded men in the rooms around him reminded him that conflict was no respecter of gender. It was inborn – as ingrained in the bloodline as the green-eyed trait in his family.

In truth, he'd never been tempted away from his work and goals. Never too distracted from the purpose at hand to entertain thoughts of a partnership, his dreams his main focus, but war changed things...redirected dreams and focus.

"I know you're tired of waiting on me, but I'm almost finished."

Catherine's declaration pulled David's attention back to the laceration. The wound, freshly and poorly repaired from the Front, had contained bits of shrapnel and other debris before Catherine meticulously removed each shard and resutured the laceration.

She looked up, worry-lines creasing her porcelain brow. The white cap on her head barely held the massive bulk of her dark hair in place, with ragged tendrils slipping underneath the rim and curling by her ears.

"You're doing well."

"You sighed like I wasn't." One dark brow questioned his statement.

David's lips unhitched a smile. "My sigh was not at your expense."

Her gaze softened, and she studied him, those cobalt eyes of hers taking a fairly thorough inventory. What did she see? A staunch, reserved recluse? A lonely man consumed by work? A friend?

The first time he met her on the streets of Ednesbury, she'd used her unveiled, feminine charms to garner his interest, but now...now, with a past of wounds to curb her former passions and grace to temper her flirtatious bent, he couldn't tell what she thought of him.

"You need a holiday."

An unexpected response from her after his unusual mental musings. He chuckled, a sound so uncommon it caught him by surprise as well as her. "I don't foresee such a leisure in my near future."

"Hmm..." She pinched her lips tight and narrowed her eyes.

He could almost hear the gears in her head turning for a solution. Her mind moved in relentless motion, an untapped genius her family and society held at bay, but he saw it. A solver. She learned quickly, as driven to absorb new information as he was, and she held a natural aptitude for medicine. Stitching things together. Mending people. Whether she realized it or not.

"We'll see about that," came her reply. Then she turned back to her work. "But here, I'm at the end of the wound."

David blinked back to the patient and studied Catherine's handiwork. Tight, close sutures sealed the leg wound, clean and perfect. She proved the ideal student.

"Excellent sutures." He nodded toward the end of the laceration. "Now, very carefully, pull the last thread through as I've shown you before. Tie it off."

Her hands were steady, certain.

"That's perfect, Catherine. As good as any formally trained nurse."

She shot him her side-grin. "I do have a good teacher."

"It takes a quick mind paired with the right teacher to perform at this level, and so quickly." He nodded, a sudden surge of pride in her compliment.

"Don't praise me too soon, Doctor. Maybe you should check my garlic poultice first."

He examined the small compress, the garlic scent a bitter competition for the sweet hints of lavender waving from his charming nurse. "Yes, it's fine."

She put the poultice over the wound, and David hoped the herb worked to keep infection at bay. The last thing most of these men needed was another reason to remove a limb.

Catherine stood, stretched out her back, and then looked over at him in expectation. "Now you are free to compliment my exemplary skills."

His chuckled emerged again. "Excellent work, Nurse Dougall."

"Thank you." She bowed her head in acceptance, and when she looked back up at him, their gazes locked like they had several times in the past. It was the strangest feeling, magnetizing and uncomfortable all at once.

She blinked and broke the connection. "Oh…and a letter came for you. I placed it on your desk."

"A letter?" Perhaps a new benefactor providing much needed support for the hospital?

Catherine's expression dulled his excitement. "It's from Ednesbury Court, I'm afraid."

He nodded and placed the surgical scissors back on his tray. "Thank you."

"Support will come. I have every faith in you."

The confidence beamed from her gaze with the force of morning sunlight, striking, powerful, and dousing doubt with a glowing assurance. What was it about her that held him captive? That turned his thoughts from surgeries or supplies and made him take notice?

"Get your hands off me." The gruff response came from one of the new wounded. Mr. Clayton jerked his arm free from the timid volunteer, Marcia, and made as if to strike her when a convulsion of coughs wracked him back down into the bed.

David moved forward with Catherine right behind him. From his arrival, Clayton's behavior had proved unpredictable, at best, but what could one expect with a German bullet lodged inches into his head? It was a miracle the man had survived the seven-hour journey to the hospital for long-term care, but the wounds in this war kept David guessing. Could Clayton survive weeks? Months? Longer?

"We should strap him down." Catherine stepped up beside him. "He could easily attack a nurse, even without his leg."

"What options do we have? All the hospital rooms are full."

Catherine weaved between the beds along with him, lips pinched in thought. "Grandmama's study. No one's using it, and it's isolated at the end of the hall."

She moved to one side of Clayton's bed while David stepped to other, readied to use force to protect the others if necessary.

Catherine took his flailing fingers into a firm grasp, and with a soothing touch, ran her palm across the back of his hand. "Mr. Clayton, you can't go and behave badly to the nice volunteers."

He flinched, his one good eye searching frantically for the familiar voice. His other eye had been taken by the bullet, but white wraps kept the unseemly site from view.

"The Fritz cavalry. They're comin' over the bridge. They've overrun us."

He'd spoken of little else than the first British battle he'd encountered. Most of the best rifleman had lost their lives at Vimy Ridge. The tragedy haunted Clayton, so much so that the scenes recurred in his head, even a year after the devastating loss at The Mons. Of course, with a bullet lodged halfway in his skull, there was no guess as to what images worked as reality or fantasy, a truth which made him pitiful and dangerous all at once.

"Mr. Clayton, do you think a fragile lady like me would be in the middle of such a messy battle?" She tsked and lowered to sit by his bed, her hand still holding his and voice almost teasing.

Fragile? David's gaze shot to Catherine. Fragile wasn't a word he'd assigned to Catherine Dougall, especially after her confrontation with Dr. Carrier. Her untamed moments, steeped in passion and fascinating determination, should encourage his distance, yet even in those he found himself cheering her on and wishing, for only an instant, a small spark from her inner fire might alight on him.

Mr. Clayton may have wished the same. Whatever charm she wielded distracted the poor man from his previous tirade. His memory hadn't been reliable at all, drifting from the present to the past as quick as a breath, a definite characteristic of what many medical specialists referred to as 'shell shock.' Another new creation of war.

Clayton gave his mussed head a furious shake. "No, you shouldn't be there. Not a lady like you."

Catherine cast a glance to David, mouthing the word 'morphine.' David snapped out of his stupor.

"Well, neither of us are there now. We are in a hospital far from the fighting, and we need you to behave yourself. I'm certain you don't wish for me to send a wire to your wife about your conduct, now do you?

David's gaze shot up. Clayton had a wife? How did Catherine know? And sending messages to wives?

Clayton dropped his head like a penitent child. Catherine looked to David, anticipating his administration of the dosage. He stepped forward, still trying to sort her out, as mesmerized by her as Clayton. She kept surprising him, and he wasn't sure how he felt about it.

"I know the openness of this room causes anxiety for you, so Dr. Ross and I plan to move you to a room of your own tomorrow. A place where we can display all of your medals above your bed." She pulled her hand from his and smoothed his blanket. "But for now, you need to rest here while we prepare your new room."

He obeyed momentarily, taking the morphine without incident and relaxing back into the bed, but it was a calm before another storm. David had seen only a few other soldiers wounded to such an extent from shell shock, and each unique case held one similar characteristic—unpredictability.

"I'll begin readying Grandmama's office this evening," Catherine whispered to David as they walked away from the cot. "With some help from Michael, I think it's possible to have it prepared by tomorrow."

"Your Grandmama won't mind?"

She shrugged her rebel shoulder. "I see no reason why. Grandmama has no use for it across the ocean." Her smile tilted. "And what mother doesn't know…"

The glint in her eyes, paired with that smile, produced a river of warmth over David's skin, enchanting him. Moths to flames and all that…

"Would you truly send a wire to Clayton's wife?"

She stopped her forward momentum, her gaze searching his as if his question surprised her. "If someone you loved were injured, wouldn't you want to know about them? Hear of their care?"

He stared down into the sapphires, lost and wondering at this complete enigma. "Of course."

Her grin curled up on one side. "I'd be tempted to storm the trenches of France myself to find someone I loved, so I can certainly send a wire or ring a loved one for these soldiers."

He had no doubt she would consider a trip to war-torn France without a second thought. What would it be like to possess love from such a woman? His breath clutched closed at the treacherous thought…well, not quite as treacherous as he'd expected.

Her eye contact wavered and she stepped back, another strand of raven slipping from beneath the cap. "Rhodes and Brown have taken a turn for the worse. Neither of their amputations are healing as they should. I think…"

"Gas gangrene," he finished, curbing his emotions from following the dark feeling at the mention of the word. Another byproduct in a world of new and dangerous weaponry.

She took a few more steps away from him, her expression the tell-tale marker of those two young soldiers' futures. A fading hope.

"I'm going to have Grace make some more Coltsfoot tea to ease the breathing of the more severe men in the East

Room. I heard them gasping for air this morning and have to try something to help them."

"Have her add Karaway…or lavender, if she has any. It may provide additional relief."

She nodded but didn't look up again as she exited the room. He followed her movements. The simplicity of the gray dress and white apron failed to hide the well-endowed curves she possessed.

He squeezed his eyes closed against his musings. What was wrong with him?

"Using some of Grans home remedies?" Jessica emerged beside him, arms crossed over her chest. "Coltsfoot and Karaway?"

David nodded, following her gaze to the twenty beds, all filled. "University taught me carbolic acid and garlic, but with some of the wounds, it's not enough. Even if all it means is to ease someone's passing, I've found the natural options beneficial."

Jessica's sigh drew his attention. "I've been gone for two months, and the papers are sharing the same story about the war. Thousands of wounded and dead, and now months of a stalemate?" Something like a growl rolled from her curled lips. "If they'd place a few more women in charge, we'd make progress. Men think solving a problem takes blowing up the countries of Belgium and France."

"You know it's more complex than that." Though wading through the wounded and dying made one question everything and grasp for any solution, any blame. "We have news of ten new wounded in transport. You couldn't have arrived at a better time. Nurse Dougall has opened up the wing beneath the children's ward."

David looked over at Clayton's bed. The man slept an unnatural sleep, forced upon him by medicine, but his body twitched with continual discomfort, both in mind and body.

"Catherine needs to get faster if she's going to continue to provide real assistance." Jessica raised her brow. "At her pace, we'll have three men sutured before she completes one."

"She'll improve, and at an impressive rate, I'm sure. I've been training her myself since Ashleigh traveled to the

States, and she's made great progress. She's talented in this occupation….and intelligent."

"Oh…I'm sure she is." Jessica's laced her imitation with sarcasm. She released a controlled stream of air through her nose, a better sign than the sirens of the village warning of an impending explosion. "We need to talk."

The tone set David's spine straighter. A storm of conflict brewed behind his sister's expression – one he didn't care to weather at the moment.

"After I make rounds."

David barely had time to skim the letter from Aunt Maureen before Jessica barged into the small former breakfast room he now used as an office. Aunt Maureen's note was short, but a stinging reminder of her wager…and the power she brandished.

Your presence is requested for luncheon this Friday at The Rose House. Your great grandfather has sent you a letter concerning important information for you and your father. Please arrive promptly at 2.

Sincerely,

Maureen Cavanaugh

David groaned as he slid the card back into the envelope. His aunt had wasted little time to begin spinning her wheel of control, not waiting a fortnight before involving James Cavanaugh, the patriarch of the Cavanaugh family. It didn't help that his only X-ray machine had stopped working three days ago, and he had no funds to replace it. For the sake of the wounded as well as the workers, he couldn't maintain this threadbare hold on monthly expenses.

"There you are." Jessica marched into the room, her green eyes shooting enough accusation to cause him to brace his hands against his hips. She walked up to him and did the same. "What do you think you are doing?"

David blinked from the impact of her words. "Saving lives? Tending the wounded? Attempting to find a few seconds of solitude?"

She looked up at the ceiling in exasperation and then crossed the room to stand in front of him. "Is there some understanding between you and Catherine Dougall?"

Of the list of accusations he'd imagined, this one hadn't entered his mind. "To what are you referring?"

She stared at him as if weighing his sincerity and then dropped her head into her hands. "Oh, David, for such a brilliant man, you are impossibly oblivious." She rested her hand on his shoulder. "Catherine is weaving a web to ensnare you, and you can't even see it. Do you truly believe she's interested in helping dying men in a bloody hospital for nothing other than service? She's out to catch you."

David allowed Jessica's words to sink into the silence, trying to take into account that his sister hadn't witnessed Catherine's change, hadn't seen the sacrifices she'd made, even when she thought no one was looking.

"I understand your concern, but I believe you're wrong."

Jessica crossed her arms, her static smile consolatory. "Brother dear, you may be two years my senior, but when it comes to the manipulative nature of women, I am much more qualified in the matter. It wasn't even four months ago that Catherine Dougall was plotting to ruin her sister life and seduce an earl's grandson into marriage. What on earth could have possibly changed to such an extent that she would lower herself to serve dying men, suture blinded soldiers, and post letters to poor families in her spare time?"

"Have you such little faith in the power of God to change people?"

Her eyes narrowed. "Most people, but not someone like her."

David lowered his head and sighed. "Does Ashleigh share your sentiments about her sister?"

The question made its mark. Jessica turned away. "Ashleigh has always been an optimist."

"And, perhaps, her vision is clear, and she's seeing the same as me. There is nothing Catherine can win from her service here or in the orphanage. Her life choices before were based on selfish ambition, misguidance, and desperation. Faith changed her, perhaps more dramatically than most, but certainly as real."

Jessica lips set in a frown. "You'll have to forgive me if I'm not as trusting as you are, and it's plain to see how she affects you. Take care."

A rush of warmth shot from his chest into his cheeks at the acknowledgement. He cleared his throat and stepped back. "I'll admit, I am attracted to her, and her kindness to me has been endearing. But attraction does not equal action. Between Aunt Maureen's offer and my plans for the hospital, my head is firmly set on succeeding in my professional goals, despite what you might perceive of my heart."

"Men know little about their hearts. Even men as compassionate as you."

"You have no faith in my choices, then?"

Jessica shook her head, her accusing finger returning to its position at his chest. "Attraction is often the first step toward action. You know her reputation, her past. *If* she is playing games with all of us, you won't be the first to fall under her spell and, I daresay, you won't be the last. I don't want to see you wounded or have your reputation sliced apart by association."

"Your concern is appreciated but misplaced. I've worked closely with her and feel I know her."

"That's the problem. You've worked close enough for Catherine Dougall to get her claws into you. She can't be trusted, especially where men are concerned."

A slight movement at the doorway caught his attention. Heat drained from his face as Catherine stood waiting, her stormy gaze moving from his face to his sister's. Her expression—too cold, too statuesque—gave nothing away.

"I'm sorry to interrupt your conversation, Doctor, but I wanted to let you know that Rhodes passed away five minutes ago, and Webb won't be far behind. Should I send for Reverend Jasper?"

"Catherine..."

David started to speak but Catherine raised her palm to quiet him. "Please, just answer the question."

David's shoulders slumped. "Yes, please send for the reverend, and understand our conversation was—"

"Private." She nodded. "Yes, and I'm sorry I came upon it. Under the circumstances, I believe Jessica or Emmalyn would be a better assistants for you in the future. I will busy myself with sutures and wound dressings."

"Catherine, please."

"You have a surgery in ten minutes." Her gaze whipped to Jessica. "If I am not needed, I'll see to the reverend."

"Please, go." Jessica said, her tone dismissive. "I'll assist him."

With one more glance of those dark, intense eyes, she bowed her head and walked away.

An uncustomary heat rose like a bonfire from his chest to his face. He turned to his sister. "You are my sister, and I love you. That will never change, but don't pretend to know my mind. I will make my own decisions. Whether they be of the hospital or the heart, they are mine to make."

Chapter Eight

Catherine steered the Model T Touring down the lane, tossing one last look over her shoulder as Roth Hall disappeared behind her. She'd left poor Mason in the wheel's dust, waving his cap and calling for her to stop, but she craved the distance and the freedom from everyone's infuriating judgments. One of the benefits of a house with too few servants was the ability to slip away to the motorcar unnoticed.

Or, at the very least, unnoticed by someone who would snitch on her.

Mason cared for his reputation far too much to admit Catherine took the car without chauffeur or chaperone…and he'd failed to stop her. She'd taken Nathanael's bottle to him after leaving the conversation with David and attempted to calm down from what she'd heard, but the walls of Roth Hall closed in.

She fisted the steering mechanism with a tighter clasp. Jessica Ross had changed the dynamics of everything. Her suspicion, though founded in Catherine's own mistakes, reopened fresh wounds. David, Ashleigh and Michael had come to accept her as a 'new creation in Christ.' Her mother's indifference held little shame or condemnation, but with one condescending glare, Jessica Ross reminded her of who she used to be, of a stained past and a tarnished future.

And her influence would change David.

The cool morning breeze, scented with pine and purpose, breathed life into Catherine's face. In the distance, the sun fell low, almost touching the layered hills, and Catherine reached out, new and stumbling, to this God who had saved her.

"I don't understand what you are doing." Her voice barely rose above the rumbling of the motorcar. "I don't understand how I can serve you…or help people if all they see is the person I used to be."

The wind whispered in her ears, and sudden awareness breezed over her thoughts.

I can use you where you are. I can use you as you are.

Catherine scanned the woods lining the lane, but nothing hinted at the voice whose words spoke almost audibly, pressing in on her spirit. Where she was? A broken, fallen woman who still fought a battle with rebellion on a daily basis. Even now, she drove unescorted toward town, knowing full well her mother would be appalled.

A grin shifted her frown upward. But things were changing. Like the binds of the infamous corset, society's hold on a woman's role began to loosen into something with a better fit. Or, at least, a better fit for her. Independence, being valued more for one's mind rather than family pedigree, brought with it a sense of rightness, like when she used to choose the perfect ensemble for a house party.

Oh, the memory of feeling beautiful! Adored.

Doubt pinched at the sweet taste of recollection. She'd destroyed that delight with her own hands, her own actions, but was it truly a dead dream? Did God have qualms with Catherine's love for fashion? Did He require her to give up those delights as the ultimate antithesis of what she used to know? In exchange for her soul?

Her thoughts took a downward turn. She'd always enjoyed making things beautiful. From her dolls in childhood to the rooms under her control. The look of sheer adoration on Meredith's face when wrapped in Catherine's coat left a gaping longing. With Meredith's young age and her menial rank in the Cavanaugh home, she'd probably never worn anything as extravagant as Catherine's silk, embroidered motoring coat with a hint of satin collar.

Had she felt beautiful, special for one moment, before all went dark? Catherine looked over the expansive, rolling countryside, stretching with layers of green all the way to the autumn blue skyline. The winding road split a gray trail through the forest ahead, with sunlight filtering golden bands through the overlapping trees, a halo for her path.

Surely….surely He loved beautiful things too.

The thought pooled with comfort over the open wounds left behind from her ravaged dream and Jessica's truth-tinged words. Bringing beauty to Meredith had fed something innate in Catherine. A need. Sending notes to the loved-ones of the soldiers, sharing in their joy of sweet words from home, brought some sort of sweetness to the wounded…and even the dying.

But what on earth could God do with Catherine and her love for beauty? She cringed at the preposterous and probably heretical notion. Wasn't she supposed to give up all earthy loves for the goodness of God's call?

I have made you beautiful.

An inexplicable comfort wrapped around her wounded soul and bandaged it with renewed hope.

The village emerged in the valley, scattered buildings wrapped around a quaint main street. She'd always enjoyed the prospect from the hill when approaching Ednesbury. Grandmama's family must have chosen this reason to situate Roth Hall overlooking the town before they were forced to sell most of Ednesbury to the Cavanaughs. Catherine parked at a distance from the main street to avoid attention to her clear lapse in proper decorum by showing up unescorted… and driving. She removed her motoring goggles and slid across the seat to the door. These automobiles, American or English, were not made with women in mind. Not at all.

After wrestling between her skirts and the narrow floor space, she finally stepped from the car, but her sleeve snagged, halting her movements. The silk ribbon embroidery lining her coat ripped off and remained hooked on the latch of the car door.

Catherine grabbed her sleeve and examined the damage. The length of the gash along the seam line forced a whimper from her throat. Her lovely, coral French design of last year? She groaned and threw her motoring goggles into the front seat of the car with enough force they bounced to the floor.

She pitched her gaze heavenward and then closed her eyes, releasing a slow stream of air through her nose.

"Use me as I am, Lord? Stripped to pieces? Threadbare?"

Her whimper melted into a sad chuckle. "What good could knowing social rules and fashion do for the kingdom of heaven?"

If memory from childhood served her, angels wore white robes without one stitch of embroidery on them.

She closed the car door and looked toward town, only to find a mother and child staring at her as if she'd gone 'round the bend and back again.

Catherine smiled. "I was talking to God."

The woman's brows shot higher.

"Sometimes, one simply must speak to the Almighty aloud, don't you think?"

The woman bowed her head, took her daughter's hand, and continued walking a bit more quickly.

Catherine sighed and started her walk. First, send the telegram to Grandmama, and second, collect Reverend Jasper. She walked passed a few streets and then turned up Old Rutland, keeping back from Main in the hope she might avoid any unwelcome collisions with Dr. Carrier or Lady Cavanaugh. Either thought left a bitter taste in her mouth and a fiery fury of heat beneath her skin. The insensitive, ruthless people!

It had only been a week since she'd found Meredith, the memory inducing a shiver. Though she'd witnessed death at the hospital, the tragedy of finding Meredith dangling from a rope and her newborn wrapped in Catherine's coat stained her heart with a deep ache. Meredith died in the utter helplessness of her position, believing she'd been branded with an irremovable blemish.

Like Catherine.

She increased her pace up Old Rutland, as if the past hurried in pursuit. Jessica's reservations burned in her ears, a painful reminder and steel cage.

"Wait. Miss, wait."

A voice called from behind her, echoing from the alleyway to Meredith's apartment.

"I know you. Stop."

A woman emerged from the alleyway, dark auburn curls refusing to stay confined beneath her worn, straw hat. Her brown wool coat, frayed at the edges, wore the same weary use, but the woman's eyes glittered with energy.

"Pardon me?"

"You're the one who found Meredith."

She was a swell, make no mistake, with her large, fine hat brimmed with enough flowers to decorate a window box. Annie Feagan took in the sight of Catherine Dougall. She'd seen this woman tending to the baby while the reverend and Gavin, the chimney sweep, took down Meredith's lifeless body.

She'd seen something else too. Compassion and understanding…from a lady.

Even in the middle of war, with the world turned tipsy, the Crow Cavanaugh kept a steady hand on the social lines of her village, but this woman—the one with the piercing eyes—defied her. That willingness, a kindred boldness or slice of rebellion, strengthened Annie's courage to cross the well-tended class boundaries. Curiosity provided the final push.

"You're the one. I saw ya that day. With the babe."

The woman studied Annie with curiosity rather than the expected condescension, and then she did something completely unexpected. She offered her white gloved hand. "Catherine Dougall."

Annie stared from the woman's fingers to her direct gaze. "Annie Feagan." Annie wiped her palm against her skirt and took the hand. "My room was next to Meredith's."

The stoic expression softened with understanding. "You were her friend?"

"Aye."

The woman sighed, and her ruby lips curved into a smile. "So she wasn't alone, then."

"We're all trying to get by with what we can, but not even the pummies from the table are enough to keep us fed with the war pinchin' purses all around. We've needed each other." Annie gestured with her chin. "I heard tell you were an American."

A mischievous glint glimmered to life in her blue eyes. "It makes it easier to be an outcast when you already don't belong."

Annie knew charity. It was one of her family's means of survival after her father died. She knew prejudice too.

Besides fighting the usual judgments against her Irish heritage, she'd fought a whole dragon of prejudice when her employer had cast her out on the street, pregnant with his child, and blaming her for his loss of money. Used and discarded.

But what Catherine Dougall presented was something wholly different. Not prejudice...not even charity. If Annie read the attitude and actions correctly, her offering smelled a whole lot more like hope than anything peddled her way in a long time.

Caution rose like a weapon to the defense. "Is that why you helped Meredith? You saw her as an outcast?"

"Partially."

Ms. Dougall's honesty sent Annie a step back.

"But more than the outcasts, I couldn't abide what was happening. Lady Cavanaugh cannot continue to regulate the lives of others as she's doing. We must find a way to protect those who need protection."

We? Annie gestured to the street, ready for the partnership. "Well, if its outcasts you seek, there are plenty here."

"Others like Meredith?" Miss Dougall stepped closer, lowering her voice. "Women who...who need..." Her gaze searched the street and then returned to Annie's face. "Assistance? Provisions?"

Annie patted her stomach, only now beginning to swell from the life within. "The very same."

Understanding dawned quickly, and then she took Annie's wrist, drawing her closer. "Are you making ends meet?"

Meredith had trusted this woman, and Annie was slowly beginning to see why Meredith not only entrusted Catherine with her address, but also with her child. The woman held the ability to pierce one's soul with a look from those penetrating eyes, to make someone believe in her strength.

"My sewing gets me by during most weeks, but the war's taken some of my business away."

"Can you obtain employment?"

"No one will hire me in my state." She chuckled. "Especially since Mr. Pickernell got finished with me."

"The banker?"

"Aye, but after he got what he wanted from me, he kicked me out and sullied my name along with my reputation."

Miss Dougall's jaw tightened, and she released Annie's arm, her fingers curling into a fist. "There are too many men in this town who've trampled their morals and women underfoot." She glanced back down the street, air coming in puffs from her nose as if she was trying to hold her fury in check.

Yes, Annie and Catherine Dougall were going to get on just fine.

"To whom do you sell your sewing work?"

"What shops here in town will buy it. Then they go off and sell it for three times what they bought it from me." Annie waved her finger, pointing in the direction of the thieves' shops. "I know what Irish lace and Mountmellick costs, as sure as rain. And they don't pay me a quarter of what they ought for the beading I do."

The high class lady flattened her palm against her expensive coat, smashing the cloth rosette buttons. "You make Irish lace *and* Mountmellick?"

"Course I do. Learned it a long time before I ever learned how to work as a secretary for Mr. Pickernel. Though I worked for him five years." Annie nodded toward the side of Ms. Dougall's coat. "And I can fix the tear in your sleeve and put the ribbons back."

"You do ribbon embroidery too? This material is fragile. It will take a well-trained hand."

Annie's palm went to her hip. "Miss Dougall, can't you tell I ain't no maiden? I've been workin' with more fragile material than that since I was a babe." Her grin twisted wide. She waved the woman forward. "Come on, then. Let me show you what I can do."

Miss Dougall fingered the loosed ribbons at her sleeve, a small hint of fragility turning down the corners of her rose lips. "It's not a lost cause then?"

"I don't believe in lost causes. But I do believe in opportunity. Setting one's mind to finding opportunity keeps the hand of hopelessness away. We're all here for a purpose, miss." Annie turned back to see Catherine following her down dusty Old Rutland. "Maybe yours is to help outcasts and vagabonds." She chuckled. "And maybe mine is to make sure you dress well for the task."

Chapter Nine

"What did you do to Jessica Ross?"

Michael's question brought Catherine's head up from her Grandmama's desk as she packed the years of correspondences into another box. She'd snuck into the house through the kitchens, sliding into the orphanage wing without Mother or David spotting her. With a quick check on Nathanael and then some persistent urging to Michael, she'd acquired his help to fit Grandmama's old study for hospital use.

"I survived the Zeppelin attack, I suppose."

Michael dropped the filled box in his hand on top of a stack of two other such boxes and quirked his brow. "She doesn't seem like the sort of person who would actually wish for your death." Michael looked up to the ceiling, contemplative. "But she has enough of a temper to cause it. Whew, fire and a whole lot of anger in that woman."

Catherine returned her attention to the envelopes. "She's concerned I might use my feminine influence to steal her brother off the straight and narrow."

Michael's laugh shook her focus from the mounds of letters. "No offense, Catherine, but David's made of some pretty firm stuff. I don't see him easily manipulated into your grasp."

His eyes grew wide in mock-horror.

"Shut up." Catherine tossed a crumbled paper at him.

"Besides, it takes him forever to make any major decision, so I wouldn't even consider a chaste kiss for at least….hmm….six months?"

She laughed. "But with my powerful skills of manipulation, you never know. Five months? Four, even?" She sobered and shook her head. "She won't believe that I have no intention of swaying her brother's heart."

He propped his elbow up against the boxes. "You've never been truly malicious, Kat. Just selfish and scared." He shrugged and tipped his grin. "Like me."

She hoped her dead stare communicated her thoughts. "You're quite the encourager. Remind me to seek camaraderie elsewhere in the future."

He feigned a wound to the chest. "You don't want to be like me?" He chuckled and dropped his hand. "I'm much better now than I used to be."

"Oh, Michael." Catherine tossed another envelope in the 'keeper' stack and slid another stack off the desk into her last box. "I'm more like you than you know."

He crossed the room, his limp a constant reminder of the external wounds he bore from his past. Surviving the sinking of the *Lusitania* and getting caught in the crossfire of a war that wasn't his…yet. He waited for her to close the box before lifting it into his arms, his muscles tensing beneath his shirt, showing off the product of all his hard work on the house and grounds. No, he was a different man from the self-consumed playboy he once was, evidence of a past and a heart-change they both shared.

"You were flirtatious, and you decided to make friends with the wrong people. But that's not enough to cost you your future. It may mar your social standing a little, but those sins…" He shifted the box in his arms and sighed. "They're not obvious. Not like mine. I have a three-year-old to show for my past. He's the best thing to come out of my mistakes, but he's pretty obvious." Michael sighed. "And busy. I can barely keep up with those hands of his."

She smoothed her fingers over the envelope, Grandmama's familiar handwriting bringing sweet consolation. "My sins will be quite apparent soon enough."

He stopped in his walk to place the box with the others and turned slowly. His gaze moved from her face to her stomach and back again, as if digesting the information. Understanding dawned in his hazel eyes, and he set the box down on the floor as he took a seat near her.

When he did look up, the warmth of his compassion took some of the bite from her confession. "I'm sorry, Kat."

The gentleness in his reaction, the softness of his words, drew the ache from Catherine's heart like drawing out an infectious fever. Tears blurred her vision, and she grappled for control with a slippery hold. *Compassion*. Such a blunt contrast to Jessica's reaction.

"How soon?"

She swallowed the sudden tightening in her throat at the admission. "April, I think."

He stood from his chair and knelt in front of her, taking her hand. "Truly, I am sorry." He pulsed his words with a squeeze to her fingers. "But you're not alone."

Madame Rousell's words from earlier blended with his in overwhelming tenderness. The tears loosed.

She shrugged off his fingers and smiled, swiping at her face. "Well, you know what mother is always saying about me. My headstrong passions get me into all sorts of trouble. But once the news emerges, and it's only a matter of time, the people I love will be tainted by association, just like those poor women in town."

"The people who really know you and love you will bear the burden with you, Kat. Believe me, without Sam and Ashleigh's support from my past, I couldn't have become who I am today. The shame burns and can easily steal any hope for a good life. A happy life. They forgave me for my deception...for leaving Ashleigh without a reason as to why I couldn't marry her." He took her hand again. "And you have that here. People who love you. Who believe in you."

She stared at him in silence, wishing his words could penetrate the doubt darkening the sliver of hope she clung to like breath. "No one in England knows your story, Michael. To them, you're a poor widower who lost his wife on the *Lusitania* and left a sweet little three-year-old motherless. They have no knowledge that you only married her a few weeks before boarding the ship. Your secret is safe with the ones who love you best. I'll not have your anonymity."

He sighed, another swell of silence passing between them.

"When I return home to North Carolina someday, everyone will know, but most importantly, I know what I did. I hold the shame." A glow in his eyes brought out more the gold than the green. "But I also know how greatly I've been forgiven." He tipped his head, his gaze growing intense. "Just like you."

She dashed another tear away. "And what happens when every person in Ednesbury knows and it hurts the ones I love? The ones to whom I owe so much?"

He shrugged. "You can't change what other people do, or how they respond. You know I've dealt with my reputation my whole life. My dad gave me little choice but to be known as the son of the town drunk who accidentally killed his own wife. With Father in prison, my grandparents had little use for me, so I lived up to my reputation with a vengeance. Sam's father and your grandmother showed me what love really was, but how did I repay their kindness? I stole money from them to pay debts, and broke their hearts by abandoning my fiancée. And what did they do?"

Catherine leaned her chin against her folded hands on the desk in front of her, the warmth of a smile touching her lips. "They loved you anyway."

"And they always have." He nodded and stood, stretching out his back. "Because that's what love is all about."

She studied him, his body strong and lean from the hard labor of carpentry and stone masonry needed to patch the crumbling manor house. As children and then youths, growing up in the small town of Millington, North Carolina, she'd seen him as Sam's tag-along friend, far beneath her attention due to his miserable parentage and circumstances. But now, in the light of her own fallen state, a kinship had bloomed. He'd grown into a true friend.

He leaned down and picked up the box he'd left in the middle of the floor. "Do you remember my story of the family who pulled me from the sea after the sinking?"

Catherine searched her memory for his reference. "Yes."

"They said when you realize you've ruined your life and someone offers you a second chance..." He glanced to the ceiling and smiled. "And when you recognize the second chance for what it is—hope and grace—there's a sense of gratitude that gives you strength and clarity, and understanding that you can do much more with this second chance than you ever did with your first, because you recognize its value." He stopped at the door and held her gaze. "Any man, Saint David included, couldn't find a woman who would love with more honesty, whole heartedly, or, I daresay, with more appreciation than you, because loss teaches gratitude if we let it."

David caught sight of Michael as he entered the main hospital ward and made a straight line toward him. He'd been in search of Catherine all afternoon, unable to bear the thought of leaving her with his sister's words echoing in her head. It was inexcusable. Unkind.

"Michael, do you know where I could find Nurse Dougall?"

Michael's brows rose, and he hesitated. "Have you been looking for her?"

"Yes, actually, I needed to discuss something with her regarding…regarding an earlier conversation."

"Is that it?" Michael looked around the room. "I'm in need of an extra bed. Do you have one?"

The change in topic caught David by surprise. "Pardon?"

"If you want to talk with Catherine, then help me move a bed down the hallway, and I'm pretty sure you'll find her."

"The office, that's right." David ran a hand through his hair. "She's been preparing it for Clayton."

"She's true to her word, Doc."

From the poignant expression on Michael's face, his words carried an undercurrent of hidden meaning, but David already bore the guilt of Catherine overhearing his sister's slight. He didn't need a reminder of Catherine's change of heart.

"Of course. I've been preoccupied with surgeries this afternoon and forgot. Let me assist you."

Michael entered the office first, and Catherine's voice rose with excitement from within. "Michael, I…I have an idea. There are dozens of contacts in these old letters of Grandmama's. Surely some would willingly contribute to the hospital and the orph—"

Her words stopped as soon as she caught sight of David entering the room.

"Carry on." David nodded her way, tagging a smile onto his gentle command.

She stepped back, crinkling the papers in her hands against the front of her blouse. "I think the bed should go by the window, don't you? We can display Mr. Clayton's awards on the wall above his bed...there."

She gestured across the room to a spot by one of the floor-to-ceiling arched windows. The view overlooked the back garden and then stretched out over the rolling countryside, easily one of the best spots in the house.

Michael guided the bed to the assigned place with David following behind. "You were saying? Contributors?"

She shot David a cautious glance which served him right. He should have defended her in front of his sister, set things in order right away, and he hadn't. "Yes, well, I discovered a large number of correspondents in Grandmama's files. Some of the names I recognize from childhood, acquaintances and family members all over the country. I think they might be willing to help."

David placed the bed down. "And you would write them?"

"Why not?" She looked at Michael, and a glint of mischief tinted her cobalt eyes. "All they might do is tell me no, and I'm getting quite immune to rejection."

A twinge of something sparked in David's chest at the familiarity that passed between Michael and Catherine. A tenderness time had forged in their friendship. The awkward emotion tightened, uncomfortable and unwelcome.

Her gaze flipped back to his, and the playful glow evaporated into a hint of caution. She offered a scripted smile with none of her personality to color it. He immediately felt cheated.

"I'll feel as if I'm doing something to help instead of watching things fall apart. I'm horrible at sitting back and waiting."

Michael's cleared throat turned into a full blown laugh. "And we're all in shock at that declaration."

She pinned him with a teasing glare, and the knot in David twisted even tighter. "And your Grandmama wouldn't object?"

"Victoria Dougall would be offended if she knew you needed support and didn't use any means to obtain it, including her contacts," Michael suggested. "And you don't want to see her angry. Where do you think Catherine inherited her gifts of persuasion?"

She shook her head with a resigned smile and then turned her attention back to David. "Grandmama's reputation is known all over Derbyshire and beyond. She's kept up correspondences for years, on both sides of the Atlantic. I'm certain there are people, influential people of her acquaintance, who would be willing to support what you and Ashleigh are doing, for Grandmama's sake if not for the war effort."

David stared into those animated cobalt eyes in wonder. "Are you a constant pool of ideas?"

"You haven't realized it yet, Doc?" Michael exaggerated a sigh. "This woman fits in with the innovations of the time. Never a quiet moment in that head of hers. If she's motivated, there's no telling what plot or scheme might emerge from thin air."

"Good intentions and schemes, Dr. Ross. Do understand," Catherine clarified.

Her doubt wounded him. He pressed a palm to his chest and steadied his gaze on hers. "I've no doubt, Nurse Dougall."

She narrowed her eyes and studied him in her curious way that thickened his breath. What did she see when she looked at him with such intensity?

Whatever her opinion, she accepted his honesty and turned her face away from him again. She gestured to the room. "We still need to clean the curtain and move the remainder of the boxes to my room, but we should be prepared for him by tonight."

"Yes, innovative and industrious are perfect descriptors for Nurse Dougall. A woman of the age."

Her lips almost tipped at his words, and a burst of pleasure in breaking through whatever barrier she'd placed around her emotions energized him. He wanted the freedom of conversation, of…friendship with her. His gaze dropped to those lips again, and a twinge of something dangerous flared to life.

Her smile faded completely, and she moved toward the door. "I need to find fresh linens for the bed. Thank you for taking the remainder of the boxes to my room, Michael."

She slid into the hallway without another word and took the warmth with her.

David cast one glance at Michael who offered a half-tipped grin as encouragement, and then ran after her. "Catherine! Wait, please."

She turned at the sound of her given name, which David rarely used in front of her. She stopped halfway down the hallway, almost to the patients' rooms. He approached her, watching her face for any anger or softening, but she remained as emotionless as a Grecian statue.

"Yes, Dr. Ross?" Her formal address kept a distance between them. He frowned in response. She used Michael's name, but not his?

"What happened earlier…" He stepped closer, lowering his voice to exclude possible eavesdroppers. "I wanted to apologize for my sister's carelessness. It was inexcusable."

She kept her gaze on him, ushering in a sobering silence, leaving him unbalanced, uncertain, and completely intrigued.

"You don't have to apologize for her. I expect her reaction."

"There is no excuse for it." David stepped closer, almost reaching out to touch her arm. He shoved his hands into his pockets. "Regardless of your past choices and mistakes, her behavior was wrong…and surprising."

Catherine released a ruthless chuckle. "Surprising? No, her response isn't surprising at all. It's exactly how I expect society to react to someone like me. I created my reputation and must live with the consequences." Her gaze searched his again. "*Your* response, however, is the surprising one."

She turned to continue her walk, words lingering in the air, but he stopped her with a gentle tug to turn her to face him. "What do you mean? Have I done something to offend you?"

"You truly have no idea?" Her smile spread wide, sweet and beautiful, disarming him as much as her statement. Her question hushed to a whisper. "Dr. Ross, you know my secrets and my reputation. In fact, you were the first person who learned of my...situation."

"But how is that surprising?"

Her expression gentled at his apparent ignorance, giving him another glimpse at her tenderness. "By all accounts, I should be an outcast, ignored and reduced to the level of the meanest servant. Your kindness, your patience, and especially your offer of friendship, to someone like me...from someone like you? Of course, it's surprising."

"I value your friendship. Besides, you don't deserve to suffer forever from the choices you've made."

She shook her head. "You see, that's exactly it. You're not responding as your station demands. You're so good, so certain. You're like a rock in a storm. Steadfast." She chuckled and dropped her head, sending a hint of lavender in his directions. "I've never understood that word before meeting you."

The look she gave him humbled and shocked him with alarming intensity. It was an expression of unadulterated admiration, turning his insides to mush. He stepped closer into the scent of lavender, toward the magnetizing essence surrounding her and calling his heart.

He stumbled through a reply. "I...I've failed in many ways to do what's right, but this I know—you are much more than what society deems. God has a precious plan for your future." Tenderness softened his voice, his attention drawn to those dazzling eyes. "Something beautiful, even—"

A scream broke into their conversation. A loud crash followed from the hospital room, sending David into motion. Everyone remained where they'd been before except the other two nurses cowering in a corner...

And Mr. Clayton.

Heat drained from David's face. Clayton stood in the middle of the room with the assistance of a crutch. His wild-eyes searched the room as if for unseen enemies, and he clenched a scalpel in his fist.

"I won't be prisoner to no Fritz. Let me outta here, or I'll kill the lot of you."

Chapter Ten

Clayton stumbled toward one of the soldiers at his right—Greystone, still unconscious from his recent surgery. Without hesitation, David plunged forward, heading directly for the madman. Clayton glared up at David, his lone eye menacing, and then jabbed the blade into Gravestone's shoulder, drawing the man from his near-comatose state with an anguished moan. One of the nurses released another scream, pulling Clayton's attention toward her.

David took advantage of the distraction and jumped on Clayton's back, sending them both toppling to the floor. A table of equipment slammed down with them, tipping cotton swaps, bandages, and tools crashing onto the hard floor.

Clayton's elbow shot hard into David's ribcage. Blinding pain launched David backwards, but he maintained a hold on Clayton's arm and kicked the man's foot and crutch out from under him as he tried to stand. Whether from Clayton's battle experience or the strength of insanity, he twisted his body in such a way that he grabbed onto the nearest bed rail, stopping his fall and giving him enough momentum to hurl himself at David.

David moved to miss the scalpel, but the blade pierced into his forearm, producing another bite of pain. With as much force as he could muster, David slammed a fist into Clayton's face, sending the man and his crutch sprawling off balance and onto the floor.

Clayton growled, reaching for another bed rail to regain his balance, and grabbing the blanket covering poor Mr. Sacks instead. The new arrival attempted to slide back in his bed, as far from Clayton as he could, but the madman turned the scalpel on him. Blood rivered from Clayton's nose as he hovered over Sacks. David charged forward to make another attack, but Catherine's sudden appearance behind Clayton froze him in place. She hadn't made a sound. Careful and precise, she raised a white ceramic bowl into the air, and without hesitation, smashed it down onto Clayton's head.

Time slowed. Clayton stared at David, a look of pure surprise then curiosity crossing his face, before he crumbled to the floor in a massive heap.

David looked up at Catherine, who looked back at him with as much of a wide-eyed expression as he must have shown. She released a long, slow breath as if she'd been holding it since they entered the room.

"What on earth happened?"

Jessica's voice pierced through the fog of the moment, and David turned to her, catching his own breath.

Michael charged through the doorway behind her. "Are you all right?"

"Clayton," David answered.

Immediate understanding curbed her annoyance and sent David's mind into motion. "Gravestone needs immediate assistance."

"What about you?" Jessica's question gave him pause.

He scanned his body and noticed the red stain on his shirt sleeve. His chest ached, his head throbbed, and the sting in his arm muddled his thinking somewhat, but they were all minor wounds compared to Gravestone.

"Michael, take Clayton to the new room and restrain him in case he wakes soon." He found Catherine's face again, offering her a moment's levity through the thick tension. "Though I doubt he'll be any trouble for quite a while."

The room took a dizzying turn, and David stumbled back, feeling, for the first time, the warm blood running down his arm.

"Gracious, David. Sit down before you fall down." Jessica moved forward, but Catherine was closer and slid her arm around his waist as support.

"Thank you," he whispered down to her. "But I will be fine."

"Of course you will," she answered. "As soon as we take care of you."

Jessica attempted to tug him away, but David shook his head. "Greystone. He needs immediate care. My wound is small in comparison. I believe Clayton stabbed him in the top left portion of his chest, very near one of his current injuries."

Jessica slid a reluctant glance between the two and then called for one of the nurses to help her tend to the moaning man.

"Nurse Randolph," David called to the other nurse in the room and nodded toward Michael. "Please assist Mr. Craven with Clayton. I shall be only a moment."

Catherine raised a brow to him, clearly questioning his prediction of time, but kept silent as she led him to a stool by the sink.

"I'm truly fine," he whispered to her. "Give me some gauze, and I shall see to the wound myself. You should help Michael."

She answered by taking his sleeve in both fists and ripping the bloody cloth up his arm. With rebel brow still raised, she looked up at him. "Is it your desire to pass out on the floor as you take care of your patients?"

He scoffed. "Of course not."

She glanced at the ceiling as if weighing his answer. "Good." She focused her attention on his sleeve. As she peeled it back and wiped away the blood, the size and depth of the gash surprised him. It was at least two inches long and had barely missed the main vein in his forearm.

"Then you must wish to develop an infection to such a degree we'd need to amputate your arm?" She reached for a bandage by the sink.

Her intention shone as clear as the needling look in her eyes.

"I'm capable of taking care of myself, Nurse Dougall. I've been doing it for quite some time before you entered my life." He attempted to pull his arm free, but she pinched down tight enough to produce a wince.

"Pressure limits the blood flow." A twinkle lit her gaze. "At least, a certain doctor in my acquaintance told me as much."

His lips twitched against his will. "You're incorrigible."

"And you're stubborn." She leaned in and narrowed her eyes. "Not to mention struggling with a hint of pride."

His smile broke free. He preferred her feisty wit over her distance any day. "Aware of that are you?

She poured peroxide over his wound, and he stifled another wince.

"Personally, I am painfully aware of pride." With gentle and confident movements, she began bandaging his arm, her fingers soft and swift. "It can cause some disastrous side effects, I'm told."

Her touch, her subtle confession, reignited the deep longing within him he'd felt earlier. Its vibrancy spread through him with a more potent and pleasurable sting than the peroxide on his wound. Attraction? Yes, but something else, an emotion with a great deal more substance. Dangerous. Powerful. And something he wasn't ready to embrace. Not with a wager hanging over his head that could possibly separate them forever.

Her raised brow nudged his reluctant admission. "Guilty."

"I hear an excellent remedy for pride is good care, hot food, and a long nap."

He tried to still the warmth branching out through his chest, to no avail. He internally repeated the words he'd so adamantly declared to his sister. Attraction was one thing, but acting on it was another. "Is that so?"

She nodded and pinned the bandage in place. "Wise doctors heed such thoughtful advice."

He looked down at her hand resting on his arm and another swell of tenderness and kinship gripped his chest. Their eyes met, tightening the growing bond, securing it against his will.

She blinked and then stood, distancing herself with a step, a shadow perched upon her brow. "We all need others, Dr. Ross. Especially when we think we don't. Where would we be without the care and compassion of others?"

She turned to watch Michael carry Clayton out of the room. The unconscious soldier's head bobbled back and forth with Michael's uneven gait.

"I hit him very hard."

"And it was needed." David slid his fingers over the firm and neatly placed bandage. "Who's to know who else he might have injured if given more time?"

She nodded, but her question sent a clear sign of the compassion she cloaked with her fiery temper. But sometimes, the hint of beauty beneath her guise shone with a strong will curbed beneath her brokenness. Gentled. Refined. A vulnerability that drew him deeper into whatever came to life in his chest when she was near.

"He could still die because of me."

It wasn't a question. She knew enough from nursing to understand the possible damage from a head trauma. Long-term damage. Coupled with the mental difficulties Clayton already sustained, there was no assurance of recovery.

He stood and touched her shoulder with his good hand, allowing tendrils of ebony silk to brush across his knuckles. "You did the right thing."

"I've been angry for so long, and there were many times I thought to kill another person. But now that I might have actually done it…"

"You made the right choice. If not for your quick thinking, we might very well be nursing more than just Greystone." He gestured toward his arm. "And this could have been much worse."

Her gaze flickered to his, her eyes holding so much depth and so many questions. What thoughts, dark or bright, wandered behind her expression? Would she tell him, someday, if he asked? Would she trust him with her fears?

"You need to attend to your attire, Dr. Ross." She tugged her arm free, her smile as counterfeit as faces on the propaganda posters plastering town windows. "And do take care, as any good patient should."

Weariness weakened Catherine and pushed her to her bed. After helping clean up Clayton's mess, making her usual nursing rounds, and visiting Nathanael, her muscles pulsed with sharp pangs of protest. Her evening sickness brought an added weariness.

From all she'd read, most pregnant women suffered morning sickness. She grinned. Of course, she would prove different to the usual.

She sighed and rolled onto her side, staring at the corner closet in her room. Her mother boasted about adding it to the room when they'd first moved back to Roth Hall. *A place for your gowns, my dear. The gowns that will rescue us from our poverty.*

Little good the gowns had done. The closet door stood open, and faint light from the buzzing electric lamp glistened off the satin materials. Some lace. Some silk. Some out of fashion and a few never worn. Several older gowns littered the floor of the closet, tossed there, not doubt, after her mother's dreams for an advantageous marriage ended with Catherine's "disgraceful situation" and rejection by Drew Cavanaugh.

The three boxes of Grandmama's correspondence sat near the closet, the top one holding the most influential connections.

At least she could try to make up for some of her mistakes. She pressed her fingers into her hair, rubbing at her aching scalp, the slightest sting of tears tingling her nose. The emotions of the day settled over her like a heavy hand.

"God, I know you're watching, and you're probably not too pleased with my motoring into town, but I did get the opportunity to meet Annie. Surely that wasn't a mistake. I think I heard somewhere how you can make even our mistakes turn out better?"

The ceiling provided no answer.

"Will you help me know what I'm to do? Please don't let Mr. Clayton die because of me, and heal Mr. Greystone and...David." She whispered his name into the room. The intimacy of it took her thoughts back to her attending his wounds. Something in his expression awakened the deepest ache of her heart, a tenderness, an attraction.

She squeezed her eyes closed and shook her head. "Lord, you know I'm not trying to influence his affections. You see my heart. You know. I don't want him to be wounded by me, because of me. Please, keep me strong." She looked back at the ornate moldings of the ceiling. "He's so good and..." The memory of his gaze, his gentle touch, warmed her face. She sighed. "Oh heavens, what would Grandmama tell me to do?"

The question worked as a blessed reminder of a letter the reluctant postman had given her in town. She sat straight and shoved her hand into her pocket.

With quick fingers, she drew the letter out and slid it from the envelope. Grandmama's familiar hand brought an immediate sense of comfort. Catherine rolled on her stomach and smoothed the pages onto her bed.

My dearest Catherine,

Ashleigh has only been with me a few weeks and already I am feeling much more like myself. I am well enough to finally write in my own hand, which I have wanted to do for some time now. Please do not worry yourself with not accompanying your sister. I am proud that you chose to stay behind and step into a position more fitting for who you are.

And what did that mean?

I have prayed for you ever since I first held you in my arms. I've watched you struggle with life's many challenges and the expectation that a firstborn always bears. I've seen you search for meaning and love in places where neither could be found, and I've seen you grasp the boldness and courage to do things that few else would attempt.

Catherine wiped a tear from her cheek. How could Grandmama say anything kind about her? As firstborn, she should have saved her family instead of ruined it. Heaven knows, she'd tried everything she knew to secure a fortune and title for her family's sake, but all of her work had failed.

I know you've been branded, and am certain you've felt abandoned at times, whether from your own guilt or your perception of others' responses, but your pain has not been in vain. It has served to transform you into the person that God has designed you to be all along.

All along? Catherine pinched the pages. God must have believed she was worth something to save her. Had he truly designed her for something good?

You mentioned in your last letter how you felt unworthy of God's grace, as we all should when we recognize the sacrifice, but do not minimize what God can do with a willing heart. I have lived long enough to see the world groan, change, grow and fail. I've seen legacies crumble, and the smallest, most broken or seemingly insignificant person make the greatest difference. I've been that broken person, my dear. More than you know.

Grandmama? Small, broken, or insignificant? Catherine reread the sentence. No, her grandmother could claim sainthood with her life, love, and compassion. How could she possibly understand the depth of Catherine's lostness and the amount of debt to repay to make amends?

God doesn't need more self-important people in his world. Your brokenness is useful to Him. You are precious in his plan.

Tears closed off Catherine's breath. Precious? Oh, how long she'd craved to be precious to someone. First her father, then to David. She'd tossed away Sam's affections because he couldn't fulfill the financial needs for their family, but now... God saw her as precious?

Your past choices bring their own natural consequences. As do your future choices. Do not let your past define you, but let it guide you to become better than what you were yesterday. God has planned your path – footsteps that only you can make.

Remember, no matter what the voices say around you, find truth in Him. The truth of who you are and who you will become. In your brokenness, he has chosen you to be his daughter. He loves you with an everlasting love and he never forgets his children.

Tears blurred Catherine's vision, dropping down to splatter against the white pages. How could he love her? She still couldn't fathom it. The hatred and pride she'd carried for years? The overt jealousy and manipulation? She clung to the words that God's everlasting love does not forget and it does not fail.

I'm sorry for the pain that surrounds you. Death is a reminder of our mortality and life's brevity. And though it is certain and constant, it is also encourages us to live well while we have life to live.

It is important to remember from where you come, but right now, in this moment, remember who – or rather whose

– you are. I speak from similar wounds, my sweet Catherine. God will see you through this. Trust Him to surprise you with more love than you could ever have imagined on your own. He will take the remnants of your life and fashion them into something new. Something beautiful.

Catherine stared at those final words through blurred tears. Something beautiful? How?

She sat up on the bed and folded the letter, placing it gently on her bedstead. Remnants described her plight fairly well. Stripped pieces of the unused and unwanted. She couldn't see how fashioning them together could ever make something…

Her gaze flicked to her closet and the gowns strewn across the floor. A thought bloomed, disconnected and uncertain. She walked to her closet door, trying to wrap her mind around the sliver of an idea. Her heart strummed a faster rhythm, fingers dancing over the fabric of a few garments. She pushed them aside and reached for the older gowns. All of them looked in excellent condition, merely out of date. Remnants…something new?

She bolted from the room and directly into David.

He steadied her with arms to her shoulders. "Whoa there, is there a fire?"

"I'm sorry, Dav…" She blinked and pinched her lips closed. "Dr. Ross. I need to see Fanny."

His warm palms covered her shoulders, sending a cascading heat pouring over her. She used every arsenal in her body to refrain from melting into his arms. His gaze searched hers, clearly taking inventory of her well-being.

"I'm fine, yes. I just need…er… I need to ask about some sewing."

Both his brows shot northward. "Sewing?"

"Exactly."

He gave her the strangest look, something between humor and tenderness. A look which sent her pulse skittering up in rhythm to a ragtime swing beat.

"You do realize it's nearly midnight?"

Well, she hadn't taken the time into account. Her hopes took a detour. "Oh, yes…well... I suppose I should wait."

His smile tipped up on one side, inciting the illusive dimple. It proved quite distracting. "Do you think you can manage that? Waiting?"

"You'd be surprised how very capable I am of self-control when I have to be." She tipped her chin. "In fact, it might be rather impressive."

His grin spread wide and her heart fluttered like a schoolgirl's. "Indeed."

Her gaze fell to his arm. "How are you feeling?"

"Well, thanks to your insistent care."

"Someone needs to take care of you, Doctor. There are too many lives counting on your wisdom."

A shadow formed across his brow. "But without support—"

"I'm sending letters this week…and, of course, we must pray."

"Of course." He pushed a hand through his hair, upsetting his curls in a rather adorable way.

"Of course," she whispered, marveling at the perfect curve of those golden ringlets on his head. Would they wrap around her finger? Her gaze dropped to his, which had taken a quite intense turn. Green and alive with feeling. Oh, heavens! He'd caught her staring.

Heat flew into her cheeks. She was in desperate need of distraction. "We should pray right now, I think."

"Now?"

"Why not? We could use a miracle now, couldn't we?" Her smile brightened so much it pinched into her cheeks. She sobered her mind, taking in the sweeping need and the weariness in David's stance. "I only recently read about God being in the midst of two or more of his believers." She waved a hand between them. "And here are two."

His gaze, so beautiful and honest, produced an ache through her chest. To hold the affections of such a man! Let alone deserve him.

"Yes, Catherine." His voice dropped low, whispered and soft. "Two."

Her name on his lips, uttered in his husky deep tones, nearly buckled her knees. Exhaustion certainly inflamed her emotions.

He took a step forward, the intensity of his green eyes peering deep. Men had looked at her in many different ways, most sending hooded glances, their intentions clear. Those looks, those moments, had sent a quick thrill that ended in hollowness and deepened her loneliness.

Now here, a man walked into her life with integrity and gentleness. A man who introduced her to faith and mercy. She wouldn't sully his reputation with giving in to her longing to love him.

"I'll start then." She bowed her head, breaking his hold on her thoughts, and fumbled into a prayer. Her words eked out in slow, careful sentences. Thanksgiving proved an easy prayer. She knew the beauty of undeserved blessing, but requests felt awkward, cumbersome, like a naughty child asking for a gift from the hand she'd disobeyed. "In your kindness, would you provide funds for us to run this hospital and orphanage to your glory? You know our hearts. You know we wish to serve in the middle of all this suffering. Please provide, and give us patience."

Warmth surrounded her fingers. David took her hands in his, soft and warm. Her mind drew blank for the next sentence, but he was quick to continue in her stead. "Thank you for your grace in bringing servants to this hospital who are more than willing to care for the suffering and dying. Please, give us the strength we need to do good and right, even if we cannot see the way."

She looked up into the warmth of his emerald gaze, soft and endearing. Her throat tightened, and she pushed her next words through a whisper. "Especially if we can't see the way."

"Amen."

A sudden surge of belonging forked through her with sweet certainty. She stuttered out a breath. He was much more than everything she could have ever prayed. Much more than a doctor, friend, or mentor. Her chest seized in painful awareness. Much more than she deserved.

She slipped her hands free of his hold, immediately bereft of his touch and moved back to her bedroom door. "I'll bid you good night then, Dr. Ross."

An expression of pure bewilderment froze his features. "You can call me David."

Her fingers wrapped around the door handle, and she swallowed down the lump of disappointment. No, she couldn't.

She firmed her resolve with a turn of the handle. "I hope you rest well and have sweet dreams."

With that, she slipped into her room and closed the door. She leaned her head back against the door and closed her eyes. Sweet dreams? How utterly ridiculous. Perhaps she could resort to matchmaking and help him find some mild-mannered, rich, God-fearing woman to steal away his heart.

The notion brought a pang. She groaned. She needed to focus on this seed of an idea for the women of Ednesbury and not the beautiful hue of Dr. David Ross' eyes. She pinched her eyes tighter, but his face stayed in view. His smile. His touch. His dimple.

She opened her eyes and looked over at her closet. With the energy of a runaway heart, she marched to the gowns and began pulling them out, one by one. Maybe, just maybe, she'd found a way to set things right. She couldn't seize her own second chance, but she could offer one to the fallen women of Ednesbury.

Chapter Eleven

David couldn't shake the vision of Catherine from his mind as he drove toward the village. Her hair falling in dark untamed waves around her face, enhancing the brilliance of those unnaturally blue eyes, branded a striking picture. Michael called her Kat, the familiarity grading on David's nerves a bit, but the pet name fit. She'd run out of her room, her cheeks flushed with excitement, and landed directly in his arms.

A surprisingly perfect fit.

Then she'd prayed, and whether out of embarrassment, compassion, or a combination of the two, her sweet words wrenched his heart into her hold. Every piece of logic thwarted deepening a relationship with her. Even by his father's standards, her background cast a shadow on the family. His mother's never did. And a child? The growing warmth stilled. By another man?

What would his father think? His gaze shot heavenward. Could God really want something so…unexpected for his life? His future?

David stopped the motorcar a few streets away from downtown, carriages and other motorcars lining the way. He'd forgotten Market Day. He parked the car and stepped out, glancing up to the sky. The gray clouds promised a usual English afternoon. David tapped his brolly against the ground as he walked, prepared for the incoming rain.

As he passed by Old Rutland, his mind wandered to how he was to get her out of his head when she continued to surprise, challenge, and encourage him almost daily?

He nodded as he met an older gentleman on the street, his suit clearly marking him as upper crust. The man gave a slight nod in return, his cane tapping a steady rhythm against the cobblestone. A woman and her son moved to the side to let the gentleman pass. He never slowed his pace, nearly knocking the poor lad over as he funneled forward. The woman steadied the boy who cried out in pain, and no wonder. His arm hung in a haphazard sling, wrapped with what looked to be old drapes or bedclothes.

The Rose House waited two streets up, and he'd arrived at least a half hour early for his luncheon. He caught the mother's desperate expression as she ushered her son further down the street. David pinched his lips tighter and turned on his heel, approaching the pair.

"Pardon me."

The woman pulled her son close and shot David a wary eye. "Can we 'elp ya?"

"Please, there's no need for alarm." He gentled his voice to dissuade any caution. "I only noticed your son's arm and wondered if he has received care from a doctor?"

"It was an accident, plain and simple." The mother's voice whispered. "He fell from an apple tree. I tried to explain it to the doctor, but he wouldn't listen."

David's gaze darted from the boy's arm to the mother. "Dr. Carrier saw to him?"

"Not for long. Not when we couldn't pay."

David's jaw clenched against the atrocity. Unpardonable. "Would you mind if I tried to help?"

"We ain't taking no charity, sir. We're good, hard-working folks."

Hard-working for half-shillings from the look of their well-worn clothes. David nodded in acceptance of her claim. "Of course not. I don't plan to give charity, but I am a doctor, trained at The Royal College, and I would be willing help your son on one condition."

Her eye widened. "I ain't no dollymop from the street. I'm a married woman. Just because my husband's off to war don't mean I'll forsake my vows for the likes of some hottentot."

David's mouth dropped in utter astonishment, and a healthy wave of heat rushed into his face. Combined with a tickle of humor over her colloquial reference to him as an unsavory sort, he had to strangle his unruly and wholly embarrassed grin. "Of course you are. I meant no offense. In fact, all I ask is you keep my assistance secret. I wouldn't want to incur the wrath of Dr. Carrier."

The reserve in the woman's gray eyes faded slightly. "You'll see to my son's arm?"

"Yes, if you will allow me."

"And that's all?"

"Unless you have others in your home who need some medical attention."

She searched his face, a faint glimmer lighting her expression. His breathing hitched in welcome. This is what he was called to do. What God had designed him to be.

"But we can't afford it. Not from some college-trained doctor."

He hoped his smile offered some reassurance. "I'm less concerned with your money and more concerned with your welfare." The confession expanded his chest. "Pay me whatever you can, whenever you can. For now, I only want to help."

She blinked in astonishment, and David breathed out a sad sigh. How long had it been since the town knew compassion from the ones who should be the examples? It fueled a new purpose, another dream.

Catherine finished her rounds, thankful Mr. Clayton had emerged from his coma, even if his overall grumpiness remained intact. She barely made it to the nursery to catch Nathanael's afternoon feeding before his nap and then rushed below stairs in search of Fanny.

She found the beloved housekeeper pouring over a menu list written in Catherine's mother's hand. Poor Fanny. Catherine used to add to Fanny's anxiety with expensive dinner plans, coaxing her mother to dine as if they were the well-to-do family they used to be, and Fanny was left to cut corners and make subtle substitutions where she could.

It was wearisome and humbling to come face to face with one's past on a daily basis. She doused the looming sadness with a pinch of purpose.

To change other people's futures as redemption had changed hers.

She grinned. *One dress at a time.*

"Fanny, I am sorry to bother you."

Pepper D. Basham

Fanny looked up from her place at the old desk and pushed a strand of wild auburn from her sweaty brow. Her gray-green eyes grew wide. "Miss Catherine? What brings you down to these corridors?"

Catherine stepped further into the room and glanced about, rehearsing her request once more for good measure. "I've come to beg a favor."

Fanny's eyes narrowed, no doubt waiting for some extravagant appeal. "Beef is too expensive for twice a week, as you well know."

"Of course it is." Catherine took another step forward. "I've become quite fond of veal and poultry, at any rate."

Fanny lowered her pen, leaned back in her chair, and crossed her arms. "What is it?"

"I only wondered if you still have use of your sewing machine."

Fanny examined Catherine for a solid five seconds. "My sewing machine?"

"Yes."

"Most of my work has been by hand recently, so no." Her ginger brow tilted. "Do you have a sudden desire to take up sewin'?"

"One's never too old to learn a new skill."

"Ah." Fanny leaned forward, braiding her fingers together on the desk. "You used to be a better liar."

Catherine slumped down in the chair across from Fanny's desk. "If I tell you, it must be our secret. Mother would kill me and Dr. Ross…" A cold rush fell over her skin at the thought of his reaction. "Well, he would probably frown upon it."

"Not a promising start, I must say."

"Most of the best things begin with unpredictability." Catherine's smile inched wide. "But I have high hopes for the results."

Fanny released a long sigh. "Well, let's hear it."

"I apologize for my tardiness, Aunt Maureen." David took his aunt's hand and bowed to it before joining her at the table. "I was engaged in a…medical opportunity which took longer than expected."

Her deep frown advertised her displeasure. "I'm not accustomed to waiting on those *I* invite for luncheon."

She wore intimidation like her constant sour expression, but this time, her eyes looked weary, an uncustomary characteristic. As David examined her a bit more closely, her pallor took on a more unhealthy hue as well.

"Are you feeling all right, Aunt Maureen?"

She lifted her chin. "Apart from waiting for a half hour on you to arrive, I'm perfectly adequate."

David adjusted his serviette in his lap to keep from looking the cantankerous woman in the eyes. "Again, I'm sorry to keep you waiting."

"Have you thought any more about my offer?"

"To be honest, I've had little time to turn my mind to it." He poured tea into his cup and added one lump of sugar, using her own weapon of silence against her. "But I do think, as I consider your...generous offer, you might entertain a scheme of my own."

Her brow twitched ever so slightly. "I think I've already made my opinion about waiting quite clear, nephew."

"What if you used your wealth to strengthen Ednesbury, even from the poorest inhabitant?"

"What on earth are you talking about?"

David leaned forward, testing the limits of her closed-fistedness. "There are many in our village, good people, who need medical assistance."

"Dr. Carrier is available for them."

"With half the men gone to war, fewer families can meet the demands of his inflated prices."

"How dare you disrespect Dr. Carrier's name with such gossip." Her eyes darkened. "I assume you're referring to those on the East side of town?"

"I'm referring to people in need, regardless of where they live or their current income. You have the opportunity to spread charity and compassion in a time where both are desperately needed."

"Why would I waste both charity and compassion on those people?"

David's grip tightened on his glass, and he met her heated glare with one of his own. "Because those people make up the majority of this village. They have been entrusted to your care."

She broke off the stare first, choosing to take a sip of her tea. "I would make Ednesbury an example. A righteous beacon amidst the dustbins of our dear shire."

"Have you forgotten mercy altogether?"

She placed her cup in the saucer and carefully took up her sandwich. "Those who are strong enough will find a way."

David scoffed. "Are you still reading the pomp in the journals? Science may have its theories, but what of compassion and helping your fellow man? There are dozens, if not hundreds, in this town alone who are struggling to survive, and your edict has only made it more difficult for them."

"Some decisions must be made to ensure the strength of others."

David leaned forward, palms against the table. "Some may have chosen a path of misery in their own way, but others were born to poverty. How can you be so heartless?"

Her steely gaze came up to hold his, ice-cold. "I would not heed your advice, nephew. You would see Ednesbury turned into a brothel with the company you keep."

She clearly aimed her not-so-subtle reference directly at Catherine. "I think our conversation is finished." He placed his serviette on the table and made to stand.

"Do you have no wish to read your great grandfather's letter?"

Her question paused David's exit.

Lord Cavanaugh, the patriarch of the Ross-Cavanaugh family, held to a strict observance of protocol and tradition, but he also wielded the power to change David's father's future as well as reverse Aunt Maureen's control.

David relaxed back in his chair and waited.

Her smile twitched to prove her victory over him once more, and he almost shot up from the table and tossed any support from her or his great grandfather out with the rubbish.

"Of course he could not travel to meet with us in person due to his health, which makes this...reconciliation of grandfather and grandson all the more immediate, don't you think?"

Her gaze boasted an excellence in getting what she wanted, whatever the cost, and if David hadn't been forced by sheer necessity for his father and the hospital's existence, he would never have met with her in the first place. But here he was, pulled deeper into her entrapment.

"His response." She handed the letter to David. "Of course, I appealed to him with the highest recommendation, highlighting your excellence in your profession as well as your upstanding moral fiber, and how you have a particular determination to establish yourself in Ednesbury." Her brow quirked. "Home."

The place he'd come every summer from the time he was eight to visit his grandparents, the only ones in the Cavanaugh family who'd thwarted the patriarch's disinheritance. They'd owned Ednesbury Court until their deaths and created a haven of acceptance with the Dougalls. All continued to run smoothly, even when David's great uncle took residence at Ednesbury Court...until his death, and then everything had changed.

"If your grandmother hadn't been his favorite child, your family would never have been shown such condescension."

David chose to ignore her slight and instead, focused on his great grandfather's letter. His stomach tightened at the subtle demands printed in his grandfather's familiar hand.

"As you can see, you have the ability to become a very wealthy man. Even more than what I offered you. Your grandfather is willing to take your father's previous inheritance and set it on you, assuming, of course, that you follow his stipulations and marry well."

Unfortunately David knew exactly what "well" meant, and it had very little to do with the heart. Or the head. And more to do with purse strings.

"I assume you need time to take in this new information, but I wouldn't keep your great grandfather waiting long." She placed another envelope on the table. "Take this as another gift to be used for your war effort, and remember, you need not suffer with broken equipment, an overrun building, and a minimal staff."

How did she know? His will fisted as tightly as his hand. How many spies did she own in this village? Was his father's peace a high enough price to pay for the hurting souls of the town? For separation from Catherine?

The latter question bloomed unbidden in his mind. Marrying for convenience had never been a burdensome notion before, but now…

He looked up at her, her dark eyes as emotionless as the chair on which he sat. And now, she'd somehow bound herself with his great grandfather to ensure David took the offer. He hated feeling trapped.

The server appeared at that moment, his usually stoic expression showing more agitation.

"I do apologize for the intrusion, Dr. Ross, but there is a courier here to see you."

"A courier?"

"Yes, sir. And he appears to be highly agitated."

At this, a young lad, no more than fifteen, burst past the tables toward them. David had seen him in the postal office before, delivering messages. "Dr. Ross."

The server took the boy by the ear. "How dare you barge in this place, boy?"

David turned to his aunt and bowed his head. "Excuse me, Aunt Maureen."

She tipped her chin in response, but her eyes never left his. "I have every faith you will choose the right course of action. You are an intelligent man." His aunt's brow rose like a knife's blade. "Desperation will bring you to your knees. Your pride can only beat so long against your noble heart. One will give way." She took another sip of tea. "And you have enough of your father in you that I know which will submit and which will conquer."

Catherine grabbed Mason and jerked him with her behind the corner of a shop as David emerged from The Rose House, a boy beside him moving his hands in an animated fashion. They proceeded at a rapid pace down the street, engaged in some intense conversation.

The poor driver nearly toppled under the weight of the heavy sewing machine in his arms, and Catherine almost dropped the set of gowns in hers.

"Miss Catherine, what—"

"Shh." She covered his mouth with her palm and focused on David's march toward his motorcar. What on earth was he doing in town this time of day? And in a suit? She paused to appreciate the view. His brown tweed suit lent a perfect cut to his masculine form, and the way his long coat flapped behind him almost gave him a regal appearance. Oh, he was fine. Quite fine.

She pinched her eyes closed and released a slow breath. *Put a stop to your train of thought, Catherine Dougall.* But in all honesty, if God wanted to keep her from temptation, why, oh why, did he place David Ross in her life?

Mason cleared his throat, vibrating her palm with his movements.

She shot him an apology, removing her hand and adjusting the gowns back in place. "I'm so sorry, Mason. This is a...um...surprise and we don't need Dr. Ross, or anyone from Roth Hall, knowing about it. In fact, once you deposit the sewing machine, you can promptly forget the entire trip."

Mason's brows creased a deep worry line. "Miss Catherine, I do not mean to contradict your plans, but we are in a most compromising position here in the middle of the street. I shouldn't wish to promote unnecessary rumors."

She stepped back and dusted off his shoulders as if she had left a mark on his gray driving coat. "You're absolutely right. We just need to keep things secret for now."

His dark hair, kept in a cut close to his head, stood a bit erratically, but he quickly swept a hand through it and replaced his crooked cap. One brow quirked high. "This may seem an unimportant question, but are we engaging in something legal?"

Catherine's mouth dropped in half shock, half laughter. "I know I've always lived on the edge of good choices and bad ones, but I can assure we are not participating in anything illegal. Frowned upon by...certain segments of society, perhaps." She patted his arm. "But not illegal."

His shoulder relaxed. "Very good then."

Catherine shot another glance in the direction David had walked, but he was nowhere to be seen. With a swish of her blue serge skirt, she made a direct line up Old Rutland, now becoming a familiar trek.

She and Mason garnered a few suspicious stares from the small number of stragglers along the street, but Catherine kept her focus on the goal. Mason looked a little less confident but, of course, it could simply be because he was struggling to maintain control of the sewing machine.

Catherine led Mason down the narrow alley to Mrs. Lancing's rugged boarding house door. Mrs. Lancing opened the door, less wary of Catherine's arrival than her previous visits, though she didn't seem to like the looks of poor Mason as escort.

"No gentlemen in the rooms. Only the entry and hall."

Catherine sent the woman her most disarming smile. "Thank you, Mrs. Lancing. Mason is only going to deliver this gift to Annie, and then he will leave the premises."

She surveyed the man and his package then gave a stiff nod.

Annie answered the door at the first knock. "Well, you haven't proven me a liar." Her Irish brogue tinted the words.

Annie's gaze swept past Catherine and landed on Mason. One hand shot to her waist in an immediately defensive stance.

"Annie, let me introduce you to my driver, Andrew Mason." Catherine said, quickly. "I couldn't have brought my surprise to you without him."

Annie's stance relaxed a little, and she nodded to the driver then opened the door to its full width. Two other women waited inside, making the space even tinier.

"Saint Nicholas, what have you brought?" Annie stepped forward, examining the cumbersome load in Mason's arms. "It's a sewing machine, ain't it?"

Annie moved to help Mason with the bundle, and his smile relaxed as she took control, helping him guide it to the center of the room.

"You brought us a sewing machine?" The blonde girl, quite young, wore her golden curls as loosely as the calico dress barely clinging to the small frame of her body. She had round brown eyes, the color of dark leather, and her smile held an innocence, a sweetness, that defied her situation. "How wonderful. And just in time too. Isn't that right, Janie?"

The dark-haired woman in the corner sneered. "What's that going to cost us?"

"Janie." Annie hushed her. "I already told you, it's not like that with Miss Catherine."

"That's what you say." Janie's dark eyes surveyed Catherine. "But most things don't come for free in this world."

Catherine sobered and turned to face Janie. She knew skeptics. In fact, she'd been one and still was, sometimes. "You're right. Most things don't come for free. I'm loaning the sewing machine until we can get you set up somewhere to purchase your own."

The young blonde stepped closer and ran a slender hand over the machine. "Do you mean to help us become independent women?"

"Fairies' stories and children's tales if you ask me," Janie muttered.

Catherine bit back a retort and turned to Mason who stood in the doorway, hands to his side as if he was quite uncomfortable.

"Mason, thank you for your assistance. I think it best if you wait for me at the car."

A look of utter relief washed over his features, and with a curt nod to the ladies, he left.

"I truly appreciate your faith in us, and your plan." Annie shook her head. "But I already told ya. No one's going to hire the likes of us in their shops."

"Us?" Catherine gestured toward the strangers in the room.

"These are my closest girls, and they board here as well. Mrs. Lancing don't look like much, but she has a heart for girls like us." Annie grinned and nodded toward the blonde. "That's Marianne." Then she gestured to the dark-haired woman. "And Janie. Both have sewing skills."

"I came along to make sure you wouldn't take them in with your fancy talk." Jane tipped her chin in challenge. "I don't trust you, and I'll say it upfront."

"I appreciate honesty. It's woefully out of practice, nowadays."

"I finished your coat last night." Annie took the garment from the back of the only chair in the room and held it up. "Stayed up most of the night, but it's done."

Catherine placed the gowns she held across the sewing machine and reached for the coat. The threading and the ribbon embroidery wrapped in perfect imitation of the other sleeve, the work impeccable.

"This proves my scheme might very well work."

"These are lovely." Marianne touched the cloth of one of the gowns Catherine had brought, a lavender overdress in need of a few updates.

"What scheme?" Annie slipped her fingers over a blue satin evening gown from three years ago. "I'm all ears."

Catherine took a deep breath, speaking her harebrained notion aloud for the second time that day. Fanny hadn't balked too badly at the news.

"I want us to redesign these gowns. Update their fashions and sell them for what they're worth to the highest bidder."

"You want us to repair them?" Marianne asked

"No." Catherine's pulse shuddered to a faster pace, her idea bringing a thrill of opportunity and challenge. "I want you to remake them." She gestured to the dresses. "All of these are out of date and unacceptable to the current fashionable lady. I think we have a better prospect if we redesign them, using remnant materials, and fashion them for today's young women."

"How many gowns would possibly sell at this time of year?" This from Janie who'd taken a few steps toward the middle of the room.

"Parties and balls are at their height in the Winter Season."

Annie pulled her hand from the gowns. "It's a great idea, Miss Catherine, but we're seamstresses, not designers. We don't know the latest fashions."

Catherine drew close. "But I do."

"And what do you get out of it?" Janie remarked. "Assuming we can even accomplish this."

"My reward is seeing the ideas from my imagination turned into something real." Catherine's grin broadened, the possibility teasing a warm flush to her face. "I'm going to plan an Autumn Bazaar to raise money for the war hospital at Roth Hall. If we show a few of our refashioned gowns off at the bazaar, to create interest, I'm certain we will have opportunity to make a new start for you all."

"But if this scheme works…" Annie bent to examine the sewing machine. "And if the bazaar creates interest in our gowns and your designs, where would we sell them? Most of the shops won't allow women like us to set foot inside, let alone sell our wares."

"That's the only unanswered part of my plan. We need a supporter. Someone who is willing to take risks to do what is right."

"Someone who isn't afraid to defy "Lady Catterwall," Annie added with an eye roll.

"A sponsor." Catherine paced on a small patch of floor in the tiny room.

"Someone who wouldn't cause a stir in town, of course," Marianne chimed in, a sweet smile tagged on for good measure. "And one who already owned a shop would certainly be an asset."

"Right." Janie huffed and turned toward the door. "And it would help if she was mad enough to let us use her own business to support this preposterous idea. Maybe she even tosses out fairie dust with the wave of her hand."

The perfect answer arose in Catherine's mind straight from the Almighty himself, with a little nudge from Janie's imagination. A figure, complete with extravagant costuming, stained lips, and a French accent. "Janie, you're brilliant."

Janie nearly toppled over from Catherine's shout.

"You know someone cracked enough to support us?" Annie waved her arm at the three women.

"Well, 'cracked' might be a bit too extreme, but I prefer the term…passionate." Catherine laughed and offered a quick, silent prayer of thanksgiving. "I think, ladies, I might know the perfect person, but I'm going to need you to trust me…to work a little magic."

Chapter Twelve

Where was Catherine? David made another walk through the corridors, even taking an uncharacteristic trip below stairs in search of her. He needed her. She knew which rooms to open for more soldiers and which remained off limits by Mrs. Dougall.

Her laughter lilted up the stairway as he descended. She stood in the hallway with Mason, the driver, with her hand in his? David increased the pace of his descent. Catherine turned at his approach and David saw more clearly she was giving Mason a plate of food.

"Dr. Ross, what brings you down to the belly of the house?" Miss Loudon, the cook, peeked up from her place at the oven. "Supper's still a good two hours off. Did you need something else, sir?"

David attempted to shake his frustration at the mere thought of Catherine holding Mason's hands, but a trace of it clung to the tension in his chest. The same knotted burning he'd experienced with Michael. It took control.

"I need my nurse's assistance instead of her spending her time below stairs."

Catherine's eyes grew wide, and she turned fully around to face him, one hand sliding to sit at the juncture of her long blue skirt and her white blouse. A hint of fire bloomed in her eyes and hit him square in the chest.

"Dr. Ross appears to have his nose out of joint." Her tone of sweetness failed to cloak the steel in those blue eyes. "Or else he wouldn't speak to you in such a fashion, Miss Loudon. It's quite out of character for him."

He stepped closer, a deep-set anger boiling beneath the surface. From his confrontation with Aunt Maureen, the sudden influx of new wounded, the unpredictable manner of Miss Dougall, and the limited space of Roth Hall, the last thing he needed was to see Catherine laughing with the driver!

"I would expect one of my lead nurses to help me welcome new wounded instead of cavorting with the servants."

He almost felt the heat from her glare. "Cavorting with the servants?" She edged closer to him, unyielding. "Why wouldn't I choose servants? They won't judge me like the rest of world will."

"You seem quite familiar with a great many men." Had he truly spoken that out loud?

"You too?" She made to march past him. "Well, I am full up with people placing me back in an old mold instead of having some faith I'm not what I used to be, especially you."

David caught her arm and swung her around to him, the power in his movement bringing another wide-eyed stare from her. She was close, surrounding him with lavender, softness, and suffocating fire. His throat went dry, and the flint of anger died a sudden death. He loosened his hold and froze, his gaze taking in the contours of her face, the heat in her eyes…the humbling conviction behind her words. For the briefest moment, he had the urge to pull her to him and make amends with a kiss. Warmth scorched his face at the unbidden and sudden need.

"Catherine, please, forgive me."

She attempted to pull free, and then he saw it. The wounds she placed underneath her fury. Her expression hardened, but not her eyes. Those round gems swirled with…pain. Pain he'd caused with his madness of the moment.

"You're only treating me as I deserve, isn't that it?" The granite hold of her anger quivered with a tremor of her lips.

"No, that's not it. And you should fight, no matter who it is." He rubbed his palm against her arm. "I'm only ashamed it was me."

He had pulled her close enough to notice a speck of lighter blue around the iris of her eyes. "Please, Catherine. I don't know what came over me. The events of the day? My exhaustion? Neither are an excuse for what I said. I saw you with him and I…I…don't know what happened."

She paused a moment, then a new expression moved across her features. A wariness. "I do," she whispered, succeeding in pulling free from him. "But you are stronger than this. Better than this. I'm not worth your anger."

Why did she say that? She spoke to him as if she knew something he didn't. "Catherine."

"You mentioned something about new wounded?" She refused to look at him, the moment broken. He hung his head, berating himself with a mixture of complete confusion and immense regret.

"Yes, a Zeppelin bombed the hospital in Lancet last night."

'No."

"They've requested to have their survivors transferred here as we are the closest war hospital."

"Such as we are." She shrugged, starting for the stairs. "I'll make what arrangements I can."

He covered her hand on the stair railing with his own. "Please forgive me."

"Don't forget, dear Dr. Ross, I would do anything in my power to keep your opinion of me at its highest." Her smile turned sad. "Of course I forgive you."

Chaos reigned above stairs, with Mother's voice echoing above everyone else's. Catherine stopped in the middle of the vacuous entryway with its grand chandelier and ornamented crown molding and pinched her eyes closed. Jealousy. David Ross was jealous. Three months ago, the thought would have sent a thrill of victory through her, encouraging her to keep the green monster alive and well with a healthy dose of flirting, but not now. And not him. She cared too much for him to ever toy with his tender heart.

What was worse, he didn't even understand what was happening, which meant she still had time. Time to save that kind heart of his. If she could. The longing to be close to him drew her with more force than anything she'd ever known from their first discussion at her sister's sickbed to now. She'd never known such desire to *belong* with anyone else, to talk with him, to feel his arms around her.

Catherine opened her eyes and took inventory of the house. The far right wing held the orphanage and all the family bedrooms, including David's, Jessica's, Michael's, and the other two nurses. Part of the left wing lay in disrepair, but the functional part held the current wounded and hospital offices.

She heard steps on the stairs and darted for the back of the house, a perfect place to stay clear of David. Her mother had placed the South Wing off-limits to hospital work, almost as an unhealthy memorial to Catherine's father, but necessity continued to force her mother's stubborn hand.

The dark hall led past rooms and memories. Her father's rooms darkened the very end, almost their own section of the house. Catherine stifled a shiver, as if his presence walked the hall, reminding her of her inability to measure up to the love he'd dangled before her. Her hatred of him had curbed with time and knowledge of his depravity—the liberties he'd take with her sister, the love he'd withheld from her.

And now, her mother kept the corridors unused almost as a shrine to the memory of the exalted man she'd created in her head. Not the true one.

Down a hallway to the left sat a few unused rooms, and then she came to a large double door. With a deep breath, she placed both hands on the door handles and turned. The doors opened and welcomed her into the grand ballroom, once the pinnacle of her family's social success.

The bittersweet surge of pleasure and disappointment pulled her into the enormous space, dark and dusty from disuse. Grand, granite fireplaces framed the two sides of the room, and windows hung high above on two walls, allowing natural light to compliment the three crystal chandeliers.

She'd hosted a ball the first autumn she and mother returned to England, welcoming Grandmama's acquaintances and people who remembered the former grandeur of the Spencer family home. Drew Cavanaugh had been among the throng. His dashing good-looks and charm stood out among the others, and over time, once Catherine had learned of his vast inheritance from his great grandfather, patriarch of the Cavanaugh family, she'd pursued him. Determined to restore her family's social status and financial security, she'd given everything in the pursuit...including her self-respect.

But never her heart.

Her smile grew with another look around the beautiful room. It was time to reform the uses of this room as God had done with her. It suited her new life – forego the beauty and elegance for a deeper beauty. Hope.

Catherine worked miracles. David was sure of it. He watched her out of his periphery as she took the role of hostess away from her anxious mother and readied the house for an uncertain amount of new wounded. Mrs. Dougall refused a part of anything which would defile her husband's sanctuary, which left the brunt of the burden on Catherine. And she took it without a flinch. She'd even garnered a few somewhat unlikely recruits from town to help with the transition. A fiery-headed Irishwoman, who was with child, and a young waif of a woman named Marianne. David wasn't too certain how much help either would be, especially the bright-eyed girl with her soft smile who looked much too young and idyllic for the world of war.

"The motorcade is approaching, Miss Catherine," Jackson, the butler, announced from the doorway.

Catherine turned to the group before her. One nurse stayed behind in the ward to see to the current patients, but everyone else stood in a line at the entry, awaiting orders. Including David.

"We aren't certain what sort of injuries we will see today, but it will take all of us to manage it for the good of these poor lads." She glanced at David and quickly away, which served him justice. "Dr. and Nurse Ross will meet each patient at the door and direct the stretcher bearers to one of two rooms. The long-term wounded will go to the ballroom." She nodded to Fanny. "To which Fanny will escort them."

"Severe cases, who are in need of immediate care, will be taken to the back library by Nurse Randolph."

The older, dark-haired nurse nodded.

"Miss Annie and Miss Marianne will provide assistance as needed, as well as Michael and myself."

117

The front door ground open, and the first wave of wounded entered. The first patients' medical needs proved extensive, much more than the capabilities of their current staff and resources. With abdominal wounds, facial damage, and tragic limb removal, so many were in need of immediate care that Catherine redirected the more severely wounded to the ballroom instead of the library. At one point, David looked up to see her staring at him, the gravity of their situation reflected in her eyes, asking an unspoken question. *How are we going to take care of all these people?*

Annie proved to be as decisive and quick-witted as Catherine, making quick and accurate decisions for the soldiers' comfort, and Marianne flitted from one wounded to the next like a sunbeam into the gray, offering a cool cloth or a soft word. Where Catherine had found them, David had no idea, but at the moment, he didn't care.

The final automobile arrived, running behind the others, but its passengers weren't wounded soldiers. Three women, in their typical blue and gray nurse's uniform, emerged from the back of the motor. Both held a somber air of tragedy and experience and fit the typical mold of dour and no-nonsense David had seen in training. A tall, lean man exited the front, placing a bowler on his dark head as he did so. He surveyed the house with a quirked brow and then swept the extended countryside an appreciative look. The nurses stood at his side as if waiting for his orders.

"Well, I must say, the facilities aren't as up-to-date as I'm accustomed, but the view is spectacular." He grinned and offered his hand. "Dr. Christopher Hudson, plastic surgeon to what was previously Lancet War Hospital."

David took the proffered hand. "David Ross, lead…well, only doctor here in Ednesbury."

Dr. Hudson's light brown eyes grew wide. "Only? What a job! Well then, sir, I suppose I'm under your direction for the present."

"You're staying to help?"

"Of course." Dr. Hudson's smile grew with genuine warmth. "You don't think Dr. Patton would leave you to handle his wounded on your own? He's the good sort. Top notch."

David grasped for a response. Help? A surgeon and three trained nurses to add to the staff? David almost grinned his reply but quickly doused it. He hadn't accounted for them. Was there room? He caught Catherine's gaze again as she sent another wounded man in the appropriate direction, and his chest expanded with confidence. She would make certain there was room.

"It's been a long time since I've enjoyed the company of a colleague. Our accommodations may not be your customary fare, but we hope to provide some privacy for the staff."

He showed them toward the doorway, his step a bit lighter at the thought of another doctor on hand. One pleasure he'd missed from leaving his grandfather's practice in Warm Springs, NC, and then the London practice, was the camaraderie of other professionals.

Dr. Hudson followed him into the house and took his time measuring the people in the room. With a tilted grin, he leaned close to David. "I don't know what you grow in this part of the country, Dr. Ross, but your nurses are exceptionally better looking than mine."

David followed the direction of Dr. Hudson's stare, the small fire in his stomach swelling to flame. Catherine.

Catherine felt his stare before she turned to confirm it. The new group, one man and three nurses, stood in the doorway of Roth Hall with David. Though she couldn't place his occupation in the middle of the swarm, she read the message in his smile clearly. Interest…and not in her medical knowledge, either. He was young, her age or a few years older, and definitely not a social recluse like David.

They walked toward her, the stranger keeping his dark eyes on hers, and she refused to look away, matching his forwardness with her own. She knew the social expectation in showing interest. The woman smiled shyly and averted her eyes, but she didn't want him to receive the wrong message. She wasn't interested.

His smile only curled with more confidence, and her insides curled for a whole different reason.

"Nurse Dougall, I'd like to introduce you to Dr. Hudson and his nurses." David gestured to them. "They've come to help us."

Her attention flitted to David, and the weariness around his eyes pulled at her compassion. He worked so hard with such long hours...if these new additions would alleviate some of his efforts, then she'd manage it.

"Welcome to Roth Hall." She reluctantly offered her hand.

"We are most appreciative for your readiness to house our patients...and us." Dr. Hudson's palm warmed hers, his gaze as intense as ever.

She'd almost forgotten the sway of such unadulterated attention and the heat in the game of seduction. The pleasing warmth pearling beneath her skin, the power in her own womanhood to turn a head or change a reaction. An art she'd formed into a lifestyle for so long. The touch of it mingled with bittersweet longing for such affections, even if shallow and temporary.

But she knew the emptiness afterward. She breathed out her clenched air and offered him a smile. "We are pleased to have your services, Dr. Hudson."

Her gaze returned to David's steady, familiar face, but his eyes held nothing steady or familiar in them. Steel. Kempt fury.

"Dr. Ross, I know you must see to the new patients as soon as possible, but I need your approval of accommodations for our new staff." Where to put them? Not on the staff ward near her room, that was for certain. "Might I snatch a moment of your time?"

"You'd better snatch away now, Nurse Dougall. There is another motorcade of wounded arriving in about an hour, and I can assure you, neither Dr. Ross nor I will hold liberality on time at that point and neither will you." Dr. Hudson's brow rose with an unspoken question, one which hinted to finding him within the hour.

"Then I suggest, Dr. Hudson, you make yourself acquainted with our facilities so you can find your way in the middle of the throng." Her smile pinched. She turned to David. "Shall we, Dr. Ross?"

She heard him follow behind her, but she wouldn't dare look back and possibly give Dr. Hudson any fuel for further pursuit.

"There are four or five old servants' rooms in this back wing which will provide ready access for Dr. Hudson and his nurses to reach the patients." Catherine wove through the corridors and ascended a back stairway. "They're not as grand as our new guests might be accustomed to, but they'll provide privacy."

Silence greeted her comment. She stopped at the top of the stairway and turned to see if David still followed. He stayed a few steps behind, his progress at a more thoughtful pace and his head down.

"Are you well, Dr. Ross?"

He met her at the top of the stairway leading into a long hall. "Well enough."

Catherine studied him a moment and then continued her walk down the hall at a slower progression, waiting for him to catch up. She'd seen that look on his face before. He was mulling over something and working up the words or courage to speak it. Was he concerned about how they would manage this new change in their lives? Most likely, but that could easily be voiced.

"Why does he look at you that way?" His voice rumbled from behind her.

She slowed her pace until they walked as a pair. "What are you—?"

"Dr. Hudson."

She feigned ignorance and paused her walk. "What way does Dr. Hudson look at me?"

"Like a wolf at his prey." He whispered the words, but his voice loomed dark through the corridor.

She tossed off the façade and resumed her walk. "I suppose he finds me attractive. It isn't all that uncommon between men and women in general. Nothing for which to be troubled, I assure you."

If she could only believe her admission as well.

David stopped walking. "Do...do you find him attractive?"

Catherine turned to face him, hoping to add some levity to combat David's serious mood. "He certainly isn't difficult to look at, if that's what you mean, but I have no intention of making him *my* prey."

David's brows crinkled together. "I see."

She sighed. "Attraction used to be a ruling force for me, but I...I would not wish such vain, empty affections in my life any more. Of course, I want to be attracted to the man I love, but I also want much more. Friendship, like-mindedness, shared...passions? Something to last much longer than one evening." She walked up the hallway and opened a narrow door into the former servants' quarters. When the house was in its grandest era, as many as forty servants kept the home in tip-top shape. Those days were long gone.

"A lifetime friendship?"

She smiled. "Yes, that's right. A lifetime friendship with..." Warmth blushed into her cheeks. "With a good measure of passion, if God allowed. I might be blind at times, and stubborn, but once I learn a lesson, it sticks." She took in a breath and cleared her throat. "Now, to the topic of accommodations."

He approached her slowly, his gaze fixed on hers, probing for something. "Catherine?"

She shivered as his voice rasped and low, caressed her name like he enjoyed saying it. As if it meant something far more than sounds and letters.

"Yes?" Her own whisper echoed back to her, breathless.

He stood, emotions warring through the expressions on his face. His hand came up as if to touch her face, his breath as shallow as hers. A collision of retreat and yearning paralyzed her body. And then... his hand dropped and he released a long breath.

"Thank you for all you've done." He continued to search her face. "I don't know how I would have managed without you."

Every fiber of skin on her body stood at erratic attention, but she played the game and shrugged a shoulder in response. "It's the least I can do for my dearest friend."

Her heart wrung out the admission. *And the man I love.*

122

Chapter Thirteen

Dr. Hudson's prophecy regarding the next patients proved true. Their wounds came with the greatest severity David had yet seen. His father's letters from the Front had alluded to such grisly wounds that they caused grown men to turn away.

The gentleman's war died with the first explosion of chlorine gas.

Dr. Hudson spoke of an incoming surgeon who specialized in reconstruction. He would be given the most gruesome cases on which to operate, but as for the rest... Dr. Hudson and he stood alone. Christopher, as Dr. Hudson asked to be called, encouraged the staff with the news that another doctor and theatre nurse were to arrive within the week.

If they survived the week. Three men had already died in as many days, one from injuries sustained during the Zep attack, the other two of the long-term effects of the gas, a horrid weapon with sustained effects of breathing difficulties, blindness, and possible mental defects.

And his previous concern about Dr. Hudson and Catherine? At the rate they were both working, neither would have opportunity to converse, let alone spend time together. Not that he mistrusted Catherine, but he wasn't certain about Christopher and his easy smile.

But his skills as a doctor were impeccable.

Still, as David thought back on his conversation with Catherine, the heat simmered beneath his skin afresh. Catherine thought Christopher Hudson attractive. He grimaced. Did she think he was attractive?

"I need some assistance here," Catherine called, barely keeping a patient from toppling to the floor.

David made eye contact with Jessica as they ran toward her across the ballroom, the glossy floors now littered with bandages and cast-off clothes.

"He ripped off his eye bandages and must have ruptured his sutures. His...his loose eye has come free from its place."

Catherine struggled with the man's weight as he sank toward unconsciousness, but as he jerked, his hand came up to hit his own face.

He screamed from the impact and blood spattered in all directions, landing across Marianne's apron. She looked up, pale blue eyes wide before they rolled back in her head and she began a free fall.

"Grab her," Jessica screamed.

David ran toward her in a vain attempt to catch her head before it slammed against the floor. Dr. Hudson appeared at the doorway behind her, as if by magic, and swooped her into his arms.

He stared down into her face and then looked at David, his usual quirked grin appropriately absent. "Is she wounded?"

David moved over to Catherine, taking the majority of the soldier's weight. "She must have fainted from the shock. We need get this man to surgery immediately. Can you see to him?"

"Nurse Reynolds has me set for a surgery this moment." He looked down at Marianne and then back to David.

Catherine struggled with David and the wounded man to the doorway. "You can place her on the chaise in Dr. Ross' office."

"Jessica," David called behind him. "I'll need both you and Catherine to help with this surgery. Now."

"What can I do to help?" Annie called from behind them.

"I was re-bandaging Clark and Stephens." Catherine answered.

"I'll see to it, miss," came Annie's quick reply as they pulled the unconscious man down the hall to the smoking room-turned-second-surgery.

Jessica ran ahead to ready the table, in this case a true mahogany desk which had been re-christened as a suitable operating surface. After a few minutes, the three of them were able to get the bleeding under control and the eye replaced in its sphere. David began tending to one reopened suture while Jessica began re-stitching another, all the while with Catherine handing appropriate tools or cleaning away new blood.

"Are you all right?"

David's question appeared to surprise Catherine from her focused occupation. "Yes, thank you."

She smiled in a way that caused his own to respond, but the weariness around her eyes spoke of more. Had she gotten enough sleep? Rested? Nothing about her physical appearance hinted to the life growing in her, but the existence he'd heard it produced exhaustion in the strongest of women.

Jessica cleared her throat and shot him a severe look which he promptly ignored, but of course, his sister was anything if not persistent.

"Aunt Maureen invited me for luncheon last week."

David almost dropped the tweezers in his hands. "Aunt Maureen? She hasn't spoken to you since you started your nurse's training. How many years has that been?"

She paused to pull another suture through and then shot him a grin. "Long enough to know that if she's inviting *me* for lunch, she's desperate for something."

David returned his focus to the wound at hand. "What did she want?"

Jessica tossed a side-glance to Catherine, and if David wasn't mistaken, she stifled a grin. "She wanted to introduce me to a young woman who wishes to volunteer at the hospital."

A flash of warning stilled David's movements. "And she talked to you instead of me about this?"

Jessica averted her gaze. Not a good sign. "Perhaps she wished to speak freely among women."

"You've always been a horrible liar." David's voice ground low. "The lady wouldn't happen to be single and from an esteemed family, would she?"

"I'm sure I don't know about her pedigree," Jessica bit back. "But she seemed very nice and mild-mannered. A perfect lady."

"I can't believe you're joining Aunt Maureen's ranks."

"I'm not. But you're never going to find a wife by staying in this hospital unless a woman comes to you. The choices are rather slim, and certainly not up to your quality."

She slid Catherine another glance, and Catherine promptly responded with an unaffected eye roll. David almost grinned...if he hadn't been so angry.

"I will accept anyone who wishes to serve here. Clearly, we are in need of help." He sent his sister a narrowed-eyed look. "But only for service to the hospital. Do you understand?"

Jessica ignored his warning. "I think you've met her on several occasions at church or one of the very few socials you've attended over the past few years. Adelaide Moore?"

David examined his work on the wound before answering. "I have no memory of someone by that name, particularly someone Aunt Maureen wishes as a possible bride."

"Which speaks for itself," Catherine muttered, keeping her attention focused on the tools at her disposal.

"What did you say?" Jessica shot back.

"Pardon me. I spoke out of turn," Catherine answered, offering her most brilliant smile.

"Do you suppose every woman should leave a lasting impression on a man's heart?"

Catherine kept her gaze and voice low. "She certainly should on the man she's going to marry."

She glanced up at him for a moment, long enough to show a hint of humor. Oh, if she only knew the trouble she brought on herself with his sister, she wouldn't find such wit in her troublemaking. Though he had to fight his own desire to grin.

"Dr. Ross." Nurse Reynolds stood in the doorway, her expression emotionless. "Dr. Hudson needs you immediately."

Her monotone contradicted the message, so it took David a moment longer to understand its immediacy. He turned to his sister and Catherine.

"We'll manage this. Go on." Jessica waved him away.

"I know what you're doing."

Jessica Ross' threatening tone came as no surprise. Catherine tried to place a positive sheen on the veteran nurse. Well, at least she despised Catherine in front of everyone – no pretense. There was something to be said for consistency.

"I'm devising a very careful scheme to steal your brother's heart and then run away with his vast fortune."

Jessica pointed the sewing needle in Catherine's direction. "He's not some witless boy you picked up off the streets of Ednesbury. He's a good man, and though he may not show it, he feels deeply for the people around him…even you."

"Even me?" Catherine's laugh held no humor. "How magnanimous of him, and much more than I can say for his sister."

She leaned close, her green eyes narrowing into sharpened slits. "You haven't earned magnanimity from me. I know your history, your ill-treatment of your family…and I'm not the one who gave myself to the highest bidder."

Catherine winced inwardly but refused to back down. "I recognize that I've done nothing to garner your trust, but I can honestly tell you I've also done nothing to obtain your brother's attention or affection." Catherine stood taller, taking the truth and the pain that came with it. "And I would dissuade my brother from a relationship with a woman like me, so I understand your protectiveness. But, unlike you, I also understand second chances."

Jessica blinked and stepped back. Catherine followed.

"I understand what it's like to crave approval and love – and to search for it in any place to gain one taste, even a cheap imitation." She pressed her fist into her chest, aching to communicate the truth to a hard-headed and angry woman. "And I gave up what was most precious to me for a counterfeit because I was desperate and selfish."

"At least we agree on that." Jessica retorted, but her gaze didn't boast as much confidence as before.

"But you know what else?" Her smile grew. "I also know the beauty of forgiveness, of being seen as someone new, and bearing the brunt of my past choices has not only humbled me, but awakened me to the needs of others around me, of those who are searching for the same type of beauty, the same type of forgiveness. And now…now I know exactly where to find the source."

Jessica shook her head. "You just expect me to believe God's changed you from the manipulative woman you used to be into some saint within a few months?"

"I'm no saint. I'm as broken as the next person, but I'm aware of my brokenness. Some people never see their own." Catherine took another step, a flash of heat spiraling through her. "And brokenness is something of which I think you have little experience or you wouldn't hold your gavel with such fierce judgment."

"Don't compare my past with yours, Catherine."

"Why not?" Catherine shrugged and offered the challenge liberally. "Don't we believe in the same Gospel? The same Savior? Does he not say *all* have sinned and fall short of His glory? So, from His perspective, we're the same. Both broken souls in need of forgiveness and hope. And I know you don't like being lumped into my category, but perhaps, if you thought more of your needs instead of your self-righteousness, you might recognize what your grace *can* do to change lives instead of offering lofty platitudes that only inflate the rich minority of women who would rather be seen than serve." Catherine laughed. "You spout the ideals of women's rights and yet neglect the fallen women who could benefit from your grace the most."

Jessica stumbled back against the wall, mouth pinned closed. Catherine took the needle from her hands and slammed it on the table. "What else should a nurse, let alone a Christian, do if not bring hope and healing to the ones who need it most?"

She marched from the room, her head pounding with a fury she hadn't experienced since Drew Cavanaugh rejected her…right after he'd ruined her. *Help me, Lord. I need one moment of solitude to clear my head so I won't go mad.*

"Catherine!"

Her mother's voice echoed down the long corridor, certain to aggravate some of the resting wounded. Catherine ran to the entrance of the hallway to catch her before she entered further.

"I'm here, Mother."

128

Her mother smoothed back her faded golden hair and took a deep breath, shooting Catherine a look of stern disapproval. "I have been trying to find you all morning. Where have you been?"

"I've been assisting with surgeries. I'm certain one of the other nurses could have given you my whereabouts."

"I will not ask these woman I don't know! And there is one who is with child."

Catherine squeezed her eyes closed. "Annie, Mother. Her name is Annie."

"Is one of the wounded her husband?"

"No, Mother." She decided to skip added drama. "Annie isn't married."

Her mother's complexion deepened to carmine. "Do you mean she's a…"

"She's a hardworking woman with whom a man took unprovoked liberties, that is who she is."

Her mother's eyes grew wide, and she waved her handkerchief toward the hallway. "And the other one? Is she with child also?"

"No, Mother. Her father was a brothel owner in Lancet."

"Oh…." Her mother waved the handkerchief like a flag before her face. "My house is being overrun by wounded soldiers, orphaned children, and loose women."

"They were willing to give an honest day's work. There is nothing for which to be ashamed or frantic. Our situation is changing, and we have the opportunity to change with it to help others."

She released a humorless laugh. "You think I don't realize the world is changing? I was a debutante in society. I had lines of suitors waiting to court me. My family boasted a twenty-seat dining table which remained full and overflowing for each and every dinner party my mother hosted. And now?" Her mother's voice broke, and she pressed the handkerchief to her face. "Look at me. Barely money to buy beef, in this dilapidated old building filled with dying men and now harlots? It's too much."

Catherine grabbed her mother by the shoulders. "Life has thrown us some lumps and we've made some of them ourselves, but this is where we are, and we can choose how to spend the days that we have. It's time to accept where we are now, with what we have now, and pray God helps us change the Dougall reputation."

"Change our reputation?" Her mother's voice hardened. "How will we do that when my daughter engages in secret meetings in town?"

"How did you know—?"

Her mother pulled a paper from beneath her arm and thrust it into Catherine's face. The headline brought a cold chill with it.

A Secret Rendezvous? The article flaunted a dramatic story about Catherine engaging in a clandestine meeting with a certain 'driver' of Roth Hall. Catherine pressed her eyes closed and released a long stream of air through her nose. *Mason.*

She took the paper and shook her head, keeping her volume low. The wounded and staff worked only a few doors down the hallway. "I was discreet."

"You are many things, Catherine, but discreet is rarely one of them."

Catherine gave the paper back to her mother and snarled. "Mr. Dandy is a vile man who is in the employ of Lady Cavanaugh. His sole purpose is to weasel into the underbelly of Ednesbury and taint the lives of the people who dare stand against her demands. He wishes to ruin us."

"We don't need his help with ruining our family name." Her mother's words hissed. "Your impulsiveness and lack of propriety does enough on its own." The handkerchief returned to her mother's eyes. "Oh, what will we do?"

The sting of her accusation inflamed Catherine to the defense. "Mother, we're no more ruined than we were before. People will see this for what it is. Smoke and rubbish. It will pass."

"Haven't I suffered enough with my reduced circumstances and your father's death? Must I also bear the brunt of a daughter who continually crosses the boundaries of propriety?"

"Mother," Catherine warned, glancing down the corridor for eaves droppers. "Not here."

"Then to carry a child of a man who wouldn't even pretend to know you now."

"Mother!"

Her mother buried her face into her handkerchief. "How will we ever rise beyond the trouble you've brought on us?"

Catherine took a steadying breath and held in a myriad of wrongs she could easily lay at her mother's feet. "How will my past stay in the past if people, even my own mother, are constantly reminding me of who I *should* be rather than who I hope to become?" Her voice pinched to a pained whisper. "I will not yield to your despair, though I am tempted. I will not."

Ashleigh had once told Catherine that the way to battle self-doubt was to uncover God's definition of His children – as a reminder of his love. As Catherine drew her Bible into her lap, she poured over a verse, drinking in hope like a parched wanderer.

For as high as the heavens are above the earth, so great is his steadfast love toward those who fear him; as far as the east is from the west, so far does he remove our transgressions from us.

She dropped back on her bed and allowed the tears to flow. They rolled heat down to her temple to pool in her hair, but she didn't care. She needed the release. No one proved as steadfast as God. His love did not falter with social rules or propriety. It did not fade with her failure or remind her of her shame. He saw her heart, and although there were many hateful flaws still in need of eradication, He knew her desires held a nobility she could only reach with His help. A knock broke into her prayers. She moaned and rolled over, pulling a pillow over her head. She waited, hoping the disrupters might leave her alone. The knock sounded again, louder. She sat up in bed and threw her pillow at the door. She knew it was a vain attempt. Her door stood on the other side of the room, but somehow, the effort made her feel a little better.

"I don't feel as though you've crowned me with love and mercy right now, Lord." She growled to the ceiling and then sighed. "But I trust you're quite capable of helping me show it...even when I don't feel it."

The knock came again.

"We know you're in there, lass. We followed you all the way up the stairs." Annie's distinct Irish accent resounded from the other side.

"Well, not the entire time. First we stopped in at our room to fetch something for you," came Marianne's correction.

A sweet warmth spilled through Catherine's middle, and the tears threated to return all over again. Is this what friendship was like? She grinned. A most unlikely pairing. But still, these young women came to find her. She'd never been good with friends – at some point or another, she succeeded in stealing the boys they admired or saying something rash. Could God create a new opportunity in this too?

She dashed away the loose tears clinging to her lashes, took a deep breath, and opened the door.

Annie stared at her a moment and then walked into the room. "I'm not usually an advocate of slapping women, but your mother might tempt me."

Marianne's big eyes widened even more as she entered, toting a garment in her arms. "Oh, don't say that, Annie. She's not nearly as bad as Lady Cavanaugh."

Catherine closed the door behind them, her smile growing with the warmth in her chest.

"The Crow Cavanaugh would tempt the Pope towards murder." Annie collapsed in one of Catherine's cushioned chairs by the window. "But she'll get hers someday. If there's any justice in this world, she'll get hers."

"It's good to see you." Catherine nodded to Marianne. "Are you feeling better?"

A sweet blush touched Marianne's cheeks. "Yes, thank you. Dr. Hudson was very kind."

"He has her seeing daydreams and twinkly stars." Annie flittered her fingers in the air. "I told her that he's too posh for the likes of us."

Catherine touched Marianne's arm. "Daydreams are good, Marianne, but keep your head. We know very little of Dr. Hudson."

Marianne looked down at the garments in her hands, her face growing redder with the lengthened attention. "Of course. My aunt used to say 'hold your heart close but hold your head closer'. She knew the truth of it, having watched my mother and father's horrible ways."

"I won't let her get caught up in a mess like me, you can be certain of that." Annie's pale eyes darted a warning. "One hint of cad I see in that man and it's..." She made her hand like scissors cutting in the air. "The end. But no matter, we came here for another reason."

Annie stood and nodded toward Marianne.

"We thought this might lift your spirits." Marianne unfurled the gowns in her arms and Catherine's breath caught.

Two gowns, both displaying her own designs, draped before her as if a daydream had materialized. "Oh!" She reached out to touch the red gown. "You've...you've made masterpieces. How on earth did you find the time?"

Annie chuckled. "I used to work in a factory before I became a secretary, and in both, you worked long hours. Besides, sewing is something we both love. It's easy to spend a little extra time doing something you love."

"And I don't need much sleep," Marianne chimed in with her usual brightness.

Catherine nodded, unable to take her eyes from the display. The first, dark blue, bore brocade sleeves instead of the unadorned older model. Gathering material of various shades of blue draped at the hips with a few flashes of gold mingled in for effect. The neckline draped with a braid of pale blue and gold, lowered from the more Victorian neckline.

The second gown, a dark red, held a touch of oriental flare with multicolored cloth of golds, dark blues, and red draped from one shoulder across the front to gather at the opposite waist. The sleeveless gown kept a straighter line skirt, but not as tight as the hobble skirts from a few years ago. The entire ensemble boasted unique elegance.

Catherine's palms came up in appreciation. "The designs may not have the same flare as Paul Poirot, but they could easily compete with House of Worth in their style. You've done remarkable work."

"Well, I told Marianne, I wasn't going to make them like those mummy skirts." Annie shook her head. "No mind about fashion if you risk safety."

"The blue one is my favorite." Marianne said. "And we've started on two more of your ideas."

"Getting the hems off the floor for the two other skirts will make a world of difference. Women won't have to replace the bottom lace nearly as often." Annie walked around the gowns, examining them again. "But I can't think that they're any worse than things I've seen in shop windows."

"I think they're a great deal better." Catherine pulled her gaze away. "The real test will be to see what Madame Rousell thinks."

"And if she'll be willing to help with a Bazaar." Annie added.

Catherine's minded started working out an idea. "I wonder if I could sneak to town this afternoon. We could put on the gowns and wear our coats over them, so we'll look a little less conspicuous. Marianne, the blue one would look lovely with your hair and eyes."

"And I'll cover for the two of you." Annie's nose curled with discomfort. "Madame terrifies me with all her…" Annie waved her hands in the air as if imitating Madame. "Flair."

"She's a very passionate lady, to be sure."

"Won't you be missed here?" Marianne asked.

Catherine reached for the red gown and shot them a grin. "After the catastrophe downstairs with my mother, I'm pretty confident no one will be expecting me for the rest of the evening. They'll assume I'm ashamed to be seen in public." She tipped a shoulder. "Perhaps Mother's nervous fit was quite timely indeed."

Chapter Fourteen

Catherine could hardly catch her breath as she rushed down Main Street toward Madame Rousell's. Marianne had agreed to meet her at the French boutique once she made a stop at her apartment to collect a few things, but it gave Catherine time to prepare her persuasive argument for the benefits of this venture. Surely Madame would see the good of it. After all, she wasn't one of Lady Cavanaugh's underlings and maybe—if Catherine and Madame kept the personal information about the seamstresses quiet—it wouldn't impact Madame's business dealings with Lady Cavanaugh.

What could Catherine lose in asking?

She shrugged and looked up the lane as she crossed. A mixture of motorcars and carriages permeated the street as people bustled across the cobblestone and dirt. She loved the activity and life of the village. Her grin stretched. Oh, how she'd thrived off of the fashion and glamour of London, before... She sighed and forged ahead, directly into the path of a particularly well-dressed lady in a gray day suit. The large hat obscured Catherine's vision a moment, but as soon as she reexamined the sour face attached to the thin frame walking toward her, her entire body braced for the attack.

Lady Maureen Cavanaugh.

Lady Cavanaugh came to an abrupt stop and firmed her pointy chin into battle position. Three confrontations within the same span of time? What on earth was God trying to teach her that she clearly wasn't learning fast enough?

Catherine stood a little taller and proceeded forward, never allowing her gaze to stray from the menacing slits of Lady Cavanaugh's dark eyes.

"I see you're dressing the part of a lady now. I barely recognized you."

The stone-cold timbre of Lady Cavanaugh's voice spurned Catherine's anger with its clear innuendo to her previous choices. She cast off the social gap with a smirk.

"Well, it's good to know one of us hasn't changed. You've still not learned to behave like a lady."

Lady Cavanaugh blinked, the sting unexpected. "If it wasn't for your American upbringing, you would know your place."

"And if it wasn't for my American upbringing, I'd let you keep me there." Catherine took another step closer. "The last time I spoke with you was in the presence of your grandson about my...situation, and neither of you did anything except cast me out."

The woman looked down her nose, her lips curling as if she had a continual bitter taste. "What else does one do when there's rubbish in the house?"

The woman's tongue proved as sharp as the points of her dark brows. "With such strict rules on riffraff, I'm surprised your grandson is still living at home, then. Perhaps your discernment isn't what it used to be, my lady."

Lady Cavanaugh drew close, her teeth bared. "My discernment is clear enough to keep my grandson away from vultures like you."

"You're the only vulture in this town." Catherine worked to keep her voice from drawing attention. "I'm not afraid of you. With all your pomp and power, all you really are is a bitter old woman with a dying idea of how the world should be run." A sudden peace flooded through her, stealing the edge from her fury. "I used to be like you – fueled by my own need and bitterness. So angry I didn't care who I wounded or what the cost. All my anger ever did was isolate me, as it has done for you. People don't respect you. They fear you, and the fact that you would rather have their fear than their respect speaks volumes of how very small of a person you truly are."

"You dare threaten me?" She laughed, or a poor imitation of one. "I hold your life in my hands."

"You have no power over me, no matter what you think. I've already been broken and shamed in more ways than you can imagine. I have nothing to lose."

"Except your newfound friendship with David Ross, perhaps?"

"Dr. Ross is a noble person. You may have the power to push around his choices as far as his professional future, but you can't choose his friends for him."

Her false laugh returned. "You really do not know with whom you deal. Money is power, dear girl, a commodity which you woefully lack. Besides, your past alone gives me adequate ammunition to destroy any ties you have with my family, including David." Lady Cavanaugh's next step brought her within slapping distance. "All your boldness is nothing. You are a blemish on your family and friends. What would they do if they knew the truth about you? How you seduced my grandson—and who knows which other men in this town—only to obtain a title? Money?"

The tiny bit of fear Lady Cavanaugh had erected in Catherine's heart crumbled. "Is that all you have on me? Surely, with your long reach of insults and threats, you can do better."

Lady Cavanaugh took a step back, her eyes growing wide.

"We are broken. All of us. No matter how we try to hide it beneath the latest fashions or the power in our social status, we're each just as broken as the other." Catherine tilted her chin, confident. "You and I."

"Don't be so impertinent as to assume you know anything about me, or David." Her sneer returned. "You may boast of your friendship and service at the hospital, but I wouldn't cling to that little dream too tightly, my dear. David may be magnanimous, but he isn't a fool. He knows the hospital cannot survive without funds, and I'm counting on his generous nature to do whatever is necessary to keep his sweet little *charitable* organization afloat."

"He won't be bought."

"Men are such predictable creatures. One must only know which points to push, and he will crumble. Even David has his price." Her gaze raked over Catherine. "And you certainly haven't the persuasive abilities to change that."

"So you've decided to tug at his heart? With his patients?" Catherine drew in a deep breath at the realization. "Or with a bride."

"I see you set your sights at him, but just like Drew, you will never win David's heart." She shook her head. "Gentlemen only marry respectable women. They may dabble with their share of affairs, but the ones who truly hold their hearts are the ones they wed, not the ones they bed."

"Well, you would know more about such things, would you not, Madame?" Madame Rousell stepped into the conversation, her emerald gown taking glints of sunlight and highlighting the impish glow in her eyes.

Lady Cavanaugh's grimace deepened into harsh lines on her face as she examined Madame as one would the underside of a shoe. A French shoe at that. "No, I would not."

"Of course, my mistake." Madame pressed her palm, her nails glossy from the lacquer. "For my grievous error, may I interest you in a silk scarf from China? A lovely shipment arrived last week—"

"I only wear English-made clothing."

Madame's expression turned sympathetic, "Ah, I see. This is the reason for your sour expression, yes?"

Lady Cavanaugh snarled, turned on her heel, and marched down the street.

"She makes some sort of wager with the young doctor?"

"How did you—"

"You should not have such conversations on the street where anyone can hear." Madame waved her fingers as if her argument gave perfect justification.

Catherine's grin twitched. "We were not loud, Madame. Only eavesdroppers might hear."

Madame tipped her manicured brow. "I am quite an expert at eavesdropping. It was, what should we say, a great skill to me when I was young in a family of nine." Her smile took a mischievous turn, then she looked to the sky. "It is time for tea. Come."

"I have someone who is going to join us." Catherine searched the street and saw Marianne hidden in the shadows of one of the buildings, waiting, no doubt, for the argument with Lady Cavanaugh to end.

Catherine gestured her forward, the long coat covering Marianne's fashion masterpiece just as it did Catherine's. Madame turned a questioning eye.

"Madame, this is my colleague and one of the reasons I wished to meet with you. Her name is Marianne Lavoy."

Madame's palm returned to her chest and she gasped. "Lucille Lavoy's great niece?"

Marianne's sweet smile responded. "Qui, Madame. Vous vous rappelez ma tante?"

Madame released a delighted laugh at Marianne's response. "But of course, she was my contemporary as well as a dear friend to Catherine's Grandmama, Victoria Dougall. Before your aunt's social decline, she was quite the grand dame. Did she teach you French?"

"Oui."

"I never knew what happened to you after her death. You should have come to me." And then Madame walked forward, gesturing for them to follow and chattering on in French.

Catherine only understood bits and pieces as she followed the pair through the lovely fashions to the back of Madame's shop. They ascended a narrow stairway with a door at the top. Madame opened it into the massive sitting room of one of the most extravagant apartments Catherine had ever seen.

"This is where you live?"

Madame called to a woman in the kitchen. "Tea, Nanette, *s'il vous _rand.*" And then she gestured toward the lush, leather chairs covered with pillows and furs. She drew out her fan and waved it slowly in front of her. "I had these apartments designed last year, after my dear Patrick passed. He was Irish—warmhearted, kind, passionate." Her gaze went to the distance and her fan moved with more fervor. "Yes, he was so passionate."

"You…you own your building?" Catherine slid to sit on the leather sofa, followed by Marianne.

Madame snapped from her reverie. "Mais oui! You see, many years ago, your dear Grandmama offered to sale to Patrick and I this place. She offered to several faithful patrons of this town, and a few were able to purchase. Ma cher Patrick, he always doted on me and was quick to respond. So, you see, this is mine, and there is nothing the Lady can do to take it from me."

Catherine nodded her thanks to Nanette for the cup of tea. "If only others had the option of purchasing their property. I've heard it is happening more and more throughout the country."

"Oui, the estates are much too large to manage the costs." Madame nodded. "We used to let Beacon House from your Grandmama when we hosted house parties and had many guests. You know her grand town house?"

"I've never seen it, but she's spoken of it before."

"It is tres grand. Not as large as Roth Hall, but glorious in its own right. Church Street and Spencer Avenue. You should know it, ma petite. I spent several years in that grand home after your _Grandmama moved to America." Madame took a sip of her tea and peaked a brow. "But you did not come to talk of the Lady or my home. I think you were meant to find me, non?"

"Yes." Catherine set down her teacup and steadied her palms against her knees. "This might seem like an impertinent question, but what do you do with the gowns that are out of fashion or do not sell?"

"This *is* an interesting question." Madame paused in her answer and studied Catherine, her fawn eyes filled with a playful curiosity. "Some of the items I can send back to Paris, but most, if not purchased at a reduced cost, I must put away."

Put away? Catherine's pulse jumped a little, seizing the hope. "Put away? And you lose money on them?"

"Oui."

"What if you could still make money on the gowns you had to put away? What if they could be reinvented into something of more popular fashion? New designs."

Both Madame's manicured brows shot high. "You have someone in mind who could do this?"

"Yes." She sent a smile to Marianne. "I know some seamstresses who can create works of art. You wouldn't lose money, and they would earn some." Catherine readied

140

herself for the next sentence. "We only need someone who's willing to display the gowns in a proper shop."

Her eyes slid into slits. "And why do the seamstresses not have their own shop? Either they are people of questionable means…or questionable talent."

"They have the talent." Catherine stood and began unbuttoning her coat. "They want to earn money and also…help hold a Bazaar to raise money."

"Raise money? *Pourquoi?*"

"For the hospital," Marianne added cheerfully.

"And what does the hospital need?"

"Everything. Funds, staff, space…"

"Oh la la." Madame gasped as Catherine pulled the coat from her sleeves to reveal the beautiful silk masterpiece. Madame stood and crossed the room, examining Catherine from head to foot. "It is like nothing I have ever seen."

"Just as I said. True talent." The words came slow as Catherine searched for the right thing to say. "Don't you see, you have the opportunity to make a difference and to get back some of the money that you've lost."

"Unusual and fascinating." She ran a hand over Catherine's skirt, fingering the embroidery. "Did they make the designs too?

Catherine hesitated, working up the courage to force the truth from her lips. "No, I did."

She shot Catherine a wide-eyed look. "You? This is your design?"

"Yes, and she has many more ideas." Marianne offered another encouraging smile. "She designed this one too."

Marianne removed her coat and Madame went across to fawn over it as well. "It's exquisite. They are both exquisite. *Magnifique.*" She brought her hands together with one clap. "Are there more like this?"

"They can make more." Catherine pinched her lips tight and then took a deep breath for strength. "They only have need of a place to sell them."

"With this type of design, I'm surprised they do not have their own shop."

Now came the test. Could she trust Madame with her secret—as a confidant and a comrade? "I'm sorry to say that the ladies have found themselves in a predicament which prevents them from selling their own items or owning their own shop."

Madame opened her mouth to respond and stopped, her gaze slipping to Marianne. "Experiences which would keep them from the public eye? Public acceptance?"

"Most certainly, especially in this town where Lady Cavanaugh is draining the poor dry." Catherine motioned toward Marianne's dress. "You can see for yourself they have skills, they just need someone to believe in them."

Madame sent Catherine a poignant look. "It seems they already have someone." She turned away and paced the room, stopping to touch some trinkets on the shelf and then the table.

Marianne looked at Catherine, her expression filled with questions. The silence filled the room, except for the sounds of Nanette in the other room. Catherine held her breath.

Madame turned, finger pressed to her lips and a twinkle in her eyes. "I find myself in need of some good dressmakers."

Catherine couldn't contain her laugh. "Truly?"

"Madame does not lie." Her grin grew. "When my shop was large, the previous dressmakers worked from the back. It has two apartments which would fit three to five women quite comfortably. It is private and still has one unused sewing machine they can share until their work merits my purchase of more."

Marianne's mouth dropped wide in wonder. Catherine's smile stretched to aching. A dream coming true for Annie, Marianne, and Janie? And she got to be a part of it?

"Madame, you are the most remarkable French woman I have ever met."

Madame's lips curled wide in response. "Then you have not met many French women."

Catherine squelched the urge to grab Madame in a huge hug, but instead, gave a heartfelt squeeze to her hands. "I think you and I are going to be great friends."

"Thank you," Marianne added, doing what Catherine refused, taking Madame into her arms.

A look of pure delight crossed the older woman's face, and she dashed away a tear, stepping back from Marianne's arms. "We have much to do. Can you return in a few days to discuss the particulars of the women and finalize plans for the bazaar and ball?"

Catherine paused with one arm into her coat sleeve. "Ball?"

Madame's grin took on an elfish twist. "Oh, if we are going to sell ballgowns, we *must* have a ball. In these dreary times of war, what a better way to lift the spirits than women dressed in their best elegance and men wearing their tuxedos?" She gave a ferocious wave. "Divine."

Catherine barely remembered the drive home. The world had suddenly shifted from dark to light in a few hours. A dream come true. Her smile refused to tame itself.

Marianne sang all the way up the road, one French tune after another, dotting each melody with her light-hearted laughter. "Annie and Janie will be so pleased. It's much bigger than we ever imagined."

"God blesses abundantly, Marianne." Catherine nodded, a sweet warmth of pleasure rippling through her at the fresh knowledge of His love. "More than we can imagine."

They slid into the house, going their separate ways to change into something less conspicuous. As Catherine buttoned her blouse, she noticed a telegram on her desk. She reached for it and broke the seal.

A knock came to her door. "Nurse Dougall, you're needed downstairs for surgery at once. Dr. Ross has been trying to find you for the past half hour."

"I'll be right there." Catherine pulled the card from the envelope and the whole world crashed.

Grandmama has left this earth. She sent her love at the end. I will follow in a few weeks. Ashleigh.

Another knock came to the door. "Please, Miss Catherine. The new patients have arrived."

Catherine bit back the harsh sting of tears and swallowed the gathering emotions. She slid the telegram in her pocket and turned for the door.

Chapter Fifteen

David kept watch on her, each passing moment confirming his suspicion that something was dreadfully wrong. Her usual acuteness in responding, her typical focus, waned toward a melancholy stare into the distance. She completed her tasks and anything asked of her, but without one sarcastic retort or lighthearted quip.

An awareness of her mood, her presence, burned clearer—no doubt spurred on with a little more force by the argument he'd overheard earlier. It must have wounded her—and from her mother? His chest ached with the need to comfort her, but why would she come to him? After hearing how his sister and great aunt shared the same goal of marrying him off to Miss….Whatever-her-name, why would she seek out his company?

The new nurses brought a great deal of knowledge and added relief to the burgeoning hospital, enough relief that David fully expected to sleep six or seven hours tonight. His entire staff needed a long rest, even as he tried to sort out how to keep the hospital running. Dr. Pike had brought a moderate sum with him to help cover the expenses his patients added, but it still wasn't enough for long-term provision.

David washed up after his last surgery for the day and bid his sister good-night, but as he started up the stairs to his room, he caught sight of a figure in pale blue walking in the back garden. As the moonlight shone down on her face, his breath caught.

Catherine.

Her dark hair, pinned back at the sides, fell in a mass of ebony down her back as she stared up into the night sky, a lonely and sad angel. Angel? The emotions in his heart squeezed out a smile. Yes, an angel to the men she served here and…

He ran back down the stairs and opened the large wooden door to the garden, attempting to hold her privacy in reverence. The faint sound of crying drew him closer to her place on the stone bench overlooking the countryside. His chest tightened, his steps faltering.

She must have sensed his approach because she rushed to brush away the tears on her cheeks and turned to look at him. His throat wouldn't work. All he could do was stare. The moonlight haloed her face and glistened in her exotic eyes still swimming with tears.

"Did…did you need something, Doctor?"

He swallowed through his dry throat and approached another few steps to give himself time to gather his thoughts. "I saw you…out here."

"It's a good place to think."

"Or…weep?"

She offered a weak smile and looked away. "The remaining flowers don't seem to mind."

He slid next to her on the bench, leaving ample space between them for propriety's sake. "Is it your mother?"

She shook her head and dabbed at her eyes again. "No, I should be used to her by now."

"Hmm... I doubt anyone gets used to her."

Catherine stared over at him, her smile growing. The simple fact he'd inspired her smile encouraged the compulsion to bring another.

"No, I doubt anyone does."

"Is it the work?" He studied her profile, the softness of her skin, the turn of her nose and pink swell of her lips. "It's been a difficult week. I don't believe we expected the severity of what we've seen lately."

"No." Her voice came quietly back to him, almost like the evening breeze itself. "So many unsung heroes who will never make it back home."

David's hand fisted at the injustice of it all. Young men fighting an impossible war, dying on barren wastelands that used to be verdant countryside. Young women forced to witness atrocities beyond the realm of medicine. What nightmares waited for them tonight?

He closed his eyes to stave off the rising heat, but to no avail. "Heroes?" David shook his head and ran a hurried hand through his hair. "How on earth do we define that word now? War has changed. We're fighting an invisible, debilitating gas that doesn't just rob a man of his breath but, if he survives, it steals his future. And now….now the Hun have developed some metal machinery that lays waste wherever it goes. How can anyone be a hero when it's a pointless march into death?"

"Don't you dare minimize what they've done." Catherine's reprimand snatched his attention. "I daresay, most of them knew they were going to die when they went over the top. This war has gone on a long time. Too long for naivety. The entire thing is horrendous and wrong, and half the soldiers are cheating or being cheated. Disheartening? Painful? Unjust? Yes, but not a lost cause."

He lowered his head, a flash of anger and shame knotting in his stomach.

The gentle touch of her hand brought up his gaze. "They risked everything to do what was right. That's a hero, Dr. Ross." A wistful look crossed her face, sweet and filled with such longing, he felt the sudden urge to caress her cheek. She steadied her jeweled gaze on his. "It doesn't get any nobler than that."

Oh, the emotions she bottled inside could saturate a man's needs and desires for life. "No, it doesn't."

He held her attention a moment and then she turned away, staring out over the garden again, the same sadness darkening her countenance. Silence whispered between them.

She pushed a loose strand of ebony behind her ear.

His fingers twitched.

"I know my faith is small and weak, but if what the Bible says is true about God, that he's not forgotten these men or us, or the time in which we live, then we must cling to the truth that there is hope…even now, even in this."

The evening quiet surrounded them, only interrupted by a momentary rustle of the leaves. "Catherine." She looked up, those glossy eyes becoming even glossier with a fresh sheen of sudden tears. "I would not call your faith weak or small." He smiled, reveling in the sudden love stealing his breath. "In fact, I don't believe there is anything weak about you at all."

A tear slipped from its fragile hold and trailed down her cheek. She tossed it away, but not before he saw the tremble in her hand. His chest deflated as if punched.

How many times had her heart been broken, bruised, and no one knew except the Almighty. He ached at the thought of his sister's careless words and her mother's angry criticism. And though Catherine appeared to ignore them, how often had she borne the brunt of such harshness alone in the privacy of her room or this garden?

He took her hand, desperate to quell the tremble. "You are not alone. Whatever you bear, please know, I will not let you bear it alone." He pulsed his promise with a squeeze to her cold hand. "What is it, Catherine?"

Her fingers pinched around her handkerchief, and the quiver in her breath matched the one on her lips. She searched his eyes, waiting for some hidden nudge to give her courage, he supposed.

"Grandmama." A sob hitched her words. "Grandmama is…"

The implication rang clear as Catherine buried her face into her handkerchief again, new sobs wracking her shoulders.

"Oh, Catherine." Her name on his lips, whispered hoarse with emotions he couldn't define, breached some gap he'd placed between them. Whether by his ridiculous class assumptions, her fallen past, or his poorly constructed theology of brokenness, he'd erected a list of dos and donts which held up to argument like paper to flames. Here was living proof of something…someone who defied his assumptions and brought to light compassion, and something infinitely more dear.

Somehow, she must have felt it too…the closeness, the fragility in the darkness. With the slightest tug forward, he held her in his arms, and she gave way to her tears. Entrusting him with her weakness. Her tears wet through his shirt, warm against his skin, and quenched a longing he'd held for her, a tenderness reverberating to his very core.

She trusted him. The woman whose past choices mimicked all of his vain virtue. The woman who, by all social accounts, should be shunned from proper society. This strong, brave woman somehow made him feel brave and strong by offering him this olive branch of trust.

He tightened his hold, wrapping her closer against him, imbuing strength to her, if he could. The scent of lavender swelled around him, and he lowered his cheek to her soft hair. Tenderness and protection braided with determination within him, and a new resolution regarding this aunt's hateful notions of class and the grand 'deserving' emerged like an epiphany. Life was made of much more than 'those people' and 'our people'. God came for 'people' – broken, outcast, and fallen, including him. Including Catherine. And her unborn child.

In God's eyes, they were all the same. In need of grace and love.

Love?

David had never paired the word with any other woman outside his family, but a small jolt of awareness brought the word to mind. Here. Now.

Catherine's sobs drew to silence, but still, he held her. All the world outside faded into nothing but darkening blurs and distant mutters, but in this garden-haven, David began to understand, for the first time, what his father had mentioned about his first meeting with his mother. A sweet contentment. A buried passion lit. Love.

She pushed back from him, and he quickly offered his handkerchief. She smiled and took it, adding it to the one she already held. "Thank you."

"Why were you bearing this pain alone? There are people throughout the whole house who would comfort you."

"Haven't they borne enough from me?" She looked up, eyes glistening with a mixture of tears and moonlight. "I've brought shame and hurt on so many people, the last thing I want them to give is more pity."

"Pity?" His palms took her shoulders in a loose hold. "Pity? Oh, Catherine, stop this! Do not confuse care and compassion with pity. Your truest friends wish to help bear your burdens and comfort you in them."

"But when will the next burden be too much? They've already had to bear so much for—"

"Stop." His finger to her lips silenced her, and him. The touch brought a fire with it, moving down his arm, directly to his heart. "Stop listening to the lies. You are a beautiful woman in God's eyes...and in mine."

Her sapphires grew wide and she pulled back from him. "Dr. Ross, I—"

"No, please." Her professional reference kept a barrier between them. A hedge he wanted to crush. "Call me David."

A remnant of unshed tears highlighted the vulnerability in her eyes, and he saw it. The questions, the pain, the undeniable battle against her own heart. "No. I can't."

Her hesitant, painful admission whispered the truth he'd refused to see. She loved him. He could almost feel it binding him to her with a sense of belonging. Sweet, powerful, and overwhelming.

He took her face in his hands, and she looked up, frozen in place in full astonishment. Those lips, full and rosy, seemed to invite him forward as her breath pulsed against his chin. He was wonderfully lost in those eyes, with the enchanting linger of lavender drawing him closer, nearer to a taste his entire body anticipated.

"Catherine," he whispered, their breath mingling in expectation of more to come.

"No." Catherine's breathy response barely slipped between their lips. She pressed a palm against his chest, encouraging him to an infuriating distance. "Please." Her whimper stilled his movements. "You don't want this."

"You know what I want?"

"A woman carrying another man's child?" She winced at her own declaration, then challenged him with a raised brow. "No, I don't think that's what you want."

"Life has taught me to find the blessings in surprises." He held her gaze, searching his own heart for any hesitation, any doubt her words unearthed, but found none. "You think I haven't weighed my choice? For both you and your child?"

An apology shimmered in her eyes, her breath shaky and warm. "I know you well enough that if you make this decision, one inspired by the high emotions of the last few days, you'll wake tomorrow to regret it."

"You can't see the future, Catherine, or my heart. The only regret I'll have tomorrow is not seizing the opportunity to express my...my sincere affections."

Her palm stalled his closeness again. "Don't you see, dear Doctor, pairing yourself with me will change things for you. Forever. Once your reputation is marred, it cannot be undone. I would never wish that on you."

"You can't keep denying what's happening between us. I know you feel it."

She placed her palm against his face, her thumb caressing his cheekbone, a sad smile offering him little encouragement. "Acting on what I feel is exactly what got me into my current situation, and I've learned a clear lesson. I can't...we can't..." Her words trailed off, but the unspoken ending blazed with implications.

Her hand dropped back to her lap, but he covered it with his own. "I know you care about me. It isn't only a feeling. I see it in your kindness. In your concern. In all of your actions."

Pain and grief carved deeper lines in her brow, and she stood. "Exactly. And I'll do whatever is necessary to protect you, even if it means protecting you from yourself."

With that, she turned and ran toward the house.

Catherine's pulse hammered at the same speed as her feet. One more touch, one more look of such unhindered and beautiful affection, would rip her self-control in half from the sheer craving. Oh, how her heart wrenched with love for that ridiculous man! Why did he have to trick his mind into thinking he cared for her?

The sweet pull from those emerald eyes! The rush of warmth over her skin as he whispered her name. The endearing appeal of his tenderness which proved almost intoxicating.

If she gave in at all, she'd succumb altogether...and forever. She wouldn't chain him to her failures and reputation. Not a man whose every choice was weighed with a sense of rightness. No.

She ran up the stairs to her room and closed the door, leaning against it, eyes pinched, until air came without a tremor into her lungs. All her attempts to keep him at arms' length had failed miserably.

Lord, why? Her soul ached with a battle between her mind and her heart. One knowing she made the right choice to run away and the other wondering…what would his lips have tasted like?

"Like peppermint?" she whispered, palm smoothing over the small, hardening bulge at her abdomen. Her hand stilled. And how could David ever accept both of them?

A knock to her door sent her spiraling from her momentary rest. Had he followed her? She didn't have enough strength to stave him off again. She pressed her palm against the door and leaned close, listening.

"It's not him," Fanny's voice answered. "Open the door."

Catherine groaned and turned to place her forehead against wood. "It's probably best if I'm left alone right now, Fanny dear."

"And I'd imagine you don't want me to ask you these questions out in the hallway where anyone passing by can hear me."

Catherine pressed her eyes closed again and sighed out the fight. There was no use in it. Fanny knew the entire family so well, she predicted movements like a prophet. Catherine opened the door, allowing the ginger-haired woman inside.

"I saw ya run in from the garden," Fanny said, moving to the bed to turn down the coverlets. "Thought a wolf was on your heels from the pace you set up those stairs."

Catherine walked to the other side of the bed, helping with Fanny's work but silent.

"Then I noticed Dr. Ross *was* the wolf when he came in a few seconds behind you, lookin' like he didn't rightly know whether to chase you or leave you be." Fanny glanced from across the bed with that piercing gray gaze of hers.

Catherine considered redirecting the conversation, but with Fanny's background, it would have done little to deter her. "He's momentarily confused, but it should pass."

Fanny responded with a raised brow and went back to her work. "Are you certain about that? What I know of Dr.

Ross, he doesn't seem like the sort of man who is easily distracted from his plans."

Catherine placed the pillow on the bed and then dropped down into her high back chair. "I mean to make certain his plans change. He's having a temporary lapse in his good judgment."

"And just what sort of calamity does he wish to bring on himself?" The glint of humor in her eyes told Catherine that Fanny knew a bit more than she displayed. "Or perhaps you?"

"He fancies himself…attracted to me." Catherine picked at a loose thread on the arm of her chair. "It's ridiculous really. If he had his regular wits about him, he'd never make such a choice."

"I take it you're not keen on his affections?"

The undeniable humor in Fanny's voice pricked at Catherine's annoyance. "No, I'm not. It's a horrible decision, really." She shot Fanny a narrowed-eyed stare, but Fanny's grin only grew wider. "Any logical man would give a wide berth to a woman with my past." She patted her stomach. "And future. I can't see why he'd even toy with the idea."

"He doesn't strike me as the sort of man who toys with anyone's emotions."

"No." Catherine sighed and rested her chin on her palm. "So the only other reason would be he's been driven mad by his work."

Fanny laughed. "Or the simple fact he sees the good of such a match."

"There is no good in such a match, Fanny. David would be ruined by association." She shook her head. "I should run away. Leave him to find another beneficiary for his beautiful affections." Her voice softened at the memory of his palms touching her face, the closeness of his breath and lips.

"I see."

Catherine blinked from her daydream. "It would be what's best for him."

"What's best for him?" Fanny tapped the bedpost as she stepped closer. "Or what's best for you?"

"Of course what's best for him! Can you imagine the repercussions of his aligning himself with a woman who has a reputation of being a notorious flirt, compounded now by the fact she's expecting another man's baby?" Catherine raised a finger to add to her mountain of reasons. "Not to mention the reduced social circumstances of my family and the inevitable neediness involved in being attached to my mother in any possible way."

Fanny sat on the chair near her and nodded, pinching her lips closed in thought. "But for love, could not any of those be overcome?" She pinned Catherine with another stare. "I wonder if the true reason is you're scared he might actually overcome all your objections...and then what? When you have no shame to hide your heart behind, what will you do?"

"That's preposterous, I—"

"You've just been so good at keepin' your emotions in amiable control, prided yourself on never givin' too much of yourself. Even with the nasty Master Drew, you always planned out your decisions, carefully, keeping your emotions far from your heart." She took Catherine's hand in a gentle hold. "But haven't you learned by now you've never been in control of your own life? And that maybe, in this, you've pinched off the sweetest part of what God's offering you."

Catherine pulled her hand free. "I've never been the fairytale sort."

"No, but you're the redeemed sort now, Miss Catherine. Even better than a faerie story. Don't underestimate God's ability to work miracles, but most importantly, don't underestimate his joy in overwhelming you with his love."

"The idea of David's love is *too* beautiful." A sudden rush of tears caught her words and she paused, looking away from the hope on Fanny's face. "*Too* good a gift."

"Do you think he is incapable of weighing his own choices?"

Weren't all men? But the doubt sliced through her middle, nudging at a hope she dared not taste. She turned to face Fanny, slamming her fist against her chest, tears trickling down her cheeks. "I love him in some dangerous way."

"And how can that be bad?"

"How can it be good? He deserves someone with a full heart."

Fanny chuckled. "Dear girl, I don't think it gets fuller than yours. Your life is overflowing with purpose and passion. What could be grander than to give it to the man you love? This godly man who cares for you in return?"

"I don't deserve him." Catherine rubbed at the tears. "Not someone like David."

"Isn't that what grace is all about?" Fanny took Catherine's hand again, warming Catherine's face with the glow of her smile. "God loves extravagantly. He's a generous father. Why can't you accept this gift as you accepted his grace in her soul?"

The tiny sliver of hope trembled with life. No, she couldn't hold on to it. "What if David lives to regret his choices? What if he becomes bitter at the thought of this child? What if—"

"There are many dreams and years of peace that have died at the doubt in 'what ifs.'" Fanny gave Catherine's hand a squeeze and then stood. "If David doesn't mind your past, then perhaps it's time for you to let it go too."

Impossible. She pressed her eyes closed, releasing a new rain of tears. Wasn't it? *God, it can't be that easy.*

"And I ought to mention," Fanny said as she opened the bedroom door to leave. "We received a letter at the house today informing us that Miss Adelaide Moore will arrive tomorrow to offer her kind services to our hospital." Fanny's lips quirked along with her annoying brow. "If you're bound to relieve David's suffering in his affections for you, then perhaps you can give him over to the woman his aunt wishes him to marry. After all, it would make Maureen Cavanaugh happy indeed."

Chapter Sixteen

Somehow, Catherine Dougall inspired a vast mixture of feelings, starting with frustration and ending somewhere around fascination. The gamut produced in one glance nearly distracted David from completing his thoughts, though the glances were few since last night's near kiss.

He felt unsteady, like there was unfinished business between her lips and his. The idea nearly drove him to march across the crowded hospital and abate his curiosity. And then there was the absolute certainty stamped in his mind from comforting her in his arms. Why did she run? Protecting him? He released an irritated puff of air through his nose and watched her exchange a smile with Christopher as she assisted him with his rounds.

David's mind set with purpose. He'd never pursued a woman in his life, but that was about to change.

"David." His sister's voice brought his attention round. A young woman stood at her side, walnut-colored hair tied back beneath her small dome-style blue hat, a hue which brought out the periwinkle of her eyes. "You remember Adelaide Moore?"

David had no recollection of the petite and pale-featured woman before him, but he took her hand and bowed his head over it ceremoniously. "Miss Moore. It's a pleasure to see you again."

Her smile bloomed along with a blush to her cheeks, her interest as obvious as the hat on her head. "Thank you, Dr. Ross. I've often recalled our meeting with fondness. You are quite an impressive horseman."

She saw him ride? That must have been months ago, in the spring. Was it at his aunt's last dinner party? He'd tried to wipe those hideous parties from his memory as much as possible. The social repartee and ingenuity exhausted him. Give him one-on-one conversations, or books to discuss, or work to do, and then he thrived, but music and—he shuddered—dancing? No, he was his father's son.

"I understand you've come to offer your services to our wounded?" David swept a hand to the first hospital room. "These are our patients who have been in rehabilitation the longest. We hope to send half of them home or to the long-term hospital in London by the end of the week."

She gave a wide-eyed look to the room. "I hope I can be of some help."

"All assistance is appreciated." David gestured for her to follow him down the hallway.

"But you'll only be expected to do simple tasks, since this is your first visit," Jessica added, shooting David a warning look. "Take dictation for letters, engage in conversations with the wounded, or fetch small comforts."

"I don't think I could manage much more than that." Her voice held a frail quality, almost afraid. "I must admit, I've had little practice with sick people, so I do hope I won't faint at my first trial."

David raised a brow to Jessica who rolled her eyes but quickly offered Miss Moore a manufactured smile. "We'll be sure to keep you to less…challenging tasks."

David led Adelaide through another doorway for more advanced cases, noting exactly where Catherine was in the room. "This is our other ward of patients."

"You won't be in this wing as much as the former," Jessica added quickly. "These particular cases require more medical intervention than you're prepared to give."

Miss Moore nodded, lifting her gloved hand to her nose. "Then perhaps we should return to the other ward."

David shot his sister another severe look. Did she truly believe he'd feel an attraction for this fragile flower? No doubt she was all the things his aunt thought good and right as far as social standards dictated, but his emotions felt as cold as an ice block.

"Of course, but first I should introduce you to some of the staff." He made a direct line for Catherine, his grin twitching. Perhaps Adelaide's presence would spark Catherine's jealousy as Christopher's had his?

Catherine knelt near Lt. Davenport. She wore her usual pale blue gown, white apron, and white cap that barely contained her mass of hair.

"Must all volunteers wear such…unseemly frocks?" Adelaide grimaced. "They're cotton."

"Cotton washes easier than most other fabrics." Jessica intervened. "And they're durable. There are none of us in a fashion show here, Miss Moore."

David almost laughed. He could already tell Jessica regretted this decision which gave him all the more pleasure. "What would you suggest, Miss Moore?"

Jessica shot him a heated look which he countered with an expression of mock innocence.

"Well, they aren't very flattering, are they? More like servants' gowns than something as prestigious as a nurse."

"And a servant's gown will not do for our nurses," David stated with a little dramatic emphasis added to nudge his sister's annoyance deeper.

"Of course not. My mother has always made it quite clear that there are those who have, and those who have not. We must be attuned to the difference and distinguish ourselves."

"Your mother sounds like a true product of our times."

Miss Moore seemed oblivious to Jessica's sarcasm.

"Truly, she has set the standard of a modern lady quite high for me, but I strive to attain it."

David resigned himself to the notion of having Miss Moore with him for at least the morning. He doubted she'd last until noon, but if she held to her mother's convictions, she might persevere to tea time.

He quickly approached Catherine and gestured toward her work. "This is Nurse Dougall, one of the head nurses of our hospital."

Catherine stood, keeping her hand on Lt. Davenport's arm dressing to hold her place.

"Nurse Dougall, this is Adelaide Moore. She's come to volunteer."

"Welcome, Miss Moore." Catherine's astute gaze took in the woman and then flitted to David.

His smile spread and her lips fought an obvious battle with a response. *Oh, I will win her.*

"What is she doing?" Miss Moore asked, backing away from the Lieutenant's bed.

He gestured toward the man. "Lieutenant Davenport suffered an arm wound from the debris of an exploding shell, so Nurse Dougall is redressing the injury to decrease the possibility of infection."

Miss Moore gasped. "How dreadful. I wouldn't be asked to do such work, would I?"

Catherine and Jessica exchanged a glance.

Yes, his sister was receiving the just desserts of her little scheme. Miss Moore for him? His arm brushed against Catherine's shoulder, and he looked down into her lovely face. No, his sights were set on a much more challenging fare.

"Nurse Dougall." Marianne nearly ran into the room, face as bright as electric lights. "I have a letter for you." Her voice lilted. "And some news."

David had never seen a smile so broad. She looked to each face, nearly bouncing with a wave of uncontained energy.

"For heaven's sake, Marianne. What is it?" Catherine laughed. "You're brimming."

"Overflowing is more like it." Marianne held up a note. "We've only now received confirmation from..." She hesitated and focused a shared, secret smile on Catherine before continuing. "Our contact in town says that both the bazaar and ball have been scheduled and completely outfitted by local benefactors. The date is in three weeks."

"To what is she referring?" David watched Catherine, knowing exactly where the scheme had originated...but why? "A ball? What would any of us need with a ball?"

Catherine cringed a little as she took in all the curious faces before her. Suddenly, everyone's attention felt a little overindulgent. David, Jessica, Miss Moore, and even Dr. Christopher, leaned in to hear the tale. This was not exactly the way she'd intended on sharing her grand ideas. "There are also plans for a Bazaar," she clarified. "Both to raise money for the hospital and orphanage. Until we receive more support from benefactors, this is one way to raise money. I've had several successful bazaars in North Carolina, and I thought—"

David's full laugh burst into her explanation. "Catherine Dougall, you are easily the most interesting person I have ever met."

"Interesting?" Clearly, the poor man was mad. "It's because there is so much to reform you have no idea where to begin."

"On the contrary, I think it's more about how unpretentious and determined you are."

The tenderness in his gaze held her fast and quickened her pulse. Oh, to give in to the draw, to fall into such admiration. The memory of their near-kiss drew her gaze away from his with a rush of heat.

"I'm afraid I've always had a mind of my own."

"Which I suspect caused most of the trouble," Jessica murmured.

"And that's exactly what I presume will cause all the greatness too," David countered. "Secretly making plans to bring in the support of the town? A fundraiser which will not only help financially but boost morale. It's brilliant."

Her smile escaped. "My deviousness is brilliant?"

"When channeled in the right direction, yes." Their gazes held before Catherine looked away again, sliding another step away from him and all his magnetism.

"I don't support the idea of deviousness being brilliant in any form. It sounds sacrilegious." Adelaide pouted out her words, her porcelain brow in a pucker, but just as quickly it cleared into a smile. "But the thought of a ball puts a shine on these dark times of war."

Catherine studied Adelaide a moment, trying to follow the poor girl's conviction jump, but David's scrunched brow distracted her.

"You don't fancy a ball, Dr. Ross?"

David frowned and looked away, rubbing the back of his neck. "I can do with the balls, it's the dancing"—he winced—"that I'm ill-equipped to appreciate."

"Dancing?" She lowered her voice and searched his face. "You can't dance?"

"Of course you can," Adelaide responded with more energy than Catherine had seen since the poor girl entered the room. "You're a gentleman. Every gentleman can dance. It's in his very blood."

"If dancing is a prerequisite for being a gentleman, I'm afraid I might not be as gentlemanly as you suppose, Miss Moore. You see, I've never learnt."

"It looks simple enough." Jessica nudged back into the conversation. "Surely, with a few lessons, we can both be prepared for one ball."

"And it is for a good cause," Catherine added, bringing his attention back to her in all of its warmth. Oh, she nearly melted from the sweetness.

"Wouldn't that be wonderful?" Marianne almost left the floor, the youthful joy in her expression contagious. "Who would teach us? I only had a few lessons from my aunt, but I've always dreamed of truly dancing. And at a real ball."

If Cinderella could take human form she would materialize as Marianne McIvoy.

"My dear, I'm not certain the ball would be for common folk," Adelaide added with enough false sweetness to inspire Catherine's nausea.

"That's exactly the sort it is for, Miss Moore. Who better to have the joy of participating in a ball than the ones whose lives have been most impacted by this war." Catherine challenged the small woman, taking advantage of her few additional inches in height. "Their men are the ones risking their lives."

"But the benefactors…"

"Are well aware of the audience and the purpose," Catherine nodded, certain her conversations with Madame and the letters she'd sent painted a clear understanding. She turned to Marianne. "And I suspect Marianne can have her Cinderella ball to her hearts' content, along with any fine lady who has the stuff to come and support a good cause."

"Well, if you put it like that, I don't see how anyone should refuse."

"Nor I." David's grin grew to laughing point. "I'm determined to attend, even if I cannot dance a step."

Oh, how she loved their banter. "I would expect no less, Dr. Ross."

"I have a brilliant plan." Adelaide came alive. "I don't see that I can be as much a support with the wounded as I can with dancing. I am quite good at it." She moved a fraction closer to David. "And you will have no need to feel the embarrassment of coming off as uneducated or a country bumpkin."

"Thank you, Miss Moore. I certainly wouldn't want to appear as bad as that in front of the whole town." David's voice took on an uncustomary sarcastic edge. Catherine had the sudden urge to kiss him.

As if he read her mind, he sent her a secret wink, and she covered her smile with her hand. How dare he? He was supposed to distance himself for his own good, and here he was flirting. Flirting? David Ross! "I suppose you can dance, Nurse Dougall?"

She couldn't help but catch on to the impish spirit he cast. "I'm an excellent dancer." She smiled sweetly. "What money-hungry debutante wouldn't be if she wanted to snatch the best catch, right?"

Adelaide Moore set a firm look of disproval on Catherine, scanning her simple nurse's attire. "I don't think you quite understand the meaning of debutante, so *I* shall teach them to dance." Her teacup chin lifted high. "It will be my service in the war effort. After all, what could be worse than a gentleman who cannot dance?"

Catherine avoided both Rosses and the generous Miss Moore for a good part of the morning, still chuckling at the young woman's idea of sacrifice through teaching dance lessons to the less fortunate of Roth Hall. A third of the men in the hospital had not only lost their sight from chlorine gas attacks, but possibly their future employment as well. Another third had lost limbs, and a conglomeration of the last third held a mix of mentally unstable to possibly returning to the Front. Dancing? Certainly not the highest social priority on the list.

She slid into a quiet corner of the hallway and drew out the letter Marianne had given her. The handwriting wasn't familiar, but the name was. Lady Eleanor Hollingsworth. Catherine held her breath. She'd written to Lord and Lady Hollingsworth three weeks before, explaining her relationship to Grandmama and touting the wonders of Dr. Ross and his hospital. From her myriad of correspondences, she'd only received two responses thus far – one from a woman in Cornwall who explained that she was already funding a hospital in her country estate, and another from a kindly old cleric who sent a small donation.

The paper, boasting a monogramed 'H' at the top of the page, slid through Catherine's fingers with the smoothness of its expense.

Miss Dougall,

I was pleased to receive your letter and learn of your work with Dr. Ross in the Ednesbury War Hospital and Roth Hall Orphanage. I would like to hold an interview with you regarding the work you and Dr. Ross are doing in Ednesbury, as I grew up in the town and have great sentimentality for its general welfare. Please wire if you are available to attend an interview on Thursday.

Sincerely,

Eleanor Hollingsworth

Thursday? Catherine folded the paper. Two days? Her thoughts spiraled through possibilities. This could mean an important opportunity for the hospital and orphanage….and with David's interest, the timing couldn't be better. Hopefully, her absence would clear his head of this ridiculous attraction, and maybe Adelaide Moore's dance lessons would turn his head. Catherine nearly lost her laugh. Poor David, but Adelaide Moore, with her spotless pedigree, would make a much better adornment to David's life. Catherine frowned, disappointment rearing its ugly head. David wasn't some playboy after a title and prestige. His intelligence required an equal partner, and his subtle humor needed a quick mind to truly appreciate it. His heart reflected the essence of a gentleman in every way that mattered most. Could Miss Moore recognize that above her concern for the appearances?

Catherine shook her head and quickly put her London visit into motion. She made arrangements with Fanny, entrusting her with the secrets of the mission, wired Aunt Josephine to secure lodging, and asked Marianne to accompany her down to Madame's to leave three new designs and ensure Annie and Janie were settling in to their new positions.

Mason was kind enough to take her bags down to the car without drawing any attention. She left a note for her mother and then started for the servants' stairs.

"What are you up to?"

Jessica Ross' voice paused her movement. She turned and adjusted her expression for an excuse, unable to hide her escape when she wore one of her most fashionable coats, a small rim hat, traveling gloves, and her favorite black boots with silk laces. If Jessica knew anything about fashion, it was as clear as air Catherine was off to some well-to-do occasion.

Jessica took a few steps closer, examining Catherine's attire with renewed suspicion. "You're up to something. I knew it from this morning."

"This morning? What did I do this morning?"

Jessica crossed her arms. "Don't play innocent with me. You spent a solid hour trying to dodge David, even complimenting Miss Moore on her hairstyle to draw David's attention to it. Why would you do that?"

"You've made your intentions clear that an advantageous marriage for your brother is of the utmost importance." Catherine rested her hand on the servants' door latch. "I want what's best for him too. And it isn't me."

Jessica stared at her in silence, whether seeing her with fresh eyes or trying to determine Catherine's honesty, Catherine couldn't tell. "And now you're holding a bazaar and ball as a benefit for the hospital?"

Her words came slowly, almost contemplative.

"The hospital needs the help, wouldn't you agree? Even with the funds the new staff brought with them, we are not an up-to-date facility by any means. From what I've read, some of the best options are smaller rooms with fewer wounded, as well as available plastic surgeons and specialists for those with breathing conditions. We can't offer any of those things, but with the proper support, we could."

Jessica lengthened her measured look for a few more seconds. "And now you're leaving?"

Catherine sighed. "It isn't something underhanded as you suspect. I just don't want to garner any premature hopes. I received a letter today from a possible benefactress who has the means to endow us with a substantial amount of support – more than anything your great Aunt might offer."

"So it's a competition against Aunt Maureen?" The skepticism returned with a glint to those green eyes.

"No, I have nothing to prove to your hideous aunt, but I would not see your brother entrapped by her. Not if he can stand on his own feet and use his clear-headedness to run his own hospital. He has the capabilities to be great…he only needs the means to prove it." Catherine placed her palm over her heart. "I know the type woman she is because I used to be one. She's dangerous and will go to great lengths to ensure she gets what she wants. We must make certain we are holding as many cards as we can."

"So you're doing all this for David?"

Catherine looked down and adjusted her gloves. "I should be gone three days, maybe four. I hope this will give you ample time to sway David's heart in the direction of Miss Moore if that is your wish."

Jessica shuddered and rubbed a hand into her forehead. "I can't believe I agreed to bring her here. The woman is a pillow sham with nothing but social drivel on the brain."

Catherine grinned. "But she'd look lovely on his arm. And, of course, she'll teach him how to dance."

Jessica's frown inched upward. "Good heavens, as if that will win the war. She's the very example of the female mindset I fight against. It was such a stupid mistake to listen to Aunt Maureen…but you are right, she is devious."

"I'm an expert at stupid mistakes." Catherine held Jessica's gaze, making her point. "I'm sure you'll make things right."

The woman was smart. One of the reasons Catherine couldn't quite dislike her as much as she wanted to do. "I'm not sure which one of our mistakes is worse." Her grin grew broader. "Yours or mine."

Catherine relaxed her smile even more, a faint kinship coming to light between them. "Time will tell, won't it? If your poor brother ends up marrying the pillow sham, I think your choices might end much worse than mine."

Catherine turned the latch for the servants' stairs.

"Catherine."

Catherine braced herself and turned.

Jessica stepped forward. "You love him, don't you?" Her voice held no accusation. No disgust. Only an honest curiosity.

Catherine drew in a deep breath, preparing to jump the chasm between knowing a truth and speaking it aloud. She didn't need Jessica's approval or even her good favor, but knew the woman wasn't all prickles and stings. She may be an overprotective sister, but for all the right reasons. "Yes, I do, and I'll fight as hard as you to make sure he's happy."

Chapter Seventeen

"Do you have a few hours free?"

Jessica pushed off her cap and shook loose the mass of blonde waves so her head could breathe.

David took her by the arm and drew her down the hallway. "Maybe three?"

He wore his intensity with such sincerity. She loved that about him. Focused. Certain. Her frown bent. Stubborn when he wanted something. From the way he teased and stared at Catherine Dougall, he knew what he wanted.

Most days, he was brilliant. Not today.

"What did you have in mind? You're hardly the pub sort."

His glance down the hallway had her reconsidering the pub slight. "David?"

"I have this...venture I've started. Something I need to keep quiet, but I need a nurse."

"You need a nurse."

"One who can keep a secret." His stare added an exclamation mark to his statement.

Oh, good grief, what had he done?

"You need a nurse, and have to keep it secret?" She placed her hands on her hips. "David Ross, that combination does not bode well."

"Shh..." He waved a hand to quell her volume and pressed his words into a whisper. "I'll explain along the way."

Jessica barely believed his story until he brought her into the abandoned shop on Ellis Street. The building appeared vacant by design, but when he opened the back door to allow her inside, the dim candlelight revealed a small group of people. Their worn and simple clothes labeled them as working class at best.

"How have you done this?"

His smile turned sheepish. "I haven't. Aunt Maureen has. She's funded every quid." He winked and gestured her forward. "Let's see to our patients, shall we?"

It was a remarkable endeavor. People of all ages, the poor who needed medical attention for various ailments and who were simply, due to their social status, considered unfit to be seen. The injustice of it fueled and added determination to follow her brother in this preposterous scheme.

She treated some of the humblest of the patients—a widow's burn wound, a boy's broken nose—and as she watched her brother, a fresh awareness for his love in his work humbled her. He held the same passion as their father – the same desire to go against the grain to serve. He couldn't help it. A swell of pride brought tears to her eyes and provided a new understanding of his ability to make his own future.

She hated to admit it, but Catherine was right.

David needed freedom to do what he did best – without the restraints of a power-hungry aunt to control him. She saw how the people's suspicions melted away within the first few minutes of his care, and how they repaid him with whatever they had—a knitted scarf and gloves, a pie, a sack of potatoes. He took each offering with the grace of a king. A sense of shame fell over her. She'd created a box for her own brother. In trying to protect him from the hurt she saw in their father, the struggles, the devastation in being an outcast from one's family, in trying to keep him clear of heartache, she'd neglected to see how very capable a man he was.

He had the skills to administrate his own hospital, he only needed a partner with the ability to make the right connections, gain benefactors, and navigate the social world of which David knew very little. But not Adelaide Moore.

Which left another uncomfortable confession in her spirit she would *not* voice.

A last patient arrived as they were closing up the doors, hidden in the shadows, waiting for her opportunity. She was a plain sort of woman, with a dour expression and sturdy frame.

David approached. "May I help you?"

"I…I don't trust doctors." She bit out the words, but the worry lines around her face seemed to bring her another step forward. "But I've been told you are good and…and I think something's wrong. I'm too large for what I'm eating." She placed a palm on her extended abdomen.

David nodded. "I understand. Come inside, Mrs…?"

"Call me Janie. That's what most people do."

"Very well, Janie." He glanced to Jessica. "Get a cot prepared, will you?"

With the utmost discretion, he examined her. When he had finished, he stepped back and helped her to a seated position. "Janie, you're in good health, though I would suggest you try to eat a few more vegetables. You're going to be extra busy in two months, I should think."

"The baby is fine?"

"Both babies seem to be fine."

"Both?" Her eyes grew wide, and then her entire expression fell. "I can't care for one, let alone two." She stood, adjusted her modest, clean gown, and walked toward the door. "But I know where they shall be cared for. Thank you."

"Is there no way you can keep them? Perhaps your husband could—" Jessica stopped when the woman shook her head.

"The vile man who did this to me ain't interested in me nor any children. I don't think his wife would think too kindly of it." Janie walked to the door. "But I appreciate your good work, Doctor. There ain't many of the poshies who lower themselves to help the likes of us, but Roth Hall's proven itself with you and Miss Catherine."

David paused as he wiped off his hands. "Miss Catherine? You know her?"

"Oh no," Jessica blurted. "What has she done?"

"Done?" Janie's calmness disappeared behind smoldering eyes. "She's done more than anyone else in this town would do to help women like me. We're rejected from the day people know we're with child. We live with shame and grief, and worry how we're going to survive from one day to the next. Miss Catherine's found me a good job when everyone else would as soon spit on me. She's shown that

God's not forgotten the lowliest of his people. That's what she's done."

Aunt Josephine greeted Catherine like the prodigal, her usual exuberance accompanying a grand display of affection she never received from Mother. Catherine used to view it as a rite, a deserved crowning of regard since their great uncle owed his yearly allowance to Grandmama's good graces, but now, with vision less consumed with pride, Catherine took a new view of her widowed aunt and saw a fading beauty who had longed for the children that would never come.

And her aunt had always opened her home to Catherine when she wished to visit the city. Her aunt also knew of St. John's Wood, the luxurious area of London which housed Willow Tree Court, home of Lord and Lady Hollingsworth. Her aunt had not exaggerated the immensity of the homes or the grandeur of the area. Willow Tree Court stood as one massive home in a line of others, each with a well-tended and elaborate front gardens and entry gates. The tall brick Georgian rose above her as the car deposited her at the doorstep. Catherine had visited Ednesbury Court a handful of times, had grown up in Roth Hall, but the opulence displayed from the massive windows to the golden glow of the bricks of Willow Tree shot a tremor through her.

In the past, she'd waltzed into other homes with arrogance, but now an awareness of her station humbled her. *You may be subject to your past, but you are not controlled by it.* The whisper smoothed over her soul and bolstered her courage. No, with God's help, she could be brave, no matter the sins darkening her shadow.

An aged, lean butler greeted her. He stood tall, with the same expressionless demeanor as Jackson at Roth Hall. "Miss Dougall?"

"Yes."

He gave a slight bow. "Welcome to Willow Tree Court. Lady Hollingsworth is waiting for you in the parlor."

Catherine looked around the dark mahogany, two-level entry. A chandelier hung in the center like a mass of crystallized teardrops. Higher fashion fit Willow Tree Court.

"This way, Miss Dougall."

The butler led her through the entry which opened into a fabulous hall with a split grand stairway spiraling up on either side like tree branches to meet the upper level. Catherine worked to keep the awe from her expression and thus mark herself as ill-equipped for the task at hand, but her heart leapt with the sweet scent of such opulence.

The butler ushered her into a room of morning light, rose curtains, and pale furniture that brought a sense of spring into the autumn day. A slender woman of her grandmother's generation stood and welcomed her with a poised smile. Her pale gray gown boasted simple elegance and complemented her silvery, russet hair.

"I'm glad you could come, Miss Dougall." Lady Hollingsworth gestured toward the chair close to hers. "Won't you join me for tea?"

"Thank you." Catherine took the proffered seat. "I can't tell you how delighted I was to receive your invitation."

Lady Hollingsworth nodded to the maid who poured out the tea. "I must say, your letter piqued my interest. I've supported several hospitals since the war began, but none so far from London as Ednesbury."

"I can assure you, the quality of care received and the opportunity to recuperate in the country carries its own benefits. There are more wounded than hospitals can treat. Dr. David Ross and his sister are both quite capable administrators. They not only run the facility with efficiency and quality, but will ensure that your money is used in the most productive way."

"Miss Dougall, I have no doubt of your passion for the hospital, or the abilities of Dr. and Nurse Ross. In fact, from first receiving your letter, I've had it in mind to support the hospital."

Catherine released the tense air in her throat. "You'll find Dr. Ross a most grateful recipient."

"Yes." She took a sip of her tea and watched Catherine over the rim, expression giving away nothing. "But my particular reason for this interview was to meet *you*."

Catherine set her cup down. "Me?"

"Yes, you. I am no stranger to Ednesbury or the Dougalls. In fact, your grandmother has been my dear friend ever since we were young. I called Ednesbury my home until I met the Duke at a dinner party held at Roth Hall and hosted by none other than Victoria Dougall."

"I didn't realize you were so intimately acquainted with my family."

Lady Hollingsworth's hazel eyes turned sad. "I received a letter from your grandmother only a few weeks ago, at which time she explained the seriousness of her illness and also encouraged me to contact you."

A mist fogged Catherine's vision, the fresh wound of her Grandamama's death dangling her emotions over a fragile ledge. "My sister sent me notice of her passing only two days ago."

"I see." Lady Hollingsworth paused her cup in mid-air and placed it back on the table. "I am sorry for your loss. Her generosity of spirit and tenacity will not be easily forgotten."

Catherine smiled through the growing warmth in her eyes. "No, I should think not."

"She wasn't one to wait around for ideas or adventure. She made them happen."

"And brought other people along with her, whether they were ready or not."

Lady Hollingsworth chuckled. "Quite right. I was among some of those early schemes of hers, particularly her undying devotion to the lost art of matchmaking. She held a remarkable power of persuasion."

Matchmaking? The very idea of Grandmama's subtle fingers in everyone's lives inspired a laugh. "Yes, she did."

A sliver of silence sobered the conversation, with only the 'ting' of Lady Hollingsworth's spoon stirring in her cup. "She was quite proud of you, you know."

Catherine looked up from her sip of tea. "Proud of *me*?"

"Yes, she said as much in her letter."

Proud? Of her?

"I can see by your confusion that you neither know your _Grandmama or yourself as well as you think."

Catherine returned her cup to its saucer, her hand growing unsteady. "I'm not certain I understand what you mean, my lady."

171

"Your _Grandmama apprised me of certain information about you and your previous choices that have somewhat overshadowed your future."

Catherine lowered her gaze to her lap, the same shame washing over her at another reminder of her sin.

"You have no reason to lower your head now, Catherine. If I understand correctly, you have been made right in the eyes of God, and he sees you as whole and healed. I will not condone your previous behavior, but neither would you, I suspect."

Her gentle tones, her quiet encouragement, brought Catherine's gaze back to her face. "No, I'd never choose to repeat my behavior, except…." The knowledge, the sudden awareness came out of nowhere. "Except that I wouldn't wish to go back to the person I used to be, and if…and if it took these circumstances to open my eyes to God's grace, then I am…" She released a surprised brush of air. "I am glad for those circumstances."

Her heart twisted from the contradiction she'd voiced. Glad for the wounds her choices with Drew caused? Grateful?

Her throat tightened. Her eyes burned. Yes! Without her brokenness, she wouldn't have her sister's relationship, her service to the hospital, or the seamstresses, her grandmother's pride, or David's admiration. No, this side of brokenness was much better than the place before, when she'd mistakenly believed she was whole.

"Would we all have such clarity?" Lady Hollingsworth took a sip of tea then placed her cup back on the table. "And your statement only proves the more your grandmother's faith in you."

Catherine pushed away a rebel tear. "Faith in me?"

"Your _Grandmama came from a long line of strong and courageous woman who were all refined by trial, mistakes, and suffering. They understood the power of grace as well as their place and purpose in the hands of the Almighty."

"So even the struggles are worthwhile, then?"

Lady Hollingsworth leaned a little closer, her eyes taking on a fiery light. "Great people do not come from smooth seas, dear Catherine. They never have. Whether by the uncontrollable tempests that blow through life or our own vain attempts to control our worlds by selfishness or pride, the greatest strength is born out of suffering, or rather out of learning from our suffering."

"I'm certain my personality resembles more of a tempest than a calm sea."

Lady Hollingsworth's light laugh fit the airy brightness of the room. "I would suspect that humility has taught you well then. God has brought you to this place, and you are using the courage he's given you to serve His purposes." She opened her palm and gestured to the room. "You wouldn't be here otherwise, finding support for a group of people who can give you little except gratitude in return."

Catherine's smile bloomed. "It's amazing how one's perspective changes when you're stripped of your dreams."

Her brow lifted. "And given new dreams—better ones, I daresay."

Catherine basked in the new understanding. So much like Grandmama.

"Let me comfort you with the knowledge of your four greatest strengths. You have your Savior's spirit to empower you, your grandmother's heart to encourage you, a solid memory to remind you from whence you have come, and the promise of a future secured in unending grace."

"That's beautiful." Tears blurred Catherine's vision, the weight and the freedom of those words pressing in on her.

"*That* is truth." Lady Hollingsworth's smile crinkled at the corners of her eyes. "I do wish to support Dr. Ross' work and your sister's orphanage, but even more, I want to support you, Catherine Dougall. Your unfailing devotion and courage displays the very heart of strength in these great times of trial. You, in more ways than blood, mirror your grandmother."

"I hope you're right and that your memory isn't failing."

Lady Hollingsworth darted a grin. "My memory is the only thing that isn't failing in this body of mine." She nodded. "Your Grandmama's spirit may have softened over time, but she was your equal in determination and strength. And, I daresay, stubbornness."

"I don't think her stubbornness ever softened."

"She was also a woman who valued redemption and second chances." Lady Hollingsworth drew in a deep breath. "Those who learn from heartache and mistakes value grace with a greater affection. Your _Grandmama knew a similar brokenness as you and grew from it."

"What brokenness? Her father's early death?"

Lady Hollingsworth folded her hands in front of her and paused, tilting her head to the ceiling as if in thought. "Her father's death certainly influenced her. It was then that she became the sole heir to a historically male entail. The responsibilities of salvaging a failing fortune and estate was a heavy burden on a young woman's shoulders."

"But what of her husband? Didn't he help her? Who suggested she sell parcels of land to keep the bulk of the estate safe? The Cavanaughs?"

Lady Hollingsworth studied Catherine a moment in silence before continuing. "She was not ready to marry after her heartbreak. You see, your _Grandmama was engaged to the late Lord Cavanaugh, the man whose widow now resides at Ednesbury Court."

Crow Cavanaugh's late husband? Catherine gripped the side of her chair. "Did he break their engagement?

"What do you know of Lord James Cavanaugh?"

Catherine blinked from the sudden change in topic. "I only know him to be the father of the late Lord Jeffrey Cavanaugh of Ednesbury Court. Dr. Ross' great grandfather."

"Yes, Jeffrey Cavanaugh was the second-born son. The elder son died fighting the Boers and left no heir, thus relinquishing the estate to Jeffrey. Lord James's daughter, the man's pride and joy, married well to a Mr. Avery Ross."

"Dr. Ross' grandfather. Yes, I know that part of this story, but how does it impact Grandmama's engagement?"

"A falling out happened between your grandmother's father, Captain Davidson Spencer, and the elder Lord Cavanaugh due to both parties' desire to control the town of Ednesbury, which the Spencer's owned at the time. The disagreement was so extreme that both men refused to allow the engagement between their children to continue, thus dividing the estates until this day."

"Was it a love match?"

Lady Hollingsworth's smile grew sad. "Oh yes, very much so. I don't think either forgot the other."

Catherine sat back in her chair to take in the information. Well, this certainly explained some of Lady Cavanaugh's hatred toward the Spencer family.

"When the disagreement occurred, the fathers prohibited the two young lovers from seeing one another again. The rift in the relationship, followed by the sudden death of Captain Spencer, left the estate in dire need. Your grandmother was young, heartbroken, and lonely. She made choices, some good, and some which stung with lasting consequences, but as you have said, circumstances have a way of refining and reforming people. It fueled her generosity, but also her determination to save Roth Hall."

The story became clear. "So to save the estate, she sold of parcels of land?"

"Yes."

"And Lord Cavanaugh was happy to buy them."

"The expansion of land is a country gentleman's gold." Lady Hollingsworth leaned forward, keeping her gaze focused on Catherine's. "I shared this with you to bring you courage, that out of the most dire circumstances, a person with a vision will see a way to make things right."

Lady Hollingsworth stood and took an envelope from a small tray, giving it to Catherine. "Here is a letter of intent, along with some monies to help ensure your purchase of a much finer x-ray machine as well as any other immediate medical needs the hospital may have. I hope to send more monies within the next month to help support the orphanage, but my present commitments keep me from offering more."

"I'm grateful for whatever you've given."

"There are names of five other such patrons here in London. I have provided references for all of them and suggest you visit with them and speak of your cause."

Catherine fought the urge to take Lady Hollingsworth into her arms. "I can't thank you enough. You've been…truly a Godsend."

Her smile softened. "I am pleased to have met you, Catherine Dougall, and hope this will be a valuable connection for both of us in the future."

"Are you leaving us too?"

Michael looked up and David stepped further into the room, examining Michael's bag of materials. "What do you mean?"

"I was just informed by my sister that Catherine has gone off to London on some mysterious mission, and now I come in to see you packing up supplies?"

Michael released a sigh as he propped his elbow on his knee. "Annie Feagan hasn't given me much of a choice. She practically ordered me to help with some repairs at Madame what's-her-name's shop."

David pulled a chair closer and took a seat. "Madame Rousell? How did Annie become associated with Madame?"

"How do you think?" Michael pinned David with a stare and slowly stood. "Catherine's save-the-world scheming."

David smiled despite his current frustration at the woman's behavior. Why did the thought of his scheming American bring such pleasure with it? "The very thought of her alliance with Madame Rousell should instill fear in all the residents of Ednesbury. What a pair!"

"Oh great." Michael ran a hand through his hair. "Now I'm even more excited about visiting the local *dress* shop. It's bad enough to have Catherine giving me orders, but now Annie's taken lessons. Bossy women must be my punishment for past mistakes."

David laughed, a welcome relief from the agitation Catherine's absence posed.

Michael turned and looked up. "Any news from the Front?"

"Nothing good. It seems our boys are hitting a wall at every turn. There's been an enormous loss of life this year, and Father's letters reiterate the need for more assistance."

"I won't be surprised if America doesn't join up soon. In fact, I hope they do so we can end this horrible waste of life."

"It makes one set his priorities and perspectives in order." He watched Michael stuff a few tools into the bag, deliberating whether to broach the subject with him. He certainly needed perspective, and his sister wasn't helpful. Michael had easily earned David's trust over the past few months, patiently fulfilling his responsibility as caretaker of Roth Hall as well as chipping in wherever else he might be needed.

"Before you set off on your adventures as an indentured servant to the French and Irish, I'd like your…" David cleared his throat, his face warming with discomfort. "Your thoughts about a certain…um…delicate situation I'm trying to puzzle out."

"The one about Radcliffe and his notorious cigarettes?"

"Um… no, it's actually of a more personal nature."

Michael closed his tool bag. "If it's about your sister, I want no part of it. I've already told you my lot in life with bossy women."

A little of the tension dissolved from David's shoulders. "No, not that particular female."

Michael's grin started on one side and made a slow, knowing slide to the other. "It wouldn't be in regards to a certain scheming, raven-haired American, would it?"

David drew in a deep breath and placed his palms on his knees, leaning forward. "Let's say that it was."

"I already feel sorry for you." Michael sat down across from David and crossed his arm. "So, what's the…delicate situation, and please spare both of us the time and just say it."

"I'm in love with her."

Michael's brows shot high. "Good for you. That was about as direct as it comes. Does Catherine know?"

"I'm fairly certain she does, which is what's caused the problem, it seems."

Michael's expression turned skeptical. "She doesn't reciprocate?"

"She's pushing me away with a very firm hand and even encouraged my affection for Miss Moore."

Michael grimaced. "The dancing woman?" He rubbed his chin. "Oh she must *really* love you."

David stood and raised both palms into the air. "Then, for heaven's sake, why is she running away from me?"

177

Michael stood and placed a palm on David's shoulder. "For such an intelligent man, you don't know a great deal about women, do you?"

David rolled his eyes with his grin. "I'm afraid I'm quite at a loss most of the time, but I'm a fast learner."

"It's a long and somewhat painful process of discovery once you start the study, and most of the time, you'll probably still get it wrong."

"You're quite the encourager."

"I've been accused of that before." Michael shrugged off a smile, his face sobering. "David, I've known Catherine a long time, and I don't think I've ever seen her as terrified and confused as she is around you, which speaks volumes for her care."

"Why would she be terrified? I've done nothing to frighten her as far as I know."

Michael shook his head as if David was a hopeless cause. In regards to the complexity of women, perhaps he was. "You know her better than you think. If she purposes in her heart toward something, what is she going to do?"

"Fight for it with a veracity that's almost maddening."

"Exactly, and sometimes, like with the poor chauffer in town, she doesn't think out the consequences of her well-intended plans, but she will make up for her weaknesses with fortitude. I think, in this, she's fighting for you. Your reputation, your future happiness."

"I've already weighed the consequences, and I don't care."

"That's not the point. She's *not* going to put you in jeopardy. She cares about you too much, and the importance of social acceptance has been a constant diet in her life. You may have weighed the consequences, but so has she, and she's not willing to risk your future."

"Why should she care if I don't?"

"Probably because she doesn't believe anyone would sacrifice that for her and then live without regrets." Michael stepped over to his bag. "You're not the only one jumping social hurdles here. Do you realize what she's going through? Her whole life, she's been taught to behave a certain way. You've met her mother—can you imagine what sort of nonsense she heard and what was supported?"

David groaned.

"She's also been told who to shun and why. Drilled into her. Not from her Grandmama, God rest her soul, but from her father and mother. Believe me, I heard and saw plenty when I lived near them in North Carolina. She was always trying to measure up to, not only to her mother's expectations, but her father's too."

Quiet followed, Catherine's arguments mounting higher.

"What about the baby?" Michael's voice entered the silence, brow raised in challenge.

What about the baby? David had asked himself the question many times in the dark of night as he prayed over his decision, his choice. With each prayer, each consideration, the answer cleared.

The little one had invaded his heart with as much certainty as Catherine herself, etching out a tender place in him he couldn't define.

Michael continued. "The baby's father doesn't want him, so he's going to be as much an outcast as Catherine. Are you ready for that?"

"No, in all honesty I'm probably not ready to be a father." David shrugged, the daunting task tightening his throat. He drew in a deep breath of purpose. "But I'm willing. I'm willing to give my heart to that child as I do to his mother." He chuckled. "As a matter of fact, I've developed a particular fondness for outcasts.

"Doctor, I think you've found your perfect match."

"Then how do I convince Catherine of my sincerity?"

Michael threw his bag over his shoulder. "She's as stubborn as you, probably more so. If she's harboring that much insecurity, she's going to need more than your words."

Michael's innuendo tugged at David's smile. "You mean…"

Michael winked, his grin growing like a sly fox. "I reckon you're going to have to show her how serious you really are."

"Perfect." David marched toward the door, determination in his steps. "There's only one thing I have to do first."

"What on earth could be better than finding the woman you love?"

"Ensuring that all ties to someone who might hurt her are broken." David's grin unfurled. "And then I plan to find Catherine Dougall and celebrate."

Chapter Eighteen

Catherine stepped through the door of Madame's shop, an unwavering smile on her face all the way from London. After the letters, and the waiting, and all the sacrifices to use menial supplies to serve the patients, they were finally going to have a steady flow of support to supplement Grandmama's allowance. She breathed in the scent of perfume and new cloth, the bell over the door jingling as it closed behind her.

"Ah, *ma chère*. You have returned?" Madame, resplendent in a bright display of pale purple and green, tapped her nails against the counter as she rounded it. "I sold your first two dresses as soon as they decorated my window. Poof." She snapped her fingers. "They were gone. And more people come every day to see your creations. Busy…busy."

"Is there something I can do to help?"

"Help?" Madame repeated, with a dismissal of her hands. "Why would I need your help? I only need your designs. Annie runs the sewing room like a work house, and Marianne is an excellent shopkeeper."

Catherine nearly dropped her satchel. "You put Marianne out front? But Madame, what about her name? Her father was the biggest brothel owner in this part of England."

"What's in a name?" She wiggled her fingers in the air as if the argument fluttered away. "We changed it. Now, she is Miss Marianne Harrington, my niece."

There was no point in arguing with the woman, and as Catherine thought about it, Marianne had been only twelve when her father left her in his aunt's care. Perhaps those who knew her then would not recognize her now.

"And your new designs?"

Catherine reached into her satchel and produced her portfolio with some more sketches. "I have three."

Madame's hands came together. "Ooh la la, you are magnifique. Does your mind ever tire of ideas?"

181

"I can't seem to quiet them." Catherine handed the sketches over and Madame took them, cooing as she slid from one paper to the next.

"You know, we have already sold eight of the new designs since you left for London and have orders for five more. News of the ball will only add more requests, and soon, the entire town of Ednesbury will be wearing Dougall Designs."

Catherine rolled her eyes heavenward. "Dougall Designs? Is that what you've named them?"

"Do you have something more eloquent?"

"I never imagined using one, but perhaps...well..." She cleared her throat, a bit overwhelmed by the actuality of it. Maybe there was something to be said for fairytales. "We could use my middle name? Maybe something like C. Everill Designs?"

Madame stared at her for a moment, tapping her stained nails onto her chin. "Oui, I like it, but I prefer Catherine Everill, if you must, or simply Everill Designs?"

Catherine drew in a deep breath. Hearing her name spoken in connection to her designs almost buckled her to the floor. "Very well, Everill Designs it is."

Madame turned to the window display. "Fantastique. Now, I must prepare the shop for the next day and then make arrangements for my sisters' arrival."

"Your sisters are coming?"

Madame slid a beautiful oriental scarf around one of the blouses on display. "Oui, they hope to be moved before the festivities." Madame sighed. "They are such lovers of a good ball."

"They're moving here?"

"Oui. Younger, and what would you say, same face sisters?"

"Twins?"

"Ah, yes, twins. And when one decides, the other is quick to agree on a new adventure." Madame shook her head and adjusted one of the gowns on display in the window. "When my kind-hearted brother-in-law, Dr. Burr, heard of our war hospital, he decided London did not need his services as desperately as Ednesbury."

"Your brother-in-law?"

"Oui." She bustled over to a row of blouses on her way to the counter in the shop. "Dr. Randolph Burr, a surgeon, I believe. You can tell the good Dr. Ross to be prepared for a man with as big a heart as his stomach. And he has quite a sizeable stomach." Madame chuckled and then waved Catherine toward the back of the shop. "Go, see what my wonderful seamstresses are doing. They create, and all I have to do is smile, decorate, and convince women to open their purses."

Catherine stepped into the back and stood to take in the changes. Four sewing machines, two brand new, stood before her, Janie at one and two new girls employed two of the others. Cloth, ribbons, lace, scissors, and a whole host of other gorgeous remnants fell in various disarray across the sewing tables, with a few on the floor. Two partially completed gowns hung on display. Catherine's palm pressed into her chest. They looked even more beautiful than her sketches. Perfect.

"They're good." Janie's voice broke into Catherine's daydream.

"I'm pleased at your approval."

Janie's smile quirked almost imperceptibly. "Just speaking the truth."

Michael emerged from the back, hammer in hand and covered in sawdust from cap to boots. "Well, well, look who's back from the big city."

"Michael? What are you doing here?"

"You mean besides becoming acquainted with this passel of lovely ladies." He bestowed a lingering glance on a few of them. "I'm also helping Madame expand some rooms to accommodate the newest seamstresses."

"How did you know about—?"

"Don't worry, Kat, your secret's safe with me." He topped his declaration off with a wink.

She released her clamped air into a sigh. "How safe might be another matter."

"Oh, you know you can trust me. We're both much improved from who we used to be." He peered past her to the shop door. "Which reminds me, have you seen Dr. Ross since your arrival?"

She narrowed her eyes, studying his less-than-innocent expression. "No, is he well?"

"For the most part." Michael shrugged. "I was only curious if he'd had a chance to speak with you yet."

"Michael, have you done something?"

"Not much, if you ask me." Annie answered, entering the room and sending him a sizeable glare. "He keeps flirtin' with the ladies and taking his grand old time on any repairs. He's completely useless."

Michael shrugged off her insults without a hitch. "You say that now, but you've been happy as a clam with what I've done so far."

She placed her palms on her hips. "Just imagine how ecstatic I'd be if you worked more than you talked."

"You can't complain about the cost or the work." He leaned close, eyes narrowed. "And you have to admit, I make a fine distraction in the middle of all this cloth and lace."

Annie's mouth dropped wide for a moment, speechless, which caught Catherine's complete attention. Annie? Speechless?

Then the ginger-headed snippet narrowed her own eyes and matched his posture. "Oh, you American men think you're so irresistible." She imitated a man's pose and tossed her head. "Those poor women need a strong man like me to rescue them out of their heartache."

Catherine laughed as she imitated a southern American accent perfectly.

"Let me sweep in and watch 'em swoon for the loss of me."

Despite himself, Michael grinned. "It's uncanny how well you change your accent. Can you do any more?"

Annie turned to Catherine and winked, immediately tossing her hand in the air and walking forward with such flare there was no mistake who she mimicked. "Mes petite, white does nothing for anyone unless she is a bride. Bring me red. Bring me violet, but do not bring me colorless fashions."

Catherine laughed. "It's absolutely brilliant."

"And imitation is the sincerest form of flattery, my little parrot." Madame sashayed through the door. "She should only aim for the best." Madame's peaked brow and sly smile gave away her good humor. "And she has an ear for languages. She has been learning French with the speed of a child." Madame waved a hand at the sewing tables. "But where are my new gowns?"

"You've added two more seamstresses?" Catherine scanned the room. "No wonder you sought Michael's assistance to convert part of the storage rooms into bedrooms."

"Your designs are selling with the same flair in which they were created."

Annie walked closer. "And the women needed jobs. Two of them got the sack from the Cavanaughs."

"It seems Ednesbury Court is not immune to the effects of war," Madame added, nodding toward a young woman with gold braids pinned atop her head. "Eight have been released from service in the past week."

Catherine knew more servants were leaving service voluntarily due to the freedom in other jobs, particularly in factories or as typists, but sacking eight in one week? That seemed extreme, even for Lady Cavanaugh.

"We will not be able to house them long in these cramped conditions. Especially as your designs spread in popularity. One woman arrived from Manchester yesterday who was so enamored with your work, she promised to send new buyers. We will need more space."

Catherine looked to Madame. "I'm not certain what options we have for expanding until we locate more funds."

"Well, we will make do for now and pray for blessing." Madame's manicured brow rose. "And *beaucoup de patience.*"

Catherine slipped in through the servants' door and up the back steps, careful to keep as far from the hospital as possible, but Michael's impish question niggled an aggravating curiosity. She'd convinced herself to go directly to her room and change upon arrival, but her Pietro Yantorny shoes turned her in the opposite direction. Clearly, the Italian designer set Cupid's bow on the tips rather than the cloth buckle. She should have worn her practical English black leather lace-ups.

Her plum traveling suit caught the attention of almost every soldier she passed, and she tried to ignore the small thrill of pleasure. Their small gaze of admiration certainly did wonders for her confidence.

As she drew close to David's office, the sound of music slowed her steps. Music? Suddenly, from behind, Jessica took her arm and pulled her to the office door.

"I can't believe I'm saying this, but I'm actually glad you're here," she whispered and gestured toward the room with her head. "You have to fix this."

Jessica? Glad to see her? Something must be very wrong. "What is it?"

"Look."

Catherine peeked around the frame of the door and almost lost control of her laugh. In the center of the room, Adelaide Moore danced with David…or at least, Catherine thought the aim was dancing.

"I'm no expert on dancing, but that doesn't look like anything I've seen before." Jessica grimaced. "He's as stiff as a nutcracker. In fact, so is she."

"They do appear rather clockwork, don't they?" Catherine lowered her laugh into her hand. "Your poor brother."

"It's fine for you to laugh now, when no one can see him, but I will not have him be made the fool." Jessica's harsh whisper grew in volume. "Go in there and show him the proper way."

"What?" Heat drained from Catherine's face at the thought of David's arms around her. "No."

"You would rather him dance in front of the whole town like this?"

Catherine cringed.

"Exactly."

"You should be the last person asking me." Catherine took another look at the pair. Dancing might have been Miss Moore's goal, but it certainly wasn't the result.

"Then it's pretty obvious how desperate I am." Jessica's eyes took on a fire. "Go, help him."

Catherine clutched Jessica's arm and pulled her along. "On one condition. You must stay in the room at all times."

"Why? Are you afraid you'll do something irresponsible?"

"Not me, but I have the uncanny ability to inspire your brother toward ridiculous notions." Catherine gave Jessica's arm another squeeze for emphasis, hoping her steady gaze proved her point. "And both of us want him far from the ridiculous, right?"

To Catherine's surprise, Jessica's lips twitched into a smile. "You attempt the impossible. I just don't want him looking like...that."

Catherine shot Jessica an annoyed glance and stepped into the room. "Miss Moore, I am so glad I found you."

Adelaide blinked her large eyes. "Found me?"

Catherine tried to avoid looking at David. Those eyes. His smile. "I'm afraid Nurse Ross has been beyond help with her nerves regarding this ball."

Adelaide looked to Jessica. Jessica stared at Catherine and Catherine nodded. "Oh yes, only one week left before her very first ball, and she has no idea how to dance. Can you imagine the catastrophe?"

Jessica's eyes narrowed into green daggers before she turned to Adelaide. "Yes, I...um...really don't think anyone has the experience to teach someone as uncultured as myself." Catherine stilled her smile as Jessica transformed her expression into a pleading look. "I'm afraid I'm a hopeless cause."

Adelaide reached forward and gave a stiff pat to Jessica's shoulder, as if Jessica might be unfit to touch in her nurse's uniform. "No one is a lost cause. I was quite inept at dancing, but look at me now. It's as natural to me as breathing."

Catherine dared not look in Jessica's direction for fear of bursting into laughter.

"What a relief, Miss Moore. Do you think you could spare a few moments for me and allow Nurse Dougall to take over with Dr. Ross?"

Adelaide hesitated, looking back at David for clarification.

"I certainly don't want my poor sister to be embarrassed by her lack of skill."

Adelaide sighed. "Of course not. Come over here, Nurse Ross, and I will see if Dr. Pike can be your partner. He is quite spry for his age and a known dancer." She pushed Catherine toward David. "He doesn't have long before his next surgery, so every minute is valuable practice time."

David held out a hand and his smile teased her forward. The sweet dizziness of his presence shot a delightful wave of pleasure over her skin. How she'd missed him.

"As Miss Moore said, I haven't much time, and I need my practice."

She pinched down a swallow and stepped into the perimeter of his arms. He slid one palm to her waist, drawing her close. The action must have caught him by surprise as much as it did her because she heard his quick intake of breath. Or was that hers?

The tenderness in his gaze distracted her from the scripted and shallow conversation she'd planned. His warmth, his gentleness, his humor, fed her heart with the most painfully beautiful hopes.

"I didn't peg you as the jealous sort."

She tried to create some space between them, but his endearing scent of peppermint seemed to hold some magic power over her good intentions. "I'm not jealous."

"Are you certain?" He searched her face. "Not even a little?"

A swell of heat between them took her breath. "What? No." She cleared her throat and tilted her chin to fight status. "In fact, I've been hoping you would see the many virtues of Miss Moore and eject me from your head."

His grin turned more lethal than cannon fire. "But I'm quite fond of having you in my head." And then he took his time examining her gown. "And you've greatly improved the view from my perspective."

"You're not very good at doing what's best for you, are you?"

"I don't think you know what's best for me as well as I do."

She straightened like a seasoned schoolmistress and drew in a breath. "Loose your grip on the hand, dear Doctor." Catherine squeezed his fingers. "You don't want to communicate an intensity you shouldn't."

He loosened his hold but not before returning the squeeze to her hand. "If you're not jealous, why are you suddenly in my arms instead of Miss Moore? And don't patronize me with the same excuse you gave to her."

Catherine shot Jessica a look. "Because your sister doesn't believe Miss Moore's dancing skills are as exalted as she claims, and she wanted me to....improve upon them."

"My sister?"

Adelaide reentered with Dr. Pike behind her. "Ah, I see you are making a nice start together." She offered a tight smile. "Good, very good. Keep practicing now." She turned to Jessica. "Let's see to you."

"So you're to improve my dancing?"

"Yes, if I can." She studied his shoulders in an attempt to avoid focusing on his lips. "You have good posture, if a little stiff at the moment, but I think that might have been from poor modeling."

"You mean it's not supposed to feel like you're dancing with a tree?"

Catherine turned her head to try to hide her laugh. "No. It's definitely not."

He tilted his head closer, a teasing glow in his eyes drawing up fire through her middle. Oh, the man would be the undoing of all her selfless intentions. "And you're to show me the proper way."

A delightful thrill sparked a responsive tremor over her skin. She'd definitely been a bad influence on him. He was actually learning how to flirt, a dangerous weapon in his arsenal against her self-control. Oh, this would never do!

She set a rule in her mind that after this dancing lesson, she would make every attempt to avoid him. If he wouldn't protect his heart, she certainly would.

David could barely believe the sweet hand of Providence. One minute he was struggling through an uncomfortable attempt at dull conversation and awkward dance-steps, and the next, Catherine appeared in his arms as an apparition from his daydreams. Gone was the usual nurse's uniform, replaced by a rich purple suit tailored to her curves. She embodied the picture of a lady. And, oh, how he'd missed her.

"I don't think I've properly thanked you for all you've done to help the hospital."

She avoided his face, staring instead at his shoulders. "Dancing is supposed to be an enjoyable activity where two people move as one." She ran her palm down his arm, ignoring his statement. "Relax this."

Her touch worked magic and warmth down his arm. "Catherine."

The hitch in her breath caught his attention. She was not immune to his presence any more than he was to hers.

"I have two additional supports coming your way."

"Two?"

"Feel the music with your partner. See?" Her hand on his shoulder guided him, their bodies moving more fluidly. "Madame's brother-in-law, Dr. Randolph Burr."

Air left David's lungs in one gush, and he stumbled. "Dr. Randolph Burr is her brother-in-law? The renowned osteopathic surgeon?"

"Steady there." Her gaze came up then, smile flashing. "Yes, I believe so, and there's the simple fact that I received a donation today that will purchase you a better x-ray machine than the second-hand one we currently have."

He stopped completely. "Truly?"

She tapped his shoulder to get him moving again, but her lips kept their pleased slant.

"Truly. The benefactress plans on continuing her support indefinitely."

The dance steps suddenly fell, obsolete. "All those letters? Your trip to London?"

"Yes." She raised a brow. "Don't look so surprised. I'm known to be quite convincing when I put my mind to it."

He pressed her back and drew her a little closer. "Of that, Miss Dougall, I have no doubt."

He held her gaze for a moment longer, but she looked away quickly.

"Thank you, Catherine."

She fought an obvious battle, keeping her gaze from his. Those enchanting twin sapphires focused on his chin or his shoulder or something just beyond his shoulder. There was a vulnerability and uncertainty, and the awareness increased the protectiveness inside of him.

He always observed dancers from the far side of the room, taking in the intimacy of the movements and the touch. But never had he expected it to feel like this, a sweet connection. A perfect fit.

"Fantastic." Her smile bloomed anew. "I believe you're starting to feel it."

Most certainly. "All I needed was the right partner."

Her gaze flashed up to his and a rush of rose colored her cheeks. "Um…yes, well… Now, you try to lead."

"You'll actually allow me to lead?"

She nailed him with a smirk. "Desperate times and all that…"

What did reputation matter when there was such a woman! She'd be the making of him.

"Go on, Doctor, or you'll have me taking over the lead again."

He looked down to check his movements in an attempt to keep in step. "Dancing in the arms of a friend is one thing, but dancing with in a roomful of high-class socialites is quite another."

"Stop right there." Her hand squeezed against his shoulder. "You have no reason to let them intimidate you. You are one of the best men I've ever known. I have every faith you can do this in front of the king, if need be. Now, feel the movements with your partner, together. A dance can only be beautiful when it's done together."

The confidence in her gaze brought his chin up. Her full smile rewarded him, urging him into motion with more certainly. He cast another glance at his feet for clarity.

"No, no," came her quick reprimand. "Look at me. Focus on me. We can do this together, David."

From the widening of her eyes, she never intended to say his name, but she had. And the sweetness of it, knowing her struggle, drew him closer. He forgot all about rhythm and movement, except a nearer step to her lovely face. Her passion, her spirit for living, proved as much an aphrodisiac as the lavender scent surrounding her.

"Catherine." Her name whispered out on a rattled breath, from his soul.

For a moment, her entire body softened against his, her lips drawing temptingly close. Those sapphire eyes glistened with nearness and interest and sweet adoration, but then she stopped. "I can't."

"I see the truth of it now." The thunderous tones of his great Aunt Maureen exploded into the room. "You dare refuse my generous offer for someone like her?"

The threat in her tone sent a blast of ice through David's veins. "I will not be ruined once again by this family. You have no idea what you've done, David Ross." Her glare switched to Catherine. "I will not allow you to win. Not ever."

Chapter Nineteen

Catherine awoke from a deep sleep, grasping for air. It had taken her hours to fall asleep after the dance lesson and Lady Cavanaugh's threat. Her heart thumped in a wild tangle of extremes from an unexpected fairytale to the sobering look on Lady Cavanaugh's face…and now she was awakened because she couldn't breathe?

As soon as she opened her eyes, her vision blurred with a veil of smoke. A gulp of soot-filled air sent her into a coughing spasm. She shoveled back a fistful of her eiderdown and blinked her teary eyes to gain her bearings. Smoke? Stumbling to the door, she snatched her robe from the bedside chair and cinched it tight around her waist. A sudden memory from the Zeppelin attack a few month ago faltered her steps. Oh no!

She jerked her bedroom door open and met the same foggy scene in the hallway, except the smoke grew thicker toward the East Wing. The children! She ran in bare feet down the hallway, banging her fist against the doors as she passed.

"Wake up! Fire!"

She nearly collided with someone coming from the next room. David! He grabbed her by the shoulders, taking inventory of her from head to foot. "Are you all right?"

"There's a fire in children's wing."

"I sent Cook to call the fire brigade." Fanny's voice broke into their conversation from down the hallway. "Michael's gone to wake Dr. Pike and Hudson to help move patients from the ballroom. If the second-floor balcony collapses…"

Fanny didn't have to finish her statement. The visual imaging hung in the air like the smoke invading their vision.

"Has anyone seen Kara?"

They all looked toward the children's wing, the place Kara slept every night. David took off, with Catherine and Fanny close behind. Smoke thickened the air.

David's hand caught hers, pulling her down. "Remain low, breathing will be easier."

The cloud dissipated a little as they entered the open passageway into the East Wing. The balcony overlooking the lower floor released some of the dense air and gave them a clearer view of the corridor ahead.

A specter emerged from the sooty cloud, a child at both sides and one in her arms. Kara!

They all ran forward to help relieve Kara of the little burden in her arms as she stumbled to keep her balance. The little boy, Jonesie, moaned and clutched his arm.

"I can't"—Kara coughed—"see... It's too..."

"Jonesie's arm is severely burned." David took Kara's shoulders. "Do you know where my medicine bag is? In my office?"

She nodded, wiping her watery eyes and smearing gray across her pale face.

"Can you manage taking him with you?"

"Aye, sir."

"I'll keep the other two with me," Fanny volunteered, pulling the little boy and girl to her sides and locking eyes with her sister. "They'll be safe."

"There is an ointment inside and some morphine." David made a motion over the boy's arm as if to apply the medicine. "Smooth the ointment over his arm, and give him a very small amount of morphine to ease the pain, if necessary."

"Where are the other children?" Catherine searched Kara's face for an answer she already knew. A dreadful knowledge waited, somewhere hidden within the fog. And the fire.

"Room collapsed," Kara added between coughs.

Stephen? Charlie? Nathanael? Sarah and Bree? Lost inside the flames somewhere?

"Catherine, Fanny, stay here to help with the children once I return with them," David commanded. He placed his handkerchief to his nose and darted into the smoke.

Catherine followed without hesitation.

"I said stay behind." David half shouted. "I need you to be safe."

"And I you," she replied, keeping in step with him across the balcony. "But since neither of us are good at obeying the other, I supposed four hands and four eyes are better than only two."

They entered the West Hall and visibility dropped to nothing. Catherine brought her robe up to cover her nose and turned to him. "Take the rooms to the left, I'll see to the ones on the right."

He snatched her hand before she took another step. "Catherine." His red-rimmed eyes held hers, showing his heart, his love, without hindrance. "Be careful."

She nodded, swallowing a wash of tears. "You too."

A strange sound, like wind, rushed from the stairwell at the end of the hallway, and a dry warmth heated her skin. Years ago, a fire had taken part of the house but halted when it contacted the stone-framed center of the house. How far would this fire burn?

Her eyes stung, so she closed them and felt her way down the hallway. The robe provided some protection from the ashy air, but not enough to keep her throat from the itch and constriction of smoke. She pushed open the first door she came to and met the same hazy scene.

Catherine drew in a breath to call for any girls in the room, but the smoke took her words and turned her attempt into a harsh croak. A whimper responded. She stepped further into the room and saw them through the haze, both girls huddled in the corner, hugging each other, their matching white gowns almost ghost-like.

She ran forward and knelt before them, embracing them. "Such clever girls to stay together."

They clung to her, coughing into her shoulders. She quickly took off her robe and dipped it into the basin of water on the washstand nearby, then placed the damp robe over the girls' heads. Their small statures probably helped keep them coherent, praise God.

They exited the room and walked one door down to the infant room. She had to find Nathanael. Had David located

Stephen and the other boys yet? Catherine coughed and bent low, holding the girls before her, placing them against the wall beside the infant room door.

"Wait for me right here." Her thick voice graveled out the words. "I'm going to find the baby."

Their heads nodded beneath the robe.

The door creaked open to an aching silence. No cries or whimpers, but the room didn't show as much smoke as the others. Catherine rushed to the crib, and there lay little Nathanael, still and unmoving, his arms splayed free from the constraints of his bunting. With trembling hand, she placed the back of her hand close to his nose.

Nothing.

A cry caught in her throat. She lowered her palm, waiting, praying...and then she felt it. The slight puff of air. She squeezed her eyes closed in a quick prayer of thanksgiving, tears soothing the burn in her eyes, and then swept the little bundle into her arms.

The girls waited outside, sniffling with little sobs. The thickening smoke in the hallway awakened the baby, his boisterous cry bringing a mixture of concern and gratitude. Alive. She hugged him close and leaned down to the girls.

"Link hands, darlings." Their small finger grabbed for each other. "Very good. Now, Sarah, take my hand, and do not let go."

She could hardly catch her breath as she guided her little entourage down the hall toward the open balcony. Another explosion of coughing seared her chest and sent her head into a spin. She stumbled forward into a pair of strong arms. David appeared through the smoke, a handkerchief tied across his face like a bandit and three-year-old Stephen in his other arm.

"Can you walk?"

She pushed Nathanael into his free arm. "Take him. I'm dizzy."

"Stephen!" Michael ran into the smoke, his chest pumping with frantic breaths. "Oh, praise God, you found him."

"Daddy." The boy, golden hair smeared with gray soot, reached for his father, and Michael pulled him close.

196

Catherine tried to breathe, but air strained down her soot cloaked throat. "David?" Her voice, breathless and harsh, barely made a noise as the world began to tilt into darkness.

Catherine's pale face proved she needed air, and soon. Why wasn't her face covered? Where was her robe? He looked down at the girls and sighed in frustration. Of course, she'd protect them first. He held onto her arm, her thin white nightgown smeared with dampness and soot, her hair in a tangle of black around her face.

She raised glassy eyes to him and whispered his name.

"Michael, take the children," David commanded, barely handing off Nathanael in time to catch Catherine in his arms.

Her head fell against his shoulder. He reached around her and jerked the handkerchief from his face, placing it haphazardly over hers. *Dear God, please, don't let me lose her.*

He followed Michael down the hallway, helping to usher the children along, and placed a kiss on Catherine's head with a silent prayer. A sound outside alerted him to the arrival of the fire brigade.

David called after Michael. "The patients?"

"They've been moved out to the front garden." Michael called back. "Three are unaccounted for."

A knot of relief and grief tensed David's spine. Only three? The Zep attack had decimated the entire building and taken almost twenty lives.

Michael led them down the stairway to the lower level then outside, but he shot David a look over his shoulder. "Radcliffe, David. Some of the boys think it was him."

David groaned his response and stared back down at Catherine. The front garden was littered with patients either propped up against the stone fencing or lying flat on the grass. Jessica and some of the other nurses handed out blankets against the chill in the air.

"David!" Jessica looked up, smiling through her gray-hued face.

He nodded to her. "Do you have another blanket?"

She was at his side in a moment, covering Catherine who lay still in his arms. "What happened?"

"Too much smoke." David pushed Catherine's hair back from her face. It slid through his fingers like cool blades of grass. Soft. Refreshing after the inferno they'd left only minutes before.

"I'll bring you some water."

David smoothed off some of the soot from her face and studied her breathing. Shallow but consistent.

Her eyes flickered open, the sweetest smile forming on her face. At that moment, in the middle of such chaos, he knew he wanted to wake up to her smile every morning. "Hello, Kat."

Her brow pinched a little. "How did I obtain such special treatment?"

His thumb trailed to her chin, his smile expanding with the love and gratitude in his chest. "Special treatment always comes to those who save children's lives."

"The baby!" Her sapphire eyes shot wide, and she tried to sit up but dropped back against him.

"Shh." His fingertip caressed her lips. "The baby is fine. You? Not so much. Stay still until the dizziness is gone."

She sighed back against him, the soft smile returning, and her eyelids fluttered closed. "Well, I suppose I have the best seat for recuperating."

He found himself captivated by the vision she made, her dark hair loose and wild across his arms, long dark lashes swooped low over her soft, pale cheeks, and a hint of the smile on her rosy lips. Beauty, bravery, and kindness were all wrapped up in the woman who had stolen his heart.

"It's quite the hardship, holding you in my arms."

"Is it?" He liked this taste of her compliance, her giving in to his care without a fight, though the flirty tilt to her lips returned. "I'm tempted to think you don't like me, Dr. Ross."

"Like you?" His coarse whisper surprised him. His pulse pounded a drumroll in his ears, leading him to this moment, to her.

Her eyes opened, curious.

"Oh, Catherine, I like you very much."

Morning sunlight slipped around the curtains into the room. Catherine was in her own room, which came as a surprise because she was certain Roth Hall had burned to the ground. A trace of smoke scented the air, but the room shone clear in the faded light. A fire burned in the fireplace, creating long shadows across the floor.

A movement to her left turned her head. Ashleigh sat in a nearby chair, head lowered over a book.

Catherine smiled. "Look what happens when you leave the country for so long."

Her sister looked up from her book, her walnut eyes creasing with her smile. "You truly outdid yourself with the welcome party. I think fewer candles next time."

Catherine groaned as she sat straighter in bed. "I've always been a strong proponent of electric lights." She settled back against the pillows and sighed. "When did you arrive?"

"Last evening."

"Perfect timing. We're going to need your innovative ideas to sort out what to do for space."

Ashleigh moved over to sit on the bed, her dark hair pinned back and an extra glow on her face. Yes, she was doing well. Catherine grimaced. And most certainly a much better figure to gaze upon than herself at the moment. She reached up to touch her hair and found it splayed like a mermaid's over the pillows.

"As I understand it from a few reliable sources, you've been quite innovative in my absence." Her brow tilted ever so slightly. "Catherine Everill."

A sweet hum of pleasure pearled in her stomach. "I'm rather in awe of it."

"And the seamstresses and opening the back wing?" Ashleigh laughed. "David told me of the new surgeon and funds? You're remarkable."

"Remarkable?" Catherine shook her head, shame her constant bedfellow. "I'm nowhere close to making amends for all I've done."

"Amends? You've already been forgiven."

"But now I need to show my gratitude for that forgiveness, for God's love…for yours. I don't want to lose you again." She grabbed Ashleigh's hand. "I don't want to go back to the strained relationship we had before. I can't imagine not holding this sweet peace in my heart any longer."

Ashleigh tilted her head, her eyes pooling with sweet compassion. "Are you trying to earn love?"

"No." She squeezed Ashleigh's hand. "I'm trying to keep it."

"Oh, Catherine," Ashleigh rubbed her fingers over Catherine's. "The sacrifice Christ made didn't only provide for your salvation once, it secures it for always. You don't have to earn His love. Or mine."

"But I've failed, even since he saved me. Rebelled." She fisted the eiderdown, a renewed sense of anger burning in her stomach. "If you'd seen my thoughts about Lady Cavanaugh and Dr. Carrier—"

"Don't you think we all still fail?"

"Not you, and certainly not David."

"Not me?" Ashleigh laughed. "Of course me. I have feet of clay, just like any human. I have my insecurities, need people to love me too. David struggles with pride over his work. But the amazing thing about our Savior is that he chooses broken people to accomplish his will. Not perfect people. He uses us as we are, where we are."

Catherine scoffed. "Even me?"

"Even you. God created you the way you are, with your quick mind and your need for justice, because he knew it would take someone like you to step out of our social bonds into the world of the wounded. No one else could have bridged the gap of seamstresses and designers but you." Her grin quirked. "And from what I've heard, no one else could have won a certain doctor's heart."

"Oh no, no." She pulled her hand free of Ashleigh's. "That's a mistake. Utterly. He doesn't know what he's doing."

"Catherine Dougall." Ashleigh's sharp reply brought Catherine's arguments to a halt. "David Ross is not a man who makes rash choices. If he has given you any indication that he cares for you, then he means it, and so does God." She stood, her gaze holding Catherine's in reprimand. "His love isn't based on what you've done, who you are, or even how much you love him in return. He loves. No strings.

And…" Her smile slanted. "He finds pleasure in surprising us with His love. As for now, I need you to rest so you'll be ready."

"Ready?"

Ashleigh's smile brightened. "Oh yes, ready for a few more miracles."

"Miracles?" Catherine crossed her arms, waiting for the proof.

Ashleigh's smile never wavered. "Beauty can come from the remnants of the most painful circumstances. Remember that, Catherine."

Two days! For two days David nearly drowned under the memories of holding Catherine in his arms after the fire, her hair loose and beautiful, her slip of a gown clinging to her body in a way which produced all sorts of thoughts in David's head. He could have lost her, and it nearly broke him into a panic. Three days ago, he'd danced with her in his arms and teased the idea of kissing her in front of the entire room. Now, he couldn't seem to find her anywhere.

Of course, everyone had been busy, trying to make the remains of Roth Hall work as a hospital. Staff doubled up on rooms. Mrs. Dougall opened up the servants' hall for additional space, and, much to Mrs. Dougall's chagrin, lines of cots filled the Front Hall, crowded with wounded. He'd never been so grateful for Dr. Pike's influence. The man coddled Mrs. Dougall to such an extent, she gave in to the need without much of a fight.

But this arrangement couldn't last for long. It was neither safe nor helpful for the patients. Could the funds of which Catherine spoke provide them enough to begin building a new hospital? He groaned. And how long might that take?

He stepped out into the hallway and caught sight of her. She saw him too, because she quickly slipped down the nearest corridor.

Not this time.

He took off at a run, white jacket flapping behind him as he navigated a few cots before dipping into the same corridor. Her shadow turned the corner up ahead, and he followed. The servants' stairs. She was heading for the servants' stairs.

He ducked in through a small study that had been converted into medical storage, jumped a stack of boxes, and ran out the secondary door, cutting her off at the stairs.

"You can keep trying to hide, but spaces since the fire have been considerably reduced."

"I'm not hiding." She refused to meet his gaze, proof positive of his claim. "I'm off to speak to cook about the soldiers' soup for today."

"Of course you are." And though she tried to walk around him, he blocked her path.

She side-stepped him, into the medical supplies room, but the tower of boxes hemmed her in on one side and he blocked the doorway on the other. Perfect. Maybe a little privacy would help with this next part of their conversation.

"We really don't have time for this." Catherine turned and faced him, hands on her hips.

She probably didn't realize how appealing she looked when those hands went to her hips, and he'd never noticed how very appealing it could be on the right woman. In fact, he'd always tried to run from conflict, until now. The proper motivation truly worked miracles.

"We'll make the time."

Her eyes widened, but she lifted her chin, readied for battle. "We both have work to do, and you have a hospital to save, and renovations from the fire, and —"

"The hospital and all its troubles will still be there, but for now..." He stopped her from sidestepping him with a gentle touch to her shoulder. "I need some clarity, Nurse Dougall. Clarity that only you can provide."

Her gaze searched for another means of escape. She shrugged her shoulder, slipping free from his touch with a graceful move. "Clarity isn't my forte, really. That might be a better question for Ashleigh." Her face brightened. "Yes, Ashleigh. Did you know she had arrived?"

"I don't need clarity about Ashleigh or the hospital, or anything else except your feelings for me."

She narrowed her eyes and took another step back, turning slightly away from the boxes toward the gray stone wall, most likely working on another escape. "You're being ridiculous. This whole thing." She waved her hand between them. "You're not thinking clearly."

He closed the gap between them. "I'm cognizant of my behavior at present. And certain." His voice dropped to a deep rasp. "Quite certain."

She focused on something over his shoulder. "I think I heard someone call your name."

His grin inched crooked. The hall was as silent as a churchyard, and she was running out of excuses.

"Catherine."

The fight in her stance died at his whispered word, and it gave him an awareness of the power he wielded in his newfound and exciting love for her. Sweet power. Something he'd use to convince her of how beautiful she'd become, inside and out. She was no longer what convicting voices shouted to her or past shadows whispered. No.

She was his.

"Sometimes, the wisest choices appear ridiculous at first, but not when seen with the proper vision."

She took a step back. He took a step forward. She pinched her lips in response. "And sometimes, emotions cloud a person's vision so they can't tell what is wise." She sighed and looked up at him, pleading. "I've tried so hard not to sway your heart, but I must have done so without knowing."

He gathered her fighting hands into his, certainty growing like the fire in his chest. "That's exactly it. You never attempted seduction or flirting, and even apart from what I thought I wanted in my future, I've found you to be much more than I ever imagined my heart could feel. You've become like...like breathing to me."

She met his gaze again, eyes searching his with so many questions. So much doubt. "What if this is the worst decision you ever make?"

He took another step forward. She responded with another step back. Her heel hit the wall behind her, and her eyes widened again. Beautifully trapped.

"I don't make decisions lightly."

"Passions can lead us down unexpected paths," came her quick response, a declaration carved from regret.

He stepped another pace forward, and her lavender scent invited him closer. In all her previous pursuits, he never imagined she'd run. In her past, she'd been the instigator.

Until now.

Until him.

He couldn't help but feel a little pride. Drunk with the pure pleasure of knowing exactly what he wanted and how to show her his love. "Not this time. This time they've led us directly to our hearts' desires."

"How can you be sure?" Her fight resorted to a whimper.

He cupped her cheek. "Trust me, Catherine. Trust me for the both of us." His grin tipped. "For the three of us."

His whisper or his touch, he wasn't sure which one, broke whatever barrier she placed between them. Uncustomary tears welled up in the middle of sapphire hues. "Don't you understand, if I believe that you could care about me, that you want to be with me, and this little one…truly…?"

He placed his other palm against her cheek, reveling at the softness, the powerful nearness. "Yes?"

Her breath shivered out. "What I feel for you is…"

His palm slipped behind her neck, cupping the back of her head, his mouth tingling with anticipation. "Incredible. Terrifying? Remarkable?"

A small gasp came from those full, inviting lips, drawing him in with sweet promise. Another desperate tinge of uncertainty streamed into her eyes.

"I'm not stopping this time, Catherine. No matter what excuse you make. I *am* going to kiss you."

Without one more second for her to protest, he breached the gap between them. Her mouth, soft and tinted with the salt of tears, welcomed him, as if her body accepted much more than her mind. A thrill shot through him with the power in the connection.

He pulled back, her cool lips clinging to his, unwilling to release. Her response shocked his longing into a fury, destroying his control. He drew her deeper into his embrace and after a hitch of reserve, her arms slipped up around his neck. Nothing prepared him for the savage hunger in one taste, quaking his well-honed reserve. He'd expected many things, but not this.

Her hold tightened and they both stumbled back against the wall, sweet, salty and wild warmth mingling with each meeting of their lips. Her hands slid into his hair, her mouth as thirsty as his. The word 'passion' took on a whole new meaning and clarified one thing: there was no going back.

Chapter Twenty

His touch rendered her immobile. The way he cupped her face, the familiar and endearing tilt of his smile, and the tenderness in his gaze just before the brush of his lips wiped away all comparisons. She would never forget the look he gave her. One filled with more than desire or lust, but awash with such raw love. She felt like the most beautiful woman in the world.

He moved with excruciating slowness, careful deliberation, the surgeon's precision making an exact fit of his lips to her mouth. And oh, what a fit. He poured all of his intensity into the first careful touch, the reigned-in passion sending a dizzying pleasure from his lips downward in trails of delicious rightness. The warmth and gentleness of his caress coaxed her need to respond, so when he began to pull back, her lips lingered, almost pleading to taste a little more.

Her request seemed to release in him the same explosive need stirring inside of her. A tantalizing dream, dangled in front of them for so long, deserved a much lengthier celebration. She pulled him to her and they stumbled back against the cold, stone wall, his hand cupping the back of her head. Peppermint and a warm glow surrounded her, intoxicating and glorious.

His kiss. The man she'd come to not only love, but admire. The friend who teased her and kept her couched within the comfort of his care. The man who caused her heart to ache with such a powerful love, she thought she might explode. A fairytale? Fresh tears blended with the heat on her face. How could she ever deserve such sweet affection?

"Heaven help me, you taste like Christmas!" She breathed between them, keeping her mouth close enough to feel the warmth of his breath. To encourage another sampling.

His palm smoothed against her cheek. "Do you usually cry over Christmas?" His lips tasted the other cheek, warming different places on her face.

"The best tears." She raised trembling fingers to his face, allowing the tears to flow unhindered. "No one has ever touched my soul with a kiss."

"I would have done so much earlier, if you hadn't been so keen to keep me away."

She rested her forehead against his. "Clearly, I was the only one in her right mind."

He took her lips again, closing off her argument until she was breathless and needed the wall for support.

His palms slid down each side of her neck as he buried a kiss into her hair. "Now I can see why a man would be driven mad by you."

She groaned and pushed at his chest to get away, but he brought her fighting hands to his lips and cast her a smile. "I'm quite fond of madness at the moment."

"At the moment?" She shivered beneath his touch as his thumb moved across her cheek to stop beneath her bottom lip. "And after the moment?"

"I'll accept madness as a regular part of my life." His gaze held hers, his smile dashing her doubts. "Every day."

She pinched her lips together and stared back at him, steady and unswerving. "You can't want that, David."

His smile spread as she spoke his name, flickering his dimple. Heat pooled through her at the awareness of his pleasure.

He drew close, lips temptingly close. "Say my name again, Kat."

She placed her palm against his cheek, accepting this fairytale and all of its promises. "David."

He captured her fingers and brought them to his lips, breathing kisses over her knuckles. "I shall never tire of the way you whisper it. Something came to life in my heart when we prayed that first time together. My heart knew, much like God must have known all along, that we belonged together."

"God certainly has an unpredictable sense of humor. And at your expense."

"Stop." He tasted her lips again, silencing her argument. If he kept using that particular technique to end arguments, she'd plan to argue more often.

"Can't you see, you're not the person you used to be…and yet you are? The best parts of who you are, the passion, the diligence, the ability to take charge and see the right done – those have all remained and become more mesmerizing when molded by grace."

"You really see those things in me?"

"Of course I do, and so much more. You're the perfect complement to my awkward, bookish, driven personality." His gaze roamed her face, as if…as if he treasured all he saw. "My dear Catherine, could you reach beyond your shame and see what I see? What God sees?"

"What do you see?" Her voice squeezed out the question.

"Beauty." His fingers reached into the folds of her hair, sending a fresh wave of tingles down her neck. "Layers and layers of beauty."

She sighed out her resignation and wrapped her arms around him, embracing his confidence. "You shouldn't want a future with me. And I should love you enough to push you away."

"No." His gaze met hers, unswerving. "You should trust me enough to believe I've considered all of your arguments and don't care a whit for them."

He sealed his words with another kiss…or two.

Catherine remained fairly useless for at least two hours after her rendezvous with David in the medical supplies room. Even the massive disaster of trying to clean up after the fire or the impossibility of locating her sister among the many workers failed to dampen her daydream.

"I understand you are quite fond of Christmas."

She looked up from her suture and grappled with her smile. "It's my favorite holiday."

He nodded, emerald eyes twinkling with leprechaun mischief. "And why is that?"

She stood from her position and turned to face him. "I do enjoy celebrating the Savior's birth."

"Of course."

She tipped a brow. "In addition, I'm fairly intoxicated by the scent of peppermint."

His gaze darkened, and he took a step forward, but then seemed to remember he was in the middle of a room filled with patients and stopped. His smile spread to showcase his dimple. "Ridiculously intoxicated?"

"Most certainly."

"Catherine."

Catherine reluctantly turned from her handsome knight to her sister. "Yes?"

"Do you have a few moments so we could talk?"

"Of course." Catherine followed Ashleigh, but not before casting a glance back to David who did nothing to hide his interest in watching her walk away.

She must have worn the most idiotic smile in all of Ednesbury.

"How is Sam?"

Ashleigh's smile turned mischievous. "See for yourself." She gestured toward the West Wing where Sam and Michael constructed a door to close off the side until repairs could be made. Sam looked up as if he knew they were speaking of him, and the grin he sent to Ashleigh nearly melted Catherine on the spot. So sweet. Such a dear friendship and romance between them.

"He's here?"

Ashleigh shrugged and held out her hand. "It wouldn't do to leave one's husband behind."

"You're married?" Catherine grabbed Ashleigh's hand and examined the beautiful ruby on her finger. "When?"

Ashleigh resumed her walk to the stairway. "About two weeks before Grandmama's death. I knew it was something she'd love to witness, so we wheeled her out to the garden and had the ceremony there." Ashleigh led the way back to her bedroom, probably the only space for privacy in this overcrowded house. "I'm sorry we didn't wait until you could attend."

"No, please. I understand."

Ashleigh smiled and opened her door so Catherine could enter first. "I'm glad you do, and…and…" She sighed the sweet sigh of contentment. "I love being his wife."

With the residual warmth of David's kiss still humming over her skin, she could certainly imagine the benefits of belonging to the man you loved.

They took their seats in two high back chairs facing the tall windows and their late afternoon light. Some papers waited on the table between them.

"So, your wedding was one of the miracles you spoke of yesterday?"

"One." Ashleigh took the papers from the table. "But I have more. Miracles that are going to change everything."

"What do you mean?"

"Grandmama had two wills drawn up years ago." Ashleigh pointed to each stack of papers as she spoke. "But had rewritten them within the last three months. One will related to her assets in America and another for her properties in England. Sam and I met with Mr. Graves, her English solicitor, before coming to Ednesbury."

"What of the American one? Who will take care of her home in Millington?"

"Grandmama thought of everything." Ashley offered a sad smile. "Knowing his dislike for England, she left the Millington House to Scott."

"Of course she did." Catherine laughed, imagining their brother's response to the gift.

"But Sam's father is to be the guardian of the inheritance, as well as of Scott, until our little brother comes of age."

"Abram Miller is a king among men."

A pleased blush colored Ashleigh's cheeks. "Yes, he is. One of the dearest. I know Scott is in good hands."

"And Roth? She must have left it to you."

Ashleigh nodded. "Yes, as well as a small yearly allowance."

Catherine's brow tilted. "Small?"

She shrugged. "Large enough to cover costs. Small enough to keep me from overspending."

"I wish I could have seen her once more." Her vision blurred. "If only long enough to apologize in person. I never took the time to appreciate her, to show her how much I cared."

Ashleigh grabbed Catherine's hand. "She talked of you, all the way to the end." Her eyes glistened with unshed tears. "She was proud of you, Catherine. Proud of the woman God was making you. Proud of how you desired to place as much passion into serving others as you had in serving yourself."

Catherine's tears escaped their hold. "I feel as though I left her little for which to be proud."

Ashley's eyes brightened with her smile. "Oh, I don't know about that. Grandmama always had a way of seeing greater things in people than they saw in themselves. She told me once, near the end, when we were talking about you, that you reminded her the most of her young self than anyone else in the family."

"Me?" Catherine shook her head. "She must've been confusing me with you."

"She was lucid until the day she died. She knew of whom she spoke." Her sister's smile grew impish again. "And she knew exactly what *you* needed."

"What do you mean?"

"I love being the one to share Grandmama's gift to you. It's almost as if I can feel her smiling down on us." Ashleigh's face almost glowed. "After all we've been through." She laughed. "Catherine, Grandmama knew you loved town. She knew you loved fashion and the social world."

Ashleigh placed one of the papers in Catherine's hands along with a set of large iron keys. "She left you Beacon House."

"Beacon House?" A faded memory of the house flickered through Catherine's mind, one of brick walls and manicured gardens. "The...the small estate near town?"

"It's only five miles from town, unlike Roth which is fifteen. It will put you nearer the train station and the dress shop."

Catherine tried to take in the information. A house? She owned a house? "How...how will I keep it?"

"Grandmama thought of that too." Ashleigh placed another paper in her hands. "You'll receive this monthly allowance, along with wages for five servants."

Catherine blinked down at the number in disbelief. It was more money than she'd imagined having in an entire year, let alone each month. "How could she afford this? She barely had enough money to maintain Roth Hall and her home in Millington."

"That's the miraculous part." Ashleigh tapped another paper in front of them. "It appears that all of these additional monies were secured in an account tied to Uncle William, but at his death, the funds went to Grandmama, who created a protected account when she realized mother and father were incapable of managing money well. It was a safeguard for her grandchildren and the future of the estates, only to be released at her death. The money has continued to accrue up through last year, when it suddenly stopped and no one gave any reason as to why."

"Not the solicitors?"

Ashleigh shook her head. "No one. They were very tight-lipped about the entire affair, so I supposed it had something to do with Uncle William."

Catherine stared at Ashleigh, then back at the papers, trying to make sense of it all. "But Uncle William was a missionary. How did he possibly obtain money like this?"

"I don't know. All Grandmama told me was that a private benefactor had provided for William, should he ever choose to return from the mission field to a normal life, to keep him well situated for as long as he lived."

Who could spare such money? A church patron, or someone with a great deal of devotion to William's missionary work?

"How could she—or God—give me these things? I...I don't deserve them."

"As I told you before, sister dear." Ashleigh smiled through her tears. "Love. Love works miracles and overwhelms as nothing else can." She squeezed Catherine's hand. "God knows that now you'll use this for His purposes, not your own advantage. Just imagine what you could do with these resources that you wouldn't have done before.

The opportunities to change lives, to make a difference." She laughed. "With your energy, you could transform the entire town if you wanted."

"The town?" Catherine stilled, her gaze locking with her sister's. "Yes. Imagine." She pushed up from the chair and started a slow progression of pacing about the room. "All the possibilities."

"Catherine?"

Catherine kept walking, her mind a whirl of possibilities. Almost giddy. "Beacon House must be sizeable, yes?"

"I...I think Grandmama mentioned it had sixteen rooms."

"Sixteen?" Catherine looked up to the ceiling, both hands in the air. "Sixteen rooms. And probably a large hall, perhaps a ballroom," she muttered to herself. "But I'd need to see it to be sure."

"What are you thinking?"

Catherine pivoted on her heels and let a victorious smile creep into place. "Opportunities, my dear sister. I have one request. Would you keep my part of this inheritance a secret for now?"

"Why?"

"Lady Cavanaugh already thinks she has the better hand, so if she feels further threatened, I'm afraid she'll grow increasingly more desperate to hurt this hospital or the orphanage, let alone our family. Besides, I think anonymity will be a valuable ally for us when dealing with the Cavanaughs."

Ashleigh crossed her arms and raised a brow. "What are you planning?"

"A marvelous surprise." She rubbed her palms together. "A surprise I'm certain will ruffle Maureen Cavanaugh's crow feathers."

Catherine hardly recognized Marianne. Clothes truly transformed. Marianne stood behind the shop counter, assisting a customer, her golden locks pinned back in a stylish array and showing off her long neckline which was enhanced by the pale pink walking suit she wore.

A suit Catherine had designed.

Catherine bit her bottom lip in an attempt to quell the excited squeal waiting to erupt from her soul. *Her* design. In fact, as Catherine glanced around the shop, she noticed Madame had even created a sign sectioning off one part of the room to Everill Designs.

As Marianne looked up and noticed Catherine, her smile bloomed, and Catherine was struck by how beautiful she'd grown under the tutelage of Madame in such a short time.

"Miss Dougall." Marianne almost ran around the counter to take Catherine in her arms. "I am so delighted to see you. When Annie told me I'd missed your last visit, I was terribly disappointed. Do you see? Do you see how well your des—" She stopped and covered her mouth, glancing about the empty shop. She proceeded on a whisper. "Your designs are selling so well. We had an order for four just this morning from London."

"That's wonderful news, Marianne." Catherine matched the girl's whisper. "But why are you whispering?"

Her bright blue eyes grew wide with sincerity. "Madame says we must be very careful to keep your name separate from Catherine Everill to protect your sales from the ill-effects of Lady Cavanaugh. Madame's exact words were "For now, Catherine Everill must remain a mystery. An anonymous benefactress to the world of fashion.""

"An anonymous benefactress of fashion, is it?" Catherine laughed. "If nothing else, Madame provides drama."

Marianne's golden brows wiggled. "Heaps of drama. It does keep life fairly exciting."

"Without a doubt." Catherine stepped over to the mannequin who wore Catherine's sleeveless ensemble of midnight, layered and falling to the toe. Its princess waist, new to many of the most recent designs, was completed in silver, the perfect complement to the midnight color. They'd chosen the best material, silk duvetyn, shimmering with colors of starlight. "It's even more beautiful in reality. The colors, the style, are exactly as I imagined."

"It has drawn many curious shoppers off the street, as well as the one beside it." Marianne nodded to the walking

214

suit similar to hers, except in fawn. Madame had draped a scarf of dark tones over the shoulder, bringing out the complimentary colors. "You give such excellent instructions for material and options. For example, one can add a tunic to the gown here." She touched another of Catherine's designs, an evening gown in periwinkle. "And it changes the entire look of the gown."

The inexplicable pleasure of a dream come true lodged a reply in Catherine's throat. How she longed to tell David, share her success, but something kept her waiting. If this secret placed him at enmity with his aunt, it might be a better choice he remain ignorant.

The sudden jarring of the door nearly knocked the entry bell from its roost. Madame marched in, her French exploding at an impossible speed. Something about ridiculous women and buttons for brains?

"Madame? Are you well?"

"Well? Well?" Her volume grew with each repetition. "Non, I am furious. The idiot Inn refuses to hold the ball, even after we had secured it."

"What?"

Her words trailed off in another fit of French, then she turned to both of them, her scowl almost tangible. "I received notice that the Inn cancelled our reservations for the ball, so I made my way to them to speak my mind about such horrible behavior. They told me they would not support a man of low repute, even if he was a good doctor."

"A man of low repute? How did they—"

"The Lady." She said the words like a curse. "She has wounded yet another plan, another good deed. Passing around the news of your situation."

She waved toward Catherine's stomach.

"But that shouldn't impact the Inn's decision."

"It should if she had Mr. Dandy created the rumor that Dr. Ross is the father."

Catherine braced herself against the counter. "What?"

"He resurrected Alexander Ross' disgrace to the family by marrying beneath his station and tainting the family with bad blood, thus proving his son to be tainted as well and participating in less than desirable behavior with"—she gestured to Catherine—"yourself."

Catherine's face grew so hot, tears welled in her eyes. "Crow Cavanaugh and her disciple Dandy dragged David's father into this?" Catherine slammed her fist against counter. "What a deplorable lie!"

"Annie says Lady Cavanaugh could make any God-fearing woman lose her Christianity," Marianne added, her sweet voice barely making a dent in Catherine's fury.

"What can we do to such power? How can we possibly fight this?" A sudden fear tickled through her middle, her worst fears ignited. What would David think? Her reputation had brought ruin to him? Pain to his dear father? No. She offered a silent plea. *Please, no.*

"The bazaar can go on, but there is no knowing who will come. The timid will stay away." Madame flipped her wrist in the air in her customary way. "If only more people owned their own shops, then her influence could not be as strong."

"And the only way to do that is buy the shops from her." Catherine sighed. "Is there any way to salvage the ball? It would have drawn the most people. Perhaps it would set this ruthless rumor to rest if people saw David as he is, recognizing his kindness and generosity?"

"Unless we have another benefactor or benefactress who could produce a sizeable space for a ball *and* not be intimidated by the Cavanaughs, I do not know what we shall do."

Catherine placed her head in her hands, praying for help and a heavy hand to quench her desire to go flail Lady Cavanaugh with a strong chord of cheviot fabric. Leaving the sheep smell on Lady Cavanaugh's clothes would be an additional benefit.

"Do you know of any benevolent rich in the area? Any homes with ballro—" Catherine paused, and looked up. Marianne's words filtered through her haze of red. *Anonymous benefactress?* She turned, breath pulsing as quickly as her heartbeat. "Madame, I…I believe I have a place we can use." She began a round of pacing in front of the shop counter. "I've not been in it for years and have no idea if we can prepare it in time."

"A place? Large enough for a ball?" Madame blinked her long black lashes. "Roth Hall will not do in its present state, non non."

"Not Roth." Catherine's smile stretched to ridiculous proportions as the idea formed. "I have a different home in mind. One I've only just obtained for my inheritance."

Madame's smile slid into place. "Beacon House? Oui?"

"Oui."

Madame trailed off in a long line of French exultation and then turned to them. "It is perfect. Georgian elegance, magnificent décor, if the décor is still there from the days we let the house from your dear Grandmama."

"And do you recall if it had a ballroom with enough space?"

"Mais oui, a divine ballroom. Smaller than the Inn, but well situated for our purposes." Madame frowned. "Especially if The Lady scares away our patrons."

"We can't let her intimidate us. We have to still try."

"And we can invite anyone. Whether they are from our town or another." Madame's dark red grin perched. She scrutinized Catherine a moment. "You do not begrudge your sister the big house with all of its property?"

"What would I care for that big house when I can be close to town?" She sighed and took a few steps toward the door. "Besides, Catherine Everill can cause much more trouble in town than she can so far away."

Madame Rousell's chuckle grew ruthless. "Oh, *ma chère*, we are kindred spirits."

Catherine opened the door and turned to Marianne and Madame with a raised brow. "And after the ball, I do believe it would make an absolutely perfect war hospital."

Chapter Twenty-One

David had spent the last few hours attempting to not only be an administrator of a damaged hospital, but a carpenter as well. Progress happened, but with aching slowness. Between himself, Michael, Sam, and even Christopher Hudson, as well as a few able-bodied soldiers, they'd managed to secure the beams in one of the smaller rooms and rehang the back door.

He welcomed the physical occupation because it gave his mind freedom to sift through the current needs and the added space constraints. Lady Hollingsworth's additional funds would help them scrape through to the next month, but the loss of materials, cots and linens required them to purchase more on credit. At least the magnanimous benefactress promised another installment the next month, though that amount would go toward paying the credit debt and restocking supplies.

But Catherine had faith in this fundraising bazaar and ball. And as his mind turned toward Catherine, he made another round about the house in hopes of spotting her as soon as she entered from town. Their playful conversation from earlier teased his thoughts in a direction which required privacy.

He caught her entering the front door. Outfitted in a green walking suit, the skirt one of the newer styles that came at least five inches off the floor, she didn't notice him as half of her face hid stylishly behind a large, ivory hat. Beautiful and enticing.

"You're not trying to avoid me, are you?"

She turned at his voice, quickly readjusting her surprise. "It would be extremely sensible of me, for both of our sakes. You're quite dangerous, and I'm dangerous for you."

He stepped closer, taking her arm and drawing her into the shadow of the alcove. Her dangerous for him? Oh no!

She'd brought him to life in ways he'd never known. "I'm dangerous, am I?"

Her ebony brow rose with a tilt of her lips. "Clearly, you enjoy trapping me."

"Trapping you? No. Kissing you?" Emotions reduced his voice to a harsh whisper. He tipped her hat back from her face. "Definitely."

He took his time, familiarizing himself with the feel of her lips on his, the fit of her in his arms, and the pleasure in the taste of her. How could anyone tire of such intoxicating delicacies?

She drew back first, resting her forehead against his chin with a sigh. "Quite dangerous, David Ross."

He fingered a lock of her hair, loose from an intricate design crowning her dark head. "Where have you been? Off flittering your time away in Madame's dress shop again?"

Her lovely lips slanted. "Did you just say 'flittering'?"

"I did, in fact." He leaned to kiss her smile. "Causing trouble in town, were you?"

The teasing glint left her expression. She placed her hand against his chest, causing distance he didn't want. "Unintentional trouble, I'm afraid."

"What is it? What's wrong?"

"I tried to warn you of the consequences of a relationship with me." Catherine shook her head, the fear in her eyes tightening his middle. "And now…now the worst has happened."

"Catherine, it can't be as bad as you've imagined."

"Your aunt has done her worst. She's spread lies throughout the entire town." Catherine took his hand, her gaze pleading. "She said you've followed in your father's disgraceful footsteps by…by—"

A fiery heat flamed through him. "Tell me."

"Fathering my unborn child."

"What?" He ran his hand through his hair, staring at her as if she'd gone mad. "That's preposterous. How can anyone believe it?"

"They'll believe what she tells them too, unless they know you, of course. No one would ever believe such bosh if they knew you."

"How did this happen?"

"Somehow, she learned of my mother's declaration of my pregnancy, which wouldn't be difficult with the amount of people we have in this house." Catherine's brow pinched. "Then she saw us dancing... I can only assume she—"

"Took her revenge." He ground the words out and slammed his fist against the stone wall. When he'd counted the cost of a relationship with Catherine, he'd expected consequences against his own reputation, but to slander his father? To stir up the hatred of the townspeople he'd known his whole life? "This...this is deplorable."

"I will find a way to make things right." Catherine stepped back. "There has to be a way."

"I don't see how you can change what's happened. Aunt Maureen has the power to intimidate." He shook his head at the weight of such a blast against his family's name, his hospital's future. "I think this damage is irreversible."

How could his aunt stoop to such a level as to stains his father's name?

"There has to be something." Catherine distanced herself with another step, her face unreadable. "I won't allow her to hurt you, or your family, because of me."

The finances? The fire? And now this? His head squeezed with a pressure for control and for understanding. "I need some time to think. To sort this out, if it can be sorted."

Catherine ran to her room, refusing tears access until she'd made it safely inside. She'd wounded him. The slander of his father's name, of David's reputation, was all due to his association with *her*. Her mother's accusing words haunted her. Catherine always caused trouble for the people closest to her.

She lay back on her bed, the warm tears sliding down her temples to the eiderdown. *I've failed again.*

Suddenly, something fluttered in her stomach. She sniffled but didn't move, and the sensation returned. It was the slightest of movements, the faintest squirm. There for the briefest moment then gone.

She held her breath and placed her palm over the spot. It happened again. Within the pain of all that had occurred in the last few moments, something sweet bloomed inside her. An amazing and inexplicable kind of tenderness. Her baby.

For four months, the little one had been nothing but a secret thought, but now…now she became real. She? Catherine smiled, even as fresh tears formed. Why did she think the baby was a girl?

"It's the two of us, little one," she whispered. She breathed out a long stream of air and looked up to the ceiling, hoping her prayer reached far beyond those confines. "Please, rescue this moment. Protect David and his father. I'm so afraid of…" She closed her eyes, searching for the pinpoint problem. "Letting go, but I will…I will."

A knock sounded at her door, and Catherine tensed all over. She couldn't bear more hurt on David's face. More failure.

"Catherine, are you there?"

Catherine's body relaxed at the sound of her sister's voice. She smudged away the remainder of tears. "Come in."

Ashleigh walked in wearing her nurse's uniform. It was as if she'd never left, and yet, the peace in her countenance spoke of a deeper contentment. Married life agreed with her, but she'd also somehow reconciled the wounds of her past, their past. Perhaps Sam's love had brought about the reformation, in part. She grimaced. All she'd brought to David's life so far was a stained reputation. She paused on the thought. Well, and some wonderful memories associated with the supplies room.

"Are you feeling all right?" Her sister examined her with those acute eyes.

"I'm a bit tired." Not a complete lie. "There's so much happening."

"Yes. My head's spinning with repairs and the hospital." She laughed. "Jessica is thrilled I've returned, because she had the overwhelming fear she'd be asked to help with the orphanage."

"Not the child-type?"

"She's terrified of them." Ashleigh stepped forward and placed her hand on the post of the bed, her smile sobering.

"Speaking of children, I wanted to see how you were doing after the news this morning. I suspect you'll miss Nathanael."

Catherine's head lifted. "Miss him?"

Ashleigh's expression stilled and then swelled with a compassion which tensed Catherine's throat. "I thought Fanny had already told you. We received word this morning of a poor mother in Matlock who lost her babe yesterday. Her husband, a kind cleric, contacted us about—"

"They want him?" Catherine stood, hand pressing against the blooming ache in her stomach. She knew this was the hope for every child in their orphanage. A home. A family. Her mind understood, but her heart?

Ashleigh moved to her side, sliding a palm down her arm. "Fanny knows them and they're a kind, loving couple. They've desired children for years only to have their only child taken."

Catherine withered back onto the bed and pressed her fingers into forehead, praying logic might override the sudden urge to weep all over again. Yes, she knew, and had even convinced herself it would be for the best if he was adopted, but she'd not prepared for the sudden stab of loss.

"He will be loved, Catherine."

"Yes. Who could help but love him." Tears invaded her vision and clouded Ashleigh's face. "When will he go?"

"The couple arrive in the morning. They must attend to the burial of their child first."

Catherine's hand returned to her stomach, to the new connection made in the movement of her little babe. "I shall spend my evening rocking him tonight, for my memory and heart's sake."

"Solid practice for the future. You will soon fill your arms with your own sweet child." Ashleigh's smile warmed with comfort.

Catherine swallowed down the tears and nodded, pushing the grief aside until later, until the dark of night cloaked her sadness. She placed her hand on her stomach. "I think I felt her move."

"Her?" Ashleigh's eyes grew wide.

"I mean...the baby." She blinked away the tears and shrugged, tagging on a wobbly smile. Nathanael would be loved by two parents, something Catherine couldn't give him. "Of course, I can't know."

"I've heard of some mothers who knew from the very beginning."

"It's rather remarkable that something so...precious could come from such a mistake." She looked up, grin lifting with her spirits. "But I suppose God's been proving His hand in many ways lately."

"Even with Nathanael."

Catherine sighed, accepting her heartache with another intake of breath. "Even with Nathanael."

Ashleigh sat beside her on the bed. "Have you visited Beacon House yet? I've never been inside."

Her sister's gift of distraction proved fairly effective. Catherine's grin grew. "And you're curious?"

"A little. Grandmama gave it such high praise." She nudged her sister's shoulder with her own. Maybe seeing Beacon would distract her from the sadness of saying goodbye to Nathanael later in the evening. "Aren't you the least bit curious about your new house?"

"Of course." Catherine nodded, accepting her sister's well-meaning diversion. "In fact, I think we should go right now."

"Now?"

"Why not? You told me earlier that Grandmama's solicitor had informed the servants of the results of the will. And...I may be in need of a ballroom sooner rather than later."

The car passed between two ornate stone pillars, through a pair of wrought iron gates, and into a front garden surrounded by hedgerows on either side leading to the central point of Catherine's view. The house. It towered before them, a beautiful sandstone with tall, impressive windows framed in white to match the front doors. Beyond, the hedgerows lined a protective wall of beech trees, secluding the house even more.

Enchanting.

Catherine fell in love with it at first sight.

She sat forward in the automobile to get a better look as the car brought them around where a reception line of three waited by the front door. This would be a magnificent place to start over.

"Grandmama mentioned a walled garden in back."

Catherine shot a look to her sister. "A walled garden?"

"I know how you love those."

"You've an excellent gift of distraction." Catherine laughed. "And a walled garden?" She stopped, afraid to give away her little secret plan.

"Yes?"

She kept her voice low so Mason wouldn't overhear. "A walled garden is also beneficial for recuperating soldiers."

Ashleigh's eyes widened. "What?"

"Once the ball is over, I plan to set up Beacon House as the new hospital. It's closer to the village for supplies."

"And the railway station."

"Exactly."

"Catherine." Ashleigh stared at her until the car came to a stop. "You'd give up this house for the hospital?"

Mason opened the door for her, so she leaned closer to her sister before exiting. "The house will still be here after this war, and I can enjoy it then, but I think, for now, it needs a more useful occupation. And…David needs it."

They met a thin yet sturdy-looking woman first, her simple, black dress identifying her as Mrs. Bradford, the housekeeper. Next stood a tall, lean older gentleman, brown hair frosted with hints of gray. From her previous experience with butlers, this had to be Mr. Palmer, who'd worked for her grandmother as both butler and steward. Lastly, and quite out-of-his element, a broad shouldered man with a ruddy complexion and a shock of ginger curls greeted them. She grinned. Mr. Coates, the gardener.

Ashleigh gestured her forward. "Well, Catherine, it looks as though you finally have one of the things you always wanted."

"What's that?"

"Your own home near the village. A lady's home." Though her words came with a light voice, her intention rang deep.

She owned her own property! She'd become her own mistress. It might not have come with a title, but it added credence to one truth she was learning very slowly. God dreamed bigger dreams for her than she ever could.

Catherine's face hurt from smiling. The tour of Beacon House proved it the perfect location for hospital use. Ten bedrooms, most with southerly facing windows– half for patient rooms and half for staff. In addition, several of the larger rooms could be converted. It housed plenty of space for recreation, both indoors and out, with a walled-in garden to enjoy and footpaths for walks.

As she sat down with Mrs. Bradford to discuss the ball, Catherine barely kept her voice calm.

Mrs. Bradford's wide-eyed response confirmed the daunting nature of the task at hand.

"For that kind of quick work, miss, you're going to need people with a background in service."

"Exactly, Mrs. Bradford." She took a deep breath and forged ahead, hoping the housekeeper caught on. "And that's where your wisdom will be invaluable. You wouldn't happen to know anyone who might have lost their positions on a large estate recently?"

A light emerged in the woman's pale eyes, and if Catherine wasn't mistaken, her lips even pinched back a grin. "I do. Quite a few within the past few weeks."

"And they're accustomed to a house this size?"

"Bigger, in fact."

The Cavanaugh estate. Catherine's smile grew with the perfect unfolding of her plan. "My Grandmama trusted you with this house and its care. Do you think you can hire enough quality personnel to make this house what it used to be? To prepare for the ball in time?"

"Yes, ma'am." The woman stood with immediate purpose. "I'll do my best."

Mrs. Bradford exited the room, and Catherine reclined back into the chair, taking in a deep breath of new freedom.

She could help people find work, even with a marred reputation. The power to make a difference, a good difference, fueled her decisions with purpose and joy. Why would God be so good to her?

"Well?" Ashleigh asked, entering the room.

"She thinks she can do it."

"Of course she can."

Catherine glanced about the room as she stood. "But it's still going to take a lot of planning on my part, so I intend to stay here for the next few days."

"Stay here?"

Catherine stepped toward one of the cabinets and examined some trinkets on display. "I only have four days to plan, and with you back to help in the hospital, the additional nurses, as well as the arrival of Dr. Burr today, I won't be missed. Nathanael will leave tomorrow." She looked up from her perusal and forced a smile. "I gather my things tonight once he's asleep and return tomorrow early to finalize the plans?"

"I know what you're doing." Ashleigh crossed her arms, daring her sister to argue.

Catherine brushed off the glare with a shrug. "Planning for a fundraiser? Trying to save a hospital?"

"You're running away." She stepped closer, directly in Catherine's path. "You think staying away will help David?"

Catherine turned, hands on her hips. "I will not keep hurting him."

"Why don't you let him decide what he's willing to sacrifice instead of trying to make the decision for him?"

"Maybe I'm afraid of what he'll choose." The tears welled up in her eyes. "Before his care…" Her palm went to her chest. "His kiss…I could pretend it wouldn't hurt so much if he chose someone else." Catherine slid back into her chair. "But now? Now, I can't imagine anything hurting as badly as having him ripped from my life. If I stop things now, before I fall deeper and harder, before he even considers anything like love, then maybe I can protect both of us."

Ashley's stare penetrated Catherine's excuses. "You're scared, and you're playing it off as self-sacrifice."

"Scared?"

"I never imagined you to be a coward, but that's what this is all about."

Catherine shot back to her feet. "I'm trying to do what's right."

"Right? All I hear is that you're trying to keep yourself from being hurt. You're not giving David or God enough credit."

Ashleigh paused in the doorway. "Love hopes and perseveres. It doesn't seek its own, it believes. Look what God has proven so far." Ashleigh gestured toward the room. "Running away only takes you further from the truth. If you love David, have faith in him...or, if nothing else, have faith in God."

Chapter Twenty-Two

"There is one way to resolve the rumor no one has mentioned in this discussion."

Catherine looked at Madame across the table where they sat in the back of her shop. Annie, pen in hand, waited to list possible options for increasing the fundraiser's attendance. Marianne sat to her left, adding snippets of sunshine to the frustrating conversation.

One sleepless night in Beacon House gave Catherine ample time to ponder possibilities to counteract Lady Cavanaugh's hideous rumor. Somehow, she needed a way to create her own information and disperse it to the village. True information, instead of the negative and biased drivel coming from the general direction of Ednesbury Court. Discovering how to do that posed a quandary, however.

She'd entered Madame's shop readied with purpose and hoping for answers. So far, the answers proved less than helpful, and one of Madame's even bordered on illegal.

"What resolution is that, Madame?"

Her sliver of a brow rose, expression impassive. "You could marry him."

Clearly, the answers edged to the ridiculous. "Marry him?" Catherine looked to Marianne, whose smile grew with fairytale musings.

Annie's raised brow provided some solid grounding. "Next option?"

"Is there any legal way to have Mr. Dandy called up for active service?" Catherine offered.

"None of which I am aware." Madame tapped her fingers to her chin. "But my brother-in-law is in town now, and he works for the British government. He might…what do you say, pull a string."

"A few strings?"

"Oui." Madame grimaced. "I have not liked Monsieur Dandy since he put my good friend out of business. Pierre,

228

the other lone Frenchman in town, ran a respectable newspaper. Then, once Lord Cavanaugh died, Madame enlisted Dandy's allegiance in reducing poor Pierre to nothing."

Annie tossed down her pen and sat back in the chair, palms splayed on the table. "Well, since Dandy's the only local paper now, I don't see any way to counter Crow Cavanaugh's influence apart from starting a paper ourselves."

Catherine paused. "Madame, does Pierre still live in Ednesbury?"

A light of understanding brightened in her eyes. "Oui, though his shop is one of the Lady's properties."

"Do you know if he still has any of his equipment?"

She blinked. "Certainemant, but his shop is—"

"Owned by Lady Cavanaugh, yes, I know." Catherine stood. "But what if…what if it wasn't?"

"What do you mean?" Annie posed the question.

Catherine turned to them. "Mrs. Bradford, my new housekeeper, gave me more information about Lady Cavanaugh's finances because many of her friends are servants at Ednesbury Court…or were servants there, until recently, when Lady Cavanaugh began sacking them. And, of course, servants tend to overhear conversations."

"I had a tendency to plant scandals for my servants to hear." Madame sighed as her gaze faded in memories.

Catherine pinched her grin, not prepared to delve further onto the topic of Madame's past scandals, real or not. "If Ednesbury Court is in need of money, they might be desperate enough to sell some"—Catherine shrugged—"unimportant outlying buildings to someone who is willing to pay handsomely."

"Zut alors!" Madame exploded from her chair and came to take Catherine by the arms, kissing her on either cheek. "You should have been my daughter!"

Catherine laughed and then sobered in order to plan. "But would Pierre be willing to consider reopening his paper? And quickly?"

"I'd imagine he'd approve of the change in his landlady," Annie said.

"And we could advertise your gowns, Catherine. Like a proper designer." Marianne's glow shone.

"Wait," she raised her palm. "That might be the cover we need, because Lady Cavanaugh would never sell it to Catherine Dougall."

Annie stood, grin tilted like the perfect plot. "But Catherine Everill?"

"Oh la la," Madame tossed up her hands. "*C'est parfait!* You will go in disguise."

"I don't think there is a costume made well enough to disguise me from Lady Cavanaugh's hawk-eyes." Catherine took another round of pacing. "But couldn't someone go in Catherine Everill's stead? Wouldn't great ladies have liaisons of some sort who completed their business for them? Secretaries, perhaps?"

"Surely Catherine Everill will be extravagant and unlike the English." Madame snubbed her nose. "She's American, after all, so her behavior will not be questioned as much as ridiculed later."

Catherine grinned. "And I'm well-equipped for that."

Madame continued. "And you could use your grandmama's solicitor to complete the paperwork for the transaction, should the lady be amenable to the terms."

The possibilities spun an untapped thrill. Perhaps this was the beginning of something bigger…something to truly turn Ednesbury around. "But who do we know that could play the part of an American secretary?"

Everyone turned and looked at Annie.

Her palms came up and she shook her ginger curls. "Me? Oh come now, you think I could play a part like that?"

Catherine closed in. "You've been a secretary before, and to a wealthy land owner at that."

"And we know you can imitate accents." Madame hedged her in on the other side. "Though the American accent will not have as much elegance as the French one."

"You can also wear some lovely outfit, a suit designed by Catherine Everill, no less." Marianne's bright smile brought enough optimism to light up the back corner of the store.

Catherine leveled her with a pointed stare. "And you would be taking away some of Crow Cavanaugh's power and giving it back to the people."

"Giving back a little of what the Crow has chucked at us?" Annie's smile took up the challenge. Even her freckles brightened. "I think this idea is gaining merit."

The bell chimed in the shop to announce David's presence, but the only person to notice was a young lady at the counter. She offered a welcome smile and then froze, eyes widening. After a moment's examination, he realized the shopkeeper was none other than Marianne, one of Catherine's emergency assistants.

Her pale blue gaze drifted to a display of a mannequin in an elegant, deep purple gown, but standing near the gown was the reason for his venture into the unknown world of women's fashion.

Catherine stood, running her fingers over the gown's sheer sleeve, staring up at it as if concocting a plan. His smile expanded along with the warmth in his heart. She'd disappeared from Roth for two days, and finally, after some carefully worded questions to Ashleigh and a few threats to Michael, he'd deduced where to locate his runaway American.

His beautiful runaway.

Her navy skirt cinched at her waist and her white blouse, with a low collar, highlighted her neckline. Only a trained eye, or an admiring one, would have noticed the added roundness at her middle. David shed his coat and made a stealthy approach. No more running. No more hiding.

"Pardon me, miss, but do you happen to carry men's shoes?"

Catherine turned, a sardonic expression in place, before recognition dawned in the depths of cobalt blue. Her rose lips dropped open and then snapped closed before she took a few steps back. "What are you doing here?"

"I thought it fairly obvious." He lowered his voice to match her whisper.

"Men's shoes?" She needled him with a glare and slid until the mannequin separated them. "You are not helping rumors by being seen with me."

He attempted to step around the mannequin, but she moved to keep the display between them. "What if I don't care about the rumors?"

That answer paused her escape. "You have to care. It's your father's reputation, and yours. Please, leave."

"What if I don't wish to leave? In fact, I think I'll purchase something for my sister."

David made his way over to a display of blouses and plucked the first one, a bundle of pink ruffles. "What about this one?"

Catherine's derisive chuckle answered. "She'd as soon die as wear something like that."

At least she kept talking to him. What about another try? The next blouse he procured was a confection of lace in a unique combination of pale green and yellow.

"Don't even consider it." Catherine's voice came from behind, closer. "If you're truly looking for something for your sister…" She marched past him to another display and tossed a narrow-eyed glance over her shoulder before taking a pale blue blouse from its place. "Then this might be more appropriate."

Catherine knew his sister. The simplicity and elegance of the blouse matched Jessica's practical personality. He held Catherine's gaze and stepped forward, placing his hand over hers on the blouse. "Perfect choice."

She stared up at him, the fight fading for an instant, both frozen in place, as much a display as the one next to them. She finally tugged her hand free, leaving the garment in his hold, and her expression turned pleading. "Please go."

He didn't budge. "Why did you leave Roth Hall?"

"I don't want to hurt you anymore."

"What else? I know there's more than that."

She pinched her eyes closed and sighed. When she opened them, a sheen of tears glossed the sapphire blue. "It…it's too much to be near you and not be…"

He edged a step closer. "Yes?"

"With you." She blinked and looked away. "And being with you causes horrible things to happen, as I knew it would, so I...I won't stay."

He cradled her chin in his fingers and tipped her face up to look at him. "I want to be with you, no matter the consequences."

She stepped back, dashing a tear from her cheek. "You can't mean that."

David growled, shoved the blouse back onto the display, and took her by the arm. "Let me prove something to you." He started for the front door of the shop.

"What are you doing?"

"I'm removing all of your excuses."

Marianne tossed a coat over the counter to him as they passed and, in a flash, they stood on Main Street together.

"What are you—?"

"Put this on." He wrapped the coat around her shoulders, drawing her close enough to drink in the sweetness of lavender. "We are going for a walk."

She attempted to pull back, but he held her trapped inside the coat, leaning forward in an almost inappropriate public display. "Upon reassessment, perhaps I do enjoy trapping you."

Her narrowed eyes meant to put him off, but only endeared her to him all the more. She slid her arms reluctantly into the sleeves of the coat, and before she could slip away, he linked her arm through his and started walking toward down town.

"You are... This is..."

"Good morning, Mrs. Regan." David nodded to two older women approaching them on the street corner. "Mrs. Ramsey, how is your daughter?"

The woman's typically sour expression transformed with the personal touch. "I'm so glad you recommended Coltsfoot for her asthma. Dr. Carrier kept giving her some useless tonic."

"I'm glad to hear it was helpful. Sometimes natural sources provide a perfect alternative." He gestured toward Catherine. "Have you had the opportunity to meet Miss Catherine Dougall?"

Both women peered down their noses, inciting David's defense.

"Catherine is the woman I spoke of, who helped save the orphans during the fire."

Both women's eyes widened, and they looked to Catherine in reassessment. He turned to Catherine, her forehead a wrinkle of confusion. "Mrs. Regan and Mrs. Ramsey serve as the Women's Mission Leaders for orphaned children of war."

Catherine tilted her head and, if he wasn't mistaken, nipped back a smile. She, then, raised a brow to him in challenge, turned to both of the ladies, and offered her hand. "It's a pleasure to meet women of like passions."

Heaven help him! Her double entendre nearly evoked his laughter.

Mrs. Regan stared at Catherine's hand, unmoving, but Mrs. Ramsey took it after a moment's hesitation. "A pleasure."

The man was off his trolley!

He ignored her blatant and somewhat annoyed stare as the two women bid their good-days and walked on.

"You think yourself clever in some way with this...plan of yours." She smiled at the passersby and then continued her whispered battering. "But it is apparent you're either sleep-deprived or going mad. This will unequivocally inspire more rumors of the same theme, Dr. Ross."

"And I'm proving to you that it doesn't matter, Miss Dougall." He eased her down a step, his palm on her elbow, and then relinked their arms.

She loved the strength of him and the way she fit by his heart. And though his scent of peppermint softened her annoyance a little, it failed to stop her from fastening another scathing stare on him.

Unfortunately, it wasn't as scathing as she'd planned because his beautiful smile hit her scowl with some sort of melting force.

"My past doesn't matter?"

He stopped their walk and turned to face her, his teasing glint replaced by a flash of fire in his green eyes. "Not to me.

I've allowed my aunt enough influence. I don't need anyone else's approval to know what is right. She may control this village, but she won't control us."

"Us?"

He angled his head, studying her with such tenderness, her thoughts fogged into sweet oblivion. It wasn't a fair disagreement if he used such a potent weapon.

"Yes, Catherine." He breathed her name, and the fog thickened until she wanted to sway into those strong, safe arms and remind him of the supply closet. His thoughts must have turned in a similar direction, because his gaze dropped to her lips, evoking an anticipatory tingle. "Us."

Laughter from down the street pulled them out of the trance, and he cleared his throat, continuing toward the pinnacle of Ednesbury's quaint village, the public park.

It's manicured lawn and trimmed trees brought people from all over the village to enjoy the refreshing green. Rich and poor alike sat on the grass and enjoyed a bit of nature, though on separate sides of the park and never speaking to one another.

The November breeze brushed against Catherine's cheeks, dousing some of the pleasing side effects of David's presence and giving her back a bit of clarity. "Everyone will see us here."

"Yes, Kat. They will." He kept his face forward, jaw set.

Her nickname, paired with his certainty, turned her emotions into a complete puddle.

He guided them across the street and began a promenade about the park. "I've wondered, the past few days, what can be done. There are only two answers." He released a long sigh, as if the next words came with difficulty. "We go on with our lives regardless of anyone else's disproval. And we attempt to show my aunt something she doesn't understand."

"Poverty? Sacrifice? A conscience?

He chuckled and placed his warm hand over hers on his arm. "Love. Real love."

"Why would you show her love when all she's done is hurt people?"

"The very nature of love is giving it even when that person doesn't reciprocate. Or God's sort of love is, at any rate." He smoothed his fingers over hers, almost methodically. A gentle, caring touch. "I suppose it's the heaviest blow against our pride, but it is also a powerful force, and most unexpected in this selfish, war-torn world. It has the ability power to turn people 'round."

Uncharacteristic tears warmed her eyes. She placed a palm against her stomach, and the familiar sweetness of her secret love for this unborn child flooded through her. Yes, the baby couldn't love her back, but she loved the little soul growing inside her with an inexplicable strength.

"You have more faith than I do."

He led her to a bench nestled under a large oak in the center of the park and sat down beside her, keeping her arm tucked within his. "Although it feels rather bleak in relation to my aunt, God's love has the power to change any heart."

"Yes, but you're assuming she has one."

His full laugh broke the quiet of the park. "You, my dear, have a heart large enough to take on every hurdle with the tenacity of a new army." He scanned the overcast sky and then bathed her in another beautiful smile. "And any man would be honored to be the beneficiary of such affections. Please, don't run away any more. Don't make excuses. Don't hide in some vain attempt to protect me."

She studied him, looking for any chink in his sincerity, any doubt in those eyes. His words wove in perfect synchrony to every line of his confident face. "Promise me."

Could God truly give her this? Her stains still hung with an aura of newness from the townspeople and even her mother. Would God gift her enough with David's love?

She placed her arguments under the steadiness of his confidence, and with a trembling breath, gave up her heart. "I promise."

Chapter Twenty-Three

"Good morning."

David looked up from his father's most recent letter, his note posing an unnerving question: how many lives would be saved if caught sooner? Catherine emerged through the doorway, breathtaking in dark blue, with tea tray in hand.

He pushed himself up to a standing position from his desk, drinking in the vision of her. "Good morning."

She offered a coy smile as she approached. "I suppose you thought I'd disappeared again since I didn't return to Roth last night, so I decided, in case you think I'm not a woman of my word, I'd make my presence known."

He rounded the desk and took the tray from her, his fingers brushing across hers in the exchange. "Very chivalrous of you."

"Quite, especially owing to the fact that I'm threatened with entrapment any time you're near."

He placed the tray on the small tea table and turned in time to help her with her suit jacket. As it slid from her arms, he lowered his mouth to her ear. "Don't forget the kissing part."

A tremor passed through her, teasing him to indulge a little longer. "Practice does improve one's skill."

She turned to face him, the blue in her suit deepening the color in her eyes, leaving him drowning in a sapphire sea.

"I assure you, Dr. Ross, I am not the type of woman who takes pleasure in being trapped." She hesitated and then stepped into the periphery of his arms. "Unless it's by you."

In that one moment, she relinquished her heart. He saw it in her stance, felt it in the certainty of her stare. She'd made her choice, and heaven help him, that awareness shook him to the core. Such contained passion deserved a strong man. As he studied her face, he knew God would make him strong enough.

He touched the tip of her chin and closed in, keeping his gaze locked with hers until her eyelids fluttered closed in sweet acceptance. Her mouth encouraged him to linger, and he complied. Nothing else moved except their lips, slowly tasting and testing each other. It was the seal of a promise and the start of something relentless.

As he pulled away, she stood there, eyes still closed, as if in reverence to the beauty of the moment. If she stood in such a posture much longer, he'd have to indulge in some more practice.

She sighed and turned to the table. "Fanny said you hadn't had your breakfast, so I hope you don't mind if I share it with you."

He took a seat, watching her hands move over the tea service without a fumble. "I can't think of anything better to start the day. On both counts."

A blush darkened her cheeks and made her even more appealing. "Cream and sugar, yes?"

"I love you, Catherine."

"Oh," she whispered. The stirring spoon crashed against the tray, drawing her attention back to her work. "You don't waste any time, do you, Dr. Ross?"

She handed him his tea, and he captured her hand between his and the teacup. "David. Call me, David."

Her smile bloomed. "David."

He took the cup and released her hand, returning to his chair. "No, I don't believe in it. Especially now, when young men are dying all over the world. Time isn't a commodity, and I don't want to take it for granted. If I love you, I want you to know."

She kept her focus on her task of pouring her own tea, though the rise and fall of her breathing hitched as she worked. "Do you know something? I've never spoken those words to anyone." She took her seat and studied him. "I've agreed to someone else's assessment of my feelings or written the sentiment in a letter, but…I can't recall a time where I've spoken them."

"Why?"

She took a sip of her tea, halting her reply. "Perhaps it is because what I felt seemed much larger than three small words."

His smile broke free. And his next challenge began. "If you choose to speak them, then, I'll know their significance."

"Fanny said you received a letter this morning that distracted you from breakfast." She waved a hand toward the tea service with scones and bread aplenty. "Is everything well?"

"My father. The conditions at the Front are abysmal. The Casualty Clearing Station in which he serves isn't equipped to manage the inflow of patients, nor the extent to which they are wounded."

"I'm sorry, David." Her compassion poured a calm over him.

"He's a strong man, careful and good-natured." David grinned as Catherine served him a scone. "He would like you."

She raised a brow in doubt.

"He appreciates strong personalities. My mother was very much like my sister."

Her other brow rose to match. "Then there's hope for me."

He stared back down at the letter. "I wish there was something I could do to help him. I can't leave the hospital in such a state, but what else can be done in support?"

"We can pray for God to provide help?"

Her offering touched a deep place in his soul, her request effortless and genuine. He put his cup down and took her hand. "Yes, we can." And with that, he brought her wrist to his lips and left a lingering kiss there. "Of course, we can."

Catherine had promised the dark green walking suit would bring out Annie's natural beauty, but Annie Feagan had barely recognized herself. With her hair twisted in some intricate knot, a posh suit, and a small, fashionable black hat to top it off, she looked the part of an American heiress's secretary, even if the massive walls of Ednesbury Court reminded her of her true station in life.

She'd inwardly chided Catherine and Madame for their intense conviction that clothes and physical care made differences, but the proof stared back at her from the deference shown by each servant she passed on her way to Lady Cavanaugh's parlor.

It brought her stance a little straighter and her head higher. There may be something to be said for a touch of fashion.

Annie fought a million distractions upon entering the grand house, from the dark floor-to-ceiling wallpaper to the expensive furnishing. Everything carried the scent of money…old money.

"I understand you wish to purchase the old print shop on the far east-side of Ednesbury?" Lady Cavanaugh sat behind a massive desk—large enough to place three full dress patterns—her dark eyes severe. Annie fought against her instinct to lower her gaze.

"My employer, Miss Everill, wishes to make the purchase." Annie formed each word with precision. "She's recently acquired a home near Ednesbury and desires to expand her property to provide additional housing for servants as well as other business ventures."

The woman peered up over her glasses. "Why would a person of such means wish to settle this far from London?"

Annie refused to break eye contact, no matter how steely Crow Cavanaugh's gaze. "Miss Everill enjoyed a rural life in the American south and finds more inspiration in the quiet of a country evening than the bustle of London's streets."

Lady Cavanaugh lifted her chin. "I have never heard of this designer."

"Her designs are rather new to this part of the world." Annie kept her gloved hands in her lap, refusing to fidget. "However, if you doubt her existence, you need only visit one of your local shops to see some of it on display. Madame Rousell's is a-bustle with interest in Catherine Everill's designs."

"Madame Rousell? I don't see how a connection with such a flagrant or base French woman could serve Miss Everill well?"

Heat began a steady climb up Annie's throat. Madame might be odd and extravagant, but she'd shown nothing but kindness to Annie and half a dozen other women.

"Madame's openness to new ideas is the crux of her long-standing success, I should think."

The Lady narrowed her eyes before dismissing Annie with a wave of her hand. "Since Miss Everill is such a new success, I don't see how she can make a competitive offer for any of my properties. Have her come back in a year or two."

"I assure you, she's examined fair offers for such property." Annie brought another paper from her satchel, the one Catherine had provided to use as a tease. It listed some of Catherine's additional holdings from her inheritance. "She's willing to offer this amount."

Lady Cavanaugh's solicitor took the paper and examined it. His bushy brows took flight, and he slid the sheet to Crow Cavanaugh, whispering.

Lady Cavanaugh adjusted her glasses and pressed a fist to her chest. "I...I believe you've given me the wrong paper, Miss Feagan." She reluctantly returned the paper.

"Did I?" Annie looked down at the paper and gasped. "Oh, I do apologize. That was private information from this quarter's accounts. Forgive me."

"This quarter only?" Lady Cavanaugh's eyes widened behind her spectacles, and Annie gripped her smile tight.

The bait worked. Catherine Dougall was as clever as a fox.

"Here is the actual offer."

Mr. Clark's wide eyes confirmed the generosity of the bid.

Lady Cavanaugh scanned the number and then removed her glasses. "How soon would Miss Everill wish to make the purchase?"

"As soon as Mr. Clark can draw up the papers." Annie countered. "You know how we Americans can be." Annie smiled. "Overly ambitious."

Lady Cavanaugh hesitated and touched her fingertips together as she gave Annie another unnerving perusal. "I can have Mr. Clark draw up the papers immediately."

"Perfect. I'm sure I can return them to you by tomorrow."

"Tomorrow?" Lady Cavanagh's voice lilted.

"My employer is industrious. Most designers are, you know."

Lady Cavanaugh sent Annie another measured look before answering. "Very well."

"I'll be certain to let Miss Everill know how agreeable you were to her request. It's important to make the right connections."

"Of course."

"And should you have any properties you'd wish to sell in the future, please come to Miss Everill first." Annie offered her card. "She's highly interested in expanding her interests and dealings with the…right connections."

"I brought the gowns you requested." Ashleigh entered Catherine's bedroom, or at least the one she'd claimed at Beacon House for the last few days. "And I thought, perhaps, we could prepare for the ball together."

Catherine turned from the dressing table, still surprised by this new and missed camaraderie with her sister. They'd lost so much because of their father's hideous choices and Catherine's unyielding bitterness. So much. But God redeemed relationships, and perhaps, he could redeem time too.

"I would love that."

Ashleigh placed the gowns on the bed. "The ballroom downstairs is remarkable, the entry way lined with the loveliest décor of lace and flowers." Ashleigh shook her head. "No wonder you were the one gifted with the social eye."

"It will take all the social sense I have to make this plan work." Catherine stood and walked to the bed, glancing over the gowns.

Ashleigh examined her again as if through new eyes. "And I suppose you used some of that sense to inspire the new paper which arrived on Roth Hall's doorstep this morning? I believe it was appropriately titled *The Beacon?*"

Catherine's smile twitched and she moved to the dressing table. "Actually, the designer, Catherine Everill, is the mastermind behind the paper."

"And Catherine Dougall is the mastermind behind Catherine Everill?" Ashleigh laughed. "I have no idea how you managed it all. Amazing."

"It all brings such...joy with it, more than I ever imagined." Catherine stared at her reflection, a welcome glow on her face with this truth. "Not only the designing, but serving others too. Quite a change, isn't it?"

"So much has changed." Ashleigh dropped to sit on the other side of the bed. "Even Mother is different. Do you realize she's taken a fancy to Dr. Pike?"

Catherine turned, hairpin in hand. "I tried to ignore it, but it's impossible not to notice."

"I think it might do her some good."

"No doubt." Catherine turned back to the mirror. "But what about poor Dr. Pike?"

Ashleigh chuckled. "Mother is the type of woman that needs a doting man. He seems to lighten her mood and steady her emotions."

"I should think a doting man would improve any woman's mood."

They both broke into laughter, and Catherine removed enough pins to have her hair falling around her shoulders in a blanket of black.

"I'm glad to hear your laugh again." Ashleigh smile grew. "Your true laugh. It's been a long time."

Catherine tossed off the compliment with a shrug and stood, reaching for the buttons of her skirt. "Do you remember what Grandmama used to say about good laughter?"

Ashleigh steadied her shoulders, taking on the posture of their dearly departed _Grandmama. "A room without healthy laughter is like—"

"—a picnic without salt." Catherine's skirt dropped to the rug. She stepped out of it and began unbuttoning her blouse. "Which mother would readily correct." Catherine attempted to imitate their mother's voice. "It is infamous to show all your teeth in a laugh."

Ashleigh began taking out her own hairpins as she moved her lips to cover her top teeth. "I still haven't sorted out how one laughed without showing one's teeth a little."

"Neither have I."

Silence sobered the moment. "Fanny told me that Nathanael is adjusting well to his new home."

"Yes. I heard the same."

"And they are doting on him like mother over a new gown."

"Then he'll be well-loved, you can be sure." Ashleigh stepped toward Catherine and waved toward the gowns littered across the bed. "Speaking of gowns, which one will the infamous hostess of the ball wear tonight?"

Catherine rounded the bed to take in the options, the ache less when couched in her sister's comforting presence. "I'm not officially the hostess, remember. Catherine Everill has been kind enough to offer her home for our fundraiser."

"Ah, yes." Ashleigh shook her head. "I wonder how long you'll be able to maintain the charade."

"As long as needed, I hope." Catherine examined the gowns. "You brought three more than I requested."

"Your choices weren't elegant enough."

Catherine had intentionally kept her requests to the less extravagant side, quelling the inner-debutante into submission. "And which would you choose for me?"

"This one." Ashleigh brought Catherine's favorite from the mass. A deep red, sleeveless evening gown, with a v-cut neckline and swaths of glorious silk running in a diagonal pattern down the skirt. The princess waist of the dress accented all the natural curves Catherine used to flaunt, and the color complimented her hair and eyes in a flattering way.

"Oh no, I don't think I could wear that one."

"Why not? It's a perfect gown for you. The style, the design…especially the color. Your figure is still well intact, without showing your pregnancy at all. No man would be able to keep his eyes off of you."

Which was reason enough on its own. But oh, how she loved the sweet memories of turning heads, the rush of pleasure at feeling beautiful. Her hand reached for the material, almost of its own accord. What would David think?

She smiled at the thought. "I've worked so diligently to separate myself from the woman I used to be and this…this elegance is a luxury I can give to other women, but I shouldn't indulge it anymore."

"What do you mean?" Ashleigh came to stand close to her. "The gown didn't cause you to sin. Celebrating the beauty God has given you…" Ashleigh's index finger pointed along with her brow. "Celebrating, I said, not flaunting, won't take you back down a path you left."

"I've been mostly content with fashionable walking suits. Fine with the clothes of everyday, but an evening gown?" Her gaze went back to the dress, inspiring a longing to slip back into the elegance. Her palm moved to the small bulge at her stomach. "Do you think he'll accept this baby? It's one thing to take me with all of my scars, but what about her?"

"It's time you trusted David to be as big-hearted and certain as we've seen. You have this beautiful opportunity to start over, for you and this baby." Ashleigh took her by the shoulders. "David knows what he's doing, Catherine. Enjoy this love you've always hope to find. You don't have to keep living with guilt and fear. Christ's love for you comes without strings. He's given you a gift for fashion, a personality to regale a roomful of people, a mind to use to glorify him by helping others. He's made you beautiful, inside and out. Find joy in that knowledge instead of guilt and condemnation. Celebrate this second chance." Ashleigh gestured with her chin toward the bed, her gaze poignant. "And wear the red gown."

Chapter Twenty-Four

From David's perspective, the bazaar was a success. It might not have brought in the largest amount of financial support, but the positive hum from the people of Ednesbury brought its own rewards. Support. The type money can't buy. Positive, word-of-mouth support.

And he wanted to shake hands with whoever owned *The Beacon* newspaper. Somehow, its recruitment of people from villages on all sides of Ednesbury, many of those elite, spurred another bolster to David's hopes. Perhaps a proper hospital was less than a struggling year away.

Surprises continued to mount, as well as a deeper appreciation for Catherine Dougall's intricate creativity and unrelenting energy. How she'd coaxed the owner of Beacon House to host a ball on such short notice, he'd never understand. The massive, wood-paneled doorway welcomed him into an extravagant entryway, decorated with seasonal bouquets of delphiniums, paper whites, lilies, and roses.

The house stretched with elegance in all directions. Music rose from a room to his right, another massive room opened to his left, and a grand stairway ascended in the center, curving up into the recesses of the house. A figure on the stairs brought his breathing to a full stop.

Catherine.

His Catherine.

He'd always known she was beautiful, even from the first moment they met on the streets of Ednesbury, but never had he imagined something as breathtaking as her in ravishing red.

He finally understood why every social circle within Ednesbury's vicinity spoke of Catherine Dougall's infallible beauty. Why men waited in lines to enjoy her company. Why a man would hover on the brink of impropriety to gain her favor.

And this vision of beauty was smiling at him – the bookish, introverted, nearly penniless surgeon. The word 'captivated' took on new meaning. She bypassed the crowd congregating outside the ballroom and made her way to his side, bringing her lavender scent and lovely glow with her.

Her lips were tinted a darker shade, like a forbidden fruit. He placed his palm to his chest and took in every detail. Overwhelmed.

"You look quite fetching in your tails, Dr. Ross." Her gaze of approval kindled a deeper smolder in his chest. "A definite improvement from your surgeon's coat."

"Catherine." He took her hand and brought it to his lips, never taking his eyes from hers. "If I've been hesitant to respond, it's only because I fail to find words accurate enough to describe how beautiful you are."

Her cheeks darkened. "The tails must bring out your romantic side." She meant to brush off the intensity of the compliment, but the impact lingered in her sapphire eyes. "You should wear tails more often."

"And you should wear evening gowns more often."

"I'd be happy to comply." Her brow peaked with her smile. "As long as you'll remain my escort."

He drew her hand into the crook of his arm. "To which *I'd* be happy to comply."

Their gazes held for much longer than appropriate before she turned to the room. "What do you think of Beacon House?"

He pulled his gaze from her face and took another look around the entry as they followed the masses into a room filled with music and dancing. His throat tightened. Catherine sent him a look from her periphery, a question in the tilt of her grin.

David swallowed through the tension and gestured toward the ballroom floor. "Would you do me the honor of continuing our dancing lesson in a more formal setting, Miss Dougall?"

"Oh." Her smile fell and she slipped her arm free from his. "I thought you meant to choose one of the other ladies. Not me." Her palm flattened against the bare skin beneath her neck. "I don't know that you should stand up with me in front of these higher society couples. If they don't know of my indiscretion already, they might learn of it and refuse funding—"

"Should I reiterate my earlier argument?" He regained her hand, rubbing his thumb across her knuckles and tugging her back toward him. "I care about *you,* not their assumptions." He stopped her protest with a shake of his head. "Dance with me, Catherine. I have no intention of dancing with anyone else, so if I'm to learn, you must be my teacher."

She hesitated and glanced about the room before releasing a sigh. "With a solid argument such as that, how can I refuse?" Her chin tipped, teasing fire returning to her eyes.

He guided her onto the floor, fighting against his own insecurities beside such an expert in the social sphere. No doubt, she'd been through dozens of these experiences, standing in the middle of a room with people tucked against each wall, staring at those who attempted to make a spectacle of themselves, but one look into her eyes changed his focus. There was only the two of them.

A small orchestra began Blue Danube, and he took his place as the leader, bringing her into his arms with the sway of the music.

"As I told you before, you have natural ability."

He lowered his head to whisper near her ear. "I had a very good teacher."

She looked up at him, their faces inches apart. "Miss Moore's skills were certainly...unique."

He laughed and stilled the urge to place a kiss into her midnight hair.

"I have a surprise for you." Her teeth scraped over her bottom lip in an evident attempt to contain her delight. He loved watching how her intelligence and excitement shone through her eyes in a thousand hues of emotion.

"I don't know if I'm equipped to manage much more excitement today."

"You've been waiting for this news, dear doctor."

"Have I?"

"The owner of Beacon House, Miss Everill, wishes to offer the house to you for your hospital."

He froze in place, heat leaving his body.

She laughed but urged him back in step.

"Beacon House? My hospital?"

Her broad smile confirmed it.

"But how could we afford the rent for...for this?"

"She doesn't need the home at present and feels very deeply for your cause. It's her wish that you have the unhindered freedom to serve those suffering from this war."

David blinked against the shock and took another glance about the massive, elaborately decorated room. Gold embossed carvings, tall windows, a ceiling displaying an artistic masterpiece. He stumbled again. "Can this be true?"

"Completely. It would give her the greatest pleasure to see her home used in such a noble endeavor by such a noble doctor."

He stared at her, somehow feeling a deeper meaning behind her words. What hidden sacrifice had she made to bring this about? What painstaking work?

"I have no doubt this magnanimity is due to your efforts."

She gave a quick shake to her head. "It's almost all due to your good name." She tipped a brow. "See? A good reputation carries above the stuff and nonsense of rumors."

"And I'm certain this generosity has your fingerprints all over it." He gripped her closer, tempted to pull her into an embrace in front of every person in the room. "This place, the location...it's perfect. How soon can we move?"

"Within the week, if you like." The pleasure she received from relaying this news shone all over her lovely face. "It is vacant except for the servants, and they are at your disposal."

He placed her hand against his chest, squeezing it close to his heart, the world around them fading into music and blurs. "I don't know how you managed it, but I will forever be in your debt."

"There is no debt, David, and the pleasure is all mine. I know serving people is what God's called you to do, and I would support it with all I have."

The monies raised by the bazaar and the tickets to the ball met the bottom of their expectations, but at least the donations would supply two new surgery theaters. And, of course, Lady Hollingsworth's funds would help pay staff, which finally allowed some financial breathing room.

She'd given Mrs. Bradford the day off and sent all the servants fine gifts, nothing like the second-hand material or cigars her mother used to give. In this changing world where a factory job gave more freedom and similar pay as service, Catherine would take every opportunity to show her gratitude.

Two lodges stood on the grounds of Beacon House. Lovely little cottages, probably meant for the grounds staff at one point. Mr. Coates lived in the smaller of the two houses, the one closest to the garages, but the other stood vacant.

Catherine asked Mrs. Bradford to prepare the additional cottage for her – a quiet refuge away from the bustle of the house and a safe haven to keep Catherine Everill's information separate from Catherine Dougall's. She'd have Mr. Palmer deliver mail to the cottage and, perhaps, keep up the façade long enough to sort out how to purchase more properties from Lady Cavanaugh.

Preparing for the move snatched away any private moments. With her staying at Beacon to prepare for the move and David at Roth to pack up patients, there was little time for sweet, clandestine meetings, and though her head understood, her lips ached for his kiss.

But as she moved from room to room, reveling in the success of the move, the certainty of her choice to offer the hospital became even more secure. David's steady administration to make the transition smooth proved his abilities and calling all the more, and with Ashleigh's assistance, Catherine had purchased extra beds and fresh linens to provide each patient with his own bed instead of a cot, because she'd read how comfort encouraged faster healing.

As the quiet hum of evening closed the first night of Beacon War Hospital, Catherine slipped out into the garden, her favorite part of the house. Unlike Roth's back garden, with its crumbling walls and untamed plumage, Mr. Coates had kept Beacon's garden in lovely order. The hedges were trimmed, the fountain clear, and even the seasonal flowers bloomed late. She walked the pebbled path to a corner of the garden where a gazebo waited, pulling her coat against the mid-November chill.

Suddenly, from behind, she was wrapped in a pair of warm arms.

"I never received a good-night kiss at the ball." David's breath moved against her neck, and her body responded with a shock of delightful tingles. "As the guest of honor, I expected a more thorough closure from the esteemed hostess."

She leaned into him, her head dropping back against his shoulder. A million stars blinked down from the dark sky, glimpsing their secret rendezvous with twinkling interest.

"How remiss of me." Without hesitation, she turned, took his face in her hands, and stood on tiptoe to meet his mouth with hers. Warm and familiar, their lips found each other, over and over again, making up for lost time. She never tired of his face, his taste, the very feel of him.

"Will the honorable guest be satisfied with the hostess' answer?"

He leaned his forehead against hers, lights from the house casting a shadow on his face. "On the contrary, satisfied is the last thing I feel." He ran his thumb across her cheek. "I've missed you, my dear."

She closed her eyes to appreciate his touch even more. "And I you."

"One day, perhaps, we will have more than snatched moments."

She brushed back his hair from his forehead and then slid her fingers down his temple to his ear. "I'm grateful for all moments, snatched or no."

"Each one counts." He sighed and embraced her, resting his head atop hers and surrounding her with mint.

"What is it?"

"Letters from my father remind me of the need...of the value of loving in the present." His voice held a sadness she couldn't touch.

"Is he as well as can be expected?"

"Yes." David wrapped one of her ringlets around his finger. "But they desperately need more doctors."

Her stomach cinched into a knot at the shadow in his words, the trembling foreboding. "We can certainly pray God sends more doctors."

He paused before answering. "Yes, we can." The silence sifted between them with an intermittent dove call breaking into the stillness.

"I love you, Catherine."

She opened her mouth to respond in kind, but her voice caught on the words. 'Love' was such a small word for the feelings pressing in on her heart. She leaned in and reclaimed his lips, hoping he understood without words.

"You plan to go to the Front?"

Jessica blocked his exit from the room. "Oh no, my brother. You don't make an announcement like this and then expect to dash for cover. No, no, no." She pointed toward a chair in the room. "You're going to explain."

He groaned and kept his stance. "I had written to Dr. Stephens last month, the lead doctor who staffs the Casualty Clearing Stations, and received his reply yesterday. His assessment of the needs at the Front are similar to Father's."

"But you've had the hospital at Beacon House for only two weeks. How can it be established enough for your absence?"

He walked behind his desk and tossed a packet of papers toward her. "With the support Catherine's gleaned from Lady Hollingsworth and some of her acquaintances, we will be able to make enough to pay the staff each month in advance. We have no surplus, but this..." He shrugged. "This Catherine Everill person is allowing us to use Beacon House and its servants at no cost to us. The generosity is staggering and gives us security."

He waved his hand at the papers. "Our current staff can manage things quite well, I'm certain, especially under your supervision."

Jessica looked down at the papers, scanning over the figures. "I'm going with you."

"Going with me?" He started to round the desk. "Now, Jessica, be sensible."

"My brother and my father are at the Front. My family." She slammed her palm against the desk, eyes challenging him to disagree with her. Do you think for one moment I'm not going with you?"

God must see some sort of strength in him to surround him with so many strong-willed women. "It's dangerous."

She folded her arms across her chest, and he almost ducked from the glare. "Too dangerous for a woman but not a man?"

"Let's not make this an issue of women's rights."

"Good, I'm glad we agree." Her smile spread. "Then you shouldn't mind if I go as your theatre nurse."

"My theatre nurse."

She started for the door, a hint of victory lightning her step. "Every surgeon needs a theatre nurse, at the Front or in a hospital. I've been yours for years. I know your routines, your habits, how you work." She shrugged. "And I'm going with you."

David placed his palms on the desk and leaned forward in surrender. There was no point in trying to argue. A whole childhood with her proved it. "At least the others will be here. Doctors Pike and Hudson ran their own hospitals before the Zeppelin attack. Ashleigh is more than competent to head the nursing staff. Michael's become indispensable in the organization and function of the facility, and Catherine is…" His smile softened as he searched for a description.

Jessica rolled her eyes. "Please, I read your dazed expression with perfect clarity." She shook her head, almost in sympathy, and reached for the door handle, then paused. "Speaking of Catherine." Jessica released a low whistle, another hint to her place outside high society and nod to their rural upbringing. "You've given her the pig-headed idea you're in love with her?"

"I have."

"And now you're leaving?" Jessica stepped out into the doorway, brow tilted in warning. "What do you plan to do about her?"

253

"Do about her?" David took his coat from the chair and slid his arms through it, rounding the desk, on a mission. "I plan to marry her."

Chapter Twenty-Five

David stepped out onto the veranda overlooking the garden, the midday sun chasing the chill of the morning away. It was uncustomarily warm for the end of November, enough that David walked down the pebbled path with his coat unbuttoned in search for his elusive would-be bride.

Mrs. Bradford had directed him toward the gardens, or the cottage situated behind the garden wall. Catherine's little refuge. She must have a close enough acquaintance with Mrs. Everill to request a full cottage to herself, which piqued David's curiosity once again about the mysterious benefactress. Something felt odd about this obscure great lady who failed to make her presence known but showered him with unimaginable kindness.

He neared the gazebo and saw the object of his search. She sat inside, knees drawn up on the bench, sketchbook in hand and hat off. She'd pinned her dark hair tight today, in one of those 'knots' his sister talked about, but the style elongated Catherine's neck as she bent to focus on her work.

His steps faltered, a sudden uncertainty slowing his step. Perhaps speaking to her another time, when she wasn't otherwise occupied, would be the best course. Besides, arguing with another strong-willed woman wasn't on his list of favorite things, and he knew his news wouldn't be welcome.

He looked back at her silhouette, her profile, and his chest expanded with the desire to be with her, to shower her with affection he'd never given to anyone else. To share a few days together as man and wife.

No, he wouldn't cower.

She must have heard his approach because she looked up from her work and ushered him into the gazebo with her smile. "To what do I owe this honor?" She placed her sketchpad on the bench beside her and swung her legs around to the floor. "A few private moments of the good doctor's time? This *is* momentous."

"Don't pretend we haven't had dinner together every day for the past week." His rebel gaze scanned her body. "And a few unplanned surreptitious meetings."

"My favorite kinds." An attractive blush rose into her cheeks, and she returned his daring perusal with one of her own. "But, mind you, 'few' being the key word."

"Dear Catherine, if I spend longer without a chaperone, I'm afraid of what I might do to you." He sat on the bench, leaving ample space between them. "My thoughts take a turn which I can't seem to control."

She sighed and looked away. "I suppose you're right. We should be careful, because if your thoughts delve into any imaginings like mine, it's perfectly scandalous."

He slid a little closer, searching her face. "You...you daydream of me in a...scandalous way?"

Her lips tilted into her most alluring smile, the one full of mischief. "Your kisses inspire a great deal of scandalous daydreams, David." She waved her hand in front of her face, flattering him with her innocent admission. "And your touch?" She closed her eyes, releasing a long sigh. "Your hands on my face or my hair make me wonder—"

Her eyes popped wide as if she just realized she spoke her thoughts aloud. He felt every word blazing like a fire through him. Yes, her daydreams joined his in their abject rebellion.

She faced him, her breath shallow. "I think you ought to change the subject."

"Excellent notion," he agreed, pulling his gaze from her lips and back to her eyes. "What if we talk of war?"

"Well, that will certainly cool the conversation to a proper temperature." She laughed and looked up at him.

Her face had grown so precious, her conversation and friendship a necessity in his life. How could he convince her of his choice to leave her behind and help his father? His country?

"What is it?" She studied him, a sudden wariness tightening her expression. "No, I don't think we should talk of war, after all. Let's speak of the beauty of the day or the welcome change of Mrs. Brock as the cook over the one at Roth, but let's not talk of war."

"We must."

She stood and walked to the entryway of the gazebo, her fingers to her head. "Why must we? People volunteer to serve. They're not forced to go."

"But some are compelled by the love they have for their family, for their country. It's a sense of duty and honor to serve."

She turned on him, eyes on fire. "What about your duty to the hospital? And the ones you love who are here?" She gestured toward the house. "Isn't this also your duty?"

"Catherine."

"We see the horrific results of this war every day. The pain, dismemberment, the death." She gripped the railing, her hands shaking. "What if you…"

He stood and walked toward her. "We could die anywhere, any day. Whether on the battlefield, in an automobile, by a Zeppelin attack. None of us are promised the next breath, but we are expected to do what we can with the breaths we have."

She searched his face, the pain in her eyes searing like a knife through his chest. "Can't you do those things here? With me?"

"Oh, Catherine." He attempted to take her into his arms, but she stepped out of his reach.

"You shouldn't have given me hope of your love and a future when now…now—"

He took her by the shoulders. "You still have my love and our future. Don't kill me off and bury me before I even leave." He gave her shoulders a little shake. "I serve to secure our future, not to end it, and I plead for your blessing."

"My blessing?" She closed her eyes, and tears slipped from beneath her lashes. A shudder passed through her, trembling his hands and resolve. "When do you hope to leave?"

He drew in a breath for strength. "I plan to be off within a week."

Her hand went to her chest, and she released a sound like a whimper. "A week?"

"The sooner I can help, the better."

She turned away from him, her shoulders bent to bear this burden, and he felt her pain. All the way to his core.

"You mean to leave before Christmas?"

"Lives are lost, lives I might save if I can treat them early enough." He wrapped his arms around her from behind, attempting to comfort her in some way. "Which brings me to another request."

Her body tensed. "I don't know that I care to hear anything else from you."

He leaned his cheek against her head and whispered near her ear. "Marry me?"

Well, that certainly evoked a response. She turned and blinked up at him as if he'd gone 'round the bend. "Marry you?"

"Before I leave." He took her face in his hands, trying to make her understand. "Let me be your husband and father to this child."

"You're mad if you think, just because you're leaving, that I will drop everything and marry you." The fight in her words didn't match the concern in her eyes. Perhaps she didn't have much fight left.

One could pray.

"This war is only influencing the speed at which we marry, not the reason. I love you. I've loved you since I took your hand to pray at your sister's bedside." He caressed her cheek with his thumb and dashed away a few more tears. "You already have my heart, let me give you my name as well so that the baby will have a name too."

The glint in her furious resolve crumbled a little. "Exactly how is a woman supposed to say 'no' to a request like that?"

"She's not." He grinned, touching his lips to hers for a moment. "She's supposed to say yes and put the poor fool out of his misery, then kiss him to ensure there's no doubt."

She looked down at his lips with a raised brow, then stepped out of his arms. "It is my understanding men do ridiculous things when they're off to war."

He wrapped his arms around her, warming her cheek with his lips. "I'm not someone who makes rash decisions."

"I seem to influence your impulsivity." Her voice turned breathless.

"Only in the best ways." Without hesitation, he drew her close until their faces were inches apart. "This is the right choice, Catherine. You and me. I'll leave knowing that when I return, you'll be here."

She touched his face, her gaze pleading in ways her words didn't. It tore through him into a gaping wound, an ache.

"And your dream? This hospital?"

"I've only waited to leave until the hospital reached a stable place. It's found that here at Beacon House. We have plenty of staff to cover my absence and—"

"What?" She pushed out of his arms, shaking her head. "Do you mean to tell me you're leaving because of Beacon House?"

"It's what we all wanted. A new hospital, closer to town, with the space and facilities we need." He'd just asked the woman to marry him, and she was angry over Beacon House?

"I can't believe this!" She stepped back until she hit the gazebo railing. "If I'd known securing you a site for the hospital would send you off to war, I'd never have given you my house."

"Your house?"

She pinched her mouth closed, her eyes circling to the size of a two pound. "I mean…"

"Beacon House is yours?"

Her shoulders sagged forward in resignation. "It was my inheritance from Grandmama."

"You're the benefactress?" He stepped back, trying to digest the news. All this time, he'd thanked God for the generosity of this unknown patron, while Catherine stood before him, giving away her inheritance. "You're wealthy now? You made all this happen?"

The truth about Beacon House confirmed her love more than words ever could. She'd given him a dream, and now…now he wanted to return the favor. His smile grew with a realization. By not only making her his wife, but fulfilling her dream.

Love.

How could he make her see?

"I didn't plan on you leaving as soon as the hospital became more established, I can assure you of that. I just wanted you to be happy."

She crossed her arms in front of her, the tears in her eyes a contradiction to the defiance in her stance.

"And if you married me, you'd make me the happiest man in the world."

Her lip quivered, but she made no other response. His beautiful, broken, stubborn woman!

An idea emerged into a plan. "I see the way of it. The reason why you won't marry me." He had to convince her of how ridiculous her arguments were.

"My reason? For what? For being angry at you for stealing my heart only to break it by leaving?"

"No," he sighed, backing away and looking down at the floor. "Why you refuse to marry me."

She dashed a tear away and sniffled. "Pray tell, what is the reason then?"

"A wealthy lady such as yourself wouldn't wish to marry a penniless surgeon."

She stared at him a full five seconds before responding. "Oh, David, don't be ridiculous."

"It's true. Perhaps our relationship was fine when we were equals, both struggling, but now..." He gestured toward her and the house beyond. "How can I compare to what you have? I see I've truly been played the fool."

She marched up to him and placed her hands on her hips, her gaze a fiery blue. "David Ross, I have never heard anything so utterly preposterous in all my life. I fell in love with you well before my inheritance, and I shall love you far beyond this war. I'd marry you if I was the queen and you were a pauper, and there's nothing you can say about it."

"You love me?" He pulled her into his arms.

Her eyes widened, caught. "I..."

"That's what I heard. I also heard you'd marry me."

She frowned, but didn't fight him. "Love you? Of course, I love you. It's the only thing keeping me from

260

slapping this idiotic notion out of that stubborn head of yours."

He nudged her chin up with his thumb and snuck another kiss. "How soon could you be ready, because I'm fairly certain, war or not, I have no desire to wait any longer to make you mine?"

She wrapped her arms around his waist and rested her head on his shoulder, an embrace he inwardly declared as his personal favorite. He lowered his lips to her hair and drew in a deep breath of lavender and Catherine.

"Three days," she whispered, tightening her hold. "I'll marry you in three days, but promise me one thing."

He leaned back to see her face. "Anything."

"You'll come back to me."

It was an odd experience, preparing one's heart for a wedding with a cloud of sadness nipping at one's heart. Catherine plucked at the delphiniums in the garden, gathering the last ones to use as decoration for the ceremony tomorrow. The days moved too quickly toward David's inevitable departure. Each glance, each moment, became suddenly more meaningful and tender. The 'stolen' ones were filled with more whispered endearments than breathtaking kisses, though David still managed to inspire many of those.

But in the late afternoon, Catherine reveled in the solitude.

The weather had turned steadily colder since David's proposal, a chill to hint at the upcoming distance, but she couldn't ponder on the future beyond the wedding. She refused the tears any more access and snipped away at the lovely purple-hued flowers with renewed vigor.

"How are you?" Ashleigh knelt down beside her.

Catherine swiped the back of her hand over her brow. "I'm trying to keep my mind preoccupied."

"I can see how that might be less painful."

Catherine sat back, glancing up at the sky. "I don't know that anything can make this less painful."

Ashleigh placed her hand over Catherine's. "You're getting married tomorrow. Married, dear sister. You're beginning a beautiful journey with a wonderful man."

Catherine looked down at the scattered flowers. "For how long? We have three days together before the train takes him away." She challenged the hope Ashleigh peddled. "What if three days is all I'll ever have?"

Tears glistened in her sister's eyes. "Do you love him?"

"Yes." Catherine's breath shuddered out in a quiet, broken sob. "Yes, I love him."

"Then celebrate these days enough to last a lifetime instead of grieving a lifetime in these few days." She took the clippers from Catherine's hands and placed them in her basket. "God has given you one of the greatest blessings a human can know—the opportunity to love someone, truly and deeply. Don't squander your love on fears and worries. Seize the moments you have."

The tears came then, hard and uncontrollable. Ashleigh wrapped her in her arms. "Do you know what I'm celebrating tomorrow? I'm celebrating having my sister again. I'm celebrating God's redemption of all the time we lost and the healing power of this love He's showered on us."

Catherine pulled back to look at her, blinking against the tears. "He has."

"I'm celebrating how He's used your passion and past to make miracles happen, not only for the women in this town, but for this hospital."

"Miracles?"

Ashleigh nodded through her tears. "And I'm celebrating the sweet union of two amazing people who plan to spend the rest of their lives together, no matter how long those lives may be." She rested her palms on Catherine's shoulders, steadying her. "But I plan to celebrate, because those moments of celebration are the balm of comfort in our heartaches, and a sweet caress in our sufferings."

Catherine lowered her gaze, the realization a healthy reprimand. Only a few weeks ago, she'd raged against David's love for her, feeling undeserving and scarred, and now? Now she fought against Providence with a fury because she thought he wasn't giving her what she deserved. Oh faithless heart! "You're right. I'm wallowing in what might be instead of reveling in what is." She smiled. "I've so many things to celebrate."

Ashleigh reached for the clippers and perched a brow. "And a man who desperately loves you."

Catherine's smile grew, the revelation dawning fresh and strong to beat against her fears. "Yes, he does, poor man. Thank you."

"It's what sisters are for." She wiggled her brows with anticipation. "So, let's finish these flowers and decorate a church."

Catherine looked up at the sky, sending a silent prayer to Heaven, her heart full with forgotten gratitude. "And let's have a wedding."

David would never forget his first look at his bride as she approached him down the aisle of the small country church. Her simple white gown made such a stark contrast to her ebony hair and red lips, and somehow reminded him of Christmas. And the French tulle veil, a gift from Madame Rousell, hung like an intricate halo over her beautiful face.

Apart from grace, God couldn't have given him a better gift.

The gathering had been small, the service unpretentious but filled with assurances from Scripture about the promise they made to each other. And then, the most remarkable thing happened. When the pastor made the final announcement, something in David shifted. A deep-set awareness of not only his promise, but also his freedom.

Catherine became his wife. He now reserved the honor of protecting her, providing for her, loving her, and enjoying her with abandon. He took his time appreciating every curve and dip of her body as they rode from the church to her cottage, their haven for the next three days. Mr. Coates brought the car up to the door and then left them alone.

Alone with Catherine, and it was perfectly acceptable— in fact, the idea awakened an odd combination of longing and sweltering anticipation. He took her hand and drew her through the narrow doorway into a cozy sitting room. The fireplace already flamed with a healthy fire and someone, most likely Mrs. Bradford or the new housekeeper for the cottage, Miss Potter, had made certain to leave a meal on the table in the adjoining room. A few chairs stood by the fire, as well as an elegant settee, large enough for two. The thought inspired a grin.

He took her coat and hung it on a hook by the door, appreciating anew the beauty of his bride as she stood before him in her gown for his own private viewing.

His thoughts spiraled into uncharted territory.

"I believe Mrs. Bradford and my sister thought of everything." Catherine filled the silence, her gaze faltering. "It seems all we need to do is...enjoy each other's company."

His plans exactly. He drew her wrist up to his mouth and placed a lingering kiss against the lavender scented place. Her intake of breath each time he performed this simplest of pleasures encouraged him to trail kisses up her arm to the elbow where her sleeve began, and this time, he did. There was no need to stop with one touch or kiss. No need to listen for voices in the hall or fear a disruption. "I think we can manage that, don't you?"

He'd expected a little of the feisty Catherine to appear, so this nervous bride awakened a somewhat predatory flint inside of him. The lover. The pursuer. Oh yes, he'd manage just fine.

"I have music." Catherine whispered, her smile softened with shyness. "But first, let me help you with your coat."

He turned to remove his coat and suit jacket, but before he could face her again, she stopped him by wrapping her arms around him from behind. Her body pressed into his back and her breath warmed his shoulder. "I love you, Dr. Ross."

Those words, uttered so sweetly, turned him around and soothed a bit of the inner-predator. He tipped her chin up and brushed a kiss against her lips. "I've loved you since our first prayer together. You stood there, bearing your soul, challenging my faith, with beautiful authenticity—"

"And lostness."

"Not anymore, my dear Kat." He chuckled. "And all that time, my heart knew you were meant for me from the start. My hard head took some time to catch up."

She cupped his cheek, touching a chaste kiss to his chin. "We both suffer from the same malady, I'm afraid. A solid dose of stubbornness."

He grinned and looked at her beautiful hair, swept into a mass on her head. "May I take down your hair?"

Her eyes widened. "What?"

He took a loose tendril hanging by her temple and slid it between his fingers. "Please, allow me the honor of taking down your hair."

She stared up at him, her smile halted by surprise, and then she took his hand. Slowly, she guided him through the small dining area and up a narrow flight of stairs to a door which led into a large bedroom. The bed took up most of the room and offered much more space than the settee downstairs, and tempted his imagination. She brought him to a dressing table and then she took a seat in front of the mirror.

"Do you know what to do?"

Having a mother and sister helped him a little. Carefully, he began the process, reveling in the intimacy of this touch and distracted by watching her reaction in the mirror.

Each pin released another strand of loose, black curls falling around her shoulders against the white gown. If his fingers brushed the bare skin around her neck, she'd shiver and close her eyes, as if the touch brought pleasure with it.

It did to him too.

As he removed the last pin, he stepped back, captivated. "You're beautiful."

Her breath shivered, holding his gaze through the reflection. "You make me feel beautiful."

He trailed a hand through her hair, loose and heavy. "It's no hardship, I assure you."

She closed her eyes again, leaning back against his stomach to request more of his touch. His fingers slipped through her tresses, spreading them out over her shoulders, kissing them, drinking in the scent.

"Wait." She straightened and then stood, turning to pat his chest. "I forgot the music."

He couldn't get enough of her disheveled and intimate beauty, dark masses falling around the shoulders of her white gown in glorious disarray. His body responded with a need to draw her closer and drown his face in lavender and ebony silk. "We have music?"

"Indeed we do." She slipped from his hold to a table by the window which held the gramophone. "It made me think of you, and I longed to dance with you…like this."

Like this. Together. Alone. Where neither had to stop once the music ended.

The popular tune *If I Had My Way* crooned from the recording plate into the room. She returned to wrap her arms around him, her body melting against him, igniting a renewed curiosity. She rested her head on his shoulder and pressed a kiss against his neck, encouraging the smoldering flame in his chest to sparks.

He slid his hands up her arms to her neck, its smoothness igniting a need to investigate. Her eyes fluttered closed, a sweet sigh purring from her, and his kiss chased her lavender scent from her temple, to her cheek, her jawbone, and after a second's hesitation, he wandered to her neck, a new sense of freedom giving him boldness. Oh the taste of her skin! The intoxication of her body. He'd never imagined it could be so sweet and scorching at once.

Her hands on his back flexed, pulling at his shirt. Her gasp encouraged him to continue his perusal, reveling in this freedom to explore his beautiful wife. *His* wife. She clung to him, as if her legs failed to support her any longer, so he swooped her up into his arms and stepped to a nearby chair, settling her on his lap. No more distance. No more waiting.

He'd already loosened his shirt collar, leaving it opened and unbuttoned enough to view more skin beneath his neckline. Catherine smoothed her fingers over his chest, slipping her hand underneath the cloth and then teasing open the next button. His green eyes shadowed to a darker hue, and she released another button.

She wanted to take her time, embrace every discovery with her sweet husband. The title brought a smile. Instead of the passionate and empty encounter she'd known with Drew, this moment, this choice, was bound by something much deeper and more beautiful because of their promises. Their covenant of love, with God's blessing. This remarkable unveiling of two people committed in heart and spirit.

"I have waited a very long time to celebrate my wedding night."

The meaning behind his declaration took Catherine's breath. "You mean you've never…"

"No." He brushed his fingers down her neck, muddling her mind.

She pulled her thoughts from the glorious warmth, her heart breaking at what she couldn't offer him. "Oh David. I'm sorry I—"

He silenced her with a gentle kiss. "No, Kat." He tipped up her chin. "Focus on me and my love for you." He brushed another kiss against one cheek. "Not the past." His lips warmed her other cheek. "But us. Man and wife." His palms slipped up her neck to caress her face, his eyes a smoldering flame. "Lovers."

He kissed her again, another too brief temptation.

His brow perched in a playful way. "You're such an excellent teacher, might you be my guide in helping me make memories tonight?"

"Ones we can hold in our hearts while we're apart."

His tender gaze warmed her face like a caress. His fingers slid to the back of her gown, carefully unfastening the first button. "And I plan to take my time."

He left a lingering kiss at the juncture between her neck and her ear, spilling heat from his lips down through her chest.

Another button loosened. Then another.

Oh he didn't need her guidance. He was getting off to a fabulous start without her help at all.

His mouth moved lower, deliberate and unhurried, as if relishing the taste. "And savor each new discovery about you." His words warmed her collar bone.

Love for him pressed in on her chest with such force. Such fullness. She took his face between her palms and poured all her pent up love into the kiss. The exquisite beauty. The tenderness and gratitude. She offered much more than a lover's kiss, but a lifelong promise.

She was his. Only his.

"David, I love you as I've never loved before."

He rewarded her words with a kiss which traveled from her lips down to her neck and back again. "And I love you, my dear Mrs. Ross." His gaze shone with desire and sweet adoration. "As I've never loved before."

He stood and carried her toward the bed. "Only you." His declaration whispered in time with the song. "Only you."

Chapter Twenty-Six

November 26, 1915

My dearest Catherine,

I left Ednesbury Station three hours ago and I've contemplated returning at each train stop. The vision of you on the platform in your pale blue suit, alone, waving to me through your tears, is branded into my mind. Please forgive me. The past three days with you, I've lived and loved a lifetime. Even now, as I close my eyes against the stuffy view of the inside of this train, I feel you next to me in our bed, your hair strewn in beautiful disarray upon your pillow and your eyes showing me the tenderness and passion of your love.

I cannot tell what the days will bring, but I am certain of our love to weather the trials.

Write to me, my Kat, and pray for a speedy end to this war so we can be together soon.

With all my love,

David

December 1, 1915

My dear Dr. Ross,

I warned you in advance that I am a poor correspondent, so keep your expectations admirably low and I should meet them. I received your letters in one bundle yesterday, and I kissed each one as I opened them, hoping by some miracle you'll feel my love for you across the miles.

Mother has begun Christmas preparations for Roth Hall. Since she is only housing the orphanage now, and she has two wealthy daughters who will cover costs, she's inspired to offer another fundraiser for the town. Dr. Pike volunteered to help her, his admiration as plain as the moustache on his face. It's truly a puzzle to work out how the two of them 'found each other,' but I suppose many people say the same about us. In fact, I'm daily in awe of your love – if indeed it was love and not a massive lapse in your judgment. However, if it is the latter, you have married me, and to my eternal gratitude, you are stuck with me, for I have no plans of releasing you from your promise.

The hospital is doing well. Ashleigh and Sam have become excellent administrators, consulting Dr. Hudson and Pike as needed. I've reduced my shifts there to two days instead of four, so I can work more with my designs and manage the affairs of Beacon House. It might be wise for you to return home soon before I spend all of our money on homeless women and orphaned waifs.

Please pray for Jane. She gave birth to her twins this week and only one of the darlings survived. A boy. I helped with the delivery and had never experienced such sadness and joy mingled together. The awesome miracle of birth followed much too swiftly by the aching loss of death. Despite Madame's urging, Jane has given the baby over to the orphanage. I cannot fathom the agony of separating oneself from one's child. It is already painful enough to have you so far away, and for a good cause. To distance yourself from your child by choice? It's unimaginable.

All the more now, as this little one grows inside me, becoming an active presence in my life with each day, I can't fathom losing her or giving her away. How Jane must grieve the loss!

Well, you are to be duly impressed with my letter. I shall write to you again soon, but remember 'soon' might be interpreted with some degree of relativity. Know this: every night as I lay in our bed, I place my hand on your pillow and pray for your safety. I pray God will bless your work and fetch you home to me. I thank Him for bringing such a man into my life who is not only strong, brave, and noble, but is kind, gentle, tender, and passionate. I'm fond of all of your many attributes, but I've particularly enjoyed your passion.

Yours,

Catherine
There were no words to describe the devastation. Fields which had been green and thriving months before now stood in a wasteland of mud and half-destroyed buildings, littered with the dead or dying. The Casualty Clearing Station to which David and Jessica had been assigned was housed in an abandoned theatre. Holes from shell explosions provided some natural light into the building, but mostly, they performed surgery by lantern light.

It was a far change from the gilded halls, warm rooms, and soft beds of home, especially the bed he'd shared just before leaving. Keeping positive remained a constant battle. David had treated many war wounds, but the severity of wounds coming directly from the Front turned his stomach at times.

"The stretcher bearers are bringing in another group." Dr. Richard Cramer pushed open the tent door and marched in. "At least five new ones."

Dr. Cramer, a Belgian surgeon, prided himself on punctuality and knowledge. Anything else seemed to be a useless endeavor. He'd taken a slight interest in David and Jessica, commenting on the quality of their work, but otherwise he kept to himself and his patients.

"I'm sorry we weren't assigned to Father's station." Jessica moved next to him at the basin, washing her hands to prepare for the new surgeries. "I know you'd hoped to be closer."

"They send us where we're needed." Though he'd prefer to know of his father's safety instead of remain in constant uncertainty. The weariness of relentless death, minimal sleep, and the dark days of winter, bred a kind of lethargy of spirit.

"Any news from home?" His sister's eyes glinted with their purpose. The shadow of the Front was probably too afraid to tempt Jessica into its melancholy.

Jessica knew the way to get his mind back on good things. "I received two letters yesterday, written about three days apart." He grinned. "She's getting better."

His sister shook her head and set out a clean panel of instruments for surgery. "You've certainly motivated her toward improvement."

"The improvement is mutual."

Though Jessica kept a tough demeanor, David caught the softening around her eyes. "And with Christmas coming next week? Have you sorted out what to get this woman who has the money to buy whatever she wants?"

"Oh yes."

"Arriving." Someone shouted from the front of the station.

"I just hope it reaches her by Christmas."

Catherine's eyes threatened to close before she reached her bed. She pulled herself up the stairs, weary from a week of endless activity. Her mother's fundraiser had proved a success, but not without every staff member at Beacon, as well as some soldiers, pitching in to help. She'd purchased two more small properties from Lady Cavanaugh, and ten new wounded had arrived three days ago, adding to the hectic schedule.

The old Catherine would have guffawed at the new Catherine. A woman with substantial means serving the wounded and outcast with no ulterior motive? What a difference God's love and a good man made!

Her bed welcomed her into its pillowed comfort and she rolled on her back, waiting for her usual good-night routine from the baby. Within minutes, the typical movements began, stronger than they'd been at first, more pronounced. She placed her hand on her abdomen, trying to make some connection, the same inexplicable sweetness seizing her heart.

She sighed and looked over to the window. The dark silhouette of ridges on the horizon took her thoughts to North Carolina and a childhood riddled with anger and secrets. Her parents' relationship was tenuous at best, destructive at worst. And her mother? Not an example Catherine wished to emulate. A steady change of nannies had moved through their home, discharged at her mother's whim unless they left of their own accord. Grandmama had provided something solid. A gauge of love and truth, which Catherine rebelled against but never ceased to respect.

And now? Now she'd have the opportunity to be a mother. She closed her eyes and whispered a silent prayer for strength and wisdom to love well.

David's pillow nestled, unmoved, beside hers. She ran her palm across its cool cloth, adding another prayer for him to her list, wishing he could spend Christmas with her. Their first Christmas.

A small package on the bedside table caught her attention. She slid to the edge of the bed and drew the tiny box into her hands. David's familiar handwriting quickened her pulse. The baby even moved in a celebratory tumble. Catherine made quick work of the wrappings and opened the card atop the box.

December 10, 1915

My dearest Catherine,

I send a short note to accompany this gift, which I hope will reach you by Christmas. I had wanted to present it to you on our wedding day, but it hadn't arrived from North Carolina. Wear it knowing you are as precious to me as the love surrounding this ring. It was the one my father gave to my mother on their wedding day.

The central gem reminded me of your eyes and the surrounding gems are like starlight.

Happy Christmas. My heart is with you as you celebrate our Savior's birth and work for His good every day. May He bring me to you soon so that I may gaze into your sapphire eyes, or watch the stars with you in my arms. You and the little one are in my prayers as ever.

Until I return, my love,

David

She was a slobbering mess by the end of the note, but that didn't stop her from blinking back her tears and opening the small box. It housed an exquisite surprise. A delicate masterpiece, set in silver gold, with a cluster of tiny diamonds surrounding a sapphire. She slid the ring onto her finger and kissed it, her heart aching for his touch. His smile. Him.

She grabbed his pillow and hugged it against her chest, burying her head into it to catch any remaining scents of peppermint. *Oh, dear God, please bring him home to me.*

Weariness poured over David's body and the overall depressed mood of the day didn't help. More cold rain. The futility of his work, this war, became a constant struggle within his prayers to pursue hope. Stories rushed in from all Fronts where soldiers would agree to a truce for a reprieve in some of the senseless battling and bloodshed. Most of the soldiers held no ill-will toward the opposing forces except that it was their duty to fight.

Dr. Cramer had taken a particular interest in observing David's surgeries. Of course, the Belgian was a supervising doctor in the station which served mostly French casualties, but his demeanor meant to intimidate, adding another loathsome blow to David's battle for optimism.

Jessica helped. Her dry wit provided solace and perspective among the gray and brown hues of war….and then there were the letters. He'd received two the same day, but he reread his favorite just before falling asleep.

January 5, 1916

My dearest Dr. Ross,

It is a new year, in case you've been remiss to notice, and I have great hopes this year will bring you back to me. I am proud to report that I delivered my first baby yesterday. A healthy little girl. Annie is quite undone by the bundle of ruddy glow and round skin. She's named the angel Clara, after her mother. It was a true miracle, not only the physical procedure, but the very fact I neither killed Annie nor the baby in the process. You would have been proud, I am certain.

Also, we've had another shipment of wounded arrive and I am making space in the third floor of Beacon so the staff can move there and give more soldiers the bedrooms on the second level. You would not believe the antiquities I've discovered. There are gowns stored there which I am certain belonged to Queen Victoria in her early years. Remarkable beading, truly. Nothing as remarkable as this ring I wear with enough pride to shame my mother, but quite lovely, nonetheless.

You will hardly recognize Ednesbury, or at least the east side. There is a glow of hope and general optimism spreading from shop to shop, some in part due to Pierre Baudin's marvelous newspaper, and some in part to the people purchasing their own properties. I will tell you more of this grand adventure when I see you, but I've come to realize the great value in ownership. It is one thing to purchase properties so that the people can rent from a kinder landowner, but it is quite another to make the people their own landowners. Pierre was the first to buy, and I've never seen a man so changed. He looks at least ten years younger, and if I'm not mistaken, even resurrected a few hairs for his head.

Days are terribly busy, but I am grateful for them. It is the nights in which I long for you most. In the quiet of our little haven, I close my eyes and drown in a reminiscent state. Your smile, your touch, your kiss. Oh, to have more than memory and an empty room! I've contemplated on several occasions, if you were to be given leave, you'd never return to war, for I would lock you in our bedroom and feed the key to Mr. Coates' Great Dane. I can think of few things quite as lovely as being locked in a bedroom with you.

I trust God is giving you ample opportunity to serve your country. I know of no one so noble and kind. Please hold to your kindness until your return and keep your nobility for others. I prefer you to be an utter rogue with me in private.

I send you my love in every word...or at least every word which seems lovely. I doubt there is much love housed in Mr. Coates' Great Dane or Pierre Baudin's bald head, but in many of the other phrases, think of me. You are in my thoughts as constantly as the English rain.

Come home soon, my dear doctor. My heart has been at the trenches much too long, but more than anything, keep your hope. Your love has taught me how to hope, so I shall. I shall keep hoping, with each new sunrise, you'll make your way back to our little haven and to me.

And do not find the scent of peppermint too appalling when you enter. I have a potted plant of it in every room. Not only does it remind me of you, but I've also discovered it keeps Mother from overstaying her welcome.

With all my love,

Kat

January 15, 1916

My lovely Kat,

Three letters in one week! You know the way to my heart, darling. Words from you. Whether they are of grand news, sad news, or dull, they are from you, and I gladly drink them in. I must admit to finding particular pleasure in the ones related to bedrooms, pillows and missing keys.

You have grown so precious to me, even in this distance. Your letters bring scents of your love on every line, even the ones related to Mr. Coates' Great Dane. I can almost see your smile as you wrote about Monsieur Bauldin or the birth of Annie's daughter. Oh, to kiss your smile once again.

I find myself increasingly grateful and awestruck by this powerful love, one for which I cannot express in warm embraces or prolonged kisses at the moment, but I long for the day. Thoughts of you blow through this dreary world of war like the cool breeze of summer, refreshing my spirit and giving me cause to ponder on sweeter times.

Do you realize how the scent of lavender lingers on your letters? I keep all of them in my satchel, and when I open it, I'm flooded with the welcome scent of you, and I recall you in all of your ravishing beauty. Just the thought of our time together, even now, knocks the chill out of the billowing winter wind in my tent.

I would not wish you here, even for a second of comfort. This world is a bleeding, dying, fiery place. Each night, I pray that you visit me in my dreams. There, I find a safe and tender haven of memory for us. I cling to the hope in your words and look forward to your letters like my breath. You are such to me.

Your enamored and grateful husband,

David

Mr. Coates delivered another box to Catherine's cottage from Grandmama's third story office. She studied it, reluctant to begin another fruitless treasure hunt. Yesterday's findings had unearthed a single shoe, a moldy lock of hair, and a moth-eaten emerald hat, none of which required sorting into files for later.

At the bottom of the box, beneath the mounds of faded paper and castoff trinkets, Catherine unearthed a small, decorative box, with tiny portraits painted on each paneled side. The scenes resembled the rolling hills of Derbyshire in various seasons of the year. Catherine smoothed her hand over the designs. Finally, a bit of treasure.

Inside waited a stack of letters, tied together with a red ribbon. A chill moved over her skin as she touched the time-worn pages. Catherine untied the ribbon and opened the first letter, her breath wedging closed as the realization dawned. These were Grandmama's love letters from Lord Jeffrey Cavanaugh.

Oh dear, her dull day just took a three-volume novel turn. How delightful! But as she studied the sweet, passionate notes, the dates posed a quandary. There were ample letters from their courtship and engagement, but then a second half of the letters came after a year's absence.

Sentences began to tell a shocking story. *My beloved, how can I have you bear this shame alone, when I am the cause of your circumstances?*

My love will always be yours, in heart, soul, and body... I have led you to sin against God and your husband. Forgive me. I cannot live in this house with another when my soul burns for you. Why does the hand of a family's anger have to rip our lives apart?

Will your husband forgive you? Will he keep you from shame? I promise to provide for this child you carry – a sweet memory forged from our secret passions.

With each letter, the story became clear. Uncle William was Lord Jeffrey Cavanaugh's child, conceived while both Grandmama and Lord Cavanaugh were married to others. Their violent separation, brought on by their families' bitterness, tore them apart prematurely, but they continued a love affair for a year.

Everything started to make sense. The large sums of money to Uncle William from a wealthy yet anonymous benefactor, the hints of Grandmama's story through Lady Hollingsworth, and even Grandmama's apropos comfort to Catherine's situation through her letters.

Grandmama was a fallen woman.

Catherine stared down at the papers, digesting the information with a strange mixture of disbelief, grief, and then sweet admiration. Grandmama had ended their romance amicably, begging his forgiveness and pleading for God's, appealing to her desire to choose and love her husband better in the future than she had in the past. A half-written letter in Grandmama's hand, smudged and probably rewritten, waited at the end of the stack.

We cannot live in what was, dear Jack. We must move beyond our past and build a future, even if our hearts are torn. I have caused great pain to a good man, a man who has chosen to love me despite my unfaithfulness. I now choose to love him and pray for God's forgiveness for my sin.

Our connection was something beautiful once, but it cannot be so anymore. Please understand and know there is a place in memory where you will always hold my heart, but in memory it must remain.

Catherine thought of her Grandfather Dougall, with his kind eyes and unfettered laughter. He'd died when Catherine was only ten, but she never forgot how her grandparents doted on one another, like to young lovers, or her grandfather's tenderness toward Grandmama, or how grievously she'd mourned at his passing.

Love worked miracles, even when it was undeserved....or, perhaps, especially when it was undeserved. Just as Christ's love had done for her.

Catherine folded the letters and placed them back in the box. This secret was hers to keep, and this grace lesson hers to remember.

February 3, 1916

Oh, my dearest David,

My heart is broken. Annie's sweet Clara died in her sleep three nights ago. I have no words for such devastation. I know I shouldn't write to you of sad times, since I am certain you receive a daily helping of them, but I cannot hold back my heartache. I've tried to comfort Annie as best I can, but I would have craved your wisdom in it, for you know my tendency toward bluntness. All I could think to say amidst the gnawing ache of grief was what God has taught me over these last months of grieving my sin and longing for you.

God holds us. We are protected by his grip in such a precious way that the good and the bad must pass through his fingers to us. No harm, fear, or pain can reach us without his allowance, and yet, it is a loving grip. A loving allowance we cannot understand until time has frayed our pride and tempered our heartbreak. And even then, our only answer may be to trust His love more than our understanding.

Our world is a broken place. Young men are being killed and killing one another. The constant barrage of death and poverty appears to have no rhyme or reason. It's all topsy-turvy and shattered. That's why we need someone who can take our pieces and somehow create a beautiful portrait through the pain...in the pain.

Even in this grief, in this longing for justice, He cradles us close.

I've learned that I have two options. I can scream to the heavens of the injustice, which I am prone to do and for which God's ears must be deeply panged, and harden my heart to God's work whether down the easy path or the path of suffering...or I can trust in the One who knows my wretched, complaining heart, who loves me as I am, and understands the best way to take broken pieces and mend them back together for his glory.

I had no answers for her. I am not God, for which I'm reminded every time I try to control my world, but I wished to give her comfort...some semblance of hope in the middle of her pain. Do you think I gave the right answer? Did I pour salt in her gaping wound with unfeeling words?

Oh, I pray I did not.

You would have known what to say. You, with all your generosity and tenderness!

The conscription was introduced last week and has caused many tears among the families of our dear village. More separation. More pain. Oh, David, I wish to cry with the psalmist, how long, O Lord? How long?

Please know that I think of you throughout my day, wishing my soul could reach out to touch yours across the miles. I ache for you. I cannot wait to rest within your arms again and know you are safe.

Yours,

Catherine

Another long shift of unending work left David exhausted. Even Jessica's tireless energy waned from the strain. They'd moved north-east to a field hospital set up to serve the casualties in a place called Verdun. Along the Meuse River, it was probably once a beautiful countryside until the French artillery lines and German bombardment rendered the river banks a wasteland.

David and Jessica finished a late shift and walked together through the wet night to their tents, the tireless rain adding insult.

"Französisch verstärkungen kamen gestern. "

The words whispered in harsh German from a nearby tent. David grabbed Jessica's arm and pulled her behind him, carefully following the voice. David's German was infantile, but he recognized something in the statement about French reenforcements.

"...nehmen Sie die Westbank."

It sounded like someone was sharing French strategem. A German, working among them? The very idea burned a line of fury up through David with such force, not even the frigid air left memory on his skin.

The cold chill of metal at the base of his neck stalled his turn toward his sister.

"Dr. Ross, what a shame."

David turned to face the unwelcome end of a pistol and the sardonic grin of Dr. Richard Cramer.

"You are a very good doctor, so it gives me no pleasure to spill your blood." His accent smoothed into thick German. "We are not monsters. We value strength and nobility."

"Betraying people to mass murder is neither noble nor strong," David took a look at his periphery, praying Jessica had run for help.

"It depends on which side you're on, ja?" He chuckled and waved his gloved hand in the air for someone to approach. "Your skill will be useful to me, but I cannot keep you here to tell your friends about my duplicity."

David straightened, and a vision of Catherine flashed in his mind. *Forgive me.*

"You'll have to kill me, Doctor. I'm not going with you."

The man tsked. "Brave words. Brave and stupid."

Another man emerged, cloaked in black and midnight. David's blood ran cold. The man had Jessica pinned against him.

Dr. Cramer kept his gaze on David but turned the pistol toward his sister. "Ja, good doctor, I think you will come with me."

Chapter Twenty-Seven

"I should have known."

Catherine had barely crossed the threshold of Madame's shop before Lady Cavanaugh caught her arm. "How dare you make me the fool!"

"The fool? I make a point to stay very far out of your way."

"You insult me further by spitting your lies to my face! I should have known you would be just like her. The same feigned piety. The same deceptive plans. Oh, to see the end of such a despicable family line would be too soon for me."

Catherine stood against the insipid remarks, taking them and maintaining some composure, but only with God's help. Her initial reaction was to gather up the nearest mannequin head and toss it at the woman's atrocious hat.

"Now you too have gone behind my back and stolen what was mine."

"I've never stolen anything from you."

A humorless laugh resurrected from her wrinkled snarl. "No? What about Catherine Everill? You're not the only one with pretenders and spies, my dear. All it took was for one of my former employees to work here long enough to gain information, and, for the right price, share the truth. That Catherine Everill is nothing more than the proprietor of a whore house glossed up as a dress salon."

"I'm sorry for what was taken from you years ago. For the trust that was broken."

Lady Cavanaugh stepped back, the fight seeping from her expression like a withering flower.

"I cannot imagine the wounds left behind by such a deception. Wounds which have hardened to bitterness and revenge." Catherine stepped forward, gentling her reply. "But your pain doesn't give you the right to steal hope from others. Madame's shop is a legitimate display of not only impeccable fashion but impeccable grace. These people you squash underfoot deserve a second chance to make things right."

Her snarl returned. "There is only one way to deal with your kind." Her tone took a sinister turn. "Not all love you, Catherine Dougall. Your plans to take my property from me, to reestablish old businesses which have outshone new ones, have incurred their own enemies. This *Beacon* of yours has cost people their employment as well."

And Pierre was quick to hire Mr. Dandy's castoffs. Catherine refused to shrink under the threats and intimidation. There would always be people who battled against grace and goodness, but better still, there would be those who rise for God's truth, open-handed and open-hearted.

"My Lady, I don't own your former properties."

"I know you are the one who bought them, regardless of the actress you hired as your secretary."

"Yes, I bought them." Catherine turned to the people in the busy shop. "I'm Catherine Everill, the designer of the clothes most of you wear now. I'm also Catherine Ross, wife of the quite remarkable Dr. David Ross, and I happen to work with Madame Rousell to hire seamstresses who have no work and who would be considered fallen women in search of redemption." She turned back to Lady Cavanaugh. "Now, the damage is done. The word is out, and I'm not afraid of it. If you wish to obtain your former properties, you'll have to ask the current owners for their prices. My goal was to give this town to its people."

She offered an incomprehensible blink.

Catherine tried once more. "Can't you find it in your heart for the good of Ednesbury, if not your own heart, to forgive those who've wronged you and help build this village into the place it once was? The place your husband loved."

Lady Cavanaugh shook her head and backed to the door, swinging it wide. "Don't try your silvery tongue on me. You know nothing of the pain in my past, and I'll not give you—especially you—rest if I cannot obtain it myself."

She slung the door closed behind her with such force the bell flew across the room and landed in the middle of the undergarments section. Catherine stared at the closed door, sighed, and then turned to the shop, brightening her smile. "French shops? French drama."

But the outward humor only sank so deep against the nip of Lady Cavanaugh's threat. How desperate and vengeful could bitterness make someone?

Feb 21, 1916

My darling wife,

I have been reassigned to a field hospital in northern France and only arrived a few days ago. The hospital is a portable sort, so medical equipment is minimal, but it seems we might be entrenched here for some time. I must make my letter brief since I am called to meet with the other surgeons, but I wanted to get down a few lines before the mail went out.

I miss you. Your conversation, your pacing with an idea, your fiery spirit and passionate love.

Do you remember the night you stumbled upon me in the hallway outside your room? The one in which you readily prayed with me? It was the first time I'd seen all of your magnificent hair, free and beautiful. I was pondering the sweetness of that moment, the glint of love's taste. To touch your hair again. To unpin it and reveal all its glory. How I miss you!

Do not tease me of entrapments, for I am the captivated one. You, my darling, have captivated me with your love. Who, but God, could have designed a plan to take you with your past and me with my pride and combine the two so perfectly? Forgive my prolonged absence from you. Forgive my desperate need to conquer the world of war.

Should God bring me home, I will redeem the lost time with enough passion to compete with yours. Key or not.

Always remember how much I love you, my darling.

David

Catherine pressed the letter against her chest. It was the last one she'd received from him, followed by a month of painful silence. There had been times when his letters came in a bunch after two weeks, but a full month? She set the paper on her desk and returned to her sketch. A colorful little tea gown in linen to welcome in the spring. She couldn't imagine fitting into it at present.

A knock came from the door. "Mrs. Ross?"

"Come in, Mrs. Bradford."

The woman walked forward, a delicious bundle of letters in her hands. "I thought you might not wish to wait for these until you returned to the house, so I brought them straight away."

Catherine stood so quickly her chair almost toppled. "You are a darling, Mrs. Bradford. Remind me to bring you a box of chocolates."

"Don't tease me with such nonsense, Miss. There'll be no place for chocolates around here."

Catherine raised a finger. "There's always room for chocolates." She took the package from the housekeeper and slid her palm over the precious envelopes, then stopped.

These letters weren't from David.

They were her own.

Ones she'd sent to him, returned. The strength in her legs fled with the air in her lungs. She stumbled back into her chair.

"Miss?" Mrs. Bradford rushed forward. "What is it?"

Catherine looked up, frigid shock spreading through her. "Something's terribly wrong."

Catherine stood on the platform of Victoria Station, staring at the engine in front of her. She'd sneaked from Beacon House two days after receiving David's returned letters, making Mrs. Bradford swear secrecy. Telegrams and telephoning provided no answers to his whereabouts, growing a relentless, maddening anxiety. She'd made it all the way to London before reality seeped through desperation.

How would she ever find him?

Fruitless attempts to obtain information regarding David or Jessica's whereabouts from London, even with Madame's brother-in-law's contacts, proved the incomprehensible truth. She had to wait.

Like countless other wives with returned letters, she had to wait for the yawning unknown.

And she wouldn't risk the baby's welfare, though if she'd been on her own, she might very well have tried. It was a lonely and sobering endeavor to purchase a return ticket to Ednesbury with no more news than she had before.

"Help." A woman's piercing cry echoed down the platform line. "Is there a doctor? This man. He's bleeding."

Catherine turned in the direction of the cry, pushing the people aside.

"I'm a doctor." An older gentleman emerged from the crowd, his dusty gold hair sprinkled with gray. He leaned over a young man in uniform, an amputee.

"He fell from the train steps." The woman continued. "I saw him. Went limp as a fish."

Blood gushed from his fresh amputation and another small puddle formed at his head. Catherine moved close. "I can help you."

The man examined her with shrewd emerald eyes, a kinship in his look. "Very good." He looked passed her shoulder. "Steward, where can we see to this man?"

The steward took them to a small room inside the station. Barking orders and using what supplies he housed in his black bag, together, they managed to stop the man's bleeding.

"You are very good with sutures," her murmured as she worked.

She shot him a grin. "I've been told that before."

Her response encouraged a return smile. The first one she'd seen, and somehow, it reminded her of David. Her heart squeezed in revulsion at the terrifying unknown.

They stabilized the poor man and sent him off with medics to the local hospital.

"It was a good thing we were nearby, or I fear the lad would have bled out. Thank you for your help."

"We all must pitch in where we can." Catherine held out her hand. "I'm glad you happened to be in the vicinity to save his life. I suppose you were catching a north bound train as well?"

"You're not from London?" He scanned her body, his brow peaked. "I assumed in your condition, you'd stay close to home."

She shrugged a shoulder. "Sensible women would follow that rule, but I have a tendency to dance between sensible and irrational. In this case, I was determined to travel all the way to France and find my husband. He's gone missing."

"I'm truly sorry."

"At least I stopped before I made it to Southampton, yes?"

"So you come all this way with a plan to find, and possibly rescue, your husband?" His grin inched wider. "You're either fiercely loyal or stark, raving mad."

"I find the line indiscriminate at times, I'm afraid."

His eyes lit with a humor she somehow recognized. "But with the best intentions, I can tell."

"Most of the time, I hope."

A smile of admiration teased the corners of his blond and gray mustache. "What man could manage such passion? You could keep him alive by sheer will with the amount of determination you have in your bones. He wouldn't dare die."

"I hope you're right."

The doctor shook his head and laughed, offering his hand in introduction. "Dr. Ross, a pleasure to—"

"Dr. Alexander Ross?"

He inclined his head. "Yes?"

Catherine grappled for her next breath. "I should've known. You look just like him. He looks just like you."

The doctor's face paled, his eyes searching her face with an intensity that definitely reminded her of David. "Catherine Dougall?"

His outstretched hand paused in mid-air. A wrinkle of fear crept into her throat, and her body braced for his rejection or disdain. Instead, the man took her hand with both of his and leaned down to kiss it.

His spreading smile exploded into laughter. "I knew the woman of whom my son wrote with such admiration had to be spectacular, but I wasn't quite prepared for how very far your influence reaches, Miss Dougall...or I should say, Mrs. Ross?"

"What do you mean?"

His eyes took on a hint of mischief. Would David age with such ravishing good looks intact?

"I am on my way to Ednesbury. It's taken all these months for an important letter to finally reach me at the Front." He looked down the row of cars and back to her. "And now, to find you here? In an attempt to—" All humor left his face. "David is missing."

"I don't know."

He put his arm around her shoulders and moved her toward the train. "I want you to tell me everything, and along the way, I'll tell you how your connection with Lady Hollingsworth brought about the restoration of my inheritance."

"What?"

"In fact, you've made me an earl, my dear." His gaze grew intense. "And as an earl, I may have some power to discover where our boy is."

Catherine stared at him, numb. How could she have had anything to do with the elder Lord Cavanaugh and his choices? As they found their seats on the train, Dr. Ross began to abate Catherine's curiosity with an explanation.

"Lady Hollingsworth is a close friend to the elder Lady Cavanaugh, my grandmother. Due to her correspondence with you, she encouraged my grandparents to reconsider my disinheritance based on all the honorable choices I and my son have made for the country and well-being of Ednesbury. This conversation continued over months, at which time little discoveries began to show Jeffrey's wife's poor use of funds and the awareness that Drew is not a legitimate heir."

"What?"

"I mean to say, the lady of Ednesbury court's only son, the one who should have received the Cavanaugh entail, was not legitimate. He was conceived out of spite when the lady learned of her husband's affair with…" He bowed his head in apology. "With your grandmother."

"I know of it." Catherine said. "But not of Lady Cavanaugh's indiscretion."

"It seems very few knew of it, except those closest to Jeffrey and your grandmother. Lord and Lady Hollingsworth happened to be some of those."

"And now…now you're to inherit?" Catherine blinked, too stunned to fully comprehend it.

"Yes." His voice grave. "But I would give it all back if it meant ensuring my son's safety."

"Of course, Dr. Ross."

"Call me Alexander." He smiled softly. "After all, we're family, and we'll find him together, whatever it takes."

The car drew up to Beacon House amidst chaos. Two servants stood outside, talking together. Mr. Palmer addressed a stranger at the door, and Mrs. Bradford rushed out to meet her as soon as she exited the car.

"Mrs. Ross. It's a miracle you've turned back from your plan. I prayed you would, and just in time too." Her smile brimmed, which was quite an unfamiliar sight. "He's here."

"Who's here, and what is all this?" Catherine waved toward the stranger.

"It's the car that brought Dr. Ross and Nurse Ross back from the station."

Catherine froze, exchanged a look with Alexander, and took off as fast as her cumbersome body would allow. Alexander followed close behind.

A commotion sounded up ahead, loud voices bouncing off the high walls.

"He's disappeared again? I took my eyes off of him for one second and he's gone." Jessica marched into the entry, barking commands to the nurses behind her. "We have to find him before he takes on a flight of stairs and does more damage to himself than what's already been done."

"What's already been done?" Catherine repeated.

Jessica looked toward the door. "Catherine?" Her face paled, and the message in her eyes brought a chill.

"Jessica."

289

Jessica's gaze readjusted and her mouth dropped wide. "Father?" She ran to him, grasping him close. "You're here?"

Catherine didn't wait for answers. She charged down the hallway, scanning every room as she went. He was here? She didn't care if he came without a limb or with a broken bone. He was home.

She found him, staring off the terrace into the back garden. Except for a bandaged head and hand, he looked fine. Wonderful, in fact. She heaved a sob and ran toward him.

"David? Oh, David. I'm so happy to see you."

His smile welcomed her, gaze roaming over her face. "Hello."

She flung herself into his arms, holding onto him with every ounce of longing the past months of separation had ignited. His arms tightened around her, hands moving slowly up her back to tangle in her hair.

"This is by far the best greeting I've received since arriving here."

She laughed and looked up at him. Without any preparation, he took her lips with his, hard and passionately. The force and intimacy of the embrace shook her with its odd unfamiliarity. For a moment, she was overcome by the scent and touch of him, grateful she held him, alive and whole, but then his palms descended down her back to her hips…in public.

"What are you doing?"

"I thought it fairly obvious, dear." His lips left her mouth to trail down her neck. "You smell of lavender? I love lavender."

Something felt wrong, changed, but what? Hadn't she dreamed of his kisses? She pushed at his chest. "David!"

Her use of his name jarred him, and he released her, hands shaking in a strange sort of tremor. He stepped back, eyes wide and horrified, a haze seeming to clear from his vision. "I…I'm so sorry. Please forgive me."

Catherine fought for words amidst her breathlessness but found none.

"I…I've never done anything like that in my life. I don't know what came over me. Please, I beg you. Forgive me."

Catherine placed a palm to her chest, the rapid rise and fall slowing, the fog of confusion filtering through the residual fog of his kisses. "Yes, of…of course."

"I've sustained a head injury, and sometimes, regular inhibitions are no longer under my control." He met her gaze, his pleading and distant. "Complications from mild injuries are usually temporary. I should be somewhat corrected over time, as my brain heals, but…" He covered his mouth with his palm and lowered his face. "I'm so sorry."

"Please." Catherine stepped forward and touched his shoulder.

He flinched back, his regret paling his face. He grasped at the stone terrace railing, shaking his head.

"Oh, David, no harm done. I'm fine and so happy to have you home."

"I assure you, I've never behaved in such a deplorable manner." The regret on his face brought her a step closer. He backed away. "It's only, I felt I knew you in a special way…something I can't explain. I've never done anything remotely similar with any of the other nurses."

"Knew me?" Catherine paused, hand in the air to touch his arm. "Other nurses?" A sudden weakness nearly took her to her knees. She steadied herself against the terrace railing, air closing off in her throat.

His unknowing gaze probed hers, searching for answers. "Who are you?"

"David, there you are." Jessica emerged through the doorway, noticing Catherine as she entered, and her countenance dawned with awareness and apology.

"Jessica!" David's voice wrung with relief. He walked toward his sister, pausing in front of Catherine as he passed, his probing gaze wandering over her features. "Catherine? Is that it?"

"Yes." It was the only reply she could squeeze through her tightening throat.

He stared at her a moment longer, all tenderness, all love, gone from that familiar face. "Forgive me, Catherine."

Footsteps disappeared into the house and then a sob from the depths of her soul shook her entire body. She tried to hold back as many of the tears as she could, determined to be strong, to try and understand, but they overflowed. Breaking her. She had no words. No prayer. Nothing except the empty, gnawing realization she'd lost the most beautiful love she'd ever known.

Chapter Twenty-Eight

Catherine stared out the window of Beacon's dining room, pen in hand to make her meal order for the week, but she couldn't focus. Not since last evening's revelation. How could God do this to her? Give her a taste of such beauty and love and then rip it away?

"He's in good health. That should help."

Jessica's voice pulled Catherine from the monotonous view of a steady rain.

"And he's young, with a strong mind." A frown pinched her brow into wrinkles. "Both hopeful."

"What happened?" Catherine whispered.

"We were captured by a German spy, a doctor we met when we arrived." Jessica ran a hand over her face and sighed, her expression raw. "He forced us to work for him, his wounded, but after a few weeks, the battle became too much and half of his unit retreated. We heard the French were nearby, in the woods, so we tried to make an escape."

Jessica's usual strength and confidence fell under the shadow of her memories and her tragedy. Catherine ached for her, for David. What a horror!

"David wasn't well before our escape. Provisions ran low and he didn't eat...didn't drink like he should have." She shook her head and wiped at the tears on her cheeks. "He kept offering part of his rations. I didn't know they were his at the time."

Catherine stepped forward, drawn in by the agony on Jessica's face. She placed her hand on Jessica's shoulder, and the woman looked up.

"Cramer caught us...the spy." Jessica hurried on, new tears following paths of the old ones. "One of his men and David got into a row. David fought them to protect me and...and he managed to get one man down." Her teary green eyes met Catherine's. "But Cramer came from behind and…slammed his rifle into David's head, knocking him to the ground."

Catherine winced at the image. "How…how did you manage to get away?"

"I grabbed the downed man's pistol." Her eyes glassed, emotionless. "And I shot Cramer. Three times."

After a moment's hesitation, Catherine pulled Jessica into an embrace. The weeping woman buried her face into Catherine's shoulder, shaking and sobbing, heartbroken and scared.

As the tears subsided, Jessica stepped back and took Catherine's offered handkerchief. "Thank you." She dabbed at her eyes, shaking her head. "We have so much to do."

"We? I can help?"

She sniffed. "This is beyond my knowledge." A vulnerability softened Jessica's features even more. "I need all the help I can get with the hope he'll regain his memories."

Catherine's voice trembled, the question hovering. "What memories has he lost?"

"Mostly the past year. He's regained some, but there's no way to know what will trigger a memory or what the memory might be. Those closest to his injury are likely hardest to recover."

Catherine fisted her fear with determination. "What must I do?"

"I don't know for certain. Head injuries are unpredictable." Jessica touched her arm. "He's fragile right now, and I'm afraid to force too much at once. Perhaps…perhaps it would be wise to refrain from telling him —"

"I'm his wife?" She closed her eyes against another stab.

"Only until we have a better idea of his healing. As he becomes stronger, he can handle more."

She hardened against the tears. "If it will help him, I'll do whatever you ask."

David couldn't get the woman out of his head. *Catherine*. He'd never forget the look on her lovely face as he left her on the terrace. Shock had paled to agony in a gradual descent. Not only had he treated her with such disrespect, but somehow, he'd wounded her further. The very idea grieved him.

She moved among the patients, offering compassion. Some of them responded with harmless smiles, but others followed her movements like vultures. David gripped the cup in his hand so tightly his fingers cramped.

Then she turned those piercing sapphire eyes to him and smiled. He stared, entranced, before realizing he stared. He nodded in response. A vision of her on the streets of Ednesbury filtered into his mind. She was with Dr. Carrier, and people were angry.

Catherine? He tilted his head as a sliver of knowledge emerged from the fog. Ashleigh's sister, Catherine Dougall. The *flirt*.

But that title didn't fit the woman serving these wounded, a woman covering the curves of a pregnancy. What was her story and why did he have this indescribable need to uncover it? He placed his head in his good hand and groaned. *Dear God, help me.*

"Could I get you something for your headache, Dr. Ross?"

He looked up, and she stood before him, her expression wary, and no wonder after the way he'd attacked her. "You're not a nurse."

"Well, I've learned a few things about nursing, but I've had no formal training. Only what you and my sister have taught me."

"Me?" He searched for the connection but his mind wouldn't comply. "You're Ashleigh's sister?"

A faint light lit her smile. It was a pleasure to afford her such a small joy. "Yes. Her older, but not wiser, sister. I'm afraid I've been the black sheep of the family."

He studied her, searching for anything other than authenticity, but found none. "I remember meeting you in Ednesbury, with Ashleigh and Sam, but…I have the feeling we are somehow more than mere acquaintances."

She opened her mouth to answer and then snapped her lips closed, reconsidering it, it seemed. "Actually, you introduced me to Christ when I didn't deserve it."

"Did I?"

"Indeed. It was rather scandalous of you." Her smile spread to her eyes, the memory evidently a pleasant one. "My sister was sick with pneumonia, and I was at her bedside. I could show you the place sometime. It was at Roth Hall."

His brows rose. "I've heard going back to the location of memories can encourage them to return." He stood. "Perhaps it would be worth a try?"

His answer brought her smile back, which kept him agreeing to ridiculous things like following her into a bedroom. Then the thought of a bedroom had his rebel gaze taking inventory of her body with the same vulture thoughts of the soldiers.

"If location inspires memories, I know the perfect place."

"Yes?" He couldn't look away, somehow feeling a connection to her. It didn't make sense.

"Come with me."

He hesitated and then followed her through the house. They stepped back to the terrace and wound down the stairs, walking over the pebbled path of the garden. A gazebo stood in a solitary corner of the garden, and a flash of memory shot through his mind. Miss Dougall sitting on the bench, looking up at him in surprise.

"We've been here."

She turned and followed his gesture to the gazebo. "Yes, in fact that's where you—" She stopped and continued her walk. "We had an intense discussion about The Front and the future."

And much more in between, he'd wager.

She opened the garden gate, and sudden fear seized him. The open field beyond the garden wall, and the surrounding forest, brought on a panic.

"I can't."

She turned. "What?"

He shook his head, backing away from the gate. "I can't go out there."

She took his hand, giving it a gentle tug. "Of course you can. You've done it many times."

"No. No, I…I can't."

She tightened her grip on his hand, her eyes pleading. "Please. I know it will help you. It's an important place for us. If the gazebo—"

"Leave me alone." He jerked his hand free and ran toward the house, half in fear of the forest beyond the wall and half from the pain he'd caused Catherine Dougall.

Catherine slammed the door to her cottage and marched to her desk. A small white pot, filled with peppermint, sat on the table nearby. She stared at it through a haze of fury and tears. With one quick movement, she snatched up the pot and flung it across the room. It crashed into the opposite wall, spilling mint and dirt onto the wooden floors.

She raised her palms to the ceiling. "Why?"

She dropped to her desk and shoved her hands through her hair, squeezing her throbbing head. "How can you love me and do this? How can you love David and leave him with this gaping hole in his past?"

Her violent scream crashed into sobs as she lowered her head back into her hands. "Why?"

She wasn't sure how long she lay there, her heart warring with emotions of every color, every rage. In the silence, a question whispered through her spirit. *Have you forgotten also?*

She straightened, searching the room for something, someone. The whisper washed through her spirit again. *Do you love me?*

Her eyes shot wide, and she blinked back a new rush of tears.

A knock at her door sent her to her feet, her pulse in her throat.

"Catherine?"

Ashleigh rounded the doorway, taking inventory of the room. "Oh, Catherine, I'm so sorry."

Catherine turned away to the window, her fist pinching into her palm. "There's nothing to be done."

"Of course there is." Ashleigh walked over to the decimated pot and began gathering the shattered pieces from the floor. "I've read some things about head injuries, and there is a great deal of hope with David. It will take time and support. Your support."

Catherine kept her back to her sister, pressing her fist into her chest to stay her tears. "I hurt him when trying to help. He…he looked terrified of something beyond the wall, and then he…" She sighed. "He doesn't want to see me."

"He may have random paranoia associated with head injuries."

Catherine turned as Ashleigh swept up the dirt from the floor. "I…I don't want to hurt him."

"You're not, sister dear." Ashleigh took the mint plant's remains and brought a soup bowl out of the cupboard. "He's confused right now."

She shot her sister a glare. "He's not the only one."

Ashleigh replanted the mint in the soup bowl. "I know you want to fix this. That's what you do. You fix things." She rounded the table. "But you can't repair this. None of us can. The only thing we can do is wait, trust God, and…."Ashleigh took a deep breath. "And love David."

Trust God? Catherine turned back to the window. He allowed this to happen. How could she trust him?

"Do you love him?"

"Of course I do." She answered with enough venom to send Ashleigh back a step.

Ashley hesitated, and then drew close again. "Then love him." She placed her hand on Catherine's arm, her eyes glazed with a sheen of unshed tears. "God works miracles through love."

"Miracles? Why would he work a miracle in something he allowed to happen in the first place?" She scoffed, but the wisdom in her sister's eyes, the scars she tended beneath a past of pain, humbled Catherine. Who was she to complain when her sister didn't? "I'm sorry I lost my temper."

"I love you, but even more than my love or David's love, God loves you." She took Catherine by the shoulders. "He pursued you to make you his own. He sacrificed his life for you, even in your sin. His love for you"—she smiled—"his love for me, is far greater than your pain or anger or questions. You may feel alone and forgotten right now. But you're not alone, and you're certainly not forgotten."

Catherine raised a brow.

"Not by God." Ashleigh reached to Catherine's desk and picked up the Bible, spinning through the pages to a spot near the middle. "Read this, Catherine. David might have forgotten many things, but so have you."

Ashleigh placed the Bible down and slid a small piece of paper in to hold the place she'd chosen. She walked to the door. "Whether love restores his memory or not, it will definitely touch his heart…and yours."

Catherine walked to the desk and took the Bible into her hands.

Isaiah 49 fell open.

But Zion said, "The LORD has forsaken me; my Lord has forgotten me.

Can a woman forget her nursing child, that she should have no compassion on the son of her womb?

Catherine's hand rested on her stomach. *Even these may forget, yet I will not forget you. Behold, I have engraved you on the palms of my hands...*

"I thought you were serving at the Front." David sat in his study with his father in a nearby chair.

His father took a sip of tea. "I was."

"And they released you to come help me when you learned of my injuries?"

His father paused and took another sip, biding time if David knew him. "No. I came back to Ednesbury for a very different reason. It just so happened it was when you and your sister needed me most."

"From your cryptic reply, I assume you're not going to tell me the true reason?"

His father grinned over his cup. "Not yet, son. In time, but there is only so much you're ready to take in at once."

David released an angry burst of air and placed down his cup. "I'm not a child. Just because I can't remember a few things doesn't mean I'm to be treated with kid gloves." He stood and gestured toward the door. "She…she's tiptoeing around me now, like I might break."

"She, meaning Catherine, I suppose?"

David's shoulders sagged from the weight of his frustration. "She wants me to know her, and I...I want that, but she craves a familiarity I cannot give. And then I keep hurting her by just speaking to her. She's trying to be strong, but I see the hurt in her eyes. I can't make my mind remember."

His father studied him, sending David back to primary school when he'd missed an answer on a test he should have known. "David, you're a smart man, but you're broken. It's going to take time."

"I know that."

"Catherine is a remarkable woman. The few images you do recall, those you refer to as the flirt, were of a different time, a different woman. Your memories may not be available to assist you, but I'm certain your judgment is intact. You haven't lost your intelligence. What do y*ou* think you should do?"

Music filtered into the room from the hallway. A familiar melody.

"Do you hear that?" David walked to the doorway.

His father took the newspaper from the table. "It's most likely some of the patients enjoying the radio."

David followed the sound. He knew this song. His smile spread. *If I Had My Way.* He looked around the room, frantic. The song continued as he went down the hallway to another room with patients, looking to each nurse without success. He burst into the next room, and Catherine glanced up from her place by a man's bedside, gauze in hand.

"David?"

His breathing pulsed out in short spurts, and he stared at her. "Are you...are you all right?"

She nodded, eyes wide. "I am."

His breathing slowed. He kept examining her face. She turned to the patient. "Mr. Mabry, please excuse me."

David followed her out into the hallway.

"I...I don't know why, but I had to find you. To see you."

Her lips slanted. "You see me."

"Yes." He took a step closer, studying the color of her eyes, the curve of her cheek, the fullness of her lips, scratching for a memory just out of reach. She was beautiful. "Do you know the song *If I Had My Way*?"

She blinked as if stunned. "Yes, I know it."

He frowned. "Good." He stepped around her. "Good."

Her emotions bounced like a yoyo. One moment, she closed off her heart to keep his 'stranger eyes' from completely ruining her, and the next he asked if she knew a song…their song? She pushed back the coverlet and got dressed, sleep useless.

She slipped past her desk downstairs, pausing to reread the verses Ashleigh had marked. She felt forgotten…she *was* forgotten. If God had engraved her on his hands, what did that mean?

Beacon House lay quiet in the darkness of early morning. She walked noiselessly through the halls, listening for a need or cry. Sometimes, the nightmares seized a soldier so badly, it would take her an hour to calm him. As she passed the door to David's study, a light flickered awake and urged her forward. A dying fire sent long shadows across the room and filtered over the figure in a chair. David. Asleep.

A swell of tenderness pushed her beyond her fear. She took a blanket from a cupboard in the hallway and approached him quietly. Moonlight sent a pale glow through the tall windows and battled with the fire's golden hues. He'd fallen asleep sitting up, newspaper in hand. She grinned, carefully taking the paper and placing it on the table. With slow deliberation, she drew the blanket over him from neck to shoe tip.

The scent of peppermint hit her with breathtaking force. So painful. So sweet. She filled her lungs with another breath.

"What are you doing?"

She'd expected him to be alarmed, angry even, but he merely watched her.

She leaned closer to hear him, her fingers brushing his chin as she tucked the blanket secure. "I'm taking care of you."

His eyes, twinkling in the pale light, examined her face, half in awe, half in curiosity.

"You fell asleep reading. I didn't want you to become chilled."

"Is it morning?" He whispered in keeping with the mood of the shadowed room.

"Five, I think."

"And you're not asleep?"

"I don't sleep well right now, anyway." She gestured toward her abdomen. "So I volunteered for the early shift." She turned to walk away.

"Wait…Nurse Dougall?"

Her heart wept at his formality, at the use of her maiden name, but she mentally whispered a prayer for strength and patience. "Yes, Dr. Ross."

He gestured to a chair near him. "Would you care to talk?"

She fought against the desire to run away. The exhaustion, both emotionally and physically, put her feelings much too close to the edge to bear another flailing of disappointments, but the earnestness of his expression and the child-like lostness in his eyes pulled her into a seat. "Of course."

The crackle of the fire split the silence.

"I…I won't deny, I'm attracted to you. And I understand that you are a different person now than you were from the memories I have. But I can't force myself to remember things."

She stared back, meeting his honesty head on. "I know." Her stare never wavered, and every ounce of love she felt for him boiled up from her heart into her words. "And…perhaps you may not recognize me now, but you once told me love has an amazing power to turn people 'round."

He tilted his head, a grin almost lighting his somber features. "Why…why did I have a vision of Aunt Maureen in my head?"

Catherine smiled. "We were having a conversation about your Aunt when you spoke those words."

"I remember her wager, and…and I understand she's caused quite a bit of trouble for the two of us."

"She's tried, but we're made of some pretty strong stuff."

302

His grin twitched again. "I believe you are."

"We both are."

Silence enfolded the moment, an aching silence of words unspoken and sweetness forgotten.

"Catherine?" His whisper called out into the darkness. The way he said her name, breathless in the moonlight, sent liquid warmth running up her arms to her chest. Almost as if he knew her, recognized something in their togetherness.

"Yes?"

"I'm sorry I can't remember. Will you help me try?"

She swallowed down her tears. "With all my heart."

Chapter Twenty-Nine

"Hello, Catherine dear."

Catherine looked up from her menu for cook and smiled at Alexander Ross' greeting. "Good morning, Dr—" He raised a warning brow. "Alexander," she corrected.

"And how is my other daughter today?"

She'd shunned the endearment after finding out about her father's lurid and base past, but the way Alexander Ross called her 'daughter' gave her a newfound appreciation. Even if his son didn't have one clue who she was.

"She's managing. How about you? Have you been out to Ednesbury Court to…"

"Not yet. I'm biding my time to see if my grandfather will confront Lady Cavanaugh instead of an outcast like me."

"I know well the role of outcast."

"Not anymore, Catherine." He patted her arm. "And my son shall see it soon enough. He'll remember you. Even if his mind cannot, his heart will."

"I want to believe you, but…but it's difficult to hope."

"We live off of this thing called hope, and my son is no fool." Alexander nodded and reached for a scone off the sideboard. "There's clear proof of his affections in his letters to you."

Catherine sighed. "There's so much of him in those letters."

"Exactly." Alexander shot her a wink and took a bite of the scone. "And in his own words."

Hope dangled a precarious thread to her heart. "I'm going to take my list to cook." She tapped the scone on its way to Alexander's mouth. "And I'll ask for more of the blueberry since you are so fond of them."

His moustache twitched up on one side. "Good girl."

Catherine walked down the hallway where a few patients gathered in small groups.

A new soldier, with a pronounced limp, sidled up to her on her way. "Hello, doll."

"Hello, *boy*." She emphasized his youth, ignoring the way his gaze moved down her body.

"I'm enough of a man to know what a woman wants."

Catherine turned, brow raised, and took inventory of the scrawny lad. "Peace and quiet, usually. Perhaps a good chocolate here or there."

He stepped closer, and Catherine curbed the urge to roll her eyes. Arrogance mixed with ignorance created many a fool. "Surely a doll like you could give a poor soldier a kiss."

He gripped her arm, and she tried to pull free, but he proved stronger than he looked.

"Release me, sir."

"Name's Langley, and it's been too long since I had a kiss." He jerked her against him.

On impulse, she brought her fist around with such force, it sent him stumbling back.

Catherine took a deep breath, shaken and a bit stunned by her own behavior. Then she felt it, the sting of pain in her knuckles from the impact.

Langley growled and covered his wounded eye.

"I told you, most women prefer peace and quiet."

He started back toward her when David plowed out of nowhere, seizing the boy's collar. "Don't. Touch. Her."

She'd never seen him angry, his jaw tense, eyes flaring, shaking the boy with a power she didn't even realize he possessed. She grinned. It was terribly romantic and produced a delicious thrill.

"Did you hear me?" His voice thundered as he lifted the boy from the ground.

"Yeah." The boy pulled free and sent Catherine a scathing glance before returning to the patient room.

David turned to her, taking her hand in his good one and examining it. She couldn't help but stare at him, a little dazed that he'd emerged like a prince in a fairy story to her rescue. Even if she could have sent Langley flying again, what romantic adventure was there in that?

"Let me see to your hand."

305

She wasn't sure whether to find more pleasure in his chivalry or his gentleness, but for a few seconds, she embraced his attention without reserve.

He called to one of the nurses. "Would you bring some icings please? To my study."

He placed her in a chair and knelt beside her, his gaze intense. "Are you all right?"

"Yes, I'm fine. Truly."

"The ogre." David growled. "Doesn't he know how to treat a woman?" He examined her knuckles. "You'll have a bruise here, I think."

"His will be worse."

He chuckled and stared at her, holding to her gaze so long the air around them became thick and mesmerizing. Without breaking eye contact, he slowly brought her red knuckles to his mouth and pressed a kiss to them.

Her breath congealed to a halt. Did he realize what he was doing?

Then, as if the most natural thing, he pressed a gentle kiss to her wrist, breathing over it as he'd done so many times.

She nearly swooned, the longing and ache rising in a fury of blurred vision.

His eyes rounded and he dropped her wrist. "I'm… I do apologize for taking such liberties." He cleared his throat and looked back at her, searching her face for some hidden answer to his behavior.

Her poor David. His heart recognized things his mind didn't, like a strange and horrible game of hide-and-seek.

"It wasn't an offense." She cradled her hand against her chest and offered him a small smile, holding to the lingering sweetness of his touch on her skin.

"Catherine." Oh, how gentle his voice was. "I recognize we knew each other very well, and my sister confirms that we had a particular closeness."

She wanted to touch his face, feel his skin against her palm, and wipe away the confusion from his brow. "Yes."

"In a romantic way?" He asked cautiously.

"Yes."

He continued his intense stare, curiosity mixed with a distant kindness. He had no memory of their first kiss in the medical supplies room, or their walks in the garden arm-in-arm, or their wedding night.

His gaze drifted back to her hand and a look of utter horror paled his features. "My mother's ring?" He looked up at her face. "Good heavens! We're married?"

"Yes." She braced herself, his questions delving into unpredictable territory.

He stumbled to his feet, running a hand through his hair and sending his golden locks into as much confusion as the look on his face. "How can I not remember something so...so...?"

"Beautiful," she whispered.

His pained gaze came back to hers. "Was it?"

"And much more." She stood and offered more faith in her smile than she felt. "I believe in miracles, Dr. Ross. What God did between us was beyond any earthly means, so I have faith He'll make a way, whether by old memories or new ones, to help us find each other again."

David stared at the bookshelves of medical journals and groaned. Both Jessica and his father strongly encouraged him to remain in his study until he felt more comfortable around unfamiliar people, but the same walls and windows, day in and day out, grew painfully monotonous. Three weeks since the injury, so Jessica said. Over the past two days, he'd recalled a few images of being in a war hospital near the Front, but then the images randomly switched to the inside of a women's dress salon. Maybe he was losing what mind he had left?

Then there was Catherine. He held more images of her in this foggy unknown than anyone else. Her face filtered in and out, some staying to form a memory, but more often than not, they alighted momentarily and then faded away, leaving a sense of tenderness behind. One very clear picture emerged with welcome repetition. He had Catherine against a wall as if to kiss her.

And he wanted to kiss her, even now, but it didn't make sense. Wasn't she with child? Yes. He remembered their first full conversation by her sister's deathbed. Another man's child. His head hurt from the incongruences. *God, make it clear.*

"Excuse me, Dr. Ross." The very subject of his quandary emerged through the doorway, her usual nurse's uniform replaced with a suit of deep purple—beautiful. "I'm on my way to town, but your sister asked me to change your dressings since she's in surgery."

He sat up straighter. "Of course."

She patted a satchel at her side. "I brought a few letters too. Your father seemed to think they might help spark a memory."

"How is your hand?"

She smiled and placed her satchel on the floor, dropping to her knees before him. He should have stood. A woman with child didn't need to be kneeling at his feet like a beggar.

"It will heal."

He looked down at it, remembering the softness of the flesh at her wrist. The scent of lavender. The taste of her.

Her touch on his bandages brought his attention back to her face. Her fingers moved gently over the cloth, and he recalled a vision like liquid, of her running her hands up his arms to link around his neck. Her. With him…in an intimate way. His throat constricted. He tried to capture threads of the memory, but it slipped away, branding his mind with residual curiosity and interest.

She unleashed the last bit of bandage. His second and third finger bent in an unnatural way, and his fourth finger had been removed to stave off infection, all from a fight with a spy, he'd been told. His stomach tightened. Would he be able to work again?

Catherine seemed to guess his thoughts. "You will heal too." Her brow rose. "You might have to resolve surgery in a new way, but I have no doubt of your capabilities. You've always been remarkable."

He searched for the undercurrent of manipulation her past suggested but saw none. Felt none. "You're kind."

She grinned and went back to work. "I'm not. But you are." She chuckled. "I've seen you charm the most disgruntled patient into submission, quiet a fearful child, and soothe the anxiety of a pregnant woman."

He could drown in such sweet adoration. He saw her then, hair down around her shoulders, eyes-wide, asking him to pray, and a tenderness drew him closer to her.

"You….you loved me?"

"I still love you." She inched back from his closeness. He frowned. He didn't want her to move away. He wanted her to stay close enough to smell. Touch.

A faded sentence passed through his mind. "But aren't those words too small…for what you feel?"

Her gaze shot to his, and she dropped the fresh gauze.

"You said that, didn't you? To me?"

She moved to pick up the gauze, the fire blazing behind her.

"Wait, Kat." He stood and reached for her. "Get back from the fire."

He pulled her into his arms, her breath against his neck sending heat radiating through his body.

"What did you call me?"

"Kat." His grin tipped a little, looking down at her and enjoying her warmth against him. "Is that a name I gave you?"

Her breath grew shallow, and she stepped out of his arms. Why did she keeping pulling away? Wasn't she supposed to stay near him, as his *wife*? "Y…yes."

"I'm sorry, again. Jessica keeps telling me I've become a storm cloud. Always fearful of something bad happening."

She finished her care of his hand. "After all you've been through, I can imagine the fears you've known. I wish…I wish I could help carry them for you. To keep your nightmares at bay."

"They've grown less frequent with time." He took a random curl of her hair into his fingers, the touch sparking another blurry vision of gliding his hands through her loose hair. His throat tightened, and he released the lock.

His tenderness emerged almost-but-not-quite. It was like trying to catch water in one's hand, and Catherine's emotions were strung to the breaking point. To take his pain! To be his wife again.

He helped her stand, his gaze soft. "This must be difficult for you. Caring for a man who cannot remember you."

Tears burned in her eyes, so she lowered her head. "Caring for you has never been difficult." She took a deep breath and looked up. "You always had the hard part. I'm not an easy person to love."

He studied her. "I'm not certain I believe you." Then his grin perked. "Well, after the shiner you gave Langley, there may be some truth in your statement." His gaze distanced. "And…didn't you give quite the tongue lashing to old Dr. Carrier?"

Teasing? Well, that was a good sign. "You remember that conversation?"

"Only just." His smile grew to a dimple. Her breath caught in appreciation.

"Perhaps you are good for my memory."

"I'll be glad to answer any of your questions." She gestured back to her satchel. "And I brought your letters."

A long pause followed her statement. "I…I have one question, but it may seem…impertinent."

A thread of hope drew her closer. "Anything."

"If the child you carry isn't mine…" He paused.

She braced for the blow.

"Why did I marry you?"

His words stabbed into all the grieving places in her heart. She made a futile attempt to maintain some composure, but a hot tear spilled from its place. She drew in a quivering breath and forced a smile she didn't feel. "That's a good question, Dr. Ross. One I've asked often enough." She blinked away the gathering tears and backed toward the door. "I think…somehow, you'd convinced yourself love was bigger than…than my past."

"Catherine, please—"

"I can't." She stumbled toward the door. "Excuse me."

She moved as quickly as her cumbersome stomach allowed, dashing tears from her cheeks as she went. How could she stay? How could she win him and lose him at the same time, and repeat it day after day? Seeing herself through his unknowing eyes brought back all the shame she thought she'd overcome. Every scathing comment from the women in the village, every upturned nose, every lash of Lady Cavanaugh's tongue, every humiliating remembrance bit into her confidence as if she stood naked on the street. She had ruined her own life and believed God redeemed her out of the darkness?

Not her. She deserved this horrible end for all the wrong she'd done – for all the hurt she'd caused. No wonder God allowed this type of heartbreak. She'd even screamed in abject defiance to Him! Him, who had promised to snatch her away from her pain.

She dipped into the small empty tea room and dropped to her knees. The silence swelled around her and welcomed a sudden stillness, a stillness filled with an embracing presence.

Do you love me?

"God, please. Help me." Her voice split the tiny space, a shaky whisper into the blackness.

Am I enough?

She bent under the weight, the conviction. She'd allowed her lost love for David to shake her faith in God's love, even placing David's opinion above God's. David might see her as a fallen woman, but God... God made her whole, even when she'd deserved it least. She had to let David go...and trust God beyond the pain. Just as she'd told Annie to do when Clara died.

Trust the strength of *His* hands. Trust *His* love.

"Forgive me. Please..." The ache of her own helplessness swelled and throbbed with her pulse. "Hold me with your love."

Silence answered her. Tears cooled her cheeks and then the verses, those Ashleigh had shared, whispered in response. *These may forget, yet I will not forget you. Behold, I have engraved you on the palms of my hands.*

His perfect memory secured her. His unfailing love held her. And though she'd forgotten His truths and lost her way, He'd gathered her close. Engraved. Protected. Loved. Forever.

A renewed awareness poured over wounds. *He redeems, restores, and…and finds lost things…even lost love.*

"I don't understand your plan." A sob shook her shoulders before she took another calming breath. "But I know you love me…and you love David." She placed a palm to her broken heart. "I give my dreams of David to you. Help me love him, even when love isn't returned. Help me find hope, even in this darkness, because though David may forget me forever"—her voice trembled—"you never will."

David stared at the space Catherine had vacated, his mind and emotions clamoring for clarity. He couldn't deny the draw he felt toward her, this desire to protect and comfort her. The pain his question inflicted created a residual ache in his chest, but he couldn't make logical sense of his choices.

She loved him. Every decision to stay by him as his unawareness stabbed fresh wounds to her heart confirmed it. Love was the one explanation. But how had he grown to love her? All he remembered were his aunt's disapproving comments, a reputation, prayer, and liquid memories flowing in and out of his hold.

Her satchel lay spilled on the floor, kicked in her hurry to leave the room, scattering papers. Letters. *His letters.* He reached for them. Some had his writing, others—returned—had hers.

He brought the papers to his face and closed his eyes, filling his mind and lungs with the faint scent of her. Lavender. A warmth poured through his chest, and a flash of memory awakened for a second. The public park in Edesnbury, sitting with her on the bench, holding her hand. The memory strengthened another connection, a wordless bond, but nothing he could grasp. Nothing that stayed clear for long.

But he'd seen her handwriting before.

He rushed to his desk and drew his satchel from a bottom drawer where he'd stored it for later. When he opened it, the scent hit him again. More letters.

These told a story he didn't understand, and he needed to know. Not just for himself, but for Catherine and the little child she carried. Whether it brought them together or pushed them apart, he needed an answer.

Chapter Thirty

"Mother has decided she's to marry Dr. Pike." Catherine followed Madame to her small office at the back of the shop. "She's hosting a reception afterward at Roth Hall, and the entire town is invited."

"At your sister's expense, no doubt."

Catherine laughed. "Well, I'm helping too, and Dr. Pike brings a bit with him."

"It will be a good match?"

"I think so. It's nice to know she'll have someone."

Madame examined Catherine with keen eyes. "You seem more...at rest than when I saw you a last week."

Catherine offered a sad grin. "I...kept trying to take things into my own hands and make David love me. Force him to remember, but there's nothing I could do. So...I gave up."

"Oui, je comprends." She nodded. "You fix things. I fix things. We do not like the unfixable things, non. But God is in them, changing *us* sometimes more than changing the wounds."

She ran a palm over Catherine's hand, her smile a sweet comfort. "Do you know? Had you been a very good girl, you would not have sought to rescue those wounded in the same way as you do now. Nor come to my shop and become like a daughter to me. Or restored Lord Ross to his family. Or offered Beacon to the good doctor as a hospital." She touched Catherine's cheek, her eyes a misty brown hue. "You see, He knows. He loves. We weep, laugh, rest, trust, and He loves...and works miracles through us."

"Ashleigh." David ran up beside her as she made her way down the hall to surgery.

"David." She glanced at his hand. "How are you feeling?"

313

"Better, thank you." He moved in step with her, carefully choosing his words. "Would you mind answering a few questions for me?"

She stopped and turned to face him, her eyes as kind as he remembered. "Of course."

"Thank you." He rubbed his hands together, wondering where to begin. "I recall working with you and your sister in the hospital before the Zep attack. I even remember you training her at Roth Hall."

"Yes." Her smile encouraged him. "And she became a furious advocate of your work."

"I'm beginning to understand that." He grinned, nearly overwhelmed by all he'd learned about his wife. "But then things become hazy and out of order. There was a fire?"

"Yes, it took out part of the house."

"And Catherine?"

"She helped you rescue the children."

Which explained his reaction with her when she'd moved close to the fire a few nights past.

"I...I remember pieces. A fire, and Catherine with a baby in her arms. And there's a memory of the gazebo."

Ashleigh smile softened. "You proposed to her there."

His gaze locked with hers, another blurry moment clearing for a second. Catherine burying her head against his chest, her whispered words coming clear. *Of course I love you. It's the only thing keeping me from slapping this ridiculous notion out of that stubborn head of yours.*

He suddenly laughed. "She's quite the corker, isn't she?"

"That's quite an accurate description."

"And how did we find our way from Roth to Beacon House?"

Ashleigh hesitated. "She inherited Beacon House from our grandmother."

The air whooshed from David's lungs, awareness opening floodgates of her care. "And she gave it to the hospital?"

Ashleigh shook her head. "No, David. She gave it to *you*."

314

"Me?" Catherine amazed him, more and more, with each new detail of her personality.

His gaze flitted to the window where her cottage roof rose above the garden wall. Words from the letters came to mind. He'd taken down her hair. The image emerged unbidden, and he could even feel the silk of it on his fingers. "So she lives in that small cottage when she could be in this large house because of her love for me?"

"Love does some amazing things, Dr. Ross."

David's emotions pressed into his chest, understanding piercing his foggy memories with gratitude. "Where did we marry?"

"The stone church in the village."

"The small one?" He raised a brow, almost expecting some elaborate production, but not anymore. Not the Kat he'd unearthed over the past few days. "Thank you, Ashleigh. You've been quite helpful."

Catherine pushed the knife through the chicken breast, carving it with the finest precision.

"Don't you go ruinin' my chicken for the soup now, Mrs. Catherine. When we have to feed a flock of wounded, every bit counts."

"Of course, Mrs. Brock. And I appreciate all your efforts. Is the new kitchen maid working out for you?"

"As good as kitchen maids go, I wager."

Catherine stifled her grin at Mrs. Brock's typical melancholy view. "I've no doubt, under your tutelage, she's bound to improve."

"And that's the truth. If she's fit for learning is another story."

"Catherine?" Jessica stood in the doorway, her gaze alternating between Mrs. Brock, the chicken, and Catherine. "What are you doing?"

Catherine gestured to the chicken with her knife. "Research."

"Research?" Jessica drew closer, nodding to Mrs. Brock. "Would you happen to have some fresh thyme, Mrs. Brock? The tea may provide some breathing relief for the patients."

315

Mrs. Brock untied her apron. "Will fetch some from the herb garden straight away."

Jessica moved closer, staring at Catherine's left hand with the third and fourth fingers taped down. "What are you doing?"

"I told you. Research." She nodded toward her work. "What limitations arise from weak or missing fingers. What skills to relearn and modifications—"

"You!" Jessica stared at her, eyes wide and wondering. "You are the most unrelenting person I have ever met."

"David has a gift." Catherine bent closer to the chicken breast, examining her work with a bit of pride. "We can't let him forget that too. Someday, when he tries to use his hand again, I want him to know he can still do what he loves."

"Of course." Her voice sounded far way, small.

"And I've been reading as much as I can on head injury. One of the most important things I've noticed is that the person has a supportive environment for healing."

Catherine looked up from her work and froze.

Uncustomary tears trickled down Jessica's face. "I'm sorry, Catherine. I'm sorry for trying to shove you out of the way because I was scared for my brother's reputation…for his heart. If there's any other woman who could love him more than me, it's you."

David joined the staff for dinner for the first time since his return, and despite some anxiety keeping him on edge, he managed it well. The multiple conversations took less concentration than he'd expected and, when an agitation arose and his knee would tremor, Catherine somehow knew. She'd place her hand on his, drawing his attention to her, and follow with a question. After three instances, he realized what she was doing. She was distracting him, helping him make it through dinner.

As the footman served dessert, David took her hand. "Thank you."

"I didn't serve the dessert, Dr. Ross."

He narrowed his eyes. "You did much more than that."

"You're right." She tossed a grin over her shoulder, putting the dessert to her lips. "I ordered cook to make the bread and butter pudding."

And their teasing continued to the end of dinner when she retired for the night and left him staring out his bedroom window at her 'haven' until all the lights faded. He liked her. Her wit, her passion, her care.

He spent the next day, with Jessica's help, visiting places he'd known, finding memories emerging in slow, disjointed ways.

When Catherine walked through the garden the next morning, he was ready.

"I understand you've been doing research."

She looked to the gazebo where he sat on the railing, her palm slamming the front of her green walking suit. "Good heavens, it's freezing out? How long have you been there?"

He slid from the railing and walked toward her. "Not long."

"Were you waiting for me?" Her grin slanted crooked as if she wasn't quite sure what to make of his behavior.

"Indeed, I was." He shoved his hands in his pockets. "But you didn't respond to my statement."

She gestured toward the house. "Let me make my response inside where I don't see my breath."

"Your cottage is closer."

Her bottom lip dropped into an 'o' shape in such a fetching way, he stared a bit too long. "My cottage?"

"I've not been there yet, and my sister said I spent some time there before leaving."

Her brows rose almost to her hairline. "You did."

"Shall we?" He offered his arm, but she hesitated.

"What about the field? I don't want you to force anything."

"I think, if you're with me, I'll be fine." He pressed the truth into his gaze. "I trust you, and after all, you seem to know what I need before I do."

She looked down at his arm and, after a slight hesitation, slid her hand close. Something clicked inside of him. The fit. The feeling. It resurrected similar moments through his mind like photographs. They didn't equate a full memory, but they did ensure him of a sense of belonging. With her.

"I can only visit for a few moments since I'm wanted in the village."

"I'll take those." He placed his hand over hers against his arm. "I've been doing research as well."

They crossed over the threshold of the walled garden, and he looked to the forest beyond, pulse soaring.

She squeezed his arm. "Research, have you? And how is that supposed to impress me?"

She did it again. Distraction.

"Yesterday, I visited Roth Hall and Ednesbury's public park." His heart rate calmed and he rounded the front of the cottage, opening the door for her. "Even dared an entry into Madame's shop."

"Desperate times, I see." She shot him a grin over her shoulder. He almost melted into the floor.

"And...and I visited the church where we wed."

That news stopped her as she removed her coat. "And what great mysteries did you solve with your research?"

He helped her remove her coat and hung it by the door. "I have no memory of Madame's, but that may be more of out of choice than loss."

She laughed, a sound as welcome as the sight of her. The sitting room invited him forward with warm-colored furnishings and morning light. His gaze filtered over the room and stopped at a settee. Perfect for two? He grinned.

"There were a few pieces of memories inspired by Roth Hall, particularly related to the fire. I remember carrying you out of the smoke."

She took a seat. "You remember more than I do in that instance. I fainted."

"Smoke inhalation isn't fainting, my brave dear, and it's quite dangerous."

She avoided his gaze and picked at the end of her sleeve. "And the church?"

"Nothing, I'm afraid. Or blurry somethings. In truth, the letters provided the best insight." He placed her satchel on the table before her. "Thank you. I found them rather...enlightening."

Her grin arched in such a way that hit deep within his heart and encouraged images, and thoughts, of kissing her. "Enlightening?"

"Yes." His voice hushed, deep with emotion, watching a faint and appealing darkening of her cheeks. He sat in the chair near her. "It seems that we were very much in love."

"Oh yes, I've never been loved by anyone the way you loved me."

He caught the past tense. "Give me time, Catherine. You may not know it, but I want to love you."

"You do?"

"Of course." He took her hand. "It pains me more than I understand to see how I keep hurting you."

A wounded expression carved its way into her brow, and she stood, pulling her hand from his. "Would it be better if I went away?"

He stood and snatched her hand back. "No, no." He placed her palm on his chest. "I've been separated from my memories for too long. Don't separate me from my heart as well."

Tears welled in her sapphire eyes.

He gathered both of her hands into his. "I'm afraid it's going to take more pain first as we attempt to rediscover each other, but I'm willing to try. Are you?"

Her loving gaze drifted over his face, leaving a caress behind. "Of course I am. I've become much better at waiting, if you haven't noticed."

"You're amazing, and growing more precious by the day." He brought her hand up to his mouth, keeping his eyes on her face and slowly, with all knowledge of what he was doing, pressed his lips to her skin. Her eyes drooped closed, accepting this promise, this hope. "Perhaps rediscovery won't be as painful as we think."

Her lips tilted again. "I can safely say I've been relatively pain free in your company all morning."

He kept a hold on her hands but looked around the room. "So we were here?"

"Yes."

"And how long were we married before I left?"

319

A pleasant smile softened her gaze into enviable memory. "Three days."

"Ah." He tugged her a little closer into his embrace, enjoying the touch and closeness of her and distracted by the long line of her neck and the curve of her jaw. "And were we...um...together during those three days?"

Her bewitching gaze locked with his, impish. "Many times."

A memory of her in his mind, dark hair tousled around her pale shoulders, rushed forward. He adjusted his collar. "Really?" His voice broke.

"Mmm-hmm." She seemed perfectly nonplussed that the room temperature had suddenly increased. In fact, she stepped out of his arms and reached for her coat.

On instinct, he took it and wrapped it around her, trapping her inside. "I remember this."

"The coat?" Her voice grew suddenly breathless. Perhaps she noticed the temperature change after all.

"Trapping you." He drew her closer, appreciating the curves of her lips. "How was it?"

"You were spectacular," she whispered and then slipped free from his hold and walked to the door.

He followed in agony. "The coat?"

She ducked her head under the alcove of the door, clearly ignoring his question. "If you'll excuse me, Dr. Ross, I have an appointment."

He snagged her arm before she could get away. "David, call me David. Don't you think, after all...the togetherness"—he nodded toward the cottage—"we should be on a first name basis?"

Her smile spread wide, sweet and happy. "Yes, David. I do."

Chapter Thirty-One

And the flirting commenced.

They played this dance, passing comments as one left the room while the other entered, conversations over dinner, and an occasional walk about the garden, but to her disappointment, no kissing…yet.

Then one day, he pulled her into an alcove away from prying eyes and pressed her back against the wall.

"I remembered something this morning." His gaze dropped to her lips, a hungry look sending tingles over her skin and a blush of heat into her cheeks.

"Did you?" She was amazed she managed to speak at all. The thickness in the air at his closeness dried her throat. *So long.*

"Mm-hmm." He teased her chin back a little and pressed the gentlest kiss on her cheek. "Something about a supply closet, I think."

His lips roved a little further south, warming the soft spot at the juncture of her jaw and ear.

"That is a very good memory." Her voice disappeared into a sigh as his lips descended to her neck and she gripped the front of his shirt.

"And this is a very good reminder."

Her knees grew weak, but she tried to pull him closer…as close are her burgeoning middle allowed.

"Dr. Ross." A frantic voice echoed down the hallway.

David grimaced, his thumb caressing her lips. "I believe we might need some privacy very soon, my dear Kat."

Then she saw it. The tenderness, the endearing warmth of love returning into his eyes. For her.

"Dr. Ross." The call came again with more intensity.

David growled and then took her hand, emerging from the alcove. Nurse Render, one of the newer nurses sent by Lady Hollingsworth, met them.

"Your father was just brought in. His autocar…he had an accident."

David exchanged a glance with Catherine and tightened his hold on her hand. "Where is he?"

"We've taken him to your study, sir."

Alexander sat on the settee in the study, looking more disgruntled than hurt.

"Father?" David knelt by his father's side. "Are you all right?"

"I'm angry, is what I am." He attempted, unsuccessfully, to wrap his own arm.

David took over, but apart from a bleeding forearm and a scratch on his cheek, Alexander appeared unscathed.

"What happened?"

"Something underhanded." He barked, his green gaze shooting daggers. "I'm having Mr. Coates check on it straight away."

"What do you mean?" Catherine lowered herself to the settee beside him, and he rested his hand on hers.

Emotions tightened in her throat at the simple gesture of inclusion. He'd begun to fill the barren place in her heart where a good father belonged.

"The car was fine when I drove into the village, but when I started back, the brakes were out."

"You think someone tampered with the car brakes?" David finished wrapping the wound and sent Catherine a look from his periphery, clearly struggling with an extra dose of anxiety. "Why?"

Alexander raised a brow, his concern hitting hers like a billiard ball. "I can think of a few reasons."

Catherine shook her head. "Surely she wouldn't resort to such malice."

"Wouldn't she? I've stolen her power. Desperate people make desperate choices, I'm afraid."

A frigid silence followed his words.

"You mean Aunt Maureen, don't you?" David sat back, from the blow. "What don't I know?"

"Excuse me, sir." Mr. Coates appeared in the doorway, looking quite out of place and uncomfortable inside the great house.

"Coates?"

"It was as you suspected, sir. Someone tampered with the brakes."

David stood, tremor shaking his voice. "We must do something."

"I'll make a formal complaint to the police in the morning, but until then, I would ask you both to stay near the house."

"There's no reason to leave except for mother's house party in two days, but if it is Lady Cavanaugh, or one of her lackeys, I doubt it will be easy to prove."

"Most likely I'm the only one threatened, but I'd prefer you stay close to Beacon." He patted Catherine's hand and looked up to David. "For your own good."

"Why would Aunt Maureen threaten you, father?"

"I'm the heir of Ednesbury Court, son."

David kept a close eye on his father over the next two days. The incident with the automobile had ignited the anxiety he already attempted to keep under amicable control. He checked in every two hours until his father told him to leave and prepare for Moriah Dougall Pike's reception.

Catherine had gone early with Ashleigh to assist in preparations, which kept him on edge a little more. He wanted her close, safe, and his occasional paranoia sent the need to see her to another level. Mentally, he'd learned how to talk himself into a calmer state, but his pulse rarely listened.

He arrived a little later than anticipated and followed the butler toward the ballroom. The newly installed electric lights brightened the elegant room, a small orchestra played Strauss in the far corner, and several couples danced across the glossy, mahogany floors.

David's grin froze. He'd danced before, hadn't he? A breath of a memory teased into his mind, complete with a vision of…his bride.

He blinked. Was it a memory? There she stood, speaking with her sister, in the same gown he'd just envisioned. She glanced up then, her smile spreading as she saw him, and his breath locked in place. He knew this memory. The dark red hues of her gown, the loosely pinned hair, the smooth skin of her neck. And her eyes…tender and tantalizing all in one.

He walked toward her, focused. Certain. Images spun, one right after the other, like a moving picture show, each adding up to a night not too different than this one.

"You look ravishing." The unconventional response materialized before he could stop it. "I'm sorry, I didn't mean to voice those thoughts."

She stepped close, her daring grin covering his embarrassment. "Never apologize for complimenting your wife, Dr. Ross. It should occur on an hourly basis, at least."

Her face tilted in such a fetching way, he almost snatched a kiss in front of the entire room. "What if I'm cross?"

"Then you should complement your wife every half hour in good faith, for she's most likely the reason."

He chuckled. "I have a feeling life with you will be more adventure than crossness."

"Oh, I'm quite an expert at being out of sorts. Just ask my mother."

David looked to the dance floor for the signature couple of the evening. "The source determines the clarity of the information, my dear Kat." He gestured toward the other dancers. "Would you care to join them with me?"

"Dance?"

"Unless I'm misreading the response of half the people in the room, dancing is allowed."

She shook her head. "No, I'm not going to dance."

His hope took a tumble. "Why ever not?"

"Look at me, I'm enormous. Poor Annie had to let out two inches from this gown so I could wear it tonight."

"Look at you?" He took in the full vision of her—bare arms, long neckline and mesmerizing eyes. "I…I don't believe I should ever tire of looking at you."

A rush of crimson flooded her cheeks, and she smiled to the ground. The sense of warmth at her pleasure produced an excellent aphrodisiac.

"No matter what flattery you mutter, I will not make myself the subject of any more attention in my present state."

She waved at her stomach which still seemed quite small to him, especially when hidden beneath the glossy layers of her gown.

"Then here?" He held out his hand and gestured toward the balcony just outside the ballroom. "The two...or, rather, three of us?"

He drew her forward into the late March evening. One palm came to rest against the small of her back, his other hand took hers, and he began to sway with the music. "I remember dancing with you."

Moonlight glimmered in her cobalt depths. "Do you?"

He squeezed his eyes closed, attempting to hold onto the frayed visions in molten motion. "Were you in red?"

"Yes," she replied, her voice soft. "And you'd only learnt to dance a few weeks prior."

He stared down at her, mesmerized by all he'd come to appreciate about her in the past and the present. Not even failed memories weakened this inexplicable bond with her, and learning of all her sacrifices, her acts of love, her tireless constancy...no wonder he'd readily given over his heart.

"Catherine?"

Her expectant smile held such tenderness, he lost his train of thought.

"I love when you say my name."

He stopped moving and rested his forehead to hers. "Catherine."

Her eyes fluttered closed, and she sighed into him. "Yes?"

"Do you think perhaps...would you mind if I..." Heat crawled into his face. "Returned to the cottage with you?"

She raised a mock innocent brow, gaze darkening. "And why ever would you want to do that, dear Doctor?"

The tease in her tone warmed him clean through. "Beacon House is rather crowded, you know."

"Of course."

He cupped her cheek, holding her gaze as an unceasing longing filled his love for her. "And the noises, they can sometimes be rather bothersome."

Her grin spread. "I see."

"And I can't seem to manage my heart without you near."

"Oh." Her exclamation shaped her lips into a perfect invitation.

If they weren't outside of a crowded ballroom, he would have confirmed the hint of memory nudging him to take a taste.

"I'm sorry I've put you through so much uncertainty and turmoil." He rubbed his thumb across her cheek as if to clear away the smudge of his wounds. "You must still remind me of many things, but of one truth I have no doubt."

"That I'm quite stubborn? Impulsive?" She drew in a shaky breath. "Impossible?"

His gaze roamed her face, taking in the beauty. "You love well, dear Catherine, and no man could do better than your love."

Her smile quivered, and her gaze dropped to his lips. "I see you're finding your words much better."

"I'm finding many things better, with more clarity, but I still have one distinct and unresolved curiosity."

She looked back into his eyes, her ebony brow tilting with question.

He lowered his lips to hers in a soft and swift kiss, one that wouldn't draw attention but also encouraged his thirst for more.

The thought of being alone with his bride encouraged his speedy departure from the reception, but Catherine didn't seem to mind. She appeared as enthusiastic, bidding good-bye to her mother straight away and walking with him through the late March evening.

A quiet anticipation passed between them in the darkness of the car. The night air nipped at their faces, but he'd blanketed her into the seat for the drive. Though he'd recovered many memories, he only had faint hues of their time together as husband and wife. Perhaps, as with everything else, experience proved the best discovery, even if all he did was hold her through the night.

Car headlamps materialized behind them along the empty roadway. It approached at a fast speed for the curves, kindling David's paranoia. His mind began the internal rationale…this was only another guest leaving the reception. But his pulse shot into rapid-fire.

He rested his wrapped hand against one side of the steering mechanism and kept a firm grip with his good hand, allowing the driver to pass, but instead, the car stayed at David's side.

"What is he doing?" Catherine called over the sound of the engine.

The car nudged closer, giving a bump to David's runabout.

"What on earth?" Catherine grabbed the door frame.

The bump happened again, nearly knocking the steering mechanism loose from David's hand. It was a lone driver. Male, from what David could tell in the darkness.

"I think he's trying to push us off the roadway."

That was exactly his thought. Another bump sent them into the grass along the side of the road which led into a forest area. One hit to a tree could prove serious, even fatal.

"I have an idea, but I need you to trust me." He gripped the steering mechanism. "And hold on."

He pressed the acceleration mechanism at his right hand, moving out in front of the lunatic, and the other car accelerated to match. The runabout began to tremble from the unaccustomed driving speed. David had never gone above thirty-five mph, and now he neared forty-five. As soon as the other car began to slide over toward them, David initiated the floor brake so quickly, the other car slid in front of them, swerving out of control and only missing them by inches.

The sudden decrease in speed sent David's Model T skidding off the road, but the slower speed saved them from the other car's fate. They remained upright and jolted to a tilted halt.

Catherine would have jumped from their car and marched over to the madman to give him a piece of her mind if something quite strange hadn't happened. As the car slammed to a stop, a warm and wet liquid pooled beneath her. What had happened? Surely she hadn't…

Her stomach tightened to granite. *No.*

"Catherine," David took her by the shoulders and turned her to face him, his palms moved to her face. "Are you hurt?"

"No." Not hurt, exactly....

"And the baby?"

"I...I think we are both fine."

"Thank God." He placed a kiss to her head and reached for his door lever. "I'm going to see to the other car, but I need to leave my headlamps on to light the way. Will you be all right here?"

"Mm-hmm." Or she hoped. She grabbed his hand. "Be careful."

David walked within the dim glow of the headlamps to the overturned car. A roadster, if Catherine guessed rightly. Her stomach tightened again, bringing additional warm fluid from her body. *Oh dear God, what are you doing?* She palmed her stomach, growing more certain of her predicament. *Perfect timing.*

"I need your help." David appeared at the door and reached into the back, taking his doctor's bag. "He's badly injured."

"You're going to help the man who tried to kill us?" Catherine pushed herself out of the car. The cool air hit all of her damp places, stealing her breath. Another tightening of her stomach took away a little more.

David paused, bag in hand, and stared at her. "It's the right thing to do. And you know that too."

"My willingness is a bit more begrudging, but yes." After all, the man tried to *kill them*, in case David had forgotten. She followed with awkward steps, her body stiff and cold.

The light from the headlamps showed the roadster lying on its side. A man's body sprawled out on the ground beside the car.

"He has an abdominal wound, from what I can see." David knelt beside him. "What do you see?"

As David's shadow moved aside, it afforded Catherine a clearer view. "No, David. It's Mr. Dandy!"

David ignored the temptation to leave Mr. Dandy to his fate. The man had caused turmoil for his wife and might have been the one who tampered with his father's car, let alone the driver who almost caused their accident. But, as a doctor, his calling burned clear.

Save lives.

David reached under Mr. Dandy's back and felt for an exit wound. Nothing. That gave a little hope.

"Could you retrieve one of the blankets from the car? We can use them as bandages."

Catherine sighed. "I hope the devil of a man gets a conscience knocked into him from this." She made a stiff turn toward the car, her gait awkward.

Perhaps the baby caused additional discomfort?

Mr. Dandy's pulse grew weaker, his prognosis grave. But David had to try.

He ripped the man's shirt open to expose the full wound, the dim light of the runabout providing less than ideal clarity.

Catherine returned with the blanket. He slid one end of the cloth beneath Mr. Dandy's back and Catherine caught the other end, wrapping the entire 'bandage' around the man's abdomen. Minutes passed as they worked, Catherine more slowly than usual. A few times, she even made a pained noise, as though the efforts to save Mr. Dandy hurt or annoyed her.

Despite their efforts, Mr. Dandy never regained consciousness.

"He's gone."

Catherine placed her hand on her stomach and shook her head. "I'm sorry for it, David. Truly I am." She turned away. "I didn't like him, but I wouldn't have wished this end."

Her countenance paled to vulnerability in the headlamps' glow. He put a hand to her arm. "I know." He turned her toward the roundabout. "We'll telephone the police and emergency from Beacon."

He put her arm through his and made a few steps toward the car before Catherine stopped.

"Catherine? What is it?"

She said nothing for a moment, and then her body relaxed. "I...I think I'm in labor."

David turned her to face him. "What did you say?"

Sweat beads pearled on her forehead, even in the chill of the evening. How had he failed to notice?

"My bag of waters broke directly after the accident."

"And you didn't tell me?" He almost yelled at her. "That was an hour ago, if not longer."

"A man was dying. What did you expect me to do?" She yelled right back and then bent forward to hold her stomach again.

"Was that another pain?" He took her arm to finish the walk to the car.

"Yes. They're…they're close. Painful."

"We must get you to Beacon House."

He opened the car door and she tensed again, this time releasing a pitiful whimper. "I don't think I can make it to Beacon House."

Every ounce of heat left his body. Delivering a baby? Off the road? In the middle of the night? "Surely there's time."

"David." She grabbed his face and brought it close. "Madame gave me a detailed overview of the birthing process, as well as witnessing a few myself. I…I…." She tensed again, releasing his face, and a cry of pain erupted.

The sound sent him into motion. He adjusted the remaining blankets in the seat of the runabout in an attempt to make her as comfortable as possible, difficult in the narrow space of the car. The headlamps gave little assistance, but the moon's glow helped. Her face looked so pale in its light, so…weak.

"I need to push." She sat back, propping up on her elbows.

"No, not yet."

"But I need to," she cried, the pitiful sound ripping at his heart like nothing else.

"You need to focus."

"Focus?" Her gaze drilled into him with a sharp edge. "Don't be an imbecile! What else do you think I'm doing? Having tea?"

That was probably not his best response as a doctor…but as a husband? Fairly accurate.

He checked her, his hands having to 'see' more than his eyes because of the poor lighting. *Oh, good heavens.* The baby was crowning.

"We're having this baby here." David held Catherine's gaze. "Now."

Chapter Thirty-Two

Catherine blinked against the morning light slipping through a slit in the curtains. Her body ached, sore and beaten, but less than it had the day before. She turned her head toward the cradle near her bed and tears clouded her vision. David held a little bundle in his arms, staring down at her daughter with such tenderness, such unadulterated love, Catherine couldn't look away.

How could God have brought something so beautiful from something so broken? Gratitude crashed down on her, crushing her breath, unleashing her tears. *His* love was relentless and unfathomable and exquisite.

David ran a finger down the baby's cheek, lost in the same wonder Catherine felt every time she looked into the tiny face. Amazed. She didn't think she could love David Ross any more than she already did, but this moment, this memory brought a new appreciation for the man he was…and the father he would be.

He glanced up then, his smile as tender as when he'd stared at her daughter. "Good morning," he whispered.

"Good morning." She barely managed a response through the emotions crowding her throat.

He looked fairly disheveled, his collar loose and hair tousled. Very roguish. Her grin inched up at one corner, teasing treacherous thoughts of the future. What a perfectly sweet, dashing man! Heaven help her, how she loved him!

"How are you feeling?" He placed the baby gently in her cradle.

"Better than yesterday, but I don't think I'll plan a visit into the village yet."

"Maybe tomorrow, then?" A glint deepened the emerald in his eyes.

"On horseback."

He moved to the bed and sat down next to her, careful to adjust the coverlet to keep her comfortable. Her insides softened into pudding all over again at his nearness. "She's been such a darling, hasn't she?"

"She's beautiful, like her mother." David's warm admiration brought a sudden awareness of her early morning appearance.

She pushed back her loose hair, her face growing warm. "Right now, I look untidy."

He braided his fingers through hers, holding her gaze as he did so. "Beautiful."

"I'm ever so fond of flattery, my dear doctor, and I encourage you to use it liberally. Indeed, it might have healing qualities, for I am suddenly feeling less sore."

"Flattery for medicinal purposes, is it?"

"For any purpose you like."

He chuckled and then caught the sound in his injured palm. Catherine pulled his hand into hers, kissing it, and then she reached out and gently touched his cheek, reveling at the way her fingers remembered the contours of his precious face.

He closed his eyes, perhaps enjoying the sensation as much as she.

"Oh, don't worry for noise. She's a sound sleeper."

His brow tipped. "And she gets that from her father."

Her gaze shot to his.

"I'm a very sound sleeper." She released the hold on her caution. "Yes, you are."

He brought her wrist up to his mouth and left a lingering kiss. Their gazes locked, and the full tenderness she'd missed so much somehow found its way back into his expression. Deeper. More endearing.

Her breath shivered with frailty.

"Have you decided on her name?"

"Cecily Adeline, the middle names of two women who left us in the same year." She searched his face. "Assuming you're fine with using your mother's middle name. I thought...perhaps we could call her Addie."

Addie? Would he ever get used to Catherine's generosity? Her unpredictability? His grin tipped. No,

333

probably not, and it was one of her most appealing qualities. He looked over at the cradle. "Our Addie Ross, then?"

"It seems to suit her, don't you think?"

"Yes. It does." He pressed another kiss to her hand, breathing in the scent of her skin. "Thank you, Catherine."

"And I ought to apologize." Her words whispered, her eyes taking on a sorrowful roundness. "I'm sorry I called you an imbecile. I didn't mean it, truly." Her bottom lip pouted out in a tempting way to gain his full attention. "Well, I meant it at the time, but I didn't mean it forever. So I—"

His mouth covered hers, hungry and grateful and ready to discover all the other memories his heart knew but his mind didn't. Sweet, right, and awakening a foggy remembrance of a similar time, a similar taste. He pulled her closer, deeper into the kiss, aching to enjoy and cherish this beautiful woman, this precious gift. The muddled old memories and the precious new ones confirmed something his heart already knew. He would love her as long as he drew breath.

A steady procession of visitors filed through the little cottage at Mrs. Bradford's careful admission. Even Lady Hollingsworth arrived from London.

She sat in their little parlor, appearing as comfortable there as in Willow Tree Court. A true lady. Just like Grandmama.

"She's is a precious addition to your family." Lady Hollingsworth looked from David to Catherine. "I was pleased to receive your wire."

Catherine adjusted her hold on Addie. "I thought you might wish to know, but I never imagined you'd visit."

"It is a painful truth that as one ages, one becomes more inclined to the comforts of home than the adventures of travel, but I still find my way out of Willow Tree when circumstances merit."

"We appreciate all you've done." David added.

"It has been my pleasure." Her gaze turned thoughtful. "And now, to know you are safe from Maureen Cavanaugh's vengeance adds an additional balm of comfort."

"You have news?" Catherine walked Addie to the cradle they'd placed by the window to take in the beauty of the cherry blossoms framing the view.

"Indeed, I do, and it was one of the reasons I wished to visit in person, to set both of your minds at ease." She placed her tea onto the table. "Though no clues from Dr. Ross' incident or your own could be directly linked to Lady Cavanaugh, and owing to her passionate declaration that Mr. Dandy performed these malicious acts of his own accord, Lord Cavanaugh decided the best way to subdue her was to give her a choice."

"Prison or death?" The words slipped out before Catherine could stop them. "I'm sorry, I shouldn't have said that, but the very thought that she possibly plotted to kill David—or Alexander—unfurls every flame in my temper."

"And rightly so." Lady Hollingsworth nodded. "But again, there was no proof of her involvement, so Lord Cavanaugh offered her a solution that might prove just as unwelcome as prison. Either live on the Cavanaugh estate in one of the smaller properties, or take a townhouse in London."

"The only smaller homes at Ednesbury Court are servant's lodgings." David took a seat beside Catherine. "Like this one."

Lady Hollingsworth's smile slanted. "Exactly."

"When did she move to London?"

"Two weeks ago. With this choice, she'll continue to receive a degree of respectability without the additional...what should we say?" Lady Hollingsworth looked up over her teacup. "Grandeur?"

"And power," Catherine added.

"Indeed, and her reduced circumstances have left her former influences rather impotent."

Lady Cavanaugh's last hold on Catherine's life loosened, the threat unknotting from her shoulders. David sighed. Catherine took his hand.

"You do realize one of your grandmama's greatest dreams has come to pass?"

Catherine's grin spread unhinged. "An impotent Lady Cavanaugh? Grandmama becomes more intriguing every day."

"Catherine." David chuckled. "Be nice."

Lady Hollingsworth kept her demeanor unchanged except for the slightest tilt of her smile. "Your Grandmama had long hoped to restore the relationship between the Cavanaughs and the Spencers. That was her and Lord Jeffrey's wish when they were engaged. It would combine the families' estates for future generations to expand or recreate as necessary."

"Well, it would make sense, now more than ever, to combine," Catherine said. "Especially with the rising costs and care for managing an estate."

"And the taxes to own such property." David continued. "Father has already made plans to change the way his tenant farmers work so that the unused land will become productive farming land to increase revenue for the estate."

"Combining the families could have made such a difference for Ednesbury if Grandmama's dream had come true."

Lady Hollingsworth laughed. "But don't you see? Her dream has come true. You, the eldest granddaughter of Victoria Spencer, the blood heir of her legacy, and David, as the heir to the Cavanaugh estate?"

Catherine looked over at David as his eyes widened. They'd been so couched within their little world of new love and parenthood, the understanding hadn't made its way into realization.

Lady Hollingsworth stood. "It's very much like a tapestry isn't it? On one side there's loose strings and confused tangles, but when turned over and seen properly, it's a masterpiece.

David's hand tightened around her fingers, the fresh taste of grace humbling her yet again.

"You may only have the strings and the tangles sometimes in this life, my dear," Lady Hollingsworth looked to the cradle, her smile peaceful. "But He has the full picture, and it is something beautiful."

The last six weeks had been a slow transition for them. David stayed in the guest bedroom for the first month, his nightmares fading with time as Catherine took care of Addie and her own recovery. After a month, he awakened to her wrapping blankets around him, her hair in a black river around her face. Without thinking, he'd taken her hand and drawn her into his arms, holding and kissing her until they'd both fallen asleep. They'd shared a bed ever since, and he'd begun taking careful inventory of all the little nuances of Catherine being his.

Each day provided more open memories, and a few faint ones of their last days together before the war, but each day also deepened the craving for something more– a connection his heart understood but his mind ached to rediscover.

Little things began to tease his hunger. Her morning routine of wrestling her mass of beautiful hair into conformed styles, highlighting her neck in alluring ways. Watching her dress. The way she nudged her body close to him at night, as if she couldn't move near enough.

That particular thought kept him distracted during his hospital rounds. He wanted her to be his in every way. Not only in *her* memory, but in his too.

As he approached the cottage from the hospital, he breathed in the new flowers of spring, plucking a few pale blue blossoms from the garden and tucking them behind his back.

Catherine looked up from her desk as he entered. "How did the surgery go?"

"Very well." He shrugged out of his jacket. "Everyone managed to survive."

"I deem that an unparalleled success." Her grin arched, spiking his pulse with purpose.

He hoped to never forget that lovely smile again. "I brought you something."

"Did you?" She stood from her desk, pages of various sketches and swathes of cloth scattered about, and leaned to place a kiss on his cheek, but he caught her lips with his own, prolonging her closeness with increased intensity.

He'd enjoyed relearning the contours of her mouth, the eager return of her kiss, the like passion. She matched him so well. He drew back and revealed his small gift.

Her eyes lit with humor. "Forget-me-nots?"

"Apropos, no?"

She took the flowers and held them to her nose, laughing. "Have I forgotten something, dear husband?"

His fingers glided down her cheeks, smoothing over her skin to her neck. "Actually, it's more about things I wish to never forget again."

"Is it?" Her brow arched to tease him. "Forget your keys again?"

He brushed his thumb across her lips, and her sapphire's darkened to cobalt. "Actually, I've been thinking of much more endearing things than my proclivity for misplacing my keys."

"You are getting much better at remembering them of late."

"I have a very good wife."

She shook her head. "No one would ever believe you."

He chuckled and swept a palm to her hair, loosening a pin. "I hope I never forget your laughter." He maneuvered another pin, sending an ebony lock loose. "Or the furious light in your eyes when you have an idea, or the tender and somewhat off-key lullabies you sing to sweet Addie."

She attempted to push him away with mock offense, but he trapped her against him, pressing a kiss to her neck and loosening another pin or two.

"I hope I never forget how the scent of lavender lingers on your neck, or the way you reach to take my hand at random moments, or the way your eyes sparkle when you glance at me from your looking glass when you pin your hair."

"You watch me quite intently when I pin my hair."

"Mm-hmm." In response, he pushed his hand through the loose mass, spreading it across her shoulders. "I'm attempting to sort it out."

Her grin perked. "How I arrange my hair?"

"The memory you have that I don't." He held her gaze. "A particular memory for which I must beg your expertise and guidance."

She pressed her body close to his, palms on his chest. "And whatever might that be?"

"Is Addie asleep?"

"Yes," Catherine answered slowly, studying his face as his hands moved down her back.

Oh, she'd catch on quickly if he knew her. His grin spread. *And I do know her.* Each day, better and better. He touched his forehead to hers. "Kat, my love, what do you say we test how soundly she sleeps?"

Her brow rose in question and then understanding dawned. She placed her hands on his cheeks and offered him another smile. "And how exactly might I appease your curiosity, my dear David?"

He took her lips in a lingering kiss, a lover's kiss, one which left them both breathless...and curious. She clutched the front of his shirt, her smile inviting him to continue his expedition.

"How?" He braided his fingers through hers and started for the stairs. "You're a very clever woman. I have every faith you can sort it out."

Pepper D. Basham

About the Author

Pepper D. Basham is an award-winning author who writes romance peppered with grace and humor. She's a native of the Blue Ridge Mountains, a mom of five, a speech-language pathologist, and a lover of chocolate. She writes a variety of genres, but enjoys sprinkling her native culture of Appalachia in them all.

She currently resides in the lovely mountains of Asheville, NC where she works with kids who have special needs, searches for unique hats to wear, and plots new ways to annoy her wonderful friends at her writing blog, The Writer's Alley. She is represented by Julie Gwinn of Seymour Literary Agency. You can learn more about her at www.pepperdbasham.com.

Acknowledgements

My fantastic Street Team, you guys bring such encouragement to this journey!

To the spiciest Brainstorming Team on the planet, Carrie, Mikal, Rachael Wing, Rachael Farnsworth-Merrit, Judy, Marisa, and Charity. Wow, you guys have been such a wonderful blessing to my world. Thank you for bringing your humor and encouragement into my writing madness. We met through book 1…we created a friendship through this book. I'm eternally grateful.

Casey & Robin Miller….YES! I "done" it twice!

Uncle Randall & Aunt Tonda for giving me lessons on driving a Model T.

Dawn Crandall and Susan Anne Mason, thank you so much for your encouragement, friendships, and excellent editing skills.

Author Laura Frantz, who constantly inspires me to write beautiful stories with a heavenly purpose.

Jeane Wynn, you are an endless reserve of support, ideas, and faith in people. Thank you.

Dawn Carrington and the creative crew at Vinspire Publishing – thank you for taking your chances on me.

Kelli Johnson! Thank you so much for letting me borrow your fount of wisdom about brain injury. I couldn't have made things realistic without you.

Julie Gwinn, I cannot wait to see what 2016 and beyond has in store for us. Wow…what a start! Thank you for believing in me and bringing this dream to life.

To some of the dearest friends I've ever had, The AlleyCats. My life is richer, my journey sweeter, and cyberspace much more enjoyable because I share it all with you. I love you guys so much.

My parents for their unending faith in me.

And to the Redeemer of the broken. Thank You that no one is too broken or too fallen that Your love cannot restore them.

Dear Reader,

If you enjoyed reading The Thorn Keeper, I would appreciate it if you would help others enjoy this book, too. Here are some of the ways you can help spread the word:

Lend it. This book is lending enabled so please share it with a friend.

Recommend it. Help other readers find this book by recommending it to friends, readers' groups, book clubs, and discussion forums.

Share it. Let other readers know you've read the book by positing a note to your social media account and/or your Goodreads account.

Review it. Please tell others why you liked this book by reviewing it on your favorite ebook site like Amazon or Barnes and Noble and/or Goodreads.

Everything you do to help others learn about my book is greatly appreciated!

Pepper Basham

Plan Your Next Escape!
What's Your Reading Pleasure?

Whether it's captivating historical romance, intriguing mysteries, young adult romance, illustrated children's books, or uplifting love stories, Vinspire Publishing has the adventure for you! For a complete listing of books available, visit our website at www.vinspirepublishing.com. Like us on Facebook at www.facebook.com/VinspirePublishing Follow us on Twitter at www.twitter.com/vinspire2004 and join our newsletter for details of our upcoming releases, giveaways, and more! http://t.co/46UoTbVaWr *We are your travel guide to your next adventure!*

CPSIA information can be obtained at www.ICGtesting.com
Printed in the USA
BVOW02s2035030316

438764BV00002B/7/P